STRANGER, STRANGER

Stranger, Stranger

A collection of short stories

by

MICHAEL WASHBURN

Adelaide Books
New York / Lisbon
2020

STRANGER, STRANGER
A collection of short stories
by Michael Washburn

Published by Adelaide Books, New York / Lisbon
adelaidebooks.org

Editor-in-Chief
Stevan V. Nikolic

For any information, please address Adelaide Books
at info@adelaidebooks.org
or write to:
Adelaide Books
244 Fifth Ave. Suite D27
New York, NY, 10001

ISBN: 978-1-951896-37-9

Printed in the United States of America

Contents

Acknowledgements

A number of the stories in this collection previously appeared in literary journals. "Derangement," "If You Talk About Destruction," "My Art or Yours?", "The Whispering Space," and "The Witch Doctor of Robertsport" first appeared in *Meat for Tea: The Valley Review*, "Elusive Object" and "Laughter" in *Hellfire Crossroads*, "Lost and Found" in *Black Fox Literary Magazine*, "The Flock" in *Night Light*, "Hearts, Minds, and Spirits" in the *Brooklyn Rail*, and "An Offer You Can't Refuse" and "Into My Heart an Air That Kills" in the *Weird Fiction Review*. The author thanks the editors of these publications for permission to reprint the stories.

If You Talk About Destruction

Sherwood was eager to get back to his little apartment and open a bottle of wine. It startled him when the taxi carrying him up Morningside Drive slowed and came to a stop without a word from the driver. Hardly anyone was around up here. To the left, 114th Street extended off into the dark. To the right lay Morningside Park.

In the light from a lamp post, the driver's rough complexion made Sherwood think of the moon's surface. Though the driver still didn't speak, he clearly expected Sherwood to pay him and get out right here.

"Hey, I didn't ask you to stop here! I live on the other side of the park. You need to go up and loop around," said Sherwood.

The stranger in the front seat replied without turning his head.

"It's about four hundred feet to the other side of the park, man. Just get out here and walk it."

"But I didn't tell you to stop here!"

"No need to yell. I'm just tryin' to save you a few bucks, since you're goin' through school and all."

Sherwood hadn't told the cabbie he was a graduate teaching assistant. The driver had made an inference about a prim bookish-looking person who lived so close to the university, and had been right. While Sherwood relished intellectual discussion and debate, he rather disliked arguing with ordinary people over practical things. It never felt right to him. Besides, the cabbie was correct. The walk would take less time out of Sherwood's evening than an argument here.

He reached into his wallet, took out some bills, and handed the driver the fare plus a tip.

"Thanks, pal," said the cabbie.

"You're very welcome. Have a good night."

He got out and walked across the sidewalk to the stone steps leading down into the park. A sighing came through the canopies of leaves turning to a rust color this time of year. Soon it would be too cold to be out in a blazer and chinos.

Reaching the foot of the steps, he saw no one. He balanced his glasses on the bridge of his nose and started across the park. The cabbie was right, it wasn't a great distance at all. Already he could see the other side where Morningside Avenue snaked uptown. In two months of living in his apartment right off the avenue, he'd barely set foot in the park. Here, he thought, was a place to come with your girlfriend in decent weather, provided you had a girlfriend. As soon as he walked through the door of his flat, he'd open a bottle of Zinfandel and sit down with a Sartre play on his knee and forget the voids in his life temporarily. He picked up his pace, closing the distance.

There were four of them. They came out from behind a cluster of trees and surrounded him, two in front and two behind. One in front was white and one was black. Before he fully realized what was happening, something struck him about the young white man's rough complexion and stubbly black hair, something oddly familiar. Then he realized this was a mugging.

"Get away from me," he said.

A hard object hit him in the back of the head. He fell with a cry, twisting, landing on his back. His glasses came off as he fell. In the moonlight he saw the two other strangers clearly. They were both white, one with brown hair and a wrestler's physique, the other blond like a surfer. It was 1971 and there was lots of crime, but Sherwood had never expected trouble from a blond guy. The muscular one moved forward and raised the branch over Sherwood's trembling form.

The blond guy said, "Give us your wallet."

Sherwood didn't hesitate to comply. The pain at the back of his skull was so fierce that he felt incapable of more than simple moves to get from one moment to the next. It terrified him even to think of the squishy thing inside his skull bouncing and shifting in ways that it shouldn't. For all the barbarity of the attack, the blond guy, the little group's presumptive leader, seemed calm, almost poised.

The muggers were lucky. Sherwood had stopped by his bank in the late morning, and the wallet held nearly a hundred dollars. The leader noted this with evident satisfaction as he flipped through the wallet. But as he did so, the two attackers who'd moved in front of Sherwood both appeared to take note of something off in the depths of the park. Sherwood couldn't see what caused them alarm. A man walking his dog? Lovers out for a stroll? The blond guy and the muscular youth with the branch quickly grew aware of the danger. They had to leave at once, and if they did any further violence to Sherwood here, his cries would result in cops saturating the park and a wide radius beyond.

The blond stranger gave the others a look. All four of them hurried off in the direction Sherwood had been going when they pounced. But then one of them paused, turned back to Sherwood, and called to the others in an urgent tone.

"Wait, you guys! I *know* this asshole! I think he recognized me. We can't leave him here!"

The others came back.

"Why didn't you say something before?" asked the leader.

"I was, I don't know, eighty percent sure. Then I saw those glasses. I recognized 'em."

"God fucking damn it."

They picked Sherwood up by his wrists and ankles and spirited him away toward Morningside Avenue. It fairly amazed him how fast they could move.

Though the pain in Sherwood's head was still intense, his nimble mind began to make associations. He remembered one day when he'd been standing at the blackboard in a classroom on the third floor of one of the new campus buildings, leading a discussion about Hegel's concept of the state, when seven people burst into the room and demanded to address the class on the topic of open enrollment, a hugely controversial issue for the university. The intruders were loud and bellicose and a couple of them carried baseball bats. Assuming that most people shared his aversion to violence, Sherwood wanted to think the bats were just for show, but it was hard to be sure. One or two of them might have been students, but Sherwood guessed they were mostly hard-luck young people who hated the unfairness of things. Lacking the courage to stand up to them, but not wishing to appear to give in entirely, Sherwood said the class would have to vote on whether to hear out the demonstrators. The vote went in their favor. Now, as the four assailants carried him out of the park and up the street, Sherwood knew that one of the disruptors on that day four weeks ago was the young man here with stubbly black hair.

He had little doubt that they were going to take him someplace where they could dispose of him quietly. But what happened immediately after they exited the park, Sherwood would never know. One of the four men punched him hard in the head until he lost consciousness.

When he woke up, he felt pretty sure he was dead. In the past, he'd mused on the question of why hell had to be spectacular, why it needed any kind of grandeur, when drabness and gray were such effective means of torment. He found himself now in a standing position at the back of a dank room with stone walls, its darkness barely relieved by a bulb in the ceiling. He didn't know what they'd lashed him to by his ankles, wrists, and neck. Maybe a metal bed frame propped upright. A lot of junk lined the room's rear wall. The absence of weight at points on his person told him that not only his wallet, but his key ring and the little leather address book he kept in a pocket of his blazer, were gone. The area around his crotch felt damp, and his wrists ached acutely from the firmness of the rope.

After a while the blond guy and the thug who had recognized Sherwood came into the room and stood before him.

"How are you doing there, Sherwood?" the leader of the pack asked.

"Why am I alive?"

The leader chuckled.

"Well don't be so sure of that, now. What are you, a professor?"

"A teaching assistant."

"A living, breathing, TA. Wow. You must be fucking *smart*."

The irony invested in the last word worked like an anchor on the blond man's tone.

"A good deal smarter than you. What did you find in my wallet? About ninety dollars? What's that divided by four? No, not even by four, because you have to give something to the cabbie who's in cahoots with you," Sherwood said.

For all his fear, it felt kind of good to get this out. The blond man looked mildly annoyed.

"You wanna know why you're alive at this point? I'll tell you. I went through your little address book carefully. I know you can get more money for us. We fuckin' well need it."

Fear surged again.

"I can get you a lot more money. More than you'll ever get from jumping someone in the park. I swear. Just loosen the rope a bit, please. My wrists are killing me."

He watched their faces as they considered his plea. Then the dark-haired man stepped forward and adjusted the rope binding Sherwood's wrists, leaving his ankles and neck in pain.

"Thanks, guys. Bring me the address book. I'll arrange to get you a lot more money."

The dark-haired thug turned and left the room. Sherwood fervently hoped to resolve the crisis and save himself without anyone being violent to anyone.

"So what do you teach?" asked the blond captor.

"Modern philosophy. The German and French traditions, mostly."

The man nodded.

Sherwood wanted to appear friendly.

"Can I ask you your name?"

To his surprise, the captor answered promptly.

"Call me Deke."

"And your friend?"

"That's Larry."

Surely they'd never reveal their real names if they didn't plan to kill him. Did "Deke" suspect Sherwood's motives in posing the questions? For the moment Deke appeared to evince a mild wonder at having someone from such a different walk of life here. Maybe Sherwood needed to keep them curious and engaged. He could analyze these four criminals from a Nietzschean point of view. Larry's self-righteous stance toward the university, and the group's mugging of a middle-class man, both flowed from the same slave morality, Sherwood thought. But if he told them that, it would surely be the last thing he ever did.

Larry, if that was indeed his name, came back into the room with the address book.

"All right, man. Tell us who can make us richer."

"Can I have a glass of water first?"

The two captors looked at each other. They left the room.

Though Sherwood doubted that anyone he knew would provide enough money to satisfy these creeps, at least he'd bought some time. He wondered why he was so desperate to live, and the only answer he could think of was that his philosophical explorations had just barely begun. Whatever sophistication he had at this point was the result of his dalliances with one of the senior members of the faculty. Paul Fournier was rarely in his office at the university. People said it was because of all the demands of research, speaking, and writing, and Fournier was such an asset that you didn't dare challenge or question his invisibility. A rumor went around that Fournier had legal troubles arising from his role in the events of May 1968 in France. Whatever the reason might be, it was helpful to know Fournier personally. The professor occasionally received guests at his penthouse apartment on Riverside Drive.

It was crazy to be thinking about this now.

Deke and Larry came back into the room, followed by the other two. In need of a way to try to keep track of those other two strangers, Sherwood mentally labeled the white one Flim and the black one Flam. Now, in the light, Flim's muscles were all the more prominent, and Sherwood considered it a miracle that the blow to his head had not killed him. Of course that was still a possibility, if there was bleeding on his brain.

Larry held out a glass of water and tilted it. The room-temperature water coursed down Sherwood's throat. He swallowed. Then he noticed the switchblade in Deke's right hand.

"Hey, Deke. Please don't do something crazy. There's no need for violence. I said I'll get you money."

Larry pulled the flaps of the address book apart and thrust it within six inches of the captive's face.

"Someone here better have money."

Sherwood replied without hesitation.

"Chad Hughes. My good friend. He lives right off the park."

"Central Park?" Larry asked.

"No, of course not. Morningside Park!" Sherwood said, nearly adding, *How stupid are you?* before realizing that maybe they *were* closer to Central Park.

"He better be a real person. Show us his number."

"It's right there on the second page."

They loosened the bonds enough for Sherwood to detach his quivering body from the bed frame. His legs had gone numb and he fell right into the arms of Flim and Flam. Seconds later he was in another dank room, with a tattered couch and a couple of love chairs and a chipped wooden table with a phone on it. Deke looked Sherwood over carefully, as if to verify that he was calm and could talk in a normal voice. Then Deke spoke.

"So listen, Sherwood. You put down three hundred you didn't have in a card game, and now you're fucked, and if Chad can save your ass, you'll name your first-born after him."

Sherwood nodded. Chad was going to have to accept that after disparaging gambling a number of times in Chad's presence, Sherwood had spontaneously chosen to gamble with abandon.

Deke gave Sherwood the address. They were in Morningside Heights after all.

"What if he says he can't come now?"

Deke didn't reply. Sherwood thought he knew the answer.

He picked up the receiver and dialed, feeling four pairs of eyes on him. He heard a ring. Another ring. A third, a fourth, a fifth. He dared to raise his eyes to meet those of his captors. They were as expectant as ever.

"It just keeps ringing," Sherwood said, and began to lower the receiver.

"Keep waiting," Deke said.

He held the receiver to his ear until none of them seriously expected anyone to pick up. Deke looked at him as if he were a toddler whose toilet training had failed miserably.

"You knew no one would answer."

"Of course I didn't!"

"Come on."

They brought him back to the large room and restrained him again. Deke's gently condescending smile was gone. Deke punched Sherwood so hard in the nose that a wave of pain eclipsed the ache in the back of his head as his eyes filled with water and he barely suppressed a cry. The captor hit him three more times in the face. He felt several teeth come loose and burst into sobs.

Never had he known such pain. He thought he was going to die. Now something like pity registered in Deke's face.

"Awww. We were a bit rough on the guy. Don't want him to die of pain."

He saw a needle in Flim's hand. Flim thrust the needle into a vein in Sherwood's right arm. Within seconds the pain mellowed and Sherwood came to feel as if he were outside his body and looking down at it as if it were a long wall, with fissures too tiny to let anything in or out. The pain receded further and further like a wind on a dimming horizon.

He stopped seeing the room and the four strangers. His mind began groping, grasping for meaning, for substance, for a problem or riddle or paradox with which it could engage. How often his knowledge and training had come up short, had yielded nothing. Others out there were masters of the field of philosophy in all its unfathomable complexity.

He thought of the beginnings of his acquaintance with Paul Fournier. Just to stand in the lobby of the building on Riverside Drive and press the buzzer for the man's apartment was bracing. Once he stepped off the elevator and entered Fournier's apartment, he felt that he had not merely crossed a physical rubicon but had entered a new realm of experience and thought.

The professor sat on a couch in the orange light coming through the windows on either side of him. Taking in his host's refined intelligent look, Sherwood thought once again that here was a man of incomparable erudition, a rigorous mind with a glut of original ideas. Here in this space, in the dimming light, philosophical traditions could just as easily begin as meet their end. Sherwood had many questions in his mind as he sat down on a chair across from the professor.

In his present state of captivity in the dank room, words did not resurface with clarity in his memory but he could still recall the gist of a conversation. He saw Fournier leaning back on the couch in the still garish light and daring him, challenging him to articulate an objection to the far-left doctrines

Fournier espoused. Even if these ideas might prove lethal in their practical application, that is better than people living in ignorance, Fournier posited.

Sherwood had a ready answer. He wasn't just playing the devil's advocate here. He sincerely believed that one could construe the ideology of Marxists, and the more doctrinaire ones in particular, as a type of slave mentality, in the idiom of Nietzsche. Even in his present state, Sherwood had no trouble recalling Nietzsche's tart irony in *Beyond Good and Evil*. "'Why do you dislike him?' 'He is superior.' Has anyone ever answered that way?'"

Yes, it was a fact of human nature that people envied those who were more capable and talented. Maybe that was why the supposedly downtrodden loathed the bourgeoisie and hatched plans against them. It really had nothing to do with the unfairness of the socioeconomic order.

Fournier looked at him as if he were a particularly brash and ignorant student who didn't know when to keep quiet. Yet when Fournier spoke, he was calm, if slightly resigned. Sherwood's error, and it was an elementary one, was to assume that revolutionary Marxists found anything in the character of the bourgeoisie to emulate or wished to lead lives anything like theirs. If you want to invoke Nietzsche, you really should know something about your subject. Fournier alluded to a passage in *Human, All Too Human* where Nietzsche makes the case that those who commit the most extreme acts out of what appears to be pure bloodlust are in reality doing what future generations will rightly regard as hard and necessary work. For all their amorality, the bourgeoisie lack the firmness of character to act with such barbarity openly, without dressing up their words and deeds with moral pomp. It just doesn't comport well with their self-image as urbane, polite, civilized people. They carry out the bulk of their dirty work by proxy and utterly fail to order the world even according to their own self-interest. No less importantly, their habits, their ways of living are slothful and repellent in the extreme.

Fournier knew people in France, and here in America, who suffered from no such lack of conviction. They were hard and tough and fierce. Theirs was not a morality of the weak and ineffectual, of slaves, but one of spiritual masters who simply lacked political power as of yet.

Sherwood was curious to meet these individuals. He was also curious about reported incidents during the disturbances in Paris in which Fournier had allegedly played a role. When he brought up the latter issue, Fournier abruptly changed the subject.

When the drug wore off, the four watched him as expectantly as ever. After more of his now tiresome warnings about the uselessness of violence, he told them where to find the number of another friend, Brendan Blake, in the address book. They brought him back to the sad room with the couch. He picked up the receiver and dialed Brendan's number in the hope and expectation of hearing the voice of the bright confident young man with whom he'd so often compared the political systems of different parts of the world.

One ring. A second. A third.

"Hello?"

"Hi Brendan. It's Sherwood."

"Hey, my favorite intellectual. How are you?"

"Ah, not so great. I'm in debt, to the tune of three hundred dollars, to some guys I was playing cards with. I need your help, buddy."

"*What?!?*"

"That's right."

"Sherwood, my head's spinning. You don't even fucking play cards. You've given your friends lectures on your moral and ethical objections to gambling. Now you call and tell me you've got a gambling debt. Do you have any idea how bizarre this sounds?"

Sherwood desperately hoped the others couldn't hear any of what came out of the receiver.

"I know exactly how it must sound. I tried it once, Brendan. As a lark. An experiment. To see how the other half lives. To test all my assumptions."

"Bullshit."

"Brendan. Can you please help me out here?"

"Do you have any idea how this sounds, Sherwood? Fuck it. Is this even Sherwood I'm talking to?"

"Brendan!"

He heard a click.

They brought him back to the large room and restrained him again. The rope was so tight now he thought his hands would fall off. It was pure agony.

Deke said, "Close your eyes."

He obeyed. Almost at once he felt fingers working on the buttons of his shirt. Then someone, Deke or Larry or Flim or Flam, pulled the sides of his shirt apart and exposed Sherwood's trim but soft belly. He heard Deke's voice again.

"Don't open your eyes."

The tip of a blade danced around the upper reaches of his pubic hair. Then it moved upward, to a spot just beside his right thigh. There it paused, as if finding the spot cozy. Now it moved across Sherwood's waist to his other thigh. Pain surged but he didn't dare scream. The wielder held the knife there for a moment, turning, teasing, provoking the captive, before moving down again to his lower abdomen.

"Open your eyes."

Sherwood obeyed, and saw Deke's work outlined in blood. Deke had carved out a broad flap of skin that he could easily seize along the upper rim and jerk downward, freeing Sherwood's guts to spill out all over the floor.

"Close your eyes."

As soon as he did so, he felt the shredding of the fibers connecting the patches of skin. Then he felt the top of the flap in the middle curdling downward.

Sherwood opened his eyes and screamed again. He made a noise even louder and more desperate than when Deke had hit him. It was just possible that people outside could hear. But the captors still weren't ready to kill him. This time it was Flam who came forward with the needle and carefully pierced a vein in Sherwood's arm.

Soon the sky all around him was a deep orange once again and the only other presence was a middle-aged professor with a stern but not hostile demeanor. Fournier was aware of the questions in Sherwood's mind, of the images that flickered there, of crowds rocking cars and hails of rocks and bottles slamming into policemen. At this moment Fournier would say only that Sherwood was wrong to associate revolutionary zeal only with him. Sherwood's revised, or flipped, understanding of Nietzsche had exponents to whom the professor could introduce him if he was truly curious. Sherwood said yes, he'd love to. He was no armchair philosopher! If there were people in New York who really wanted to shake things up, he'd be grateful for an introduction.

He expected those words to mellow Fournier right away, but the professor kept a certain sternness as he asked whether Sherwood knew what Maoism really meant, what it was really about. Sherwood mentioned the titles of several books he'd read.

Fournier told Sherwood about a little group of revolution-aries whom Fournier had mentored and guided, explaining what Nietzsche's thought had to offer them, how Nietzsche could act as a gateway between traditions and schools of thought.

A party was to take place on the coming Friday. Fournier read out an address and phone number and the guest copied them down in his address book.

Three nights later, Sherwood entered the lobby of the building on West 120th Street with no idea what to expect. He pressed the buzzer for 302. When a voice demanded his name, he gave it and mentioned Paul Fournier. Upon entering the apartment, he noted the absence of pot smoke and loud noise. This wasn't at all like other gatherings. The half-dozen young people sitting around here were calm, seemingly sober. A young man in a green infantry-style jacket sat on a couch, talking with a young woman in jeans and a purple blouse. Her eyes were lucid and her hair dark and luscious like ground zero of an oil spill. Sherwood felt attracted to her in a quick instinctive way. Here, he felt, was someone whose ingenuous look did not hide for a second her wily intelligence, her mischievous playfulness. He stood in the entrance, realizing they were both looking at him, and so it seemed was the image of Chairman Mao hanging between them in a frame on the wall. He began to formulate a question about the provenance of that picture, but the young man spoke first.

"Hey, are you Sherwood?"

"I am."

"Welcome. I'm Gary and this is Miranda. Come and sit with us."

He found a place to the girl's left. Now Sherwood noticed a scent coming from somewhere, from one of the other rooms, but it wasn't pot. It was incense with a rich earthy aroma.

"So tell us about the life of a TA during these tumultuous times."

"Ah, well, some people are pretty fanatical about open enrollment. Like the fate of the planet depends on it."

As Sherwood talked with the young man and woman about life at the university and the direction of his studies, and asked questions about their lives, he really wanted to know what Mao Zedong meant to them, why of all world leaders past or present this one appealed to them. Sherwood realized he was being a coward. If he couldn't talk bluntly about real topics with these people, there was no reason for him to be here rather than at one of any number of parties where Jefferson Airplane blasted from speakers and pot smoke filled the air.

He gestured at the likeness of Mao.

"If you talk about destruction, you can count me out," Sherwood said, quoting John Lennon's famous song about revolution, thinking himself clever.

"Fournier talks quite a bit about destruction, yet you were obviously eager to meet him," Gary replied.

"Oh, I was really fortunate to meet Fournier at last. The man doesn't make time for people with three Ph.D.s," Sherwood said, realizing this could be a humble statement or a boast depending on how you read it.

"I have to say, a lot of those people with Ph.D.s don't really grasp the upshot of *any* tradition," Gary said.

"No, indeed."

"What did you guys talk about?"

"Nietzsche, and my really flawed understanding of that great mind."

Miranda smiled enticingly.

"I trust that Fournier helped you revise your understanding somewhat," she said.

"That's precisely what he did, Miranda. I already got some of the stuff about how 'morality' is really just what feels right to each of us individually. What I didn't grasp was that, even in the most literal reading of Nietzsche, someone who rejects the existing order isn't necessarily a loser trying to feel better about his limitations. And, you know, seemingly destructive forces can actually be doing necessary work."

Sherwood felt embarrassed over his fumbling account of his relationship with Nietzsche. Gary spoke.

"'The frightful energies are the cyclopean architects and road-makers of humanity.'"

"Wow! What text did you just quote?" Sherwood asked, embarrassed.

"*Human, All Too Human.*"

Now Sherwood really felt like an idiot. That was the very text he and Fournier had discussed. Gary held no degree, but had quoted a text that Sherwood could merely paraphrase.

"I guess this offers some insight into why people don't like Mao."

Gary chuckled.

"Perfectly intelligent people, who read and admire Nietzsche, turn around and shit on a leader who takes Nietzsche literally, and takes his ideas a step further."

"I'm lost, Gary."

"Mao consolidated administrative functions and took care of all the riffraff in China with myriad different political and territorial claims. He made clear there was one moral and political authority. You know what his theoretical inspiration might very well have been?"

"Tell me."

Gary quoted Nietzsche again.

"'As a bad man one belongs to the 'bad,' to a swarm of subject, powerless people who have no sense of belonging together. The good are a caste, the bad a mess like grains of sand.'"

Sherwood nodded.

"*Human, All Too Human.*"

"Precisely, Sherwood."

Two more young men came out of one of the back rooms and stood facing the newcomer. One of them, a tall blond boy with huge muscles, had enough contempt for current fashions to wear overalls. The other had dressed all in black and had a refined intellectual air, reminiscent of Trotsky.

"Ethan and Victor, meet Sherwood."

Ethan grinned, and was not at all unprepossessing though there was a gap where one of his premolars should have been.

"Hey, man. Gary here said some knuckleheads were interrupting your class. Let us know if you ever need help dealing with that," Ethan said.

An image came now of Ethan standing on a farm in Wisconsin, clutching a pitchfork, powerful and scary. A really fearsome guy. Sherwood felt full of gratitude for these champions of order, a different kind from what most people believed in, but order nonetheless.

The memories faded as the features of the dank room came back into relief. In a pleading tone he addressed Deke, Larry, Flim, and Flam.

"I know someone who can definitely come. I promise. I'll get you heaps of money."

Deke grinned without an ounce of mirth or kindness.

"All right. Last chance. If you're fucking with us again you'll be sorry."

They removed the restraints and led him, trembling and wobbling like an anesthetized patient hobbling to the bathroom mid-procedure, to the room with the couch. He dialed the number that Fournier had given him on an evening when you could think the world was burning.

One ring. A second. A third. They watched him intently.

Then he heard Ethan's voice.

"Hello?"

"Ethan? It's Sherwood. Hey, man. Remember when I told you about those disruptions in my class?"

"I sure do."

"That's nothing compared to the shit that I'm in now. You said you'd help me. I'm in debt to a bunch of guys, three hundred in the hole, and I need you to get me out of this. Will you make good on your offer?"

The swiftness of Ethan's reply startled him.

"You bet. Give me the address."

Sherwood read the address into the phone.

"We'll be there. We made a promise to a disciple of Paul Fournier."

Sherwood replaced the receiver. The four captors looked as skeptical as ever. They brought him back to the dank room and tied him up so tightly he wanted to cry.

Now there was no relief, nothing to make time pass faster or less painfully. He hung there, bound to the black metal frame, for hours and hours, feeling his defeat and disappointment build inexorably. Though he had no way to keep track of time, it felt like around six hours from the last phone call when Deke came back into the room with a switchblade in one hand and a lighter in the other.

"You really shouldn't have fucked with us."

"I didn't, Deke! I swear I didn't. I've acted in good faith every time. And you're going to get money. Please don't do something crazy!"

"Cut the crap, Sherwood. You messed with us. You condescending fuck."

"No!"

"You've condescended to us from the start. Remember that question you asked? About what we were going to do with ninety bucks divided by five? You think we're idiots, scoring chump change to buy smack."

"No, Deke, I never said that. Please put those away!"

"You condescending fuck. You think what you say is all anyone picks up on."

Deke held the blade flat and flicked the lighter on under it.

"Smart guys don't live in the moment like me and Larry. They think about next month, next quarter, next year. Right, Sherry?"

The hot blade moved closer.

"I don't look down on you, Deke!"

"Then why'd you have to put it to a vote when Larry wanted to talk to your class about open enrollment? Why didn't you say, okay, guys, let's hear what you have to say?"

The hot blade was almost touching him.

"Please, Deke. I didn't want to look like a coward in front of my class. That's the only reason!"

"You *are* a coward."

Deke put the flat of the blade on the captive's bare forearm. So sharp was the pain that Sherwood burst into tears. Next, Deke laid the blade against Sherwood's right cheek. Then his bare shoulder. Then the base of his chin. Sherwood felt as if demons were pulling off his skin a patch at a time. He screamed.

"Sherwood, my man. You think your education sets you apart from most guys, but you don't know much about the world. There's really scary shit out there. There're people you don't ever mess with."

Deke moved the lighter directly under Sherwood's chin and flicked it on. His nostrils filled with the odor of blackening flesh. He screamed, loud enough to bring every cop in the city to this miserable apartment. Within seconds the narcotic was moving through his blood again and the dark place where he had suffered so much faded away.

Now he thought he was far, far from Manhattan. Beyond that one fact, he had only a vague sense of place. He just knew that he stood in the dirt of a plain extending far out of sight in nearly all directions. The sky was red and he smelled the odor of burning structures way off in the distance, in the one area where a huge knoll relieved the monotony of fields. The homes of the landowners were on fire, and families cried and screamed as agents of the revolution, brandishing pitchforks, drove them from the houses, the symbols of bourgeois leisure, and toward the demarcated patches of earth lying in the interlocking fields of fire of machine guns propped high up on the knoll. Those who could walk no more or who tried to run off with what strength they had left received a bullet or the four prongs of a pitchfork, usually through the eyes. The screams rose and rose until Sherwood could imagine that a caste was dying here in this inferno, that the world would soon be without any of the bloodsuckers who had sought to deny the power, unity, and integrity of the revolutionary force.

He assigned a global character to these events. Even if the sky was not red all over the world, red was the driver, the impetus, on the streets of Paris no less than in China or wherever those landowners were dying. Now he watched as rocks shredded the bodies of policemen on the streets of Montparnasse, people ran screaming from the epicenter of the violence, and horns blared as drivers hoped in vain for an opening through the crowds. One of the cars actually got through the mass of rioters but there was no chance of catching them off guard again. A half dozen of them moved up on either side of a blue Peugeot and lifted it, then began rocking it back and forth. Inside, a middle-aged man gripped the wheel ineffectually as the woman beside him cried out in vain and the two kids in the back lost control of their bowels. Recognizing a few of the rioters as Gary, Ethan, Victor, and Miranda, Sherwood knew the violence now so gloriously unleashed would not stop in China or France or any corner of the world, it would spread until the skies were red over every city and town and hamlet and farm and the eyes burst from the faces of the bourgeoisie and their blood flooded the streets.

He heard the captors talking in the other room. Mingled with the voices of Deke, Larry, Flim, and Flam were a couple he didn't recognize. Maybe they had invited people to a party. Maybe the cabbie who'd given Sherwood to them was there, and further criminal plans were in development.

Deke came back to the dank room.

"You thought you'd fuck with us again, huh?"

How often since his abduction Sherwood had expected Deke to say memorable things, to share the hard-assed wisdom, the blunt philosophy of someone who lived life on the edge. But it just kept coming down to the banality of *Do this or else*.

"Please give it a few more minutes, Deke. Then you can do whatever you like."

After considering this, Deke nodded and went back to the room with the couch. Sherwood heard laughter and smelled the aroma of pot.

Time passed.

And still more time.

No one showed up to pay off the captors. Sherwood knew that by any measure his promises to Deke had proven hollow.

By the terms Sherwood himself had put forth, Deke had a right to come in now and kill him.

Now a voice in the other room spoke out, quieting the others.

A buzzer rang. Someone thought he'd heard it ring before, and had called on the others to shut up.

Sherwood heard a door open somewhere. Soon new voices made themselves heard in the other room, provoking wonder and surprise. Deke and the others must have been wondering who these strangers were. Amid the cacophony one voice rose with clarity. Sherwood was still high. He couldn't make out more than a few words at a time.

The voice of the intruder rose.

"You riffraff. You scum. You're very tough when it's four of you against a teaching assistant."

Other voices rose alongside Gary's. Those of Ethan, Victor, Miranda, and more of Gary's comrades.

"Scum!" "Garbage!" "Filth!"

Now to his astonishment Sherwood heard a pleading voice, Larry's maybe.

"Hey! You don't need that. Please put that away."

Other voices joined Larry's. Then Sherwood heard loud cries from the other room. Even in his blotto state he could make out the sounds of scuffles, the protests of those held still against their will.

He heard the sounds of power tools coming to life. Now the criminals, who had fancied themselves as possessing a monopoly on violence and being the agents of all terror in the universe, began to scream. He heard Flim and Flam wailing, and then a marked rise in their cries as if they'd just lost a finger or a hand or an arm. Others screamed and begged but the voices of the intruders carried a distinct resolve.

Blood began to seep into the dank room, some of it pulpy, laden with tissue and muscle. The cries of the criminals grew louder and louder.

"*No! Please don't kill me!*"

"*Aaaaahhhhhh!*"

Now Larry, barely recognizable with his face covered in blood, crawled on all fours into the dank room, turning his face to Sherwood in a silent plea. Someone in the other room pulled him right back inside by his feet or his ankles. The bloody face disappeared. The screams rose and rose.

Larry crawled in again, and again, and again, and on the third occasion he had no eyes and his arms were gone at the elbows.

Gary came into the room, holding Deke in a headlock, flanked by Ethan and Victor.

"How should we do it, comrade?" asked Gary, as Victor moved the tip of a machete over points on Deke's body.

"Let him live," Sherwood said.

"What?"

"Spare his life. Just let this be part of his philosophical education."

Deke's eyes expressed infinite gratitude to the teaching assistant.

Then Gary spoke.

"He's not even a useful idiot, Sherwood. He's just an idiot. A degenerate incapable of learning anything. Or maybe you disagree?"

Sherwood considered this for a moment. Deke's eyes pleaded.

"Okay, then. Cut his ears off and stick the blade down his throat."

Gary grinned with the light of a shared understanding in his eyes.

Elusive Object

Croft pushed and fought his way through the crowds toward the subway. It was the kind of cold miserable day where he couldn't make much of an effort to be polite. He navigated the slush and the filth-coated ice covering New York's streets. The city on the Pacific coast where the plane would soon take him was synonymous with rain in the popular mind. He was about to get on a plane and swap one dreary locale for another, but the prospect thrilled him. That faraway city was the home of one of the world's tabloid sensations, a young woman who had been a totally unknown kid in a foreign university town until the murder of one of her housemates brought the world's attention to her.

Once the journalists discovered that girl, they didn't want to avert their gaze from the pale smooth skin of her cheeks, her locks of acorn-brown hair, and her hypnotic blue eyes. But popular tastes are nothing if not fickle, and over the last couple of years, the public's obsession had abated somewhat as new scandals, new preposterous characters asserted their claims. Not everybody knew what Croft knew. He'd pored over buried articles, had plumbed obscure regions of the web, in the hope of gleaning a bit of data about the young woman. He'd been diligent enough to learn of changes in her personal life. She and her boyfriend of many months had parted, and here before Croft now was an opportunity, maybe the only one Croft would ever have, to meet her and spend time with her and become a person in her life. It was a longshot, but he figured that everyone you know was a stranger at some point, that the deepest most resonant relationships grow out of freak encounters.

Croft swiped his Metrocard at a turnstile, moved into the station, and mounted the steps to a platform where trains shot by every ten to fifteen minutes. He thought that in just a matter of hours, he would be in the presence of those pure blue eyes and that earthy yet ethereal Middle American voice. With the time difference between here and the Pacific coast, he hardly cared that the flight was nearly six hours. His body could get tired, but he was dictating the terms here. He stood on the platform, feeling an unwelcome rush of the giddiness that sometimes made him want to talk to strangers and get them to laugh with him. In its way, the feeling was as noxious as the rage that he sometimes feared would lead him to threaten or assault a stranger one day.

A quarter of an hour passed before the tunnel west of the platform grew brighter and the twin lights of a train peered around the curve. Seconds later he moved into a middle car of the train, sat down, and looked anxiously at his watch. Realizing he still had a nice buffer of time, he settled into his seat and tried to keep his eyes off the other riders. He'd leave them alone, and they had better reciprocate. Croft's internal life was his and no one had a right to reach into his store of minutes and seconds, irreplaceable time, and grab some of it. He slumped in the seat, watching the upper floors of squat ugly buildings pass as the train wound its way toward the airport, and he thought of the blue eyes that must at last acknowledge him when he walked into the bookstore where the young lady worked. He thought of the questions he'd pose, innocuous questions about authors and editions. The questions would work beautifully as the starting point for a discussion about the literary scene in that rainy city, the bookstore, and one employee in particular.

The train stopped at Rockaway Boulevard, still a good distance from the airport. It had been so long since Croft had taken a trip that he'd quite forgotten that not all the trains out here went all the way to the airport. On hearing the conductor say that the next stop was 104th Street, a station outside his route, he leapt up, grabbed his bags, and darted for the platform just in time to make it through the doors as they slid shut. Panting, fighting to balance himself, he thought of how close he'd come to missing his flight and extending the amount of time that beautiful woman on the opposite coast had to find another man. For his sake and those of the strangers around him, he thought, there must be no more mistakes.

He waited, his bags at his sides, ruing his lack of familiarity with the transit system of his own city. Well, never mind. Where *was* the train going to the airport? He looked around at the bundled strangers on the platform. As he continued to wait, his anxiety swelled. He just might miss his flight. Right now, that beautiful charming woman was probably greeting a customer in the bookstore, flashing the coy look Croft had noted in so many interviews, but with a critical difference. The man fortunate enough to be looking into her eyes at this moment would encounter none of the faint condescension she had shown at having even to address the question of her possible involvement in a murder. If there was one thing Croft might have coached her to do differently in her many TV appearances, it would have been to allow her beauty to speak for itself, to avoid getting upset and giving people the sense that she felt the world made gross impositions on her, even if in fact it did. How Croft longed to be that man, in that store, right now, at this moment on a meteorologically unexceptional day, a moment in the life of the universe where circumstances had parted to allow a stranger to approach her and talk to her openly, without fear, in the hope that she might recognize a kindred nature and allow the stranger into areas of her life the world didn't know existed.

Where was the train?

Where was it?

Did the people around him notice how anxious he was? He looked up and down the expanse of filthy track, thinking that at any moment now, two beams of light must come creeping around the bend and grow dramatically brighter. But the train did not come. He stamped his feet, looked around again at the bundled strangers as if one of them might be the cause of the delay. Still he waited with growing alarm. If the train didn't arrive in a few minutes, he thought he'd miss his flight. Even if the airport was not too busy, even with short lines at the checkpoints, he was unlikely to make it.

Croft waited some more, thinking almost all the world was vile and repulsive. He told himself he was overreacting. At worst, he'd have to get a later flight. But he didn't want a later flight, which would probably mean he wouldn't arrive in that faraway city until the bookstore had closed and the young woman had gone home or had gone out to one of the wine bars full of handsome, well-spoken, well-adjusted young guys. Of course Croft could have booked an earlier flight, but the situation had come about so abruptly and he hadn't been able to arrange to leave the office early. He could have called in sick, but that would have frayed an already tenuous situation at work. Croft didn't know how he'd ever appeal to the young woman if he had no job.

He waited.

Still no train.

Now an announcement came over the speakers. Because of a police investigation at Euclid Avenue, the trains were running with delays in both directions.

Well, that settled the matter. He had one more chance and that was to get a cab. He raced down the steps, through the grubby lobby, and out into the frigid air. The station was an overpass above four busy lanes divided by a narrow walkway. Cars and trucks raced by in both directions toward points in the dreary afternoon. He was desperate not to miss his flight. He stood at the edge of the southbound lane, twenty feet from the steps he'd descended. Surely a cab must pass this way before long. But as he waited, the feeling that the world was mocking him crept back. Seeing a cab headed the other way, in one of the far lanes, he flailed his limbs and jumped up and down, but it didn't slow. Maybe he needed to be over there on the edge of the northbound lanes. He moved down over the barren pavement to the intersection, waited ten excruciating seconds for the light to change, and hurried to the other sidewalk, long and desolate with a fringe of filthy ice. On this cold and nasty day, thousands of drivers were eager to get somewhere. Yet there was no cab. Not one passed in either lane. It just wasn't an area where cabbies had luck finding fares, and they avoided it. Croft would have known that if he'd done his research, or really if he'd had basic knowledge of his surroundings. He knew of the existence of a company called Uber, but he was one of the dwindling number of people who had never used it, and anyway he was unsure they could send a car out here in less time that it would take to find a cab.

He thought he must get away from this pedestrian-un-friendly artery. A few dozen yards away, on the far side of an auto body shop and a McDonald's, there were intersections where he might have a bit more luck. He moved east on a narrow street. Reaching the next intersection, he saw there was virtually no traffic here. He made the same discovery at the next two intersections. Then he spotted a street, parallel with the one he was on, with a fair volume of traffic. It was visible through an alley that ran between the walls of two large warehouses. He had to get up there. He crossed the miserable barren street leading from the four-lane artery to an unknown point in the barren gray-white. In his haste, he did not look back toward the four lanes, and so he did not see the Pontiac racing east up the street.

Croft woke up in a dimly lit room whose beige walls had patches of white where the paint had grown brittle and fallen away. He was aware of pain, oh yes, but the pain was not fierce and raging. It was one of a host of sensations. Among them were heaviness, dizziness, and a weird tingling he couldn't classify. Above all he was aware of his left leg feeling different. The limb wasn't too large but it was too much there, too infused with the odd mix of sensations that must have resulted from an injection of something or other. His head, or rather a patch of scalp above his right temple, answered the ambiguity with outrage at carelessness and stupidity. The ache was impossible to ignore. Croft deduced that the Pontiac had slammed into his left thigh and leg as he'd tried to cross the street and had sent him flying, and he'd hit his head, really hard, on the curb and blacked out.

He lay slumped in a chair in an alcove beside a disused miniature stage. A pair of handcuffs joined his left ankle to a pipe at the base of the wall. Looking at the pipe, he could tell it was sturdy and wouldn't budge an inch. Surely whoever had found him had known the right course was to call EMS or take Croft to an emergency room. This sure wasn't a hospital. There were no windows, just a bit of light from a shaded lamp in the corner, and there was something aggressively ugly about the room. The yellow and beige surfaces did not want to be pleasing. In recognition of this fact, the owner had allowed dust to gather in force on the walls and the disused stage. He guessed that the owner had brought him through a front door and thence down a hall running from west to east, but of course he could not know that.

As soon as Croft saw his captors, he knew he'd be able to think of little else. They came into the room and stood gazing at the stranger, appearing to relish his misery and hopelessness. Here was a man, like Danny Trejo with a couple of decades knocked off. His thick dark hair fell to his shoulders, without intruding on his full cheeks. His wife was a lady, about thirty-five, with rich dark hair and a bit of a paunch. To Croft it looked as if her belly was still retreating to its former dimensions following the birth of her boy, but that was absurd because the teen standing between the man and woman was at least sixteen. The kid's hair was dense as a grizzly's coat, his physique stout for a growing boy. His dingy tank top and discount-rack red sweat pants with white stripes detracted a bit from the powerful impression. All three gave signs of an unaffected glee at finding Croft so utterly helpless. Even now Croft could not fathom why they had brought him here. He blamed no one but himself for what had happened.

They were talking now, a trio of voices floated over the air, and he tried in vain to make sense of them but they were so many muffled jeers and threats. Then two of the voices disappeared and it was just the man now, speaking directly to the captive. Croft could follow little of what the man said, but he seemed to want to know whether Croft had had crossing guards when growing up. Croft looked at the captor with murderous eyes. He guessed that the man and woman would rather not have involved their son in this sordid matter, but given his presence in the Pontiac, there was little point in hiding anything.

The teasing and taunting went on for a few more minutes. Then the woman and boy turned and moved out of the dingy room, leaving Croft to face the husband. At nearly the moment the door closed behind the woman and boy, Croft felt his anxiety diminish slightly and his lucidity improve just a bit. Now when the stranger spoke to him, it was not like a weak stream of water against a glass pane. Croft could follow a bit of what the stranger said.

"Where do you live?"

"Don't you have my wallet? My information's in there."

"You can't tell me where you live?"

"Brooklyn."

"Brooklyn's big."

"No shit."

"Where is your bank account?"

"I'm sure my bank card's the first thing you looked for."

"It was. I'm asking if you know."

"Chase Manhattan."

"Is that your only account?"

"Oh no, I've got six offshore accounts."

The man grunted.

"Give me your PIN."

Croft obeyed.

"Why did you bring me here?"

"My car near fucking killed you."

"It was my fault. I ran out into the street. No one was going to fucking blame you. Why didn't you do what any sane person would do and call EMS?"

The grin that spread across the man's face was deeply unpleasant. It tried too hard, it spread too far.

"You're still pretty stoned. Running out in front of the car was the dumbest thing I've ever seen a person do. The answer to your question is, I've been driving on a suspended license for the last six months."

Croft sighed and slumped backward again in his chair as the man turned and sauntered out of the room.

He tried to get up. As soon as he did so, he realized by what margin he'd overestimated the length of the cuffs joining his ankle to the pipe running along the wall of the alcove. The cuffs snapped taut and he fell backward and hit his head on the opposite wall. The dullness, and the feeling of every part of himself being abnormally large, found a complement in a bright burst of pain. It was humiliating to make such an elementary mistake so soon after the one that nearly got him killed.

Who were these people who had brought him here rather than to a hospital? The man had decided that the consequences of driving on a suspended license outweighed all the possible ramifications of abduction and, quite possibly, murder. He was betting on those consequences not materializing, which meant he had no intention of letting Croft leave here. Then again, maybe that was just an assumption Croft made in his state of terror. Maybe the man was on the phone now with his lawyer, explaining what had happened, exploring ways to proceed and what their impact would be.

Or maybe the man was asking whether he could borrow a friend's chainsaw.

Lying back in the chair, Croft realized that he could make out traffic somewhere, a heavy volume of it in fact. An intersection was nearby, maybe the very one where he'd despaired of finding a cab. He imagined a fleet of cabs swarming over the intersection minutes after he'd left it. Then his mind wandered further, it moved westward, beyond the reaches of the city and out over across the continent. His stupidity, his desperate actions had denied him a proper experience of America and all its beauty and violence. Way out there, in the unfathomable distances, on the far side of the continent, a polite attractive woman stood in an eminently civilized setting, receiving visitors, speaking words that answered questions about books while hinting subtly at other settings, other states of being. She could answer a question about an elusive edition of Whitman or Joyce but she really wanted you to understand that she had a sensitive enlightened nature, she'd be a most interesting person to get to know over a glass of wine in a quiet café on the slope of a hill overlooking a bay, a tableau of trees and water and mist. How unbearable now was the envy Croft felt toward all the young men who could walk into that bookstore on the opposite coast with a breezy manner and pose questions about writers, the gifted and the mediocre, the canonical and the obscure, about new books and out-of-print rarities, questions that solicited information of a precise discrete nature but whose function was really to get her to fill the rectangle of space with a voice that was vulnerable yet marked with a coy jadedness about all the dumbness of the world, all the blunderings that had allowed or facilitated the jailing of a young woman whose image was incompatible with the portrait rendered by vicious prosecutors and media whores. She was out there, single, available, yearning for the companionship of a thoughtful well-read man, and now some other stranger, some unworthy chump, would get to her. Croft had no hope of arriving in that distant city in time.

He slumped in his seat, gazing at the dusty surfaces and barren walls, listening to cars race by at the intersection. Soon he dozed off. When he woke he badly needed to piss. He yelled for a few minutes, but could not disturb the monotony. Breathing furiously, feeling drops trickle down his forehead, he stared at the door. He decided he'd be happy to piss all over the floor if his hosts desired.

As footsteps came down the hall outside toward the door, Croft thought that nothing should deny him his experience of America. Right now he had no destination or person in mind. He thought, *America is so vast and great and you must take it in. It is incomparable.* You meet men and women who appear to embody all the good and wholesome clichés, and then you find out about the uncle who committed suicide, the brother in jail, the sister in rehab. People were desperately unhappy, yes, and it was a quality that spoke eloquently and directly to his sensitive nature. Why he should have these thoughts just now he had no idea.

The door opened, and the teenager came into the room with an annoyed look. The captive gestured at his crotch. The youngster came to him, bent down, and then Croft felt a merciful lessening of pressure around his left ankle. The strong teen hoisted Croft to his feet, got behind him, and pushed him forward, then right, to a dingy rectangle of space in the corner with a toilet and sink inside. On the way back from the lavatory, Croft's vision blurred and his muscles went limp, so that the teen had to pick him up off the floor and half carry, half push him back to his seat. Neither of them was really upset. They both knew that one side effect of the painkiller they were injecting him with was to make him extremely drowsy.

He had no idea how long he lay slumped in the chair while the world ground on outside, strangers met strangers and began to make associations about each other and became the opposite of strangers. Maybe it was snowing again, or maybe the dull frigidity preserved the remnants of past snows in their invincible ugliness. Though Croft could not remember the last time food had passed his lips, he did not feel hungry, at least not in a physical sense. He was thinking, once again, of the continent out there, on the far side of the streams of traffic and the sullen skyscrapers. He imagined escaping from this place and getting onto a plane bound for the opposite coast and meeting the beautiful charming woman just in time to stop any other young man from making the acquaintance forever impossible. Croft was the first to admit his limitations and flaws, yet he felt certain that if there was one thing that woman hounded so ruthlessly by the paparazzi could appreciate, it was an intelligence on par with her own. He knew she'd warm to him. He just had to get out there. He had to.

Once again he gazed around the barren space, but nothing presented itself, nothing at all, within or beyond his reach. In a real sense, he did have a continent before him, a great block of solitary waiting. Croft busied himself by reviewing some of what he'd learned about the young woman. Her life had returned to a semblance of normalcy after so many months of soulless paparazzi capturing her moves in public. The highest court in the country in southern Europe where her roommate died had cleared her, though people argued over whether this was a definitive proclamation of innocence or a finding of reasonable doubt after many appeals and the advancement of a solipsistic attitude toward the evidence. Well, if the media couldn't figure things out, that was hardly of concern to Croft. He'd been following case more intensively than most people, and his sense of things, his emotional intelligence, spoke clearly.

Though Croft had little hope of leaving here alive, he decided to indulge his curiosity about one thing. He began crying out as loud as he could, kicking the pipe, hammering the walls with both hands. This time the teen responded much faster. He flung open the door, ran into the room, gazed at the captive in stupefaction. The teen was right here in front of him, yet Croft kept up the yelling and banging. It didn't take long for the teen to reach into a back pocket of his jeans, withdraw a box cutter, and slide the blade forward out from the handle. On seeing the box cutter, Croft feigned terror and shut up.

"I'm sorry. Please don't cut me. I'm so sorry!"

The teen's look said he demanded to know what the fuck had happened.

"I had a panic attack. I'm sorry. I won't do it again. Please don't cut me."

The teen retracted the blade and returned the box cutter to his back pocket.

"I know that you keep coming in and sticking a needle in me when I'm sleeping," Croft said.

The teen grinned.

"You want to know what pain is? I'll stop giving you the drugs."

"No, don't do that. I know I need them. It's just terrifying when I feel weak and fall down."

"Then don't fucking do it, okay?"

"You seem to think it's something I can control. I can't and that's precisely why it's so scary."

The teen turned and sauntered out of the room.

Croft had the captors thinking he was woozy and weak all the time, but in reality he knew when his strength was at its peak and when it was absent. To illustrate his vulnerability to weakness and fainting, Croft staged a couple more incidents en route to the tiny lavatory. He thought he did a pretty creditable job of making his eyes lose focus, yielding control over his muscles, and spilling out onto the floor. Though the teen's annoyance was palpable he physically disciplined the captive only once. The slaps he gave Croft about the face after his third spill went beyond any effort to make Croft alert again.

When Croft wasn't asleep, he lolled in the chair wondering why they hadn't killed him. He guessed that the money from the Chase account hadn't satisfied them, they were wondering about money and assets he might still have, and they did not discount the possibility of needing further information from their captive. They'd get through their impasse eventually.

At this point, Croft had little hope of ever getting away to that city on the opposite coast where a young woman greeted patrons in a bookstore, some of whom knew who she was and some of whom had no idea, they just assumed a bright articulate young clerk was a fixture of any used bookstore in a cosmopolitan town on the coast. He relished the memory of the unsuspected thespian gifts that had emerged when he'd begged the teen not to cut him. But he knew they'd do it. So maybe he'd better indulge his interest in the young woman in that faraway town in whatever ways he could. He fantasized about traveling out there, about visiting a place whose name had had no resonance for him at all, it was just there, until the media broke the case. They produced segments where they interviewed her siblings about growing up with her. Then when the high court cleared her and she finally got to go home, the paparazzi followed. At that point it had become hard for Croft not to think about that city on the far coast.

Feeling adventurous, Croft attempted a kind of lateral thinking he'd engaged in from time to time. He imagined taking flight across the continent, heading west with all the cultural and philosophical implications that implied, to a region beckoning to all those who knew what they wished to become, if not through the crude artifice of tattoos, piercings, and hairstyles, then by resolutely acting on impulses we must never acknowledge. As Croft travels west so many thousands of feet above ground, he looks out the window and surveys a domain of gaudily lit motel rooms where so many guests have only the vaguest notion of the coast in question, they are unworthy of that coast as they languish in settings so ugly they convey for so many guests the music of suicide.

Croft sees himself getting into a cab at the airport on that distant coast and riding over a few miles of freeway to the dark sodden downtown. The self in his vision finds a hotel just a couple of blocks from the bookstore. It is far from the tech-fueled prosperity on display throughout parts of the city. As Croft wanders through dark side streets, the bundled forms of the homeless stir in the alleys, a vagrant passes him on the street, too quickly for Croft to make out the face enclosed by the hood of a thick parka, and voices come to him, making appeals to his kindness, his decency, his belief in a world where people do not hesitate to fulfill the needs of strangers. It is so very touching. But Croft ignores the addicts who inhabit these dark dripping spaces, he has no time for them as he moves toward a point on the grid. He knows exactly where he is going and has no time for distractions of any kind. The night is so vast and dark but there are squares and rectangles of light. One of the rectangles is within the façade of a store on the ground floor of a building on a desolate square, a place that gets crowded in the warm months as people gather to hear live music but now is barren and forbidding. The rectangle is not full of light, but there are bright green and orange points in the space beyond. Croft enters the bookstore, exchanges pleasantries with the owner, and finds the young woman who is eager to engage him in a dance. Of course the encounter does not have nearly the importance for her that it has for him, but for a few minutes their bodies engage, twist, turn, and face each other again gracefully, and he is a breathing tangible presence in this famous woman's life.

How to make this more than a fantasy?

How, how to make this real?

Croft felt a surge of panic, and this time it was something genuine, not a ruse to fool that simpleton who was the only human he'd interacted with in maybe seventy-two hours. He despaired of ever making it out of this dingy hell and finding a means of transport across the continent. In this room, there was a stage, but its presence here would have been far too pat a coincidence were she actually to appear on it. She did not appear on the stage or any other place Croft could see from the chair. He wondered what might appear on the stage in the absence of the object he desired most in the universe.

Yet he felt she did not spurn him. She wanted to engage with him, she wanted him to whisper secrets to her, in fact her curiosity about what he knew was as strong as her desire for his physical proximity in the bookstore in that dark cold city. Though he could not see her before him he felt the presence of all the distilled curiosity and intelligence she possessed in the dirty lightless space of this room. Her recognition of a kindred intelligence made the physical distance, the expanse of cities and towns and lakes and motels, most irrelevant. He whispered at the dusty spaces before him.

I love you and I need you.
Do you hear me? I love you.
I know. Come to me.

Croft cried out like a child. He used his voice in a way he knew that no adult, in a traditional, conservative sense of the term, had any right to do. The teen rushed into the room. Croft referred to the script in his head.

"I'm so sorry, I had another panic attack. I apologize. I really, really have to piss!"

"Okay."

The teen unlocked the handcuffs, put his hands under Croft's armpits, and hoisted the captive to his feet. Their bodies engaged in a halting shuffle across the floor in the direction of the lavatory. The teen stood outside as Croft moved inside and reached into his pants. Then he was pissing and thinking about the teen's parents, whom he had not seen for days. Maybe they were just a few feet from where he stood.

He finished at the toilet, then rotated 180 degrees in the cramped space until he faced the sink. The teen was looking at his sneakers. So the teen did not see Croft turn the hot water on full blast and begin to edge out of the lavatory. Croft shut his eyes and dropped onto the grimy floor, not emitting a sound. The teen let out a curse. He stepped over Croft's body and into the lavatory, reaching toward the sink. In doing so, he exposed his back and the seat of his jeans to Croft.

Croft got up, seized the box cutter from the teen's back pocket, and flicked the blade forward. The little device, an elusive object for so many days, was now in his hand, ready to do whatever he required of it. He did not hesitate. The cries from the teen quickly drew the man and his wife into the room. It would have been exceedingly awkward for them to call the police, but that did not excuse the elementary mistake they made by rushing in here.

Croft stood there, panting, groaning, the room quiet, the box cutter at his feet. Though he did not question the necessity of what he had just done, he had wanted his thoughts about the woman on the opposite coast to flow without interruption right up until the moment when he would meet her in person and the old memories and ideas must give way to bracing new impressions. He began to recall some of the ideas that had arisen in the course of his slavish pursuit of the case in all its complexity. For hours without number Croft had browsed the more rarified corners of the internet in an effort to attain a status denied to most people who claimed or presumed to know something about the case, or about its principals, to have a basis for an opinion. He had sat up all night, the only light in the room a square of radiance emanating from the monitor and framing his pale eager face, he had sat staring at the text and images.

Croft could not say that all of the words and images failed to achieve their intended effect on the viewer. That a publica-tion or site might have a tabloid character did not make all its content dismissible, especially not when a site managed to obtain and upload photos from the most sensitive parts of a forensic investigation. Some of the sites Croft had lingered over displayed a knowledge, a sensibility, an erudition about the case you could hardly find elsewhere in the world. In com-parison to these sites, the tabloids, the mass-market books, the trial transcripts, and even the judges' opinions fell short. Croft could not know how many members of the *Carabinieri* the authors and editors of these sites had bribed, but the images on display before his eyes within the penumbra of light were more sensitive than he could ever have imagined. What did they disclose? Oh, nothing too lurid. Here was a rare photo of the room where the murder happened. Here was the victim, the edge of her tank top resting on her belly button, a thick tuft of pubic hair visible just inches below, but that wasn't what caught the viewer's notice, at least not the first thing. The viewer more readily took in the pair of gashes on either side of the victim's throat. It was clear that someone, or a couple of someones, had stuck an object into the moist regions of flesh and tissue, spraying bloody garb all over the room, and at least one of them had not been content to pierce the victim's throat, but had acted on an urge to rake the blade back and forth and loose tissue from its ordered place around the victim's esophagus. Garb and blood had come out in such volume that the floor and bed and pillows had copious amounts all over them even after the clean-up the killers undertook.

Here were heaps of tissue, so red and rough you might have thought parts of the victim's brain had escaped through the gashes in her throat. There were close-ups of the victim's wounds, of her dead eyes, of her trimmed pussy. There were images of blood in the hall, blood on the sink in the bathroom, blood in the room where the killers had faked a break-in, and there was evidence from other parts of the cottage, including a mat with blood on it forming the image of the upper part of a foot, but with no impression of the lower region, for the killers had cleaned the floor with bleach. In these online forums Croft had found transcripts of audio recordings of statements of the principals, including one where the young woman answered a question from one of the victim's roommates, about whether the victim had suffered: *What do you think? She had her fucking throat cut.* The websites aspired to nothing more than vulgar sensationalism, but Croft saw no reason to discount the truth of what they published with such brio. He rejoiced at the purity of these sites' adulation or loathing for the young woman on the opposite coast.

Now the thing was to get to that coast. Exploring other rooms of the apartment, Croft quickly found his wallet which still had his plane ticket inside. There was even some cash left in it. He expected to have no trouble getting back to the intersection and jumping on a train to the airport. Before he left, he made a point of arranging the three heads on the stage in the room where they had tormented him.

The Witch Doctor
of Robertsport

Jonas woke up on the beach. He picked himself up. Reaching to wipe the dried vomit from his face, he looked out at the waves and wondered about the cleanliness of the water. The deep blue beneath the scrums of foam moving rapidly ashore suggested purity. It was hot for so early in the morning, and the water held out relief. Warily but hopefully, he set out down the crest of the beach.

The hand that closed around his ankle was cold, but firm, much more so than he'd have expected of a dying man's hand. As soon as he turned and saw the dark purple head controlling the moves of that hand, he had no doubt that one more member of the crowd that had gathered the night before to watch the massacre of the whites was now himself in his death throes. It had never been totally clear whether the aim of the rebel militia had been to kill the visitors or to engage in a drunken orgy. Jonas knew only that the event had gone on far too long, and people in the crowd never fully adjusted their expectations even when the rebels began shooting whites and a couple of the whites grabbed weapons from child soldiers and began returning fire. Then a few grenades had gone off, boom boom boom. Jonas couldn't remember how or when he'd lurched away from the edge of the town down to the beach. He was just glad he'd had the sense not to stay in the thick of the revelry, battle, or whatever it was. Why someone would want to kill him, Jonas couldn't imagine. He was here in Liberia as part of a mission with no more wicked goal than to expand the reach of the world's top coffee franchise.

He tried hard but could not jerk his ankle out of the purple hand's grasp. Luckily his left ankle was captive, not his right one. He swung his right foot at the dark head as hard as he could. It went further than he felt it should, as if teeth inside the diseased mouth had instantly given way on contact. He kicked again, harder, hitting the stranger in the bridge of the nose. Now the grasp on his ankle felt feeble. He kicked the hand away, to a point in the copper sands, and began to lurch on a northerly course up the beach.

Now he really had a bit of time to look around. From here none of the bloodied Westerners were visible. Those corpses occupied discrete pockets of space on the mud roads some thirty yards beyond the crest of the copper dune to his left. The Americans, Canadians, Germans, and Britons had died where they had fallen. Among them were no doubt the bodies of soldiers, including child soldiers, who'd gotten high on khat before learning to read or write.

Jonas couldn't see any of that from here. His mind was extrapolating on the basis of bits of memory from the last twelve hours. Though he couldn't recall much of the evening, there were bright spots in his mind. There was the heavy American who'd complained that booze was too pricey here, and whom one of the rebel soldiers had plied with beer after beer, in order to watch with wonder when he blew a hole in the American's belly and all the beer came gushing back into the world. There was the uppity, opinionated British woman, a corporate lawyer at a London firm, whom one of the child soldiers had raped with a garden hoe. Jonas remembered two dozen whites running out of a café in terror and alarm and into a machine gun's field of fire. The screams, the gushing blood. The joy in the maniacal features of the soldier manning the weapon.

Ambling up the beach, he felt that nature didn't care how poor this nation was. The land all around him in the brightening air was gorgeous. Looking to the northeast, where the crest of the dune fell away, he could make out the edges of an expanse of cotton trees, a forest whose density the Western furniture makers had not yet begun to erode. The leaves were motionless beneath the pastel blue flecked with clouds of odd shapes. To the northwest lay the water, with not a trawler or rig on the horizon, with nothing at all to disrupt the waves moving in with an easy rhythm. Of course he was aware of danger, but it, too, seemed to occupy a discrete space on the far side of the crest way off to his right. Let no matter what calamity happen when people had too much drink in them. It could not make the world ugly.

As he moved up the beach, it registered that his hangover was pretty much the only thing wrong with him. There was no gash or bullet wound that he'd failed to notice. It might take effort to piece together events and figure out whether he'd been a coward or just lucky. For now he reveled in the beauty of the world.

Then another hand grasped him. He realized he'd walked right over a man half-buried in the sand. But this grip was tentative and the look on the face below him and to his right was almost friendly. It said, *Hey, won't you feed me?* With minimal effort, he walked out of the hand's grip. He looked around. It was not a total shock when, thirty feet further up, he heard footfalls and the noise of pebbles flying and crashing. He turned his head just in time to see a figure come running up from behind him and to his right. This might have been a member of the militia from the night before. Then again, Jonas had moved far enough up the beach that he thought the events of the night before belonged to an alien context. He'd been admiring the beach, the trees, the sky, the clouds, and the waves, with a manner so innocent you might have thought him a tourist with no designs on the local coffee market.

The attacker's eyes had blood in their rims and his grin exposed severely rotting gums. An idea of propriety had made him tie a rag around his scrawny lower abdomen. Jonas did not see the blade until it narrowly missed the bridge of his nose. The attacker drew it back in preparation for another swing. It was littler than a machete, but Jonas had little doubt that troops had put it to good use during the civil war, that it had liberated many heads from trembling captives' bodies. This stranger was obviously high. He'd taken part in the revelry and violence of the night before and had never come down a bit. He came at Jonas in jerking, gangly moves, announcing every act far in advance. Jonas ducked as the blade flashed through the air. The blood in those diseased eyes danced. Before the blade swung again, Jonas got a look at the blood and garb coating the expanse of steel. With still greater randomness, the blade swung three more times. Jonas kicked the stoned man hard in the left calf. That did it. The attacker cried out and fell, the weapon flew through the air toward the crashing waves. Once again Jonas was the only one standing on this beach.

Praising himself for his pacifist instincts, Jonas resumed his northward course. No sooner had he begun to admire the waves and sky again than he heard the familiar clomping and displacement of pebbles. He ran down toward the water and grabbed the weapon just in time to ram it through the stoned man's left eye. He let go and watched as the man danced around the beach, crying and cursing, for a minute before collapsing onto his back. The prone, emaciated black body made a nice contrast with the uneven vastness of amber sands and the cobalt blue above.

Now Jonas was free to walk north in a leisurely manner, to take in all the beauty of this country few Westerners had ever dared to visit. His feet fell on the sand in a measured, responsible way. Looking far ahead to the north, he had a confident feeling, a sense that the country was really not so big after all. He didn't know exactly where he was, but it was north of Monrovia.

For the next couple of hours, he walked. The beach was as beautiful and welcoming a place as he could have dreamed of finding during his days as an executive of the world's largest coffee franchise. He breathed deeply of the pure air, basked in the sun, let the fringes of the waves tickle his feet at the edge of the amber sands. At length, he saw that the beach was growing really narrow and he would have to enter thick scrub and bush if he aimed to keep going directly north. Moving up the bit of beach that remained, he looked at the trees. For all their snarling branches, the trees were not so dense as to discourage him from moving right ahead, carrying on his education about the natural life of the country. He forged ahead past the tree line into a place of zigzagging paths under mottled light. To his left, light falling through a gap in the branches threw into relief a company of stones, a grotto where frogs might declare their love. To his right, a quality of the light briefly tricked him into thinking that a random configuration of the bark on one of the trunks was a likeness of the face of one of the philosophy professors he'd studied under in Munich, before he moved to America.

He kept thinking of one word: *Robertsport*. It was a real place, deriving its name from this nation's first president, and he was going to get there. Forging ahead, he looked up at the gaps where light came though and illuminated the jumble of trunks, leaves, and twigs all around. Here he felt relatively secure in the knowledge that it would be hard for any rebels to spot him. Then again, if he did have another encounter, it would be hard to run fast. He really ought to have pored over maps and gotten to know the roads, such as they were, a little better. If he'd taken a bit of trouble, he could easily find his way to a road east of here, and pursue it, ducking or hiding when jeeps full of rebels with guns and rocket-propelled grenades sped by. Jonas blamed no one but himself for his troubles. In his eagerness to break into new markets and win a promotion, he'd lied to his bosses about safety in this country, about the course of the feud between the regime and the rebels.

Straining his ears, he could make out no footfalls but his own in this place of mottled light. He repeated all the pieties to himself. Most men and women in this country don't back the government or the rebel camp. They harbor no ill will toward people from the rich countries. They just want to carry on with their humble but fulfilling lives. Respect their ways, reject vulgar stereotypes.

Jonas knew he really didn't buy any of that. This tropical country on the West Coast of Africa was beautiful but it was at best a spinoff of the U.S. The founders of Liberia were slaves freed during the administration of President James Monroe, hence the name of the capital, Monrovia. He had a creeping feeling that the people of this country really ought to measure themselves in comparison with the First World citizens of

America. It was Americans who made this nation possible, who helped train its military, and who gave it cash, and Americans represented the ideal to which the descendants of freed slaves must aspire. A spinoff society has to prove itself worthy of its progenitor. Here was the politically incorrect truth, as Jonas saw it.

Another creeping feeling was his confidence that he would ultimately escape. The rebels, those who weren't high, really had no reason to want to kill him, and before too long he must come upon a house or a settlement and appeal to someone to help him get out of here. But even here his thoughts were prone to odd reversals. He did not feel fully comfortable with the prospect of going back to the civilized land on the far edge of the ocean, where he had grown more and more aware of odd experiences in cafés when strangers appeared to find something curious about Jonas. They looked at him for longer than seemed normal or they peeked at him from behind newspapers, not quite conspicuously enough to provoke a reaction, but unmistakably nonetheless. Jonas had begun to wonder whether something was happening to his perception, he felt it couldn't just be the pressure of professional life, though he worked as hard as anyone. With the monotonous regularity of a smoker vowing to quit, he'd promised himself he'd seek out therapy.

Looking around, he saw with delight that the woods were assuming the shape of a closing parenthesis at the edge of a widening bit of beach. With great eagerness, he started toward the tree line, but he paused upon reaching it, determined not to repeat his error and walk into a kill zone. As far as he could tell, the beach was bare.

The sun on his face as he walked out onto the amber sand felt like a rebuke for all his naïve admiration of nature as it existed here in Liberia. Walking in the woods, he'd had little idea how much the temperature had climbed and the sky had brightened. The heat was almost painful. But he felt that almost nothing out there in the day was beyond his vision. Looking to the north, he could see the edges of a town. The façades and spires glowed in the sun, and their enhancement in this meteorological moment was astonishing to behold.

Here was Faulkner country, or a picturesque derivation thereof. The branches of the palm trees hung motionless around mansions with wide white porches joined to upper floors by elegant spotless neoclassical pillars. The cluster of commercial buildings at the center of the little town united fancy and utilitarian qualities, with their grand porches and their neat rows of bricks and evenly spaced rectangles of glass flanked by green or black shutters. Jonas began to wonder what Faulkner would have made of this distinctly Southern place on the far side of the Atlantic, and to imagine the passages that Faulkner would have written about the ornate munificent venerable tranquil antebellum residential and commercial buildings standing in resolute stoic indifference to the unforgiving relentless mercenary heat just beyond the approaches to the sedate spectacular undulant reflective gorgeous imperturbable copper sands assailed by the mighty shimmering lucid unending susurrant waves beneath the beautiful limitless luscious pastel sky. Yes, Faulkner would have captured it well.

At this moment, Jonas had one goal in mind, and that was to stand in the center of the town he now beheld from a distance, to ponder the importance of this place in the life of Liberia, the world, and the universe. He picked up his pace, looking around aggressively, feeling that his awe for natural beauty must not distract him from danger. But that wasn't even really the thing. The beauty must not make him forget for a moment how inferior this country was in relation to America.

The expanse of beach did not go on for long. Within minutes, he had no choice but to turn back or enter dense woods once again without the benefit of a machete. He moved on into the bush. The crackling of twigs under his feet was loud, irritatingly so. The density of trunks all around nearly made him want to turn back. But up ahead was a town whose purpose, it seemed, was to impress visitors who had passed time in America and viewed the world a certain way. He pressed ahead. The trees were so numerous that it came as a jolt when an easing of the density of trees afforded a view of a column of bright light.

He moved closer to the opening in the bush. At the center of the space was a pond with a lucid reflection of the tops of the trees and the pastel blue. At the edge of the pond, just visible through the gaps in the trees ringing the little space, a boy in a dirty tank top and a pair of red gym shorts stood warily watching the approach of the white stranger. Jonas proceeded without fear. He thought of the youngsters he'd run into in this country, and their taste for PlayStation, for the Xbox, for DVDs of blockbusters. Hong Kong action flicks were also popular. Jonas knew how to ply the young minds of this nation, it was really pretty easy. If he did not have something on hand to offer a kid, he could allude to troves of goods waiting for someone to come and take them away for commercial purposes or, better yet, for personal use. A script ran through his mind. *Let me get a bit closer, and I'll give you access to cultural treasures of a kind that you and your compatriots, members of a poor deprived spinoff society, can never hope to emulate. Let me help you make some associations, boy. Remember the music from* Titanic, *from the tender scenes between Rose and Jack? Do you want to hear that music again? I'll make you an offer.*

Soon Jonas had a better view. The boy in the little clearing had muscles and a face comprised of bold handsome features even at the tender age of thirteen. In his eyes there were none of the signs of mania or disease that Jonas had seen so often in his brief time in Liberia. Jonas felt he could relate to this kid in an easy, natural way. This impression came now, as quick and welcome as an exotic bird alighting on a visitor's arm.

The bullet sheared off a chuck of flesh from Jonas's left thigh. His body reeled so abruptly that his head jerked upward and his mind took in a patch of the perfect blue before the urgent signals reached his brain and pain shot through him. Blood drenched his left leg. More shots raced through the air around him. He'd failed to notice the Glock pistol in the kid's right hand and it was only partly because the kid had held it mostly out of sight, behind his lower back, as Jonas closed the distance. Now he cried out. Voicing what he felt at this moment at the heart of the verdant setting felt more urgent than his life's continuation. Another bullet grazed the right side of his neck before he had the presence of mind to turn and bolt toward the beach. The kid kept firing until Jonas gained ground and trees made shooting a pure waste. Cursing, bellowing, crying, gibbering, Jonas ran and jumped and dashed over the ground he'd traversed with confidence minutes before.

He looked around in bewilderment. He could not see the beach, not a sliver or a jot of it. The sky was still there, if he wanted to take in its radiant indifference, but the sand and waves eluded him. He forged ahead, fell, got up, fell again, whirled around, probed the distances all around him, and moved resolutely on. When at last he thought he could make out the crashing of waves, off to his left, it seemed the waves had gained force since he woke up in the morning. He decided he didn't want to be out in the open again. If he knew he was heading north, that was good enough. He paused to remove his shirt and make a tourniquet to check the blood flowing from his thigh. With the thing tied around his waist, his moves were more awkward than ever.

In his head, the odd visions returned. Strangers in cafés kept looking at him in violation of all norms of civility. He didn't know whether those strangers were more odious than the coffee executives who conveyed their dislike or disapproval through looks or body language, pretending to a kind of subtlety. As he lurched ahead through the bush, he felt his disordered mind was unworthy of a body that was functioning much better than he had any right to expect in the circumstances. He moved down a slope, hearing waves pound the shore with ever greater force. Then he tripped over a trunk, spun through the air, and hit the ground hard. He got a glimpse of a gull cleaving a path through the perfect blue. When the sky at last began to dim, he was unconscious.

Jonas woke in the moonlight. A hand was shaking him vigorously.

A white hand.

A voice said, "Good thing for that tourniquet, buddy. You would have bled to death. You're a mess!"

"Where did it go?" Jonas said.

"Excuse me?"

"That gull I was watching. Where'd it go?"

The white stranger turned to a pair of soldiers in U.S. army uniforms. They came forward and helped him pick up the executive of the world's leading coffee franchise and move him through a patch of shrub, onto a paved road, and into the back of a Humvee. The vehicle set off up the road under a glowing moon. The guards handed Jonas a flask and he drank eagerly from it. Whatever was in there kept him under for the rest of the drive.

When Jonas next woke, he lay prone in a sterile rectangle of a room with gray metal walls and bright cylinders running along the ceiling from end to end. He had no idea what they'd injected him with, but he felt a calm utterly at odds with all that had happened on the night of the party by the beach and since then. He looked around. The room was large, but they hadn't seen fit to provide company for him. Two metal doors faced each other, unmoving, at opposite ends of the long rectangle. He gazed at the columns of light in the ceiling, trying to recapture in his mind the radiance of the day, the image of the gull in its passage through clear blue space. He drifted off again, woke, and dozed yet again.

When he woke, that white face hovered over him again, peering calmly down.

"You owe your life to technological innovation, Mr. Eckart. We've got systems installed in the Humvees that can detect body heat and pick up the exhalation of breath from many meters away. I thought we were going to find someone crouching in the bush ready to fire an RPG at us. But look what we found instead!"

Jonas looked groggily around.

"So you damn near shot my head off."

The man laughed gently.

"I doubt you were in much greater danger than you put yourself in, wandering around unarmed and all alone. Someone obviously didn't want to have a beer with you."

Jonas winced.

"I'm sorry, does it still hurt down there?" the man asked.

"Oh, no. I'm actually in kind of an agreeable physical state. It's the memories."

"We heard about the beach party."

"Those rebels! I know they've been through all kinds of awful stuff, but anyone can see that Americans are here to help this country become something."

The man left. Jonas dozed. At some point in the next few minutes, or weeks, a pair of male nurses, recruits from the local populace, picked Jonas up and helped him ease into sleek black pants, a gray button-down shirt, and a pair of loafers, a nice touch, rounding out his likeness to a drama major. They urged him to extend his limbs and do a few exercises. Then it was time for them to escort him out of the room and along a metal plank between two luminous steel walls. They led him through another portal, up a long narrow ramp in a dark forbidding space, then through yet another portal. The rectangle rose and fell with the swipe of a card on a little pad.

Here came a maze of chambers. In most of these rooms, you could see the adjoining ones thanks to large windows. Jonas guessed that the windows' purpose was to facilitate communication among the staff of this odd outpost. But he saw hardly any staff until the two escorts brought him into a room larger and fancier than those they'd passed through on the way. Here stood the white stranger who had found Jonas lying prone in the woods and had brought him to a warm, safe, American place in the wilds of Liberia.

"Hello, Jonas. My name is John Bennett," the man said, extending a hand.

"Hi, John."

"Our names are so similar. As I'm sure you will find our views are."

"Really?"

Bennett looked at him, not critically, but with a kind of probing wonder.

"Tell me, Jonas, about your sense of this country. I'd like to know, in your view, what is the way forward for Liberia."

"The country needs to have closer ties with what they call 'the international community.' That basically means America.

If you can increase your trade with Belgium or Norway or New Zealand, then great, but let's not delude ourselves."

Bennett frowned.

"As I'm sure you know, Jonas, the government here, the current government, is heavily dependent on U.S. aid. We've got to keep them dependent on us. In the context of Africa, the regime here is a welcome exception, you see. It voices pro-American sentiments and even votes with us sometimes at the U.N."

Jonas nodded again.

"But what if the people of this country should manage finally to harness their abundant resources, to take advantage of all the bounty that Liberia has to offer? Imagine if they unified the country and developed much more effective means of cultivating the rice and the rubber, and turned Liberia into an export hub. They could decline foreign aid and, by extension, foreign control."

Jonas didn't like where this was going at all, but he kept listening stoically.

"We can't allow the weakening of American power and influence in this corner of Africa. Things are bad enough over on the far side, in Somalia, in case you haven't heard. If we have to fund and arm the rebels, to keep the government desperate and dependent, believe me, that is far from the worst option."

Jonas couldn't keep silent.

"But that's a crime! That's like—"

"Robbing Peter to pay Paul?"

"Oh, I don't know. That's not quite the right analogy. It's being highly devious to accomplish an end you could have realized more easily."

Bennett laughed, this time tranquilly.

"Well, if you can't be a little devious, you won't make much of a spook."

Jonas asked the question he should have asked at the beginning.

"What is this place, John?"

"This is where we pull *all* the strings, Jonas."

As if to underscore Bennett's utterance, a screen a few feet away, between the two men, came to life. On it a head of state appeared, a middle-aged man with a mop of black hair, wearing a dark gray designer suit. Jonas quickly recognized this person as the president of Venezuela. Even more remarkable than the apparition on the screen was the profusion of digits and codes running directly under the screen. Jonas had to study them for only a moment to grasp what they conveyed. The glowing digits indicated the president's heart rate, his body heat, the rates at which he blinked and drew breath, how long he'd been awake. For all this scrutiny, the politician had an air of professionalism and his look wasn't without warmth. The president was inside a building of some kind, which led Jonas to believe that the camera recording him must be inches away. But now Jonas reminded himself of how little he knew of the technologies that labs at odd locations in America and throughout the world had been developing while Jonas analyzed the global coffee market.

He turned to Bennett.

"So your purview is global. You contemplate, plan, and carry out assassinations all over the world. That's what this facility is about."

Bennett smiled.

"Your praise is a bit excessive. We do keep an eye on heads of state, but going out and murdering them can bring quite a few complications. We tend to take an interest in mid-level officials in countries where they never had much of a life expectancy."

"For example?"

"Take the nation of Liberia."

The screen went dark. Then it and two other screens that Jonas had not noticed were alive with vivid colors. Now Jonas was looking at a trio of men in their forties, one in the center of each screen. He guessed that the cameras had alighted on them at various times in recent months, and now Bennett was managing the feeds to make events appear contemporaneous. But, once again, Jonas realized that maybe he underestimated the resources at Bennett's disposal in this facility.

The screen directly in front of Jonas, where moments before the president of Venezuela had appeared so proud and inviolate, now framed a member of the Liberian regime. In the broadcast, the politician, the senator or minister or mayor or whatever he was, reclines on his porch in the clear fragrant evening against a backdrop of verdant bush and a sky unviolated by a single errant gull. He stands, rocks on his heels, takes in the splendor of the day. Then he raises a glass to his lips and sucks in lucid amber liquid from the glass. He has seconds of joy before the reaction begins. Its first manifestation is a spasm in his throat, which must be sending all kinds of desperate signals to his brain. Then his eyes bulge grotesquely as he cries and gasps. Blood jets from his mouth and from both ears as his eyes burst from their sockets. It does not do to ingest chemically enhanced poison.

On the screen to the left, a mid-level official, a politician or maybe a director of the security forces, is plugging a pair of earphones into both ears. His finger dances on the surface of his iPhone. Three seconds pass before the explosion. His face and scalp decorate the walls of his tastefully designed flat. Meters away from this carnage, on the right side of the screen where the man downed poison, a bizarre scene plays out. A minister's curious eyes fix on a newspaper he holds in his brown hands. The article he's reading clearly fascinates the minister, it mesmerizes him. A peculiar magnetic property in the ink fixates the man's eyes, it denies him the option of looking away. His eyes begin to protest their captivity in his sockets. They swell and bulge, they roll and spin until they can no longer resist the chemical agents inside the ink on the page and they burst out onto the newspaper, adhering to the print like a pair of magnets to a fridge door, tissue and muscle and blood following them from the man's sockets and decorating the newspaper.

Jonas turned once again to his host.

"What are you, Bennett. CIA?"

Bennett laughed like an indulgent parent.

"Oh, no, don't insult me. The CIA couldn't stop a bunch of idiots with boxcutters!"

"Well, what is the provenance of this facility?"

"You wonder how we have the power to assassinate without having to go through tiresome Constitutional channels. I understand. You'd have to follow U.S. politics on a pretty granular level to keep track of the nomination of various people as Defense Secretary, or what in less p.c. times we called the Secretary of War, or as Undersecretary of Defense, and the monetary decisions and allocations that follow such appointments in the hope and expectation that a given person will soon take office."

Jonas listened intently.

"So this facility sprang up as a result of a temporary allocation, made under false assumptions about some lunatic's viability as Defense Secretary, and by the time the nomination died people had forgotten it."

Bennett nodded.

"Precisely."

Jonas fixed Bennett with a cold stare.

"Fuck my life, Bennett. I'm going to say it. I can't fathom why you'd share any of this with me. I could go out and blare all of your secrets to the world. Unless, of course, you do plan to kill me right now."

Bennett chuckled.

"Oh no, Jonas. I'm not going to kill you. I think we could use your talents. You're a highly competent salesman."

Jonas took some time to process what Bennett was laying on him.

"I like the idea."

"Really?"

"If you think representing a coffee chain was my calling, you're crazy. But I do wonder why you'd trust me for a minute."

"I wonder what you imagine we were up to while you slept, Jonas. You've got some tiny passengers implanted in your ears, buddy. If you go astray, you'll develop a bit of a migraine. You know, the kind where your head feels like it's exploding in slow motion."

"How could you do that, Bennett?"

Now Bennett laughed, and Jonas thought he'd prefer virtually any other reaction.

"Relax, Jonas, I'm kidding. I trust you. More importantly, I think you know your life depends on me every second that you're in Liberia. Plus, there's a U.S. aircraft carrier right off the coast, and I don't think it's here on the orders of people who like what I'm doing in this little facility. I'm feeling a lot of pressure. But if there's trouble, I can say, 'Look, this coffee executive turned up, and I've taken great care of him.'"

"Oh, nice."

"I'm willing to let you go out on the town, Jonas. Just don't do anything stupid."

"Oh, I won't. I really would like to see more of the country. You know I haven't felt at home in America for many years."

"Too much surveillance, is that it? I don't think my domestic counterparts tend to pay too much attention to coffee executives."

"I wasn't talking about government surveillance."

"Okay. Whatever."

Ten minutes later, a large rectangular door in a garage within the complex slid up into the roof and a jeep rolled out into the brilliant light. Jonas didn't talk to the guard beside him in the back with an M16A4 rifle on his lap. The driver and the guard beside Jonas exchanged a few words about the *USS Kentucky*. Jonas guessed that was aircraft carrier off the coast and neither of them felt good about its presence. Still they didn't talk to Jonas. The driver declined to play the role of tour guide as they passed among the plantation-style houses and stores, the churches, the factories, the flatbed trucks piled high with logs bound for the piers. Women and girls walked on the roads with baskets on their heads, young men shot by on motorbikes, battered and weathered Fords and Citröens mingled on the dusty roads with modified jeeps driven by soldiers of the regime, machine guns poised on platforms and manned by troops probing for any flicker of rebel activity. The soldiers in those vehicles eyed the Americans with a wary respect. The civilians passing by on bikes and in cars and vans tended not to acknowledge the Americans at all. The country benefited from so much American largesse that resentment on the part of ordinary men and women was unfathomable to Jonas. He wondered how any of these people could know about the dynamic that Bennett had related, the destabilization of this country by its supposed friends and benefactors.

The jeep arrived in a square where the frieze of colors in nearly every citizen's clothes, the dance of red, yellow, blue, green, orange, and purple, challenged the eye to alight on a point for more than a second or two. The baskets were more numerous, as were the bikes, and the military jeeps, and there were many stalls with walls made from sticks lashed together with rope or elastic. In the dark interiors, brown faces peered out at the bright scene with guarded hopeful looks. For the first time, Jonas talked to the driver.

"Hey. Please don't stop here. Let's go where it's quieter."

"Okay, boss," said the driver.

The eyes of the soldier beside Jonas suggested resignation. *We're responsible for this idiot for the next hour. Let's just do what he wants.* The driver pressed on a pedal and the vehicle surged ahead through the color and movement until it reached an intersection where it was impossible not to notice how precipitously the road leading west declined as it flowed into a network of piers on dark rectangular pillars over a beach composed of fine pebbles with rocks lying around at wide intervals. Off to the north, in a still quieter setting, the outlines of huts built from branches and rice stalks were visible. As the jeep came to rest at the intersection's northwest corner, Jonas listened intently. He could hear the waves assailing the beach with a pleasing rhythm.

"This is just the setting I had in mind."

With a movement so fast the soldier did not see it, Jonas grabbed the M16 from the young man's lap and leapt off the jeep and onto the dirt. So unexpected was this move that he got a dozen yards from the jeep before the soldiers fully grasped what was going on and began to react.

"Stop now, Jonas! We'll kill you!"

"Stop! If the bullets don't get you, your head will explode!"

As he ran toward the huts in the distance, both men in the jeep fired their sidearms. He'd taken the only automatic weapon in the jeep. But they were firing aggressively with a clear intent to kill rather than immobilize. He spun around the fired the M16 until it was empty. Without bothering to take in the state of the jeep, he dropped the weapon and ran as fast as he could toward the odd shapes on the northern horizon. Remembering Bennett's words about surgery, about an Olympian technology that could kill him on a whim, he reached up to probe his ears for blood. He was all right. Scrambling, heaving, panting, cursing, he closed the distance until he was right outside a humble hut. Without self-consciousness, he pulled the door open and went inside. As he entered, he felt an intense pain in both ears and then a couple of tiny objects clattered on the ground.

The face that greeted him inside the dim space was wizened but alert. In the sublime awkwardness of the moment, Jonas paused to take in the antique radio in a corner, the masks, vases, statues, and figurines from different periods of Liberia's history on the shelves and the little tables. He spied an empty chair directly across from the owner, who regarded Jonas now with a kind of indulgent curiosity. The man nodded. Jonas sat down.

When the owner of the hut spoke, his speech struck Jonas as highly polished. He sounded a bit like a Haitian immigration lawyer Jonas had met once. Jonas chided himself for expecting a stereotypical pidgin English to come from the stranger's mouth.

"Are you looking for a place in this country where they can't find you?"

"Pardon me, sir. I'm Jonas Eckart. I'm sorry to intrude in your private space, sir. But yes, I want to stay out of the grasp of the Americans running the facility down the coast."

"Do you think that's even possible?"

"Well, of course, every inch of the country is under surveillance. I wonder why I'm still alive, with the things they said they planted in my head."

"They weren't lying. Look down there," the man said with a gesture at the floor.

Jonas spotted a pair of metal balls glinting in the faint light. He reached up and probed his ears with a finger. Both ears had bled.

"Those balls didn't fall out on their own, did they?"

"No, of course they didn't. And you'd never have gotten them out without digging half your brain tissue out."

"Bastards!"

"I can tell that regardless of what you may have told friends and colleagues, you're deeply disappointed with globalization and the growth of surveillance in tandem with that phenomenon. You've been aching to get away for a long time, Jonas."

Jonas looked with a feeling of wonder at the face peering at him through the dim light.

"That's something I should have understood on my own. Coming here had to do with a lot more than my ambitions as a coffee executive."

"Tell me, Jonas. Why would you want to get out of your comfortable life in the First World?"

"It really wasn't so nice. Especially in the last few months. I kept getting this feeling strangers were looking at me. I didn't know whether I was sick, or whether they'd find me clinically ill if I talked about what I was feeling. But I felt it all the time. I nearly attacked the last man I caught staring at me, in a café I used to like, about a month before this trip."

The stranger nodded.

"That man was no man. He was a colonial mole."

"*A what?*"

"You heard me, Jonas. You're so awfully condescending toward this poor wretched spinoff society on the coast of Africa. How can it ever live up to the American example? That's been your thinking."

Jonas nodded.

"But listen. Your world, your reality, exists through the charity and patience of shamans outside the outer bounds of what you know. They began this experiment and they can end it. Every so often, they send a mole to check up on the state of things here in this colony, this experiment. Lately, the reports they've gotten have made them more and more curious. The future of the experiment has never been in more doubt."

"How do you know this?"

"I'm one of them, Jonas."

"A mole?"

The stranger laughed softly.

"No, not a mole."

"A shaman. A witch doctor."

The man smiled at this tiny sign that his pupil wasn't hopelessly dense.

"Well, you don't need to tell me why the scrutiny is getting more intense. I can think of all kinds of reasons. I'll wager that the treatment of Liberia is high up on the list."

"The treatment of this 'spinoff society' is pretty terrible indeed."

Jonas listened hard. Far off, he could hear the rumble of mechanized attack vehicles, the whirr of helicopter blades, and men yelling.

"Protect me. Save my life. I'll try to give the moles good things to report on, I promise."

The stranger nodded again. He stood. He preceded Jonas out into the bright day. Jeeps, an armored personnel carrier, a tank, and a trio of helicopters raced up the coast toward them.

Jonas looked at the occupants of the jeeps speeding toward him and the witch doctor. They were not Americans, but locals whom Bennett must have duped or bribed or blackmailed or otherwise manipulated into taking his side out of all the sides they could have picked in Liberia. He could not see the occupants of the copters but he guessed the same was true of them. When Jonas spotted the tank and APC, he wondered what could have caused such a gross miscalculation. One soldier could accomplish the task of killing Jonas and the witch doctor, he reasoned. If the goal was to capture them, then he wondered why they'd need a tank, a metal monster designed to batter and ram its way through no matter what terrain. Maybe, just maybe, Bennett and his allies in the local populace feared an intervention from the *USS Kentucky*.

Even at such a distance, Jonas could hear the crackle and blare of radios in the jeeps. The men in the jeeps appeared to be listening intently to what observers in the copters were reporting. The jeeps began to converge on a course toward Jonas and the witch doctor. Now the tank and the APC modified their direction. How often people hear a word like *terror*, Jonas thought, without understanding what it means.

The witch doctor appeared unfazed. He planted his feet firmly on the dust, breathed deeply, and reached out with both hands as if to claw the air around his head. He managed to look at once relaxed and intense. He was both a traveler on far planes, and a master of the moment. Over the last few days, Jonas had let the rhythms of the waves lull him, had taken pleasure in their gathering, roaring, crashing, and withdrawal. Now the swelling of the waves in advance of an assault on a

physical place went on far longer than Jonas could remember
it ever having done, and he heard the noises drawing near
as if all the world's dry land had moved to an altitude many
rungs beneath the oceans. The waves shot through the space
behind Jonas and the witch doctor, over their heads, straight
at the phalanx of copters. Columns of water slammed into
the attacking aircraft. One of them exploded in midair, and
its parts fell into the path of the jeeps. The other two copters
jerked backward, spun through the air like cats chasing their
tails, and careened toward points in the forest. They crashed
on the branches and exploded. Great gusts of dark smoke with
streaks of flame at their cores shot high into the air. One of
the jeeps veered off its course, rolled over three times in the
dirt, and exploded.

Now the witch doctor raised his right palm in the direction of the tank. The armored monster altered its course until
it was coming rapidly up behind the remaining jeeps. Jonas
watched with amazement as a portal on top of the turret flew
open and four men in desperation climbed out of the tank and
jumped off it into the mud. The crew of the vehicle that had
abruptly threw off their control looked on with amazement as
the turret moved and the barrel honed in on one of the jeeps.
The barrel erupted and a shell slammed into the jeep from
behind, exploding with a fury and splendor that made Jonas
want to weep. The jeep flipped over and lay in the dust, a relic
for kids to come and play on in the months to come. Again the
turret rotated. Another blast annihilated the remaining jeep,
adding further to the density of smoke over the coast.

The driver of the APC must have been paying attention
to these events. Before the tank's turret could move again, the
APC stopped and its back door swung down into the dirt.
Troops rushed out of the vehicle and dove for cover amid the

wreckage, trees, and rocks. Within seconds, Jonas heard bullets whizzing past him. He marveled at how many troops the vehicle had held. Now a number of troops began to abandon their cover and move out into the open. They fired their automatic rifles with confidence, with something close to fearlessness. A few of them reached for grenades hanging from hooks on their chests and began to hurl the weapons.

Flames ran high into the sky all around Jonas and the witch doctor. Jonas fell to his knees. He looked up at the circle of sky enclosed by the tips of all the columns of fire. For one moment, before the bullet came, Jonas thought he made out something exceedingly odd way up there. The faces of several wizened old men peered down at him, with an intimation of pity in their looks, but also a hint of contempt. *Here are the guys who really matter,* Jonas thought. They were shamans who dwelled on the other side of the bounds of this wild depraved universe, who were quite ready to let the spinoff reality die unless they heard a compelling case against doing so.

The bullet hit Jonas in the left shoulder. With a cry, he flopped onto his back. After blinking many times, he found he could not see the shamans. Bullets shot through the air above his prone body. In spite of the bullets, Jonas propped his torso up on his elbows. He did not miss it when the witch doctor strained both arms toward the attackers and they turned into statues of sand. But the statues lacked the consistency people generally associate with statues. Parts quickly began to slide off. Soon more than half of them had collapsed, bits of sand sprinkling and mingling with the mud.

Finally the witch doctor relaxed, let his arms drop to his sides. From his look it was clear that he did feel a certain pride. Late, far too late, Jonas detected movement in the yards between him and the witch doctor, and the shore. A ragged soldier with that familiar diseased look in his eyes came up the slope of the beach, steadied his AR-15, and shot the witch doctor in the back. Jonas wanted to cry and scream. Instead, he ran up to where the sand of dissolved enemies met the mud, seized an M16, whirled, and fired at the assassin. The coward who had shot the witch doctor from behind flopped backward and lay still.

Jonas dropped the weapon and turned again to the hinterland from which the attackers had come. Now he saw that the attackers had not been idle during the portion of the raid when they'd had clear radio contact with Bennett's facility. He could see scores of jeeps, tanks, and APCs moving up the coast. At the same, Jonas was aware of a buzzing and roaring in the air behind him. He turned away from the gathering enemy forces and looked at the sky above the coast. A dozen helicopters, with fighter escorts, advanced from their carrier out on the water toward the beach. Some of the copters touched down on the beach while others forged ahead into the interior.

Jonas tried hard to ignore the pain in his shoulder as the copters landed and U.S. soldiers with fresh pink faces ran toward him. A few of them surrounded him. As he told his rescuers of the events of the last few days, as he voiced his fear and loathing of Bennett, he wondered what doctrine, what idea, could ever have force and meaning in this crazy spinoff reality.

One of the soldiers, a confident youngster of twenty-five, stepped up and offered Jonas a pair of Steiner tactical binoculars. The young man spoke reassuringly.

"You're going to be fine, man. Your wound's not even deep."

"Really?"

"Obviously. Now take a look down there. They've got that renegade. Watch, man!"

Jonas peered through the binoculars. A company had disembarked from the copters and had surrounded the rogue, the head of the extra-legal facility. The days leading up to this moment had been so crazy. Once again, Jonas wondered whatever idea or doctrine could have force in this spinoff reality.

He watched as an officer stepped toward Bennett, paused for a moment, and pulled from one of his pockets a copy of the United States Constitution.

What the Rain Said

People wondered how effective the government could be at fighting a hidden enemy when the government's nature was so hard to fathom. To project strength, you need to state your intentions pretty loudly, you must arrange public demonstrations of might, with columns of troops flanking rolling platforms mounted with sonar-guided missiles. That was the conventional wisdom, and Samuel Croft, a typical resident of the city in many ways, if highly peculiar in others, subscribed to it. *Sure,* he thought. *Let's make the enemy fear us as nearly everyone, nowadays, fears the enemy.* Operatives or whole divisions of the regime could operate in secrecy, you would expect no less, but it was strange when even the outlines of government faded into the drizzle all around.

There were rumors, whisperings in cafés and from passing cars, about what the regime might have done recently to consolidate some of its functions. Someone, or a council of someones, near the top had decided to move personnel into a hotel over on the west side of the city, near the river. One's initial reaction might be that the hotel was a most unlikely venue for anything official. The hotel wasn't for kids, oh no. Croft liked to linger on the streets around it, as late afternoon drifted into evening, gazing up at what went on behind the windows.

The hotel had a sleek modernist design, two wings of equal proportions extending out from either side of the rectangle of concrete and metal housing the elevator banks. The windows ran from floor to ceiling and a majority of guests did not close the curtains, so that from a position on the street below, you could get a pretty good view of what guests were up to inside their tastefully designed rooms. Croft liked to linger on the street directly south of the hotel, on the ramp of a disused garage. People moving along the streets perpendicular to the one he was on did not notice him, nor did many of the guests, even when they made a show of their debauchery and pressed close to the windows. So he could linger here for hours if he chose, taking in the sights. But the setting wasn't quite private. Moreover, he did not know whether the government would tolerate behavior that confirmed the nastiest things our enemies said about us. That might not have to come into the equation, because even if you did not hold the enemy's zealous attitudes about exposed female flesh, you could certainly make a case for cracking down on what went on here. Then again, maybe tolerating naked buttocks and driving cocks was a Fuck You to those who hated our freedoms, our way of life.

It was hard to ponder any of these things when you saw what he was seeing now. Ignoring the drizzle, he looked up in the waning light at the bright rectangles at dozens of points on either side of the elevator banks. In one of the rooms, a man stood behind a thin blonde as she gazed into a mirror on a dresser. She had just pulled on her underwear and bra and the man was clad only in a blue dress shirt that fell to his hips. He massaged her shoulders as he whispered in her left ear. In another room, a woman who had just stepped out of the shower cavorted around her room with a towel on her head, never once looking out or acknowledging the world beyond the window. In yet another room, a girl in a green sweater that fell to her waist made trips between a suitcase at the base of the window and a closet at the other end of the room, carrying undies and socks and pullovers and shorts. Croft watched her for a minute before allowing his gaze to revert to woman with the towel on her head. She showed only a bit more lassitude as she went about little tasks in her room or paused to sit down before a monitor and type a few words. After surfing the web, she got up and paraded around the room naked a bit more.

Croft found himself wishing he had binoculars, but then again that would make what he was doing here on this damp street way too blatant. He hadn't worked things out but in a part of his mind, he felt he'd get in trouble, maybe get arrested on one pretext or another. If it came to that, he supposed he could say he was a student of architecture, or of birds. He told himself he was being silly because there was no law prohibiting what he did now. None whatsoever. Oh, this woman with the towel on her head! He found himself quite taken with her, with a scene that was provocative yet had an indefinable domesticity about it, but he knew how flimsy a basis this impression had. From this remove, her skin looked the color of butterscotch but maybe in a light less garish it would have a different tint. She blithely went about her business though she must know that anyone who spotted her even once must continue to watch. Sooner or later, she must stop and take a look out the window, he thought. Already he had a name for her. A name that he liked, that fitted with the aura her casual nudity lent to the scene. *Emily.* He would walk the streets of the city thinking of the time he watched Emily parade around her room with a towel on her head. He wondered whether she was here for a while, as the girl unpacking presumably was, or whether she'd check out minutes from now and vanish into the gray drizzly world.

Now he let his gaze drop until it alighted, quite unexpectedly, on a room three floors below where two men were touching each other. Croft shut his eyes. Return he must. Yes, he'd return to this spot the next day, after work. But this would not satisfy him, not even a bit. He could not bear to leave the spot. His eyes roamed over the façades of the two wings standing tall in the mist. Now it occurred to him that if the hotel received enough complaints, it just might take action to keep him out of there or punish him. Well, if the guests wanted privacy, all they had to do was draw the blinds. It really took an effort to expose oneself to the public as blatantly as these people were doing. He returned his gaze to the woman's room but she did not appear. She was in the bathroom or on the side of the room where her closet was, getting ready to go out, he decided.

The next day, it rained hard until about 5:00 p.m., when you could see your breath in the cool damp and even the grittiest corners had a pleasing luminescence in the light from the lamps and traffic signals. As soon as he could break away from his office, the scene of so much babbling idiocy, Croft returned to his spot on the street running parallel to the hotel's southerly façades. Now he was indifferent to all the guests save one. But when he looked up to that window, the woman he'd spied before was sitting, dressed, in front of her computer's monitor, composing sentences. Croft stood there in the mist, feeling as light as a fluttering leaf, wishing she'd notice him. She kept busy with the flickering characters on her screen. Around Croft a couple of shapes moving through the mist grew more distinct and he briefly feared a hand would reach toward one of his quivering arms, but the shapes moved on. It was just a couple out for a walk and a breath of fresh cool air. They passed without appearing to take notice of Croft. A couple of minutes later as the woman at the monitor rose and retreated to the nether parts of the chamber, Croft saw that he had been mistaken for her body was not covered below the waist. When she returned to the monitor, she glanced down through the mist and noticed the pale trembling man with his head craning at a seventy-degree angle. As far as he could tell from this distance, her reaction was not anger, nor even surprise, but curiosity of an amused kind. In the easier light by the window her skin looked paler than on the initial encounter, and her eyebrows were thin and curving, responsive to the intelligence in her eyes. They locked eyes for about forty seconds. As they did so, one of Croft's hands probed frantically in a pocket of his coat until he found a pen. Then he snatched a cardboard box from the perimeter of the garage and wrote frantically on a side of it. He felt so isolated and afraid down here and he didn't want her sense of him to come from that alone. He must talk to her. The bemused, inquisitive look was still on her features, intelligent under coyly arching brows, as he raised the box with both hands high above his head. He'd made the characters so thick that there could be no mistaking any of them. Croft could not be sure how much she took note of, but he thought he saw her fingers glide across the keyboard. Within seconds she was gone from the window and he decided to go home.

Croft grew convinced that the pair of people he'd taken for a couple when they passed him in the mist was not that at all. They'd made a note of what he looked like and what he was doing, maybe even furtively snapped a photo of him. That must be it. In any event, he couldn't figure out the nature of the government and what this business of relocation was about. Perhaps the ruler and his advisors had wanted to take an edge off their image, an image sullied for so long by the use of controversial methods in the global conflict, that they'd devised this transfer of functions to the hotel as a way of saying, *Hey, relax, we're all human and we all need the same things ultimately. In this hotel, in this libertine place, we can unwind and you can unwind knowing that we are doing so.* But then again, he'd come across no tangible evidence of their having moved to the hotel in the first place. And if they had, the question came up again, as to whether they'd be more or less effective. He felt sure of one thing, that he wasn't ready to go back there just yet. He longed for an assertion of strength on the regime's part and tried to ignore a feeling that his logic was deeply flawed.

The grim weather wasn't about to improve. The city was bleak but he did note that luminescence here and there, and it pleased him. When he left work three evenings after the wordless communication with the stranger, he did not walk toward the hotel but in the opposite direction, toward the east side. If he went on in this direction long enough, he'd end up in a park where there were lots of people who were open about their hatred of the police. A tradition of protest, of barely leashed rage, ran through the park's history. But he probably wouldn't make it that far, in this weather. He wanted a nice place to dine, a break from his usual comfort fare. He was quite despondent. There were rumors of strikes by the enemy in distant cities. Already he had a café in mind, a point far off in the somber blue-gray, but the rain was cascading down with such force now that he took refuge under the awning of a shoe store, folding his umbrella, reeling from the gusts. The streets were nearly empty and he wasn't sharing this space with anyone. Now the phone in his front right pocket began to vibrate.

He jumped. He thought it must surely be her. But when he put the phone to his ear, he heard a man's voice. The voice of a man in his forties, hard, businesslike, but perhaps not especially well educated.

The voice told him that obviously Croft was highly curious, and that might seem like a good thing from a certain point of view, but then again our curiosity always catches up with us sooner or later. In his bewilderment Croft stood listening but did not challenge the voice. Yes, our curiosity catches up with us. Even without this heavy rain, there were worlds out there that Croft had not begun to envision, the voice told him. Imagine a man, sitting on a beach hundreds and hundreds of miles from here. Yes, a man on a towel on a beach on a glaring hot day, his long skinny legs forming inverted Vs before him. He's like many another young blond guy but his skin has caved deep into the hollows below his jutting cheekbones and around his nose, it has receded, retreated, caved until he looks like the sun has taken vengeance on him for all the voyeurism in which he has indulged, to the point where he literally HAS NO FACE.

The caller hung up. Croft replaced the phone, stared out into the shifting sheets of rain, decided he wasn't up to hunting down a good meal just now. The heavy relentless rain put his little existence in perspective, it told him, *There is far more you don't have the will to pursue.* Deploying the umbrella once more, he moved timidly out from the awning and downtown two blocks to a metro station. As he sat inside a hurtling train a few minutes later, Croft noticed that a man and woman whose nationality he could not determine were staring at him. They occupied seats directly across from him on the speeding subway while their boy lingered nearby. Every ten seconds or so, the man leaned over, grinning, to whisper in his wife's ear. She grinned in turn. He gathered that they were making jokes at his expense and he felt more insecure and unsafe and alone than ever before. As he walked out of the metro later, he wished deeply for a show of force by the regime, for an assertion, a validation of its authority. This wish, in its turn, encouraged a creeping sense that he was naive and was missing something quite obvious. He dared to hope that a sprightly intelligent guide, an oracle, would materialize out of the water and mist to explain things to him.

At last the weather turned. Spring was shading into early summer and bright days were inevitable. Soon the beer garden at the base of the hotel would be busy every night. It was now four evenings since Croft had first seen the woman, and he feared that if he didn't meet her now, she almost certainly would check out and he'd never see her again. He moved out of the shadow of the garage, crossed the street, walked up past the beer garden and stood outside the lobby. He kept up his vanguard here for hours until, sure enough, the woman strolled right out of the lobby's revolving door. She wore jeans, a blue sweater, a pair of shades. Though hurried, she projected more than ever the appearance of an aesthete and a girl-next-door rolled into one. Croft dashed up to her and began to talk about how everyone in the city was so guarded and no one wanted to open up to strangers any more. She warmed to him and talked freely even after he told her he'd been lingering outside the hotel, waiting for a business partner to call him back, when he'd happened to glance up and notice her walking about her room. After that, he said, he'd felt he absolutely must meet her and had tried to give her his number.

She had the number, she said. She'd just been on the fence about whether to call. You see my point? he said. Everyone is so guarded, and with good reason. After talking a bit more, she told him her name, Anne Danvers, and agreed to have dinner with him at a venue of his choosing, since he knew the cafés here so much better.

He had dinner with Anne on three nights, and each time he felt his desire and lust surge as he studied the depths of her brown eyes in the light of a flickering flame at their table. She had found a way to extend her business in the city a few more nights, so she wouldn't be making an exit from Croft's life just yet. They continued to dine out. They also talked by phone as Croft walked about the city and in one of these exchanges, she disclosed the fact that she had a middle name she more commonly went by, but in her relations with Croft she felt like being called Anne. That suited him, for there was no more lovely name. One thing bothered him, though. When he asked Anne over dinner where she was from, she didn't answer, and he thought it was just because she was really polite and didn't want to talk with food in her mouth, but when she finished chewing she began talking without preamble about the hotel. Even if she hated to talk about the place she came from, he felt, it would have been polite to tell him at least that much rather than act as if she hadn't heard the question. On their following date, he repeated his question in a manner that made clear he expected an answer. She told him that where she came from didn't define her at all and requested with unaccustomed curtness that he not ask her again.

He stopped walking to the hotel after work simply by default. When they didn't have plans to meet, he took zigzagging paths around the city now, not caring which metro station he ended up entering. One night, he decided on a route home, descending with a drunkard's steps into the depths of a station. Walking along a platform between tunnels, he heard feet clattering on the steps behind him but thought nothing of them. Seconds later, they were upon him: seven or maybe eight teens who hooted and laughed and rapped as they shoved Croft headlong into a pillar, then kicked and stomped on him as he wailed, first in surprise then in agony and shock. He'd never been assaulted before, it occurred to him as one of the teens split his right ear open with a kick and another walloped him in the gut so hard and fast he couldn't breathe. They rained blows on him for a couple of minutes before a final, inevitable kick to the skull. They ran off. Awake, heaving, spitting blood, he marveled that they hadn't taken anything from him, but then remembered that the game, Knockout King, had no economic motive at all.

Croft despaired of sharing anything with the police. If the regime couldn't prevent this, it wasn't good for anything at all, he resolved. At the same time, people talked about how safe the city was these days, about how they were by no means living under a reign of terror. Well now, that was bluster, they were all shitting their pants and were too haughty to admit it. The bottom line was that the regime couldn't even protect a citizen from a pack of unruly teens, and that being the case, you could never it expect it offer credible protections against an enemy far more elusive and insidious. He was desperate for a sign, any sign, that the civilized people of the city could yet make a stand.

After the attack, he began to have reservations about taking so many solitary walks, but he could hardly imagine life with little or no exposure to the rain and its rhythms. He walked for miles, studying the reflections of neon light in the puddles, the sheets of water loosed by passing tires, the mounds of dirt in the radii of trees pelted by drops. He moved through the city with no destination in mind, feeling like Scott Fitzgerald's narrator in *The Great Gatsby*, who found satisfaction or stimulation in the face of unquiet dark.

The rhythms all around built and built. In search of a place to process and meditate on all the stimuli, he turned into an alley between two big buildings. Here he saw at once that the mist and water above him were rapidly condensing. The natural substances converged at a few points in the air, forming a mouth, a nose, a pair of intelligent eyes, and the eyes studied him, appraised him, coolly but not without pity or compassion, he felt. At last he was in the presence of the rain oracle, the distilled wisdom and intelligence of the city, ready to receive its counsel. The oracle was indescribably beautiful and knew everything. The oracle had so much wisdom to dispense. That woman, Anne Danvers, is not a woman at all, the oracle told Croft. She is a sorcerer in the employ of a foreign regime with no goodwill toward the one you live under. If you wish the city around you to go on, kill her.

The features of the rain oracle grew quickly less distinct. Within moments they faded back entirely into the cool gray-white.

As he left the alley, Croft thought that there was one location where the death of Anne Danvers would be public and would help prove to everyone the strength, the invincibility, of the regime. Then again, he thought, maybe Anne has deceived me, maybe she seeks to orchestrate my death in the most public manner for psychological ends of her own.

He had dinner with Anne at the café he'd been thinking of the night he received that call from a stranger. Over numerous glasses of red wine, they discussed his plan. After eight glasses, he thought, she would practically have signed over her ovaries to someone who made a fairly eloquent case. She came off as so nice and sweet.

On a cool and misty Friday night, they walked arm in arm into the lobby of the hotel. Croft told the clerk he wanted a luxury queen suite, and promptly produced a card, drawing upon the savings of three months. Minutes later, they were riding an elevator upward through the middle of the tall vertebrate structure, to the eighteenth floor. Once in the hall outside the elevator bank, they linked arms again and strolled to the fifth door on the left. Inside was a luxury suite of an order that neither of them could have hoped to glimpse before. But they did not have a minute to stop and admire the designer lamps and chairs and toilet. Even the monitor, which flickered with malevolent life the moment they stepped into the room, was of little interest. Anne began to undress, urging him to do the same. He said placating words as he moved toward the south wall. With a sweep of his arms in opposite directions, he pulled the curtains far apart. He gazed out at the buildings with blinking lights like eyes in an asylum where all but a minority of inmates had gouged their eyes out. At this moment he had the perfect clarity of knowing exactly what he'd been longing for. Yet that old feeling that his logic was wrong still wouldn't go away. Well, just fuck it. He peeled off all his clothes, grabbed one of the tall thin designer lamps from a corner of the room, flicked it on, and began to wave it back and forth before the window. There were people on the streets below and on the promenade running from the north courtyard of the hotel to the south courtyard. He spied the red tail lights of cars and taxis receding into the vastness of the night on the street perpendicular to the one where he'd stood watching. He could see now, in the cones of light cast by streetlamps, heads rotating upward. For another ten minutes he stood there waving the lamp diligently, then leapt onto Anne on the bed. For the next half hour, they kissed and he entered her and their locked bodies rolled restlessly. He got up again, waved the lamp, banged it against the window as hard as he could without breaking it. Then he turned to Anne, to gauge her reaction. I know you're a sorcerer, he told her. I know that you came to this city with wicked intent. She smiled. He went to her.

Sliding his hands onto the sides of her pale slender neck, he told her that he'd fully expected the banging of the lamp against the window to scare her. If that had failed, maybe what he did now would work. He clutched her neck in both hands, relaxed his grip for a moment, then squeezed as hard as he could. He said he had it on the authority of a rain oracle that Anne was a sorcerer and was here to undermine and destroy. But her eyes didn't convey any alarm. They looked at him as if he were a disobedient child.

He squeezed harder, and harder still. To his amazement, she spoke with all apparent ease. She asked whether he really believed in the order he purported to defend. Everything here in this city was so lewd, dirty, and vulgar. Croft reminded her, not relaxing his grip at all, that it was her nudity that led to their getting acquainted. The woman with disdainful eyes said, *No, I just did that to get your attention. I wanted to examine a resident of this city and see whether he conformed to my poor expectations. I don't think I need to tell you the answer. If it's the other way around, and that rain oracle is really a demoness, tell me how you'd know any better, Samuel darling. The rain oracle encouraged a deluded man to defend a city that shouldn't be here. This place, and everyone in it, deserves to die.*

Croft decided that Anne was lying to save herself. He squeezed her throat with renewed fury. Anne raised her right arm and made a gesture with her palm like giving a high-five. Croft flew off her and across the room until his naked back and buttocks slammed into the wall opposite the bed. He cried out in agony and fell onto his belly, fearing his spine had sustained damage. Anne laughed.

Clambering to his feet, he could not ignore the scene outside. People were noticing now, yes. Crowds had gathered on the promenade and on the streets. He told Anne he hadn't been serious before, and he loved her. Once again their bodies locked and he thrust so hard his force carried her head within inches of the ceiling. She sank, rose again, sank, rose again, sank, rose yet again, screaming with joy. Their locked bodies did pirouettes before the window until it was time for the thrusts to resume. He craned his head toward the window as his force lifted her again and again.

He got off her and went to the window. The crowds had thickened. If he accomplished what he came here do to, they would all see. Croft decided he must kill her. He tried to approach Anne, and once again an awesome force flung him against the wall. He hit his head and nearly passed out.

There came pounding on the door, and they heard the unmistakable rotor of a helicopter which moments later made a dramatic appearance only yards from the window. It was so close they could make out the features of the pilot and the young man with clipped blond hair and a cap who leaned out of the passenger's side door. The helicopter was to forestall any escape by means of the window or the roof. But Croft did not try to formulate plans to escape even when the pounding came harder on the door, and a group of armed men rushed in, for in spite of everything Croft began to feel fully vindicated, fully assured of the regime's infinite capacity to look, to probe, to pry, to contain.

For the first time in years, he felt safe. Yet as they led him out of the hotel, he never quite succeeded in banishing the voice that said this wasn't close to the outcome the rain oracle had ordained.

And then: tragedy came to Boston.

Derangement

Dedicated to James Thurber

I cannot describe these events as I experienced them. The editing of my recollections must be rather extensive if the happenings are to make any sense to you. It was during my months as yet another actor pining for the big time that I learned firsthand of the effects of the drug called propranolol, which makes it impossible to experience much of anything in a linear way.

One might as well start with the meeting I had with a forty-six-year-old movie producer, Stan Egan, in the beachfront home of my agent, Walter Pentlow. Walt was also a participant in the meeting. Stan and I were sitting on the lush black pillows of a huge couch facing glass doors that afforded a stunning view of the ocean. Walt lounged in his trademark tweed jacket and chinos on a wicker chair beside the elegant glass coffee table on which lay a copy of *The Hollywood Reporter*. Stan was interested in having me appear in a moody, violent film set in the New Mexico territory in the 1860s. Nothing too remarkable there, but one of the clauses in the contract we were arguing about would require me to take propranolol, whose side effects and long-term effects on the user's mind were subject to fierce debate. The immediate effect of the drug was to cause the user to lose most memories up to and including ingestion of the drug, for the sake of total immersion in a setting. For producers and directors yearning for utter verisimilitude, the drug was a miracle. For many of my friends in the actors' guilds, and for my agent, it provided for potentially the most Faustian of clauses in an actor's contract.

"My client gets the same royalty structure as on *Hayseed Bandits 3*," Walt said.

"Oh, fine," Stan replied, looking bored.

"I'm going to ask you to pull that clause about the propra-whatever-the-fuck, Stan," said Walt.

"Oh why the hell, Wally?" replied Stan, the brows above his thin little glasses knit with annoyance.

"Well, for the obvious reasons. It isn't in wide use and no one really knows where it might take someone."

"Ever wonder why you're a C-list agent?"

"Excuse me, Stan?" said Walt, whose home this was, after all.

"Do you want me to dance around the subject, or be brutally honest? You're fifty-three, Walt. Whatever you were going to do with your life should have happened long ago. Nobody's ever heard of you. You're pitiful. Because you're *so fucking timid.*"

"Timid! I'm not scared of shit! It's not even about me taking the damn drug. I'd like to know since when is it timid to be a little concerned about your client."

The producer exhaled, crossed his legs, gazed out through the glass door at the waves pounding the shore. Stan had a beachfront home, like this one, but bigger and fancier.

"Your opinion is duly noted," Stan said, with a look establishing that there must be no further discussion of the clause.

"Stan. Do you remember Ivan Jankow and *Blood Red Valley*?" Walt asked.

"Ah, vaguely."

"Have you read any accounts of the actors they hired?"

"No. Did they take propranolol?"

"Yes! And since then—"

"Walt. *Your opinion is duly noted!*"

Ah, *Blood Red Valley*. That was a low-budget shocker about an alien race that comes to the Earth, to a place not unlike New Mexico, in fact, and makes a decision about the fate of humanity on the grounds of how degenerate we all are. In the aliens' view, we've sunk so low as a species that we can't even believe in ourselves or mount a convincing defense against them. In the final scene of *Blood Red Valley*, you see the aliens, which look like a cross between crabs and rats and are eight feet tall, leading endless rows of chained humans toward a giant abattoir. The slaughterhouse, for some reason, resembles nothing so much as a great fort from the 1860s. The resemblance is so uncanny you half expect to see a Confederate flag fluttering in the desert breeze.

Jankow reportedly thought he was documenting a real phenomenon, and wanted to make more films about it. The man actually believed in aliens.

But now.

I thought they were going to shoot me any second. All the eyes in this tense room were on Captain Wilkes.

Wilkes and his Confederates had captured us in the course of our failed attack on Mesilla, and I could not recall the last time I had seen Confederates with so much swagger. The sight of these boisterous rebels and their commander made me despair not just about my life but about the whole course of the war. The men cowering in a corner, watching Captain Wilkes, were in even worse shape than I was, with suppurating wounds, and the Confederate officer seemed pleased to find them without their bluster, like a president and his cabinet rounded up and stripped naked.

"Now we're going to raise the stakes a bit," said Captain Wilkes, his look shifting from the Federals to the Apache women filling the opposite corner and back again.

"I see you Federal men are terrified. That's as it should be. If we finish questioning these women, and it turns out there has been any licentiousness, any at all, then I am going to make an example of the culprit," he said.

The women stared at the captain, who rested one hand on his pistol and the other on his saber, as the Federals cowered in silence.

"If I find out one man has committed a rape, I will gut him here in front of his companions. The second man found guilty will come outside with us, and we will tie him to a tree and burn him alive, and so on for any more culprits. We'll do what it takes to bring order to this state."

Now one of our own stepped forward. Lieutenant Baylor, his wrists bound behind his back, walked up and faced Wilkes, and I braced myself for a harangue against extrajudicial means.

"Sorry, Ned, I can't let you do that," Baylor said.

Astonished, Captain Wilkes stared at the other officer, whose life he had so graciously spared on the buttes overlooking Mesilla.

"You have compassion for rogues?"

"That's got nothing to do with it," said Baylor. "I can't let you inspect these women."

We all realized what he meant, why he *must not* allow any inspection.

"My God," cried Wilkes. Before Baylor could retreat, Wilkes shot him between the eyes and his body crashed to the dusty floor. Private Martin ran over and drew the saber from the belt of his dead superior, and then Wilkes fired three rounds through the private's scrawny body and the bloodied women were screaming. I charged out of the chamber into the hot night, Wilkes noticing my flight too late to halt me, and I ran through the stony soil and the sagebrush in the direction of the creek half a mile away. I knew they were following me, but I didn't care, they had little chance in the dark with a handicap of twenty or thirty yards, and only a noisy plunge into the creek or another flagrant stupidity could do me in. As I ran, the soil began to turn to a mix of jagged rock and clay with a hue of advanced rust, when you saw it in the day's full blaze. In the dark it was a semi-soft mulch where my feet made clomping noises as the yells of the pursuers grew more distant behind me. Still I kept up my pace and searched for a place to hide amid the riot of sagebrush and the rises and pits on either side of the creek that now lapped my feet.

Shots rang out far behind me, but we all knew that they were wasting rounds. Then I made out a place on the far side of the creek that might shield me. I crouched there as the predators' yells carried through the night, cursing me and cursing one another, and I thought that they didn't have a chance. But an overwhelming sense of guilt, of having unwittingly given the dastardly Confederates moral ammunition to use against us, was squeezing the life out of my soul. Baylor, the strong, vindictive man who had taken a bullet for another soldier at Mesilla, was gone forever.

At dawn, I staggered out into the shallow reaches of the creek, kneeled, and cupped my hands. I poured water over my matted locks, and then drank laboriously. The sun was high and even at this hour, I knew today would be a reckoning. I drank and drank in the silent valley, and then I looked up and saw them. Wilkes's mind writhed and seethed behind the slits under his gray cap, while his three subordinates glared sullenly and clutched their glinting guns and sabers. For a moment, we just gazed at each other, myself knowing what they knew I knew, and then came the mental image of Baylor crashing to the ground in the red-draped chamber where the Apache women gazed in terror, and then my feet were splashing through the creek again and I expected to die. But when I stumbled and plunged face-first into the creek, it was not lead or steel that came down to meet me, but the arm of a lithe girl, who protested that I was too close to the large rectangle of earth rising amid a heavy metallic groan on the hill to our left.

Please do not be disgusted with me, reader. You may feel that I have violated a pact with you, with this ending that amounts to "and then I woke up." But in reality, this Walter Mitty experience has introduced both of us to the effects of propranolol, whose use they had written into my contract, in order to achieve an effect of reality in their film. I had frankly forgotten about the clause in question, and to this moment, I don't recall ingesting the drug. Say what you like, but it worked. The actors' guilds do not know what to make of the product, but they must decide pretty soon. Maybe you feel some of my astonishment, and the story isn't half over.

After they suspended the shoot and began their yelling match with the developers who had messed up everything, I accompanied the producer, Stan Egan, to his house on the beach about thirty-five miles south of L.A., and we relaxed in his huge black designer chairs and gazed out at the waves crashing on the sands where the mostly naked kids would begin showing up by 8:00 a.m. or even earlier. We sipped merlot and talked about the movie, the producer appearing to sense that I still didn't quite accept the use of propranolol, even if the result had been good up until the mishap. Egan was furious at the developers who ruined the shoot.

"We ought to have a party here soon," he said, when he was done venting.

I just looked out at the waves and tried to remember how and when I'd ingested the memory suppressant. No memory came. For all I knew, I had traveled back through time to the 1860s over the past couple of days. This occasioned jokes from the producer, amused that anyone could presume to find that unsettled world anywhere outside of the popular history magazines, books, and films. That was pretty much where I had found the Old South and it did not seem unsettled at all, it had stood in my mind as an example of oppressive order.

"You could have seen this coming, you could have traced the arc for a long time," Egan said. "From those reality TV shows through Dogme 95, on to the present, people wanting to see actors fully immersed, to see them just stop having to be actors. But then there's the social role to consider, of course. Educating people about the horror and chaos of war and why we had to rise up and stand tough against the bloody old Confederacy," he finished.

I thought of putting my two cents in, then just lay back and sipped some more wine and looked out at the waves. We chatted for about another twenty minutes and then ambled off to our rooms.

The next night, Egan had plans to go out to dinner with his fiancé, so that left me with time on my hands in this spacious house where you could lose yourself in the soothing cadence of those waves breaking on the beach. Before he stepped out, the producer pointed to a pile of DVDs on a table in the living room.

He said that they were films made by crews that went around to college parties and filmed portions of the festivities, then sold their product online and through the skin magazines. I loaded one of the discs into the player and watched the brief opening credits stating that the film came from a party at UC/Irvine last year. Then came the scenes: a blond girl doing shots of some substance as a bare-chested guy crept up behind her and pulled up her shirt, then another girl came up behind the guy and started fondling his groin; a shower stall as two guys in underpants and two topless girls crowded in, and then someone ran a tube from a keg over the top and drenched the hysterical four; a mostly nude duo wrestling on the floor, with alternating frisky and aggressive moves; a quartet of dancing co-eds ripping their tops off and making the guys gawk at their ripe breasts. Later on, there came shots of a young woman performing fellatio on three guys in quick succession.

I watched a second disc, a third, a fourth. When I loaded the fifth disc, I got more of the same for the first twenty minutes or so, and then there came scenes from an off-campus party. The camera alighted on a girl, and if you saw her, you'd hardly quibble with my use of *girl* over *woman*, standing on the edges of a crowd who were passing around an object I couldn't make out. The girl seemed shy. A thin creature with long golden hair, her breasts were modest, but not so modest that they would disappoint whichever horny guy she ended up with that night. When the object, which I recognized as a joint, came to her, the girl dipped her head and closed her eyes, or the lids moved so far down I thought they were shut, as if she wanted to decline but couldn't quite bring herself to say so. The offscreen partner persisted, holding it out and prodding her, and even though I could not see the others, I knew that they looked on expectantly. Finally, the edges of the girl's mouth curved into a shy smile. *No, no, you fink!*, said her look, expressing not anger but amused complicity in the breaking of a dumb rule, *Yes, I'm feeling some reservations here, but they're weak and I feel them in spite of my hip judgment.* She did what the others expected.

The film carried on through a montage of sex a bit more graphic than in the first few movies, and then we were in another room with some people offscreen and that same girl. Now the group was doing something to one of the guests, or at least I assumed that that was what he was, for the camera gave only a random glimpse of his feet, his big hands clasped as if in supplication, and his blurry face marked by an anguish, like a working-class Brooklyn kid asking his mother for forgiveness, but I saw that he was in an odd position and what his look registered was partly physical, they were hurting him, and I guessed that he was a mildly retarded guy, and now the group again turned its attention to the shy girl. I watched until I saw that timid smile creep back again, *Don't make me do this, you fink*, and I watched still further as another partier brought a kitten into the room, and then I decided to call it a night.

Stan Egan was a walking compendium of Hollywood lore. He knew how to cultivate contacts and get people to run their mouths, and if he had spent most of his life in Washington, D.C., instead of out here, he would have been one of those political insiders of whom people whisper, *He knows where all the bodies are buried.* Who knew, maybe he was aware of a grave or two in those Hollywood hills.

Egan had been making new friends, and wining and dining old ones, longer than I had been in the workforce. His rolodex amazed me, and when he mentioned someone's first name, I had to stop and ask if it was that Paul or that Jennifer or that Robert, and the answer was usually yes, though he'd brought the person up in order to disparage him or her for being spoiled, egomaniacal, impossible to work with, or some combination thereof. Moreover, Egan claimed credit for moments in some of my favorite films. He was an unbilled co-screenwriter, advisor, or associate producer who had come up with the idea or looked at someone else's script and helped force a moment to its crisis, in T.S. Eliot's words. As you can gather, I was grateful for the chance to hang around with him during this lull in our shoot, which had begun to exhaust me on so many levels. I yearned to be a star, but the route seemed more tortuous all the time. Egan's attitude toward me was a bit hard to fathom. I accompanied him to a few more parties before the weekend when he left town to attend a wedding.

On Saturday evening, I decided to drive down to the cluster of towns on the coast north of San Diego and check out the bars and clubs. Once, as a teenager, I had visited someone in La Jolla for a weekend and explored the clothing-optional beach accessed through a steep and winding trail down the face of a dune. I had pleasant memories of that trip and lots of curiosity about the region, so I jumped into my Saturn Ion and headed south through the dark desert.

After thirty minutes of listening to the disposable music on the car's radio and trying to focus on the road, I pulled into the parking lot of a club where a lot of sailors on leave from the naval base in San Diego had come to unwind. I found my-self intrigued with these guys and their tales, but afraid of ap-pearing to study them like creatures in a zoo, so I affected the most casual look as I strolled the courtyard sipping a Corona Light. No one took note of me until I struck up a conversation with a recently married couple who said they hung around in San Diego because of the husband's interest in maritime his-tory and in getting to the nuts and bolts, the structural logic, of ships from one or another era. When the couple left, I decided to go and check out some other spot before I was too drunk to drive safely. I found a second nightspot, then a third. It was at the third bar, a large, pleasant terrace partly enclosed in crisscrossing wooden slats, that I took a chance and wandered over to the table of three guys in their mid-twenties whom I figured had to be on leave from a ship or a submarine. They sat at a table at the far end of the terrace sipping mojitas as the speakers blared Jim Morrison: "Indians scattered on dawn's highway bleeding . . ."

I introduced myself, and they encouraged me to sit down. Their names were Higgins, Erdahl, and Bryce. When I mentioned that a producer I knew might want to explore the idea of a military thriller set on a submarine, they quickly set me straight.

"We wouldn't know about that," said Higgins. "I'm a radio operator on a carrier, and these guys are SEALs."

I could hardly believe it. SEALs were commandos who went on missions in Iraq and Afghanistan. Was Higgins even allowed to identify his friends as SEALs? Was he pulling my leg?

"If we'd been on a submarine for the past six months, you can have my word we wouldn't be sitting here right now," Erdahl said.

"They haven't allowed any women on submarines until just recently and there still aren't many at all. So this would be a busy night if that were the case," said Higgins.

Then Bryce broke his silence.

"Someone asked me earlier today if it's true that half of all enlisted guys are trash."

Even though the other two gasped, I suspected that they maybe weren't all that incredulous about someone thinking poorly of enlisted men.

"I said no, it's actually more like *eighty percent.*"

We all had a good laugh. The three chatted about what they wanted to do in their brief time offshore. No one wanted to think about the months that would follow, the priority for all the guys here was to lose themselves in the *mélange* of dry heat and beaches where the fine white grains stung your eyes in the infinite distances of midday. We kept drinking as Erdahl and Bryce razzed Higgins about the "dear John" letter he had gotten a few weeks ago, after his girlfriend in Wichita fell for a handsome guy named Tate. He had swept her off her feet and she had dealt with Higgins, who felt deep yearnings and thought often of future possibilities, like a bothersome detail.

"The stars don't smile on one who whines and frets," said Bryce, before getting up to fetch another drink for the love-lorn sailor. Higgins said that he knew it was wrong to wish anything bad on the sonofabitch who had stolen his girl, but sometimes . . .

He drank some more and mellowed out a bit, as the other two reminded him of opportunities sure to come. Then I asked the three about their views on Iraq, and they expressed a passive attitude. They had done their duty, men of any generation may have to make sacrifices for the sake of order, and it was time to relax and enjoy the country's gratitude, they said. Bryce drank some more and struck up a little ditty:

Imagine if all the ships did away with inspections,
Imagine if Venus gave 'em their directions,
Imagine if all the broads came from People *magazine,*
Imagine if all the seas turned to Jim Bean.

At length, Higgins decided to call it a night, and then Erdahl, leaving only Bryce and myself.

"Do you think the stars would smile on an actor who frets over a failed relationship from years ago?" I said.

Bryce seemed amused as he put away another drink, and another, and we talked on about the beaches and the bars and the high number of couples in the area that included a woman from Japan or Australia or some other place that hosted our sailors. We were enjoying each other's company, but I saw that Bryce was unlikely to make it home on his own.

"Come on, sailor," I said, throwing my arm around him, feeling as if I had known him for years. "You shouldn't be out in public like this, and you definitely are in no state to drive."

I led Bryce to my car and slid him into the passenger seat, then I climbed in and drove us back to the desert road. For a long time, he languished in his seat with his eyes shut and his head lolling slightly toward me, then he began to mumble just audibly.

"I think the stars may be set in your favor. You know, every so often, you meet someone who's got a way, an air about him, and you know that even if the guy's down, just being who he is, that's ennobling."

I wouldn't have expected this guy to use the verb *to en-noble*. I thought of quoting Aristotle, but realized that this would add nothing, that I'd merely be showing off. Bryce finally drifted off for the reminder of the trip. When we pulled into the drive of Egan's home, Bryce roused himself, rubbed his eyes, and followed me groggily indoors. I guided him to a big, plush chair and brought him a glass of water, but he just set it aside. I strode into Egan's chamber as bits of the evening's levity replayed in my mind.

Imagine if all the seas turned to Jim Bean.

Here before me, once again, was Egan's collection of discs.

In the other room, Bryce said something that I didn't catch.

Having collected a good sampling of the raunchier discs, I wandered back into the living room, when, for no reason at all, it hit me that I had no memory of ingesting the propranolol that helped me act so convincingly. Maybe the drug blocked neural transmission just like wine or beer. It was possible that the memory languished somewhere in the tissues inside my skull and would emerge unexpectedly, along with God knew how many other memories.

In the meantime, I just felt *weird*.

If I didn't remember taking the drug before, who was to say that I wasn't on it now? Who was this strange guy in the living room? But that was silly, I remembered the whole evening, and the preceding ones, and coming here with Egan from the shoot in the desert. I knew this was really Egan's house, this was where he lived and slept and fornicated, its emptiness was quite authentic.

"Egan wants to have more parties out here, you know," I told the guest.

"Yes, we all should party. Party," repeated Bryce, much further gone than I was.

"Celebrate. Every American family should cook hamburgers made from Iraqis," Bryce added.

I stared at him and wondered, again, who he was.

Who he really was.

"Every American kid should get in the spirit."

"Bryce, are you okay?"

He grinned at me. It was an *impossibly* wide rictus. Then he started shadow-boxing, feeding the queasiness in my gut, for sometimes nothing is scarier than playfulness. One of those blows would kill me or put my lights out for sure.

"Bryce, you need to drink some water and chill out."

He didn't want to relax, and now he added kicks to his parries and thrusts.

"I'd really like to show you what we felt the moment you sat down at our table."

"Huh?"

"I'd like you to know what we felt like doing to you."

"*Bryce,*" I said, "*get the fuck out of here.*"

"Yes, I'd love to fuck you out of your skin, pretty boy."

I walked over to Bryce and tried to guide him to the front door, thinking of the relative isolation of the house and the lack of anywhere else for him to go. Then he punched me in the shoulder, not hard enough to do damage, but it was no love tap. I escorted him to the door, closed and locked it.

As soon as I'd turned around to find the telephone, Bryce burst through the door, a look in his eyes such I had seen in junkies' eyes a few times, this look of *anti-life*, and in a motion so swift that I did not see it, Bryce slid behind me and got me into a headlock, and there was a hot thick sensation at the back of my pants and I screamed. Somehow I slid back and out of the headlock, then I was dashing through the house to Egan's room, slamming the door and locking it, while the blond giant snarled, and I rummaged in Egan's drawers for what I knew was there even though I had never seen it, I had just asked Egan about his safety, living out here by himself, and it was where I expected to find it. I walked back out and faced the snarling and spitting giant. He advanced. I showed him the Sig Sauer. He kept coming at me until I smelled his foul breath again, that odor like a decaying rat in brine, and he punched me in the chest, hard this time, moving me straight back into the wall, and that is when the gun went off. The giant bellowed and staggered back three paces, stunned, running his fingers over his leaking gut and sniffing the gunpowder, and then he crashed to the floor.

Within minutes, I was back out in the dark desert, the ghostlike hum of the car and my pants and cries and curses reverberating through the open window into the ominous silence, and I could think only of driving as far east as possible, of heading further into the great desert until there came a mount where God tells faltering-actors-turned-murderers what to do. From a certain viewpoint, I was no murderer. But others would say it was totally needless to drill Bryce, or that I could have shot him in the shoulder or the foot, and they were surely right. Only one person in the world knew how it went down, and God knew how many people hated me, how many felt that when I played the whore, I wasn't acting at all. The nondescript highway passed beneath the rumbling car with small shifts in one or another direction, until for a moment I felt the night locking me into its deathward course, as if distilling the just acts and the misdeeds of my whole life into a simple violent play of gross outrage and retribution by agents I had not yet met. Then I thought some more. *No,* I told myself. *No, that's crazy, that's not at all what this is about. The guy was disturbed and he attacked you, he's part of something crazy, you did what any person with the human instinct for self-preservation would do.*

Then I thought: *Bryce recognized a degenerate. We're pretty obvious. Soon there must come a reckoning for all of us.*

After a few hours, the outlines of some kind of rectangle began to materialize way off in the distance. It was a roadhouse of some kind. Minutes later, I pulled into the parking lot and tried to compose myself for a minute, then I climbed the wooden steps, entered, and sat down at the bar.

The wild-eyed kid with long blond hair two stools down from me had a hungry look. He spoke volubly without fear. He had been through scenes of hell in Las Vegas and come near to blowing his last penny, and now here he was. He was not quite one of the broke pieces of detritus that drift away from that town to commit suicide in some solitary place, but he was burnt out and dead tired from having roamed over so many miles of dust and tarmac in the wee hours of the night. I asked this desert rat to tell me more about what he had beheld, but he did not talk in the linear way I expected, but gave a montage of images and made the desert and the wind and the road at night come roaring back in a sensory tremor that almost hurt, and I yearned to know the secrets he had searched out in the night, so he told me of a place, his eyes only grazed the edges of it as he shot past in the dark, but he knew it was there, it had to be there. I bought the kid another beer before heading back out to the road, feeling my determination overcome the effects of what I had done this black night, and I was out there searching, looking for the answer to the paradox, the elliptical hell that the past swirling year contained.

I turned off the highway and drove through the desert until the car's warning light came on, and then the Saturn slowed and conked out in the middle of the dark infinity. I stepped out and started walking. I wandered over the terrain as a weird hope began to grow in the mulch of my mind. Maybe they would believe me about Bryce, maybe I could get away from the matter without a trial dragging on for months, pulling my personal life even deeper into the mud. I could continue to act, to make new contacts and cultivate a persona as a controversial, brilliant actor whose life was as dark and dramatic as his roles, or something like that. As light began to filter through the amorphous shapes above, I could really see just how remote I was now, and I kept walking with lassitude, welcoming the dawn like a harbinger of unlikely hope and promise. All around, the sands were bright, with a reddish sheen that grew as dawn set in. I made my way through the brightening air as the thought of water occurred to me, but I did not want to turn around. Soon the bright day surrounded me, and I could only gasp at the clarity making the sight ahead all the more astounding.

It was a fort such as I did not believe existed in our day, looming before me as I gasped and thought how the immediacy of the sky and air and dry heat in this place mocked all Walter Mittyish distinctions, they could scarcely take hold in this blazing reality conflating the issues and conflicts of past and present. As I beheld this stronghold of a different order, one that I thought didn't exist outside a schlockmeister's fantasies, I could not disavow its might and fury. From the odor that came over the breeze, I was fairly certain that aliens were butchering people inside. Here. Here in the ruins of that civilization that Mr. Pound referred to as an old bitch gone in the teeth. I needed to find a way, to define the parabola of the rest of my existence, and here I would do it or die. I knew I would almost surely perish in any event, as I struck out into the vast reaches of sand and sagebrush to look beyond the intrigues of Wilkes and Baylor and to find a target for the repressed fury of all my experience in Hollywood, my pitiful struggle to navigate the spaces around a hack actor in a dying world.

Laughter

What is the provenance of the strange men we glimpse at remote points on the road? The question occurs to me more and more. How often a distraction from the monotony of the highway or country road comes in the form of the bearded hobo languishing under a bridge, the solitary figure walking through a desolate field, the sullen gas station attendant with half-repressed shame over his position in the world. These strangers are catalysts to the imagination. It is a stretch to believe that any of them planned to end up as they are now, in middle age, and they must have come from somewhere. I have made my speculations into a bit of a hobby.

Sometimes, the loneliest wanderer can trace his or her history to one of the most densely populated points on the globe. Once, on a trip with my wife through a corner of eastern Quebec, I made a connection between a stranger I encountered, and a tale I heard from a friend who works in television news. Believe me, Americans have ended up in rural parts of Canada for reasons that had nothing to do with wanting to evade military service.

But we'll save that encounter for later. Let me tell you now about the protagonist of the tale, an unmarried, childless forty-year-old named Oliver Wadsworth. When Oliver wrapped up a day's work at the legal services firm that employed him as a proofreader, Oliver liked to pursue a most unusual pastime. He made his way over to the west side of Manhattan, to the Meatpacking District, an erstwhile "lunch-pail" neighborhood transformed thanks to the outré tastes of the moneyed young people who've moved in over the years. Oliver liked to find a spot between a couple of cars in a parking lot under and a bit to the west of the Highline, a place from which you can see pretty much the entire south side of a popular, chic hotel with floor-to-ceiling windows. Guests of the hotel are not known for their modesty, nor does the management encourage them to be demure. Signs all around the hotel's eighteen floors openly encourage guests to carouse in the flesh. Anyone who hangs around on the Highline or in the lot just below it will, sooner or later, catch a glimpse of bare female buttocks or of people having sex in the area behind one of the huge windows. Oliver stood there in that little lot for hours at a time, pretending to be talking on his cell phone. No one really took notice of him save for an occasional guest who waved in amusement or pulled a curtain across the window with annoyance upon detecting the spy in the lot below. Sometimes he stood there for hours without once glimpsing a woman who had just emerged from a shower or picked herself out of bed, but that did not discourage Oliver. Oh, what loneliness can drive a poor alienated wretch to do. Though his satisfaction was limited, Oliver told himself that just being who he was, a guy with solid WASP credentials, was ennobling, that a man with the surname Wadsworth could never fall below a certain level no matter how much he might appear to fail in a conventional way.

Pass enough time looking up at those windows and watching the guests, and you are likely to wonder about the clientele, who they are and where they come from. To Oliver, the place gave off a chic vibe and seemed, from the outside, to have a highly international clientele. Almost all the faces, and bodies, visible through the windows are white, but unless you have training it can be hard to assign a nationality from a distance without being able to converse. Oliver knew the place was popular with Europeans, and from dozens of feet away, some of the figures he glimpsed had, at least for him, a kind of weird indefinable pan-European exoticism. He even made a gesture toward his fascination with and admiration for Europeans by sporting a green beret while he lingered there in the grimy parking lot. At the same time, he knew some of the guests were Americans who'd come to New York for a weekend or a fortnight and weren't shy about spending a bit, or about anything else.

On occasion, something happened that delighted Oliver. A guest saw him and was openly, joyously titillating. Framed in the hard rectangle of the room's walls, the guest might drop her towel, or might stand there in only a t-shirt, acknowledging what captivated Oliver, gesturing playfully as if to say, *Here, are you satisfied?*, all while locking eyes with the odd lonely man in early middle age. But, increasingly, Oliver found himself growing frustrated as late afternoon segued into evening and guests, as if in tacit communication, began to give the windows a wide berth.

Oliver made a decision. He wouldn't really get satisfaction until he got at the mysteries of this hotel, and no one could do that from the outside. No, you had to walk among the guests and converse with them and perhaps even come to know them as people in order to understand the flippant spirit that animated some of them, drove some of them to show off at the windows, isolated and fading as those incidents were now. Perhaps he might come to enjoy the expression of that spirit more directly, if he should "get lucky." Perhaps. Oliver's pay was rather meager, the legal services firm employed him as a freelancer rather than a full-time, salaried employee, so he had to wait until his payday to make a reservation at the hotel.

At last, the Friday of the weekend of Oliver's visit arrived. It was with a feeling of rising confidence that he left work late that afternoon, knowing what the weekend held. He slept peacefully at his home in one of the outer boroughs, got up, showered, and went over to the gym five blocks away, acutely conscious of how his figure would look when the time came to shed his clothes. As 4:00 p.m. drew near, Oliver ascended from the station at Fourteenth Street and Eighth Avenue, walked west three blocks, turned south, and ambled through the stone courtyard of the huge hotel in the damp, gray air. The few people sitting at tables of the café occupying the ground floor did not appear to notice the haggard man in chinos and a short-sleeved, button-down blue shirt as he crossed the yard and passed through the revolving door into the cool air of the lobby. The two clerks at the sleek, black desk at the lobby's far end looked like twins, a male variant of the blonde Nordic appearance of the girl, and vice versa. They wore long-sleeved pristine white shirts and were impeccably pleasant and professional. But as the male clerk handed Oliver the key to his room on the 16th floor, he issued a warning in a somber voice.

"You may have heard about a minor problem at the hotel."

Oliver shook his head.

"We have a bit of a problem with a voyeur who shows up outside. You may even have seen him in passing—a weirdo in a green beret."

Oliver gave the clerk a look of utter perplexity.

"A number of guests have complained about him. If you happen to see him, the best thing is really to ignore him," the clerk added.

"Well, I wouldn't have too many choices, now, would I?" Oliver replied in a dry tone.

"Please, sir. We really do our best here," the clerk pleaded.

With a look of suppressed annoyance, Oliver grabbed the key. He walked to the elevator banks off a corridor to the left of the reception area. He stepped into a cool shiny cylinder and rode it, alone, to the sixteenth floor, where he walked out onto a strip of corridor utterly indistinguishable from those on the floors above and below. A few strides took him to a longer perpendicular hall with silver rectangles filling seven-foot frames at intervals of twenty feet. His room was about midway down the hall. He turned the cold shiny knob, pushed hard, and stepped into a suite furnished modishly with a queen-sized bed, a plasma TV on a sleek black rolling tray, a computer, and a hot orange couch with big comfortable cushions. On the north side of the room, abutting the corridor, stood a desk with a white plastic surface. Through a space in the east wall Oliver glimpsed a bathroom as sterile, as pristine, as the most gleaming chamber of the wealthiest family in Dubai. The west wall was bare. Through the windows in the south wall Oliver could make out the financial district, the towers looming in the dank gray. He put his bags down beside the desk and moved to the window, curious about a guest's perspective on the Highline and the lot below it. Forlorn figures milled about down there. The air all around had a heavy dead feel, but Oliver felt such a thrill at the novelty of being here that for a moment he battled an urge to try to get the attention of the gaggle of pedestrians way down there, to make them aware that a cool and intense guy (with what he thought were impressive WASP credentials) was in a room on the sixteenth floor, and it was an event as important in its way as a visit by Russell Crowe or the Pope would be.

Losing interest in the Highline, he walked across the room and reclined on the plush, cozy orange couch. In his ebullience over the novelty of this experience, he did not realize that he hadn't shut the door. Oliver dozed off on the couch as the world ground on in the gray day outside.

He opened his eyes. The young woman in the space between the couch and the gleaming steel rectangle had longish blond hair tied up in a big bun. High cheekbones gave a faintly defiant look to a smooth narrow face, but her smile projected tremendous warmth. She was about 5'4", not a millimeter of which went to waste. No part of her was small enough to escape notice or large enough to be obtrusive. Oliver noticed every bit of the progression of her svelte hips, the swell of her inviting breasts. So friendly and flattering was her smile that Oliver was sure he'd misconstrued it. And there was another presence in the room, the blonde's eyes acknowledged it. Oliver craned his head around until his eyes took in a second woman, 5'8", with smooth coy features and hair of the richest scarlet, standing between the couch and the north wall. They were both exquisitely pretty, and each seemed to vie to look more mischievous than the other.

"Have we become real enough to you?"

The blonde's voice was so light and soft he wanted it to caress him for hours and hours. Her accent was hard to place. She spoke English with the cool precision of a German, a Swede, a Dane, somebody for whom the language had never been far away. Oliver guessed that the other lass, the redhead, was Hungarian. Though the woman behind him was eminently beautiful, he could not help reading in her features a wiliness, a coyness, that came even more naturally to her than to the blonde. He could only guess at what thoughts or wishes might manifest themselves that way, so in one sense at least the redhead had not yet become fully real to him. Such was their beauty, their instantly accessible warmth, that he didn't care.

"I could do worse than to wake up in the presence of two stunning woman," said Oliver, thinking himself quite suave.

"We were exploring this floor and we noticed you'd fallen asleep," said the blonde.

"Well, I've had a really exhausting week. I'm so glad to be here and it's all so new I don't think my body really knows how to react."

The blonde's smile broadened. Her companion walked around the couch and they stood there on the polished narrow boards, regarding him with curiosity.

"I'm Saskia and this is Alexandra."

"Oliver Wadsworth."

"Welcome to the hotel that untethers desire from everything else."

"Where are the two of you from? Holland? Germany?"

She laughed, a pleasant sound, like a wind stirring chimes.

"Whatever makes you think that?"

"Ah, I don't know. I look at you and listen to your voice and can't pick up on any regional American peculiarities."

Again came that pleasant sound, the work of a wind utterly absent from the dead gray day outside.

"We're both American."

"I don't believe you."

"This is more important to you than anything else we might represent."

"Well, you know, I'll always have a bit of the jaded New Yorker in me."

The young women looked at each other.

"I think it's about time I called my dad," Alexandra said.

Oliver nodded toward the desk with a look acknowledging he had no qualms about Alexandra making a call on his tab. She moved to the desk and flicked a switch on the phone.

"Let's get my dad on speakerphone," she said.

Oliver repeated the last word of her sentence with incredulity.

"Of course it has that feature. Every suite is an office these days," Saskia said.

"Where exactly are you calling?" Oliver asked.

"Don't worry, when you hear my dad's voice I think you'll feel pretty satisfied with his American-ness," Alexandra replied.

Oliver sat on the couch in growing anticipation as the nubile redhead pressed buttons on the plastic phone. They listened to five rings, six, seven, eight. Somewhere out there, in America, somewhere in the gray spaces to the north, west, or south, a phone in an empty hall or on a nightstand in a bare room was ringing and going ignored. After two more rings, Alexandra replaced the receiver.

"My dad doesn't know what a cell phone is."

"We could call my parents but they're on the road. On vacation. They don't know what a cell phone is either. You'll just have to be satisfied with our word," Saskia said.

Oliver recalled a conversation he'd had at a party once in someone's garden floor apartment in the East Village. He vividly recalled talking to a Swedish girl who, just to give Oliver some information and shut him up, had pretended to be from Wisconsin, giving Oliver the opportunity to spring a trap.

"Tell me what state you're from," Oliver said now to Alexandra.

"Maryland."

"Okay, who's the governor of Maryland?" he asked, utilizing the same trap as at that long-ago party.

"I forget!"

"Shut up, you're not really from Maryland," Saskia said, grinning.

By this point, Oliver had quite forgotten how the conversation had taken this course or what the point was. Being in the presence of these women overwhelmed him with a joy he'd hardly ever known in his forty years and counting.

"I accept your American-ness."

The women turned to each other again and something passed between them.

"It's quite obvious that you only just checked in. This room doesn't have too many amenities," Saskia observed.

"Did you expect a minibar?" Oliver asked in what he wanted to sound like a playful voice, but it came out defensive.

"Come downstairs with us."

For some reason, Saskia and Alexandra seemed determined to avoid the elevators. He followed them down the hall and into the stairwell. The women led him down to the twelfth floor. They stepped out into a hall indistinguishable from the one they'd left save for the numbers on the gleaming silver doors. The two ladies' room was at the south end of the building, like Oliver's, but was a bit closer to the west side, where the elevator bank was. As they walked down the hall, Saskia's left hand closed over Oliver's right buttock and squeezed gently. Oliver thought perhaps he'd never woken from his doze on the hot orange couch.

Their room had pretty much the same furnishings, except that the couch hugged the wall abutting the corridor. The bed was big enough. They didn't mind sleeping together, he deduced. As soon as the door was partly shut, Alexandra walked over to the table on which a bottle of vodka, a bottle of peach schnapps, and three glasses rested. As she got to work mixing liquids, Saskia took Oliver's hand and led him to the window. Outside, there were even fewer pedestrians on the Highline than before, and the parking lot, the street running along the building's southern flank, looked as barren as the set of an old black-and-white Luc Besson film Oliver had seen one drizzly afternoon in Paris when he was twenty. All around were lonely patches of encroaching dimness. Oliver expected Saskia to point out something to him, to offer some kind of observation or insight, but she was content just to stand there looking out at the world with her arm around his waist.

The drinks were ready.

"Oliver, what a wonderful Dickensian name," said Alexandra, handing him a glass full of sparkling amber fluid.

"I don't know. To me it has such *echt*-blueblood overtones," Saskia commented.

Oliver reflected. Who *were* these ladies? They certainly didn't sound, to him, like unlettered girls from cow towns. But something told him that Alexandra's call earlier had not gone out to a major city, but to a place where older people still clung to anachronous land lines.

"I won't lower myself to respond to that, Saskia," Oliver said, again trying and failing to effect a playful tone.

"Come, now. Drink," urged Alexandra, as Saskia looked on approvingly.

Oliver obeyed. He mused that if he were a character in a really bad spy thriller, this would be the moment where the drugs take effect and he begins to pass out. Then he will awaken, bound and gagged, and will have to give up codes to which a handful of people in the world are privy. But Oliver did not feel consciousness dribbling away. On the contrary, he felt a heightening of sensitivity in every muscle and pore.

He wondered how long it would be before he and the women got down to what all three tacitly acknowledged they were after. He drank some more, enjoying the way Saskia's bare forearm glided up and down over the base of his spine. Alexandra joined them at the window, standing at Oliver's left side, her right arm bisecting Saskia's left arm.

Alexandra said: "Look, we might as well admit it. We're not Americans. But we're pretty attracted to a certain kind of American."

"Oh, come off it. Of course we're American," Saskia said, giggling.

"Well, fine, we are. Look, it doesn't matter. The fact is, we're so taken with a certain type of American male, who towers above all the other variants of the gender in every respect. But one respect in particular," Alexandra exulted.

Saskia giggled some more. The bare forearms of both ladies worked up and down, gently but insistently, at the most sensitive point of Oliver's spine. A cat could never get such pleasure from even the most fawning owner, he thought. Gazing up at the dimming sky, he raised the glass to his lips. The liquid was so pungent it fairly demanded that his senses engage with it again and again. A reaction, perhaps inevitable, was occurring in Oliver's loins.

Saskia's arm slid away. Her fingers clasped the base of her shirt and began pulling it upward. The reaction in Oliver's lower body picked up as he watched her reflection in the window.

"Really sexy," said Alexandra, her forearm lingering at Oliver's lower back. Out of instinct, and an idea of propriety inseparable from his identity as a member of the natural aristocracy of his country, Oliver retreated from the window to a position a few inches from the north wall. The women followed his actions with aroused expressions.

"Go ahead," said Saskia, with the most mischievous grin Oliver had ever seen.

First he unbuttoned and pulled off his shirt. He didn't think the contours of his lower torso would draw too much notice if he could get his remaining garb off quickly enough. The protrusion in his loins demanded, absolutely *demanded*, that he liberate it right now. Within seconds, his pants and underpants were gone. In the immediate aftermath of shedding his clothes, Oliver's erection fairly seemed to reach across the room. Of course it did not. It was more finite than he would have liked, but he found it impressive nonetheless and felt certain the young ladies would concur. He had to hold their attention.

For a few moments his new acquaintances stood there gaping. On some level Saskia and Alexandra did seem to appreciate what they were seeing. It appeared to be the fulfillment of the deep longings Alexandra had voiced. For a time he thought Alexandra was about to go back to the table to mix another drink. But the two women stood there. *Of course they appreciate me,* he thought. *I'm not such an unprepossessing guy. I work out, though not as often as I could. I'm part of a lineage, I have an incredible pedigree.* At this moment, there was something distinctly foreign about the way Saskia crossed her legs, in fact it reminded him of the body language of a woman he'd encountered in a village in the Vendée a few weeks after the drizzly afternoon in Paris when he saw that strange film. That French woman had wanted to be suggestive and provocative, and she'd succeeded brilliantly. Now Saskia was doing the same. That, at least, was Oliver's impression, so it was a bit hard to accept what happened next.

Saskia and Alexandra, if those were their names, both squinted. They gaped. They squinted some more, and a deeply queasy feeling, rather like alarm, crept into their features. Alexandra's mouth moved ineffectually open and closed. They were looking with *disgust* at the naked out-of-shape forty-year-old standing there in their room, and at one of his attributes in particular. Oliver waited anxiously for the moment to pass, for the insensitive joke to run its course, so they could pick up where they'd left off. His eyes made a desperate appeal to both of them. The disgust was not going away, he saw now. Oliver Wadsworth had never seen anything more genuine in his life. Still he could never have imagined what happened now. The door of this room had not closed all the way. Now it swung inward and three, no, four, no, five strangers moved into the room. Here were five women in the same age bracket as Oliver's two hosts. All but one of them were blondes. They had long curly hair and somewhat coarse features, as if drinking games had drained all delicacy from their cheeks and lips. Now seven women stood in the room gazing at a man too stunned even to try to cover himself.

Saskia made an arrow of her right arm and forefinger. The seven women began laughing so hard he thought the whole building could hear. The noise was like the shredding of costumes by an army of troglodytes.

"He's pathetic!"

"Disgusting!"

"He deserves to die!"

Oliver was too stunned to react when one of them darted across the floor, grabbed his clothes, and dashed back to the others. All he could think was that he must get away from them and get help immediately. In the eyes of the seven women there was such a naked, schoolgirl malice, that Oliver did not even think of taking offensive action, of throwing an object or a punch, as he dashed past them through the door and into the hall indistinguishable from others in the building save for the numbers on the doors. Forgetting where the stairwell was, he ran past three doors and then in his panic began banging furiously on the fourth. He felt on some level that this was what they call a "911 situation." As far as he cared, Saskia and Alexandra had stolen his clothes and exposed him to humiliation without any acquiescence on his part. In the moments before the answer to his banging on the door of #1212, he happened to glance downward. What was down there was pretty abject, a shriveled sac with a protrusion so limp it didn't even dangle, it just lolled like a punctured balloon.

Oliver was right about to begin pounding on the door again when it opened. Inside the room, indistinguishable in its proportions and furnishings from most others in the hotel, were a twenty-six-year-old guy with clipped dark hair and stubble on his face, looking as if he'd been naked and had hurriedly thrown on a button-down dress shirt whose flaps dangled, and, behind him, a slender woman of the same age, with straight black hair, wearing only blue jeans and a bra. The man looked at Oliver with uncomprehending annoyance, and, upon noticing what Oliver had between his thighs, disgust tinged with pity. This middle-aged freak had no right, no right at all, to disturb the perfect evolution of a deep personal bond between two young people who had gotten right all the things Oliver had bungled. Oliver tried to speak but was almost like a baby drooling. Spitup came, and he felt his knees buckling and a bit of wine exiting the tip of that shriveled thing. The drops hit the stubbly olive green and orange carpet and morphed into splotches quite hard to see. But the features of the man at the door curled in disgust as he saw what had happened. His air of affronted dignity grew all the more marked at having to protect the woman from this. The man looked

Oliver up and down, his gaze saying, *So this is what forty years have come to?*

"Please," Oliver finally managed to say.

"What?" the incredulous man answered.

"Please help me get my thing back—"

Oliver wanted to say *things* but that was just how it came out, and he felt lucky to be able to say that much.

"Get your thing back? Fucking freak! *Pathetic piece of shit!*"

"Please—"

"PATHETIC! Get out of here now! Go jump off the fucking building and make this a happier world!"

The man pronounced *pathetic* with so peculiar an inflection that there could be no doubt Oliver's every move, every breath redefined the term, gave it unsuspected dimensions.

Suddenly the woman inside the room opened up.

"Leave us alone."

So banal was her demand that Oliver found it almost kind. In his panic, he hurried past two more doors, still unable to recall the stairwell's location. He came to another door but paused before banging on it. If he could change his physical appearance even marginally, the effort would be worth it. He reached down with his right hand and stroked himself, thinking of the flash of exhilaration that came while he stood there in the room with Saskia and Alexandra (if those were their names) before their looks began to change. The effort was not wholly fruitless. Pounding on the door, Oliver managed to say, "Hey! Hello!"

Wrong door, was his first thought as the metal rectangle opened to reveal a balding man in his late forties, with a harsh face like that of Vladimir Putin's cousin in a line of work that never requires diplomacy. The man was quietly furious at Oliver, whose eyes caught a delicate flutter behind him. Oliver thought that maybe in this room things had gotten to an even more advanced stage than in #1212. Was this man a cop? If so, then the stranger could make everything all right.

But now, the man commanded, "Bring it here, Inez."

Oliver discerned the edges of more motion, closer this time. Then a woman with platinum blond hair and a smooth face stood directly behind the man and to his right, and placed something in his hand.

Pointing the Glock pistol at Oliver's face, the man said, "We'll have to decline a *ménage à trois*."

Inez began laughing hard, and the bald man joined her. At this point, doors all along the hall began to open, heads started poking out. Now people in at least six other rooms joined in the laughter. Something else was spreading now, Oliver could feel it, not alarm exactly but a hyper-awareness of what was going down and of the need to react. Now he thought the urine had been nothing, he was going to lose all control of his bowels, it was utterly inescapable. At the same time, he achieved what was, in the circumstances, a feat of memory and recalled where the door to the stairwell was. More doors were opening all along the hall, ten, a dozen, twenty, and heads were not only poking out but exchanging glances and words. People called to Oliver, beckoned to him, asked him to wait for a moment. In his bewilderment he lingered there, waiting for guidance or encouragement. As he did so, he could hear people inside the rooms, talking animatedly about the hilarious situation. He started. He felt he had to object, to protest, to say something. But he lingered there in his confusion until the bald man with the Glock stepped out into the hall.

Oliver bolted. He ran back toward the room he'd fled, stopped about midway, opened the door to the stairwell, and raced through. Before he climbed even two of the stairs, he heard it. Here was laugher such as he'd never heard. It came from every room on the floor, and, he was certain, from other floors as well. Something was horribly wrong. The ratio of laughs and guests was impossibly skewed. All the guests had their speakerphones on, and were in conference with friends, relatives, colleagues, perhaps even strangers, in an infinite number of locations. Oliver thought, THE WHOLE WORLD IS LAUGHING AT ME! He raced up the stairs, feeling his semi-solid member jostle and thump against his upper legs as he brought one foot up, then the other, frantically, desperately. Oliver didn't even know for certain which floor he'd reached when he burst through a door into yet another plain indistinguishable hall. To his immense relief, none of the doors were open. Those on this floor were not in on the hilarious misfortune of the pedigreed WASP, he deduced.

Oliver briefly had the presence of mind to ponder what to do. He needed to get back to the safety of his room and put some clothes on, but he had to raise the alarm over what had happened below, and besides, he couldn't even recall the floor and number of his room at the moment. He'd gone through unspeakable trauma and he needed help. Oliver thought about what he'd done wrong on the floor below. If they supposed he was dumb enough to keep making the same mistake, they were underestimating him as gravely as anyone had ever done in his life. Quickly, decisively, Oliver picked a door at random, the third to his right, moved up to it, turned the knob, and pushed. He couldn't move the door. He moved up the hall, toward the west side of the building, and tried three more doors. The third of these wasn't locked. Oliver swung it open and advanced into a room where a prim man in a tasteful black suit held aloft a glass with a pink liquid in it. This stranger was in the middle of delivering a monologue to a brunette in a mauve dress with lots of frills and a touch of the air of a refined Southern belle about her.

"So if the hotel is your podium and the world is your audience—" the man was saying.

"OH MY GOD! HOLY WORD!" the elegant lady cried as Oliver invaded their space.

Oliver realized now that he was drooling just a bit and his member had snapped to attention at the sight of this lady.

"Now, fellow, you wouldn't hurt a couple of nice people, would you?" the man said.

"Please, sir, we are eminently civilized," the lady said, with a gesture at the bottle of champagne on the table.

"I invite you to partake of this," the man added, holding his glass aloft.

Oliver relished what neither of them could deny or ignore: the fact of his huge, pulsing erection. He felt he was far more of a man than this fool in a suit, and the evidence was not hard to find at all. This woman, who might otherwise be in a position to lacerate him with ridicule, could not pretend to deny it.

"Easy, fellow—you don't want to hurt a couple of really nice people," the man repeated.

"Maybe not."

Oliver issued commands. The terrified woman obeyed. The man in the suit was far, far too timid to intervene as she removed her dress and shoes and kneeled, in her bra and panties, at the feet of the aroused guest. She proved so quickly, unquestioningly obedient that Oliver felt his manhood, his self-worth swell even further, until the woman's spouse looked on with wonder and perhaps just a touch of envy. The dapper fellow was staring, no, more than that, was obsessing over his wife's attentions to the organ she'd help coax out of its damning desuetude. Only now did it occur to Oliver that maybe people outside could see into this room, and that perhaps the noises that came to him now from outside the room, laughter and yells and the whirr of helicopter blades, plus other sounds he couldn't quite define, might be warnings to which he'd better react quickly.

But first he had to reach climax. The woman's mouth was working vigorously. He was almost there.

He did not get the chance. The noise of the buzz saw had been detectible for a few moments, but Oliver's distraction was too great for him to process it and react as a rational person would. An obese man in a blue uniform with a nametag saying "Mike" burst into the room. Oliver realized now he'd had plenty of time to take note, had he been paying attention to anything other than the workings of the mouth of the body kneeling before him. There could be no ignoring Mike now. Mike advanced resolutely toward the middle-aged freak, brandishing the buzz saw as if to say, *Nothing you have is equal to this.* Oliver had to differ. He dashed past the man in the tasteful suit, reached the table, seized the bottle of champagne, made another lithe movement, and brought the bottle down so hard on Mike's head that shards of green-tinted glass, and nearly a quart of the good stuff, gushed all over everything in a twelve-foot radius. Mike screamed and cried and dropped to his knees, feeling his head. He gazed in horror at his bloody fingers. Oliver kicked Mike in the face as hard as he could, picked up the saw, kneeled, and moved the whirring blade methodically up and down, back and forth across Mike's chest and abdomen. The spray quickly grew so dense that any attempt to wipe off blood would only smear the part of your body in question even worse. Oliver got a fair amount of pleasure from doing this and had no inclination to quit, until the lady, in her turn, forced the issue.

"I think I must excuse myself. I know I've been rather a poor host."

"No," Oliver said, rising.

She understood that she was to bring him to the consummation Mike had so rudely denied.

Thirty seconds later, Oliver picked up the saw again, thanked his hosts with unfeigned gratitude, bolted from the room, and returned to the stairwell. The laughter was faint and distant now. From that point of view, no direction was more or less inviting than any other. He strained his ears. No one was mocking him, as far as he could tell, but the buzz and rumble of helicopters was closer than he thought possible unless you were an infantryman in the Ia Drang Valley in 1965. Oliver welcomed the noise, which precluded certain others from overwhelming him or even reaching his ears. Up above, voices issued from mikes, a few copters contested the airspace. Oliver thought that a timid man's instinct would be to dash downstairs, right into the arms of the police. He was no timid soul. Several bounds took him up to a landing where a short ladder with thin rusting rungs led to a padlocked trapdoor. For a moment, Oliver strained his ears, daring the laughter to pursue him. He still had the saw. Instead of laughter, he heard ten or twelve men clambering up the stairs, muttering, growling, cursing. Without further hesitation, he climbed up the ladder, used the buzz saw to sever the lock, flung open the door, and climbed up onto the roof. It was not quite the Ia Drang at the height of a battle, but three news helicopters with eager staring occupants hovered over the roof. Oliver stuck the handle of the saw into his mouth and leapt onto the right skid of the nearest copter, a KCTV unit containing reporter Jim Donovan and pilot Bob Riggs, flung open the door, and entered the cockpit. The occupants did not have too many options if they wanted to go home in a physical form their families would recognize.

Last September, my wife and I happened to be driving through a swath of southern Quebec, not so far from the Pine Mountain region of New Hampshire. My wife, whom I love deeply, couldn't shut up about how much she loved the aroma of the pine trees and the sight of mountains with rich dense coats of green, unbroken save where granite crags poke up at random points, and, of course, the pace of life there. Not for us now were the pressures of corporate partners who must find ever more devious means to drive up billable hours. And people here were so nice. We certainly didn't anticipate any jolts. We expected local guys to be Larry or Tom or Joe or something equally déclassé. There are names we never, ever expected to encounter in these parts.

We'd been on the road for a few hours, and were both exulting in the expectation of more hours of wending from nowhere to nowhere, when we needed to stop for gas. The logical choice was a family-owned station on the right side of the road leading westward. The station was a wooden shack with a crude thatch roof, reinforced with tin against the awful winters. One pump stood out front. It would never get busy enough at this place for customers to have to serve themselves. A white-haired man in overalls sauntered out to the car.

"Fifteen dollars' worth, and could you check the oil?" I said.

"Will do. Ollie!" the old-timer called.

A sullen man in a blue outfit came out of the shack and approached the pump.

The Whispering Space

Neil and Heather gazed out the car's windows at the desert. To the north loomed the San Jacinto Mountains. To the south were the approaches to Mexico, the leaves of the Joshua trees as still as in a painting.

The screenwriter and his young wife stopped at a filling station where a beefy man in overalls sauntered outside and shared his view that the country was unlikely to see anything like the rains of the year before. Neil thought he was right. So blue was the sky that Georgia O'Keefe might have painted it. Neil drank hot coffee while studying the streak of paint extending east out of view, far beyond the penumbra of the mountains.

His young wife closed the door and pulled her ankles against the base of her seat, her legs as smooth as a birch tree stripped of bark, with a stray dimple accentuating the creaminess of the flesh. Heather's chest heaved faintly inside her t-shirt. With her light brown hair unbound, hanging at her ears, she could have passed for an undergrad. They drove on without stopping, Heather marveling often at how vast Riverside County was for people who rarely left L.A.

They passed between hills that gave way to more flat dusty lands dotted with one-story houses with American flags in their windows. Finally the car pulled onto a plateau where Neil and Heather had a view of their house on a slope at the southern end of a canyon. Flanked by a pool and a patio, the sleek conjoined rectangles had glass walls at the front and back, giving occupants a full view of the valley. But the grounds were a weed-ridden mess.

"Neil! There's the ramp."

Within minutes, Neil and Heather were carrying boxes from the trunk to the brilliantly lit spaces inside the rectangles whose ceilings seemed miles above. The bedroom shared a door with the kitchen, which in turn shared a door with the area where Neil and Heather would entertain visitors.

By noon, they'd fully unpacked. By 1:00, their locked bodies were rolling on the mattress in the room off the kitchen, light streaming through the glass wall. Anyone in the hills to the south could have watched, Heather told Neil, who laughed.

"What do you think this is, *The Hills Have Eyes*? Radioactive mutants watching us through binoculars?"

Later, over a meal of microwaved burritos and merlot, Heather asked Neil whether he was beginning to miss the bustle of L.A. He shook his head.

"No. Not at all."

Neil was forty-three, and death no longer seemed so remote. But at least he was away from the odious social reality of Burbank and Los Feliz.

The next morning, Neil dropped off Heather at the supermarket in the mall ten miles to the west. He drove on to the bottle shop on the far side of the mall. When Heather pushed her cart toward the register, she ended up right behind a handsome man in a checkered red and black shirt and jeans. He was flipping through *Guns & Ammo*. As the cashier rung up this man, Heather thought she heard the girl say *Lee Henry*

Davis in something close to a whisper, as if the kids in the store shouldn't hear that name.

Later, standing on the concrete in the loggia outside the market, Heather feigned trouble lifting some of the fatter sacks from her cart. The kindly man ventured over to help.

"Why thank you," Heather said, mustering her sexiest smile.

The bags were in a neat circle when Neil circled back from the bottle shop, the trunk of the Mercury packed with cases of red wine.

"So I'm just wondering what that girl at the register was talking about?" Heather said.

"Oh, that Davis character—are you sure you want to—why, hello sir," the man said, addressing Neil as he slid out of the Mercury and faced the two with an inquisitive look. Neil nodded. The handsome stranger went on:

"Word has spread about a drifter who entered a woman's house on the pretext of making an urgent call, then robbed her at gunpoint. People are wondering if it might be Lee Henry Davis, who broke out of prison in Texas three months ago and used to have a girlfriend in these parts. But they also reportedly sighted him in Missouri last week, so it's all guesswork. Anyway, I'm delighted to meet you folks. My name's Charles Ross."

"Neil and Heather Payton."

"Are you by any chance looking for a church?"

"Neil. I heard something."

Neil didn't want to get out of bed.

"*Neil.* Outside. I thought I heard someone laugh and fall in the pool."

"Heather, we're a *very long* way from UCLA."

"Jesus Christ, it wasn't fucking students, *please get up!*"

Neil rose and pulled on his chinos, then grabbed a flashlight from one of the semi-unpacked boxes. When he walked through the kitchen and into the long room, the desert was a black infinity in all directions.

Outside the bright moon seemed near enough you could lasso it with a rope. Sweeping the beam of the flashlight across the pool, he saw that Heather had not been entirely wrong. One of the deck chairs was lying in the pool, in such a position that an occupant would be gazing right up at that moon. Casting the beam over the driveway, toward the shed, he thought that Lee Henry Davis must be on a road in Missouri at the moment, gazing up at that same moon. He stood there in the cool crisp air until his knees began to tremble.

"Go to sleep, Heather, it's the wind," he whispered to the prone form beside him in the bed.

In the morning, Neil worked furiously at a screenplay. In an access of Luddism—longing to get closer to the essence of the creative process, to work as William Holden in *Sunset Boulevard* might have done—Neil was using a Smith-Corona typewriter rather than a laptop. Heather poured two cups of coffee, adding cream for herself, leaving Neil's black. She picked up a page from the growing stack.

RYAN: This is Roswell, Jimmy. I thought I'd seen some wild stuff in my time. You can talk about conspiracy theories all you like, but you can't convince me those shapes in the desert come from around here—

JIMMY (*interrupts*): Those bastards must have done more than condition you for combat when you were in special-ops training, Ryan.

RYAN: Luther, Newton, Galileo . . . every prophet in history is a freak, Jimmy! But I know I saw a pair of eyes looking out from behind that crag yesterday.

JIMMY: Jesus. We're going to some dark places here, Ryan.

The work did not improve with the use of "dark." Far be it from Heather to deride her husband when he was getting going, but she thought he'd abdicated his duties as a writer. Heather thought of authors she admired, Nathanael West, for example. West's work was some of the bleakest and most disturbing she'd read, but she doubted West ever used the term "bleak," or "disturbing," or "dark," for that matter.

The next time Neil and Heather visited the mall, they had lunch with a young couple who were friends with Charles Ross. Stan and Mary Cavanagh lived in Sherman Oaks for most of the year, and were renting a house a few miles west of the Paytons'. The stout, puffy-faced man was a history professor who'd taken time off to work on a nonfiction book, while svelte, feminine Mary was pursuing postgraduate studies.

"I wish there were a discipline called occult studies. That would really be cool. People are way too stubborn and narrow-minded. But there are ways around that, if you can just be a little creative in fashioning your course of study," Mary said.

"Mary's joking, of course," Stan said with a big grin.

"I really do share your passion for Fitzgerald," Mary said, looking into Neil's eyes.

When he was just about to invite Stan and Mary over, Neil remembered the state of the grounds of his new home. Fortunately Stan had the number of a local man named Wade Garvey.

Back at the house that night, Neil strolled into the long room, beaming, and said, "Did you hear the news? They arrested a drifter in Missouri this evening. They haven't ID'd him yet, but I'll bet it's Lee Henry Davis."

He grinned, hoisting a glass of pinot noir. Heather smiled with relief. Tonight Neil had the raffish charm of a younger Robert DeNiro.

As Heather climbed out of the shower the next morning, she heard Neil talking into the phone in the long room. The groundskeeper would be over at seven that evening to take a look at the property and discuss his terms.

Wade Garvey was twenty-five, with coal-black hair, several tattoos, and the physique of a construction worker. When he came over, Neil handed the guy a Corona. They talked over the state of the grounds.

"It's a Neutra house. The whole point is that it should look like something," Neil said.

The guest declined to comment.

"Of course, when I spend a lot on renovations, I always think that it's in vain, that a calamity will sweep everything away just like in the Bible," Neil added.

Garvey chuckled, parroting, "Just like in the Bible."

"Is there something funny about my referring to the Bible?"

"You seem to think there's only one that matters."

"Indeed. Are you a writer between jobs?"

Garvey chuckled again.

"No, sir. I know a born writer when I see one—I'm looking at one now. Your background is liberal arts, mine's vocational. I'm taking an IT evening class at the community college."

"Sorry, I was just curious."

In a *faux* redneck drawl, the guest added, "Well didn't one of them literary figures say that writers are always observing?"

Soon Neil was back in Hollywood, hauling his screenplays to producers' offices like Harry Greener in *The Day of the Locust* hawking cans of his Miracle Solvent. In the glare, he ambled along Sunset Boulevard into West Hollywood, then turned down toward Santa Monica Boulevard, making a right onto a block crowded with cafés.

At the time Neil was on his mission, Heather worked hard, composing pages of crisp prose, moving inside to rest in the cool comfortable expanse of the room where her husband banged at the typewriter's keys as if he needed to feel every syllable, every character land like a paratrooper hitting the earth. Garvey worked outside for a few hours, took a check from Heather, and left. The long room appealed to her. Here between the long white walls, under the high ceiling, it was so easy for your brain to fix on things like sponge.

Reclining on the coarse fibers of the couch in her undies and bra, she had the sensation of riding on a zebra's back. Beyond the transparent space where other houses would have had a thick wall, Heather could make out the crest of the hills to the north, the desert, the Joshua trees and Blue Oaks, everything the way it was before directors trapped the land on film that technicians later colorized, panned, scanned, brushed up, diluted beyond recognition. Every so often her eye caught the glint off a windshield heading east. She did not need to read now to stimulate the neurons in her brain, to fire her imagination with the possibility of a deed that would turn Neil into an angel wielding a sword in fury. In this uncluttered space, she heard her breathing amplified. Maybe in those hills, coyotes were pricking up their ears, foxes twitching their tails at the sight of this biped between glass walls, reclining, extending her legs, easing her fingers under the band of her underwear. Just maybe.

Neil ambled westward along Santa Monica, hands thrust in his pockets, avoiding eye contact.

From the tables to his right, where feet were at his eye level, came the chatter of rising studio executives and women likely to land a role in their next production. Their age made economic sense.

Heather lay back, thinking she might be making eye contact at this moment with a mountain lion. Her fingers moved. No winds came now.

Turning, Neil looked at the chirpy dates of the Hollywood elite. Two of the tanned young women in dark sunglasses turned away from their partners to look at the odd man on the street below.

Time. You are all living under a curse.

Heather pulled off her undies.

Neil stared at back at the fortunate women.

It's like this. First, you will hardly notice a change. It is not so quantifiable as what follows. Take pleasure in the moment. Soon your pallor will lack the ripeness so crucial to your self-schemata, though at first you may notice the dimming only through the juxtaposition of photos. Then the heavy shit. Pouches under your eyes, your forehead cracking like a shanty in a San Fran earthquake, your gut peeking over the band of your pants and saying "Hi!, your complexion going from cream to a churning mass of pores and blemishes. You've passed through the biological moment, and the man who held you aloft and cherished you is in shock.

Now two more patrons were looking down at the forty-something man in a dapper gray-and-black checkered blazer and a pair of tar-black slacks. The man shifted slightly but did not lower his gaze.

Heather retreated to the rear of the room, to the shelves filled with Neil's books.

Neil pretended to have stopped for the purpose of examining his watch.

Heather thought of their wedding. Guests agape.

Neil shifted, placing his weight on one foot, then the other.

Heather giggled upon spying a volume of Nietzsche on the shelves. She thought, *When you look into the desert, the desert also looks into you.*

Neil thought he saw a man at a table reaching into his breast pocket for a cell phone.

As a bit of her earlier mood returned, Heather began to reach downward again. She thought of a movie she'd caught at a retro house in Van Nuys, *Logan's Run*, about a society in the future where you can have anything you want, but you have to die when you hit thirty.

"Waiting for my date. Nobody has any manners anymore," Neil said.

Heather, who had once felt nauseas at the thought of a stranger examining her breasts, felt no one's gaze was unwelcome now. No one in the world.

Neil moved hurriedly up the street.

After dressing and getting back to work, Heather found a copy of Fitzgerald's *The Last Tycoon* on Neil's desk.

When Neil pulled into the driveway just after 7:00 that evening, it seemed curious that a light was on in the bedroom window but nowhere else. He strode through the front door, to the pole topped with a curving bulb, flicked it on, and that was when he noticed a damp spot on the middle cushion of the sofa.

Two nights later, Heather sat bolt upright in bed. She thought she could hear the desert in all its susurrant activity, hear every spider crawl, every cactus grow under the placid moon. At her urging, Neil came groggily to life, pulled on his pants, and grabbed the flashlight. He walked through the kitchen and the long room to the front patio, sweeping the beam back and forth. In trepidation, he sauntered down the slope toward the driveway, then over to the shed. Though the door was shut tight, the latch was not in the position he'd left it. Heather's face appeared at the front of the long room. Neil raised his arm to mimic talking on a phone.

While Heather called 911, Neil slowly, gingerly pulled open the double doors of the shed, aiming his beam directly ahead, then down where it alighted on the dirty pale shirt of a brown man lying face down. He shut off the beam, closed the door, and stood there panting until the squad cars rolled into the driveway. After they took away the illegal immigrant in handcuffs, Neil lay next to Heather, soothed by the caress of a finger on his rib cage.

Two days later, Neil was on the road heading west to Hollywood again. While he should have been watching the road, he saw, instead, Garvey with a penis like the trunk of a felled tree, rough and hairy and scabby, Heather crouching in awe, thinking that this virile kid could not be the same species as her miserable mousy husband with a squirming wet noodle between his legs. Garvey with that knowing grin. Sipping wine from the very glass Neil used.

For the first time in months, Neil had a promising meeting in Hollywood. The producer called an assistant into the office via intercom, asked the kid to Xerox a fragment of Neil's screenplay. After the meeting Neil set out on foot to one of L.A.'s occult bookstores. In a shop on Hollywood Boulevard, off Vermont Avenue, where he was the only customer, Neil bought a copy of Anton LaVey's little book.

Heather sat on the sofa brooding about Neil's screenplay. In fairness, it had grown more vivid, more readable, to the extent that the snatches she'd read did it justice. Again she picked up a page.

RYAN: Do you believe me now, Jimmy? This has <u>nothing</u> to do with Apaches wanting their land back. Get it through your head, man. You'd have to be some kind of freaked-out racist even to suggest that those eyes I saw looking at me from behind the gorge belong to an angry minority with its proverbial hand out.

JIMMY: I never saw this thing you claim was looking at you. Soon you'll be saying these creatures want our babies.

Soon you won't know lightning from a hailstorm, a zebra from a designer rug.

Heather wandered around the room thinking that rarely had she entered a space so uncompressed, where Hamlet could not dream of putting fetters about any fear or desire or anger or memory. She thought of a line from Fitzgerald's odd, unfinished novel, *The Last Tycoon*, concerning one of the moguls in the milieu Fitzgerald knew so well at the end of his life:

"He had watched women in screen tests and seen their beauty vanish second by second, as if a lovely statue had begun to walk with the meagre joints of a paper doll."

Continuing her amble around the room, Heather took in the brass letter opener beside Neil's Smith-Corona. She imagined it would be handy for opening an envelope containing a marital settlement agreement. As Heather thought of that gilded letter opener, the room fell completely away and she beheld the object in a cobalt blue sky without a world to give it context. If Lee Henry Davis was not knocking on the door at this moment, he might yet find a role in this drama, as Neil, with brutal male efficiency, found a means to outsource some of the gruesome and difficult tasks that lay ahead while he achieved acclaim as a writer without clinging to any relics of his years of frustration and failure. If she died, they had a handsome life insurance policy.

The phone rang. Heather froze. Another ring. Heather gazed at her reflection, a forlorn figure in the space between two tall sheets of glass.

She picked up the phone and heard a slurred, conspiratorial voice ask:

"If you found one of the gateways to hell, what exactly do you think it would look like?"

"Excuse me?"

Maybe it was Lee Henry Davis on the phone.

"Uh . . . Mrs. Payton. Heather. Would you like to come over and have a drink with us? We've got all kinds of fun going on here."

Jesus Christ, was it Professor Stan Cavanagh? Heather slammed the phone down.

When Neil got home, he looked at the spot where that stain had been, recalling a passage from LaVey's *Satanic Bible*: "The dripping of the nectar from my eager cleft shall act as pollen to that slumbering brain, and the mind that feels not lust shall on a sudden reel with crazed impulse. . . . "

His eyes met Heather's. She told him that Stan Cavanagh had called, that she'd deduced he was quite drunk, that she felt almost as if Stan had reached into her pants. She added that now that Garvey's work here was done, they could write off everyone they'd met through Charles Ross, including Charles himself. Neil studied her face, its surface uncreased by the scars of worry or anger, like clay hardening in infinitesimal gradations.

In the morning, Heather had the car again. She headed over to the post office and then the mall. Upon completing her errands, she took time to indulge her penchant for photography, taking pictures of mountains, rocks, a boy selling bottled water by the roadside, a plane landing in the desert.

Heather's absence left Neil to the wide spaces of the house of uncertain provenance. The phone rang. Neil ignored it— probably that idiot of a detective, or somebody at immigration services. Without locking the door, he sauntered down the slope toward the desert, under a sun so fierce you might imagine that the earth had strayed far off its course, that the weight of billions of sins dragged the planet toward conflagration. The land was arid. In Neil's vision, no armadillo reared its head, no spider made a trajectory toward the path of the man with a cracking pallid face and a mop of graying hair forced with a comb straight across to his forehead. *Carpe diem, for tomorrow we are middle-aged and bald*, Neil had joked. Now at intervals there were patches of sagebrush, cacti offering pitiful slivers of shadow, ocotillo plants with tall bare stalks like the fingers of a man pleading to God. He pressed ahead.

The Bible? You seem to think there's only one that matters.

Neil thought of Garvey's right arm, with its tattoo of a serpent baring its fangs, sweeping gracefully but powerfully across Heather's belly, over the cleft of her belly button, down to the abdomen and the spaces where Neil had sometimes fancied himself an intruder, whose own hand simulated the motions of a tarantula as it crept down, down to a dark patch. In spite of the heat and light, Neil felt ready to walk forever. Neil thought, *The popular perception is that in the context of a mainstream society so crass and materialistic, those who get into New Age or sex parties or the occult are so much more spiritual than everyone else. Maybe they are. And yet, the other bible, LaVey's, teaches that in some circumstances you must hate and hurt.*

For a moment, Neil caught a flash in his periphery as if someone way up in the hills to his north had tried to signal with a mirror. But scanning those hills with their patches of cacti and their dried steam beds, he felt as foolish as the evenings when he'd sat in North Hollywood nightclubs, acutely conspicuous as it grew clear to everyone that he was not waiting for a spouse or a date to return from the ladies' room.

Thinking back to the map Garvey had spread over his kitchen table, Neil assured himself that he knew the way to the Cavanaghs' place. Up ahead was a house, innocent enough from the outside. He soldiered on, fired by the thought of that tattooed hayseed, so much more welcome than the man who'd wined and dined Heather Payton for over a year, who'd brought her to the most exclusive shops in Beverly Hills and Bel Air. Neil began to think about the ineffectuality of love in the face of what was out here in the dusty world, recalling the words of Anton Szandor LaVey: "Behold the crucifix; what does it symbolize? Pallid incompetence hanging on a tree."

To the west was the kingdom of *Do What Thou Wilt.*

How Neil had yearned to protect Heather. Now when he thought of that stain, he recalled the rest of the passage that occurred to him upon first seeing it: ". . . when my mighty surge is spent, new wanderings shall begin; and that flesh which I desire shall come to me."

It dawned on him how easily he might pass out from heat exhaustion. Then dehydration might take care of the rest. *112° in the shade, what's that like?* Heather had asked not long after her move to L.A. Now Neil saw dozens of legs dangling from the altars where the host would implant his seed, Mary striding past the flickering candles with a bronze phallus hanging from between her thighs, Garvey grinning wide as Heather crouched naked on all fours to lap up the blood trickling from the chalice that had collected fluids drawn during the invocation of Baphomet, the motions of flesh pounding, slamming into receiving flesh as the ritual inched its way toward consummation. A vat as wide as a backyard swimming pool, full of naked bodies writhing, feeling, sucking. To his north, the hills appeared to shimmer and shift like curtains with sepia tones fanned by a breeze. It was easy to forget the hills, but when you retreated from the babble and violence of the world, they stood as reminders of your status as a pool of scum soon to vanish from the arid crags and plains. He pressed ahead, staring at the distances around him. Slowly, like a buzzard, his mind circled back to that map, the arbitrator of the impassable spaces. Then he looked to the southwest and thought he spied a house. Not until he was within thirty yards of it did a boy come outside in a t-shirt and shorts, wielding a baseball bat. The boy got to work on Neil.

Heather stood in the long room thinking that perhaps the Feng Shui was a little askew today. Neil's neatness hadn't precluded a violent divorce of the desk and swivel chair, or a mess of pages all over the desk, which was no longer parallel with the glass wall. The figure ambling up the slope looked through the windows of an empty house. Seen from the point of view of a bird high above, this figure might have seemed to shuffle forward in the manner of an invalid doing without crutches for the first time in months, his jerky, halting moves broken by glances around the domain. The figure disappeared into the longest of the rectangles.

Neil stood panting, gasping, his clothes clinging to his skin. He made it to the kitchen where he splashed his face before ambling to the phone on his desk in the long room. He called the home of Charles Ross. Just as he was about to give up again, someone at the other end lifted the receiver, and there came long, labored breathing. In the background, some kind of sit-com or game show was going on, with a man's words—"Doesn't anyone have a sense of humor anymore?"—interspersed with trained-seal bursts of laughter and applause. Neil quickly hung up. A car was turning into the driveway, and then the figure of a woman surmounted the slope. She came through the door and faced him.

"How did the boy's cock taste?"

Heather held up several printed pages in her right hand. Her eyes pleaded, urged, demanded that Neil sign them.

Neil continued: "I think you know whose cock I mean. Wade Garvey, resident Satanist."

"*What?*"

"*Don't play the innocent whitebread Minnesota girl with me, cunt.*"

She wanted to spit at him.

"Don't *you* ever dignify yourself as a screenwriter, Neil."

Through all the years of Neil's life, the old sensation echoed again, the sense of himself as a gnome who toiled so self-importantly to produce sheets of manuscript that handsome, driven, accomplished men would glance at, then impatiently discard. *Throw away that shit, we've got work to do.*

Heather grabbed a stack of pages from beside the Smith-Corona on Neil's desk and tore it in half, from top to bottom, then put the halves together and tore them left to right.

"You ungrateful bitch."

"Don't say that, Neil. Anyone can be generous with someone else's money—your father's in this case," Heather sneered, as fragments of Neil's screenplay drifted lazily to the pristine floor.

Then Neil was on Heather, choking her with all the rage he'd tried so hard to channel, to express in a medium that had proved as treacherous for him as running is for a turtle. Heather pulled the brass letter opener from her pocket and rammed it through Neil's left eye, splitting the retina and severing the optic cord even as it conveyed the images to his thalamus: *Woman. Eyes. Lipstick. Throat. Arm. Ring. Brass opener.* Neil's cerebral cortex was awash in hysterical signals as she jerked the opener horizontally, back and forth, until Neil got it out with his right arm, the one he'd exercised on the typewriter, and began to stab her furiously in the chest and neck, and now the red geysers came, spurting all over Neil, mingling with the blood from his gaping socket.

Two hours later, in the stillness of the afternoon, a yellow Nissan Primera pulled into the driveway, and a thin dark-haired man got out and mounted the slope to the Payton residence. Arturo Machado's associates had watched Heather take photos of their plane during and shortly after its arrival in the desert, leaving them with no doubt as to her purposes. It had taken longer than he hoped or expected to track down the Paytons' Mercury, but here was no amateur. He knew the value of what the plane carried. He was more than ready, so imagine the incongruity of what he discovered. Once inside, he surveyed the scene for a minute, shrugged, laid his MAC-10 submachine gun on the desk beside the Smith-Corona, and went to check the fridge for booze.

Lost and Found

Ed Wright was thinking about Murphy's Law once again: *If something can go wrong, it will.* He'd been desperately trying to impress his employer and hold onto his job, better mediocre wages than none, and now his car had conked out on the way back from a convention in Bakersfield, meaning he'd miss a meeting about one of the accounts they'd finally trusted him with. Ed had to crash at a motel some fifty miles from Bakersfield while the local garage rummaged around for a new alternator. As Ed checked into the motel, he felt the anguish of a lifetime of failure afflicting him like a collapsed lung. He knew how unwilling he'd been to call the thing what it was, but here, indeed, was what people call depression.

Ed sat in the lounge for a while, sipping a Coors and glancing from time to time at the football game on the screen overhead, unable to muster any interest, before noticing a man of exactly the same age studying him from a few stools down. Here was a thin guy with trim brown hair and an easy manner. Why was this stranger looking at him? Was the depression so palpable? As Ed was trying to think of an acid rebuke for this unwanted attention, the man said, "Mind if I slide over?" and before Ed could say anything, did so. After introducing himself as Jack Flynn, he spoke of damage to his car that made a shot alternator look like nothing at all.

"You'll be out of here by tomorrow. I've been here for two days."

"Hmm. Well, I'll be here tonight climbing the walls for sure," Ed muttered.

"You seem like you're not the master of your world, guy," said Jack, before inquiring about Ed's work and love life, or rather the lack thereof. Ed would have considered some of the questions quite invasive but for his mood of weary resignation.

"I can see right away you're an educated man," Jack added.

"For what it's worth. I have this day job in Placentia, but I've tried my hand at writing stories. I have yet to get one published, though."

Jack processed this for a moment before replying, "I had an interest in writing once, when I was a kid, and the world drove it out of me."

"I have no idea what you mean by that."

"I wouldn't have understood either, at a certain point in my life."

"Don't you think that a man who never reads or writes is a limited man?" Ed asked, forgetting his initial reaction as curiosity stealthily took over.

"That's one view, of course. But think about what you're not considering when you get into a poetic mood and you get caught up in the sight and feel of a rainy fall morning in the country, or some such nonsense. Somewhere else in the world, Ed, guys are sitting around, anxiously waiting to hear a decision from a bank's board of directors, and your drippy poetic state is so irrelevant and meaningless to them, to the real workings of the world."

"Well, you could of course write a story about guys whose fate hangs on a bank's decision."

"Render something like that realistically? Come on, Ed. What writer actually writes realistically about *anything*? If you were as technical and detailed about the bank's deliberations as you'd have to be to render everything accurately, it sure as hell wouldn't be fiction as most people understand the term."

"You want to be the master of a practical universe. Power to you, buddy," Ed muttered.

They ordered another round. At precisely this point, Ed noticed an attractive woman, in her thirties like him and Jack, sitting at the other end of the bar and smiling at him. Now Jack changed the subject.

"Look man, I'm a sensitive guy in some ways. Are you a light sleeper?"

"No."

"Then I wonder if you could do me a favor."

The scenario was this: The couple in the room next to Jack's had been getting it on all night, every night. Jack couldn't go another night without sleep. If it wasn't too much of an imposition, Jack wanted to know, was there any way that Ed could switch rooms with Jack tonight? Ed wasn't a light sleeper by any means, and he felt like being nice to the man, so he agreed.

"My God, thank you!" Jack said.

"No worries, man."

They had a few more rounds before Jack announced that he was calling it a night, and the two men exchanged the keys to their rooms.

"Calculate your tip correctly, all right Ed?"

After this puzzling remark, the thin man was gone. Jack had barely left the lounge when Ed turned again to the blond woman who looked as if she might have recently strolled off the set of a film with an A-list cast, and once again he was at a loss to say anything witty. The woman smiled and sipped her drink, but then she too rose and strode out of the lounge, leaving Ed to curse himself for the social ineptitude that had spawned such frustrations all his life. He chatted with the bartender and glanced at the screen, knowing that the mild boost the evening's diversions had provided would soon be gone and the rotten old despair would tighten its grip on his soul. Oh, that awful, heavy feeling! He was so conscious of all the idle talk he made with people, and felt that it wasn't putting things too strongly to compare him to an animal that must soon be put down, nervously licking and nuzzling its owner for reassurances that cannot come. He left an adequate tip on the counter and sauntered off to Jack Flynn's room on the third floor, a room exactly like his own except for a bit of overpriced luggage, and a copy of *Institutional Investor* and a matchbook on the table.

When Ed had stripped and climbed under the covers, he heard a few words from the next room, not lustful or belligerent, just chatter, and then he heard nothing.

About ten minutes later, before he could fall asleep, the phone rang.

"Yeah?" Ed said groggily into the phone.

"Well, well," came a voice, a bit like what JFK would have sounded like if he'd lived into his fifties. It continued:

"Jack, Jack. You're not so hard to find after all. Although, admittedly, I did call two other motels before this one. Process of elimination."

Ed lay listening, quite stupefied.

"But to be honest with you, my guys have given up. They're sick of this whole thing and so am I. They won't stop bitching about this endless misadventure in the desert where

100 degrees is a cool day. And we know that even if we got you, you've ditched everything in the hills God knows where. I've called it off, Jack. I want you to know that you have a standing offer: Just give me back half, and you can come back east and live in peace. No one will ever go near you, on that I swear. Just think about it, all right, guy? Here's how to reach me."

And then the voice read off a number. Ed leaned over and scribbled it on the matchbook on the table. Then he hung up and within minutes fell asleep.

The dream that came to him then was bizarre, even for a man who had had the most vivid dreams his entire life. The door of his room opened, and in stepped the blonde who'd flirted with him in the lounge. She smiled and pulled off her clothes and then she was on top of him, caressing his body as it roused in every pore, kissing his lips and cheeks and nibbling ever so lightly at his ears, and this went on for several minutes before he saw in the moonlight filtering through the window that she was really not quite as old as he had thought from the other end of the counter downstairs, no, the skin was sleek and soft and girlish, and his false sense of her had stopped him from recognizing a woman—a girl—he had once loved and then cast aside, and the thought stung him that his selfishness had inspired a dream where he could attain this experience, this object, with no trouble or bitterness, where he could set right a past that haunted him to no end. Today the woman was probably happily married and had long forgotten Ed and his awful behavior a decade and a half ago, she was married to a good successful guy with progressive views, a guy who adored her and made her know it every day, and Ed Wright, the most rotten son of a bitch in the world, knew that he would rather have the most horrible nightmare than this dream that initially gave him pleasure. But it was a dream and it was finite.

Early the next morning, as the phone call and the dream made equal claims on his mind, Ed slid out of bed and looked through some of Jack Flynn's personal effects in an expensive suitcase. He found a stack of photographs and flipped through them. To his amazement, one of them showed a little girl with a charming smile. He showered and dressed, committed the number on the matchbook to memory, and tore it up. He made his way down to the lobby, where Jack reclined in a red chair reading a newspaper and looking as nonchalant as ever. Jack had slept well. Ed pulled up a chair right next to the other man's and pressed his mouth close to Jack's ear.

"Look, Jack, what are you really about?"

Jack turned to him.

"Excuse me?"

"There's something odd about you. You're a guy who's got something to hide."

"Can you step back from whatever you're feeling right now and see how strange your conduct is?"

"No, Jack, I can't."

Jack gazed at him, a cool appraising look, then sighed briefly.

"All right, let me come clean, Ed. There's something I was going to ask you to help me do. I have to go to the hills to get something and I could use someone to help me move it. If you're in, you get a portion, and we're talking about something pretty damn valuable."

"So you're not in such a hurry to get to Van Nuys?"

"It's Saturday. Neither of us is in too much of a hurry, correct?"

Ed thought of his piles of unpaid bills, and the embarrassment that always gnawed at him because of how empty his wallet was.

"All right, Jack, I'll help you."

Half an hour later, the two men were cruising in Ed's repaired Saturn on a ramp leading off the interstate and onto one of the back roads that were not technically nameless, but were impossible to distinguish from one another. The road was an uncurving streak of gray beneath a vista of blazing sand and hills resembling mounds of clay shaped by a lunatic—so it seemed to Ed—and a sky of pure cobalt blue, a blue that never varied and could make you yearn for the seasons if you were from somewhere else. Jack was quiet until they got a couple of miles from the motel. Then he said:

"Ed, do you consider yourself a loser?"

"No."

"Okay, I'm just asking."

In the corner of his eye, Ed detected another nonchalant grin.

"I did notice that you don't wear a wedding ring. There was a time when that would seem unusual for a man of twenty-nine, forget about thirty-nine. But I know how it is with some guys in our day and age. Time means nothing to them. Mess around, refuse to grow up, treat a woman who's cared for you like dirt—and then, before you know it, your hair's falling out and your gut's hanging out of your pants and you don't have a wife or a kid—any man who's for real has both, in my humble opinion—or any prospects in that regard."

Why was Jack doing this to him? As if Ed didn't know what his life was. Still he gazed ahead at the uncurving road. Jack continued:

"I didn't believe you when you said you voluntarily left your last job. I know why you're making less than guys a decade younger. You got fired from your last job because you totally misjudged the market for those credit default swaps—you thought your job was just like selling insurance—and it really bit you in the ass. You had no idea how many claims would come in, in cases where the loan worked out fine and the customer didn't actually lose anything."

It was true. Jack continued.

"Yes, you thought it was like selling insurance. Poor fool."

"Look, this isn't my idea of constructive criticism."

"I know, I'm just razzing you, guy."

Ed *had* to come up with some kind of comeback. There must be something he could throw at Jack!

"Do you know who Ezra Pound was?" Ed asked, turning his head slightly toward his tormentor.

"No."

Now Ed tried to look a little smug.

"Caliban casts out Ariel."

"Look, Ed, it's really not that I think you're a disgrace and your parents should never have brought you into the world."

Now they were approaching a hill like something from a Martian landscape, curving and segueing into a row of other hills and buttes, cracked in places like an old clay vase, looming in its fearsome immensity over the sand and tar.

"We'd sure be in a jam if another part of this car failed," Jack said. "You do know to change the oil every three thousand miles?"

Jack let out a chuckle as that last sentence passed his lips.

"That's uncalled for, Jack, okay?"

But now Jack said, "You want to turn right up here," directing them around a gnarled and barren tree to a side road, barely visible until you reached it, leading to the foot of the hill five hundred yards away. Ed looked around and considered Jack's remark and reflected on how easy it would be to die here. The car edged over the rough terrain until they were at the base of the hill and there was no use for the car anymore. They clambered out and Jack opened a flask and drank from it, then handed it to Ed, who was in awe of the vast spaces around them. It was not a good kind of awe.

"All of this makes you feel kind of small, is that it?" Jack leered. "Listen, buddy. You may think I'm a nasty, abrasive S.O.B., but I want Ed to realize that if he had the potential to become anything, there's no excuse for being nothing."

Ed let this latest provocation pass. They climbed up through one of the scars in the hill's wizened face. It was not surprising that Jack needed help when it was practically all you could do to move your own weight and keep your balance here. It occurred to Ed now that Jack could talk to him any way he pleased because he knew how desperately Ed needed cash, and he had been naïve to expect otherwise. Yet he felt the other man's words like a lash and knew he had nothing, nothing at all, to throw in Jack's face. They kept climbing through the pass, which reminded Ed of a trail through the steep dunes that divide the glider port in La Jolla from the beaches far below. At length they came to a cave where walking was a bit easier. As Ed followed Jack the stones littering the cave made him think how satisfying it would be to bash the man's head right in. For his part, Jack had the air of a kid on his birthday leading other kids toward a stadium.

Finally they reached a heap of rocks, and without a word, Jack set to work removing them, and Ed fell in. They tossed the boulders into the nether parts of the cave, and the rocks crashed and came to rest amid the stillness of centuries. Jack had done an expert job of covering up the loot. When the last rock was gone, Ed was looking at ten bags of cash. Jack stood over them looking like a cowboy who had wandered into a saloon full of willing women. Each man grabbed five bags and then they began the trek back to the scarred face of the hill. Ed wondered if it would arouse Jack's suspicions if he did not inquire about the source of this loot, but he held his tongue. Soon they were sitting in the car with the loot weighing down its rear half, just barely fitting in the trunk, and Ed brought the tired vehicle to life once again. *Oh Ed,* came that mocking voice again, *isn't this more than you would ever have seen in your sorry life?* And now that film played in Ed's mind's eye once again, a life of stumbling and frustration and vast investments of time and effort yielding more of the same, from nowhere to nowhere, nowhere to nowhere, watching men ten years younger get married and promoted, in a world full of possibilities that flourished into breathtaking reality only for others, never for Ed Wright.

They had both grown hungry, so they decided to stop at a roadhouse about sixty miles outside of Bakersfield. It was a black and white beacon as isolated as a balloon drifting through Siberia. So little rhyme or reason guided the encroachments of people in the desert, Ed thought. The two men climbed out of the car and strode inside and sat at a wooden table beneath a framed photo of gold miners in a canyon, one of whom had a curving mustache and a grin suggestive of some measure of success in the venture. A waitress came to the table, a redhead with the jaded look of someone used to being leered at by desperadoes. They ordered beers and sandwiches and watched the attractive woman come and go, Jack notably more admiring than Ed. Two beers led to six. At this point, Jack turned his torso in such a way that Ed glimpsed a pistol in a holster sewn next to his left breast pocket. He wasn't sure if this was intentional or not, but he realized that Jack probably had no intention of giving Ed part of the loot.

"Ed, Ed. I can't say I've met a dumber man than you."

The explosion caused by this last straw drew the gaze of men and women at three other tables, when attention was the last thing they needed.

"Christ, Jack! Am I stupid because I don't make six figures? *That's most of the planet, you fucking asshole!*"

"Ed, Ed, sit down. Sit down now. I'm just razzing you. Come on, sit down, the next round's on me."

He sat down and the other patrons lost interest.

"Look, man, I'm curious about guys like you, about how you think. I thought I might actually get an insight this way. I'm sure you have all kinds of cherished memories from your liberal arts college."

"I do. All kinds of memories."

"Tell me."

Ed paused, regained control of his breathing, and then began:

"Well, I slept in a lot of beds, but those trysts aren't what I remember most often. Not at all. In fact, I think about someone I knew, in college, who wasn't as practical as you are, but had this tangible persona. If you must know, Jack, it was a young woman named Sarah Palmer, a woman I wish I'd been mature enough to treat much better. But I do relish my memories from the brief time Sarah and I were involved with each other. I ate with this schoolmate, we got into arguments in our philosophy seminars, and our experience was inseparable. I still hear her voice, crisp as if I'd graduated yesterday rather than nearly two decades ago. It was the damndest thing when I went to the town—a college town—where my classmate had grown up, because I had such a strong sense of the person from this other setting, from college, and now here I was one evening, on the streets of this town where my acquaintance had walked before, I was there all alone yet on another level not alone, and it was just the oddest thing I've ever felt. Here was a woman walking her dog, here a trio of kids on bikes, and I looked all around at the quiet streets, and I thought—well, I really don't know how to describe it, Jack."

Jack looked bemused but didn't take any of it seriously at first.

"It's not exactly *déjà vu*, it's—I don't know what to call it other than extremely strange. And if you knew a thing about literature, I'd explain it to you in terms of distinct Nabokovian personalities with a powerful sense of each other, of their complementary nature. You're not well read enough."

Jack grinned, to suggest Ed would really have to come up with a better put-down.

Ed continued:

"But, Jack, I'm quite sure that the Irish-American mobster you ripped off must have known something akin to this strange feeling when he went to St. Louis, when he explored a neighborhood in the suburbs and saw a scarf, a coat, a face on a girl that looked uncannily like a younger, female version of yourself," Ed said, recalling clearly one of the photos he'd glimpsed in Jack's luggage, showing a girl smiling warmly at the camera with a bridge in the background that clearly identified the location.

"A lean angular face with straight brown locks. It must have been strange for him to see this in an alien setting, bizarre indeed," Ed said, studying Jack's face with relish.

Jack looked as though he'd swallowed broken glass and it was just beginning to cut into his insides. His face was pale and his mouth inverted like a man sucking on an elephant's trunk. He gasped, spluttered, slammed his left fist into the table.

"No! No fucking way!"

"Yes, Jack. You would think nobody could underestimate how long the mobster's arm is, but a certain person committed that idiocy."

"How do you know this?"

Ed was really enjoying Jack's reaction. He relished the chance to push the knife in deeper, to twist it around a bit.

"I don't really feel like telling you."

"*Please, Ed!*"

"Oh, well, you know, I got a call from a rather ticked off chap. He and his men are in the area. He's got to have the money back in the next hour or he'll give the order to kill your daughter!"

"Give me the number."

"No, Jack. I'm not giving you the number or the car keys. And you know that if you shoot me your daughter will die. I told the man that only half the cash is left, and I'm going to oversee this transaction if you want to see your daughter again."

The unlettered man named Jack Flynn enclosed his burning face in his hands.

He said, "I'll never forgive you. This isn't justice you've achieved here, Ed. If you think it is, you belong in a straight-jacket in a padded room. *This is a fucking cheap shot!*"

Then he simply got up and stole out of the roadhouse. Ed would never see him again.

Ed Wright ordered another beer from the attractive waitress and thought about several creative ideas that had been germinating in his head for a while. He'd have a bit more time to ponder these ideas and reflect on his burgeoning creative sensibility before he had to get back to L.A. Ed relished the prospect. To paraphrase Saki, romance at short notice was becoming his specialty.

Stranger, Stranger

The young clerk at the hotel's front desk seemed unwilling to believe the guest's name was Rick Pineda. After so many hours on the road, Pineda knew he looked pretty ragged. But he didn't think that justified the oddness in the clerk's voice or the pauses before she said "Okay." *Maybe we're just both exhausted,* Pineda thought. *And I'm sure they do get some characters in this place.* Well, it was better not to say anything, especially since he had no idea where in this burg he might find another place to lodge and he was in no mood to go looking. The clerk wasn't unprepossessing, at least. She had dirty yellow hair and cheeks with a redness that suggested passion rather than the onset of a skin condition. But he avoided eye contact as he took the key from her and turned to mount the stairs to the upper floor.

It was a relief to hold the key in his hand. Rick Pineda had hurt and infuriated people and he was in major fucking trouble. He couldn't bear to recall the details of what he'd done, but he felt certain that consequences must come soon. On the road over the past twelve hours, Pineda had thought repeatedly, *How much longer do I have to live?* It was immensely soothing to be in a remote place where no one knew a thing about him besides his name.

On the upper floor, Pineda walked through a hall with yellow paint and a scarlet carpet until he reached a juncture with the corridor running along the rear of the building, parallel with the road a few dozen yards away. For a moment, he stood at the door of room 211, as a part of himself that held reason in contempt screamed that he must not touch the doorknob. To be slumped in a chair in this hotel, gazing at cable programs as the rest of the world ground on in the drizzle outside, was practically to be dead. In spite of this knowledge, Pineda turned the knob and stepped into the room. The banality of the dresser, the table surmounted with an oval mirror, the TV, the neatly made up bed, and the plain beige curtains of a coarse material assailed him. For a moment he'd unconsciously assumed that having a "corner room" was almost like having a corner office. He dropped his army green duffel bag on the floor, flopped onto the bed, and used the remote to flip past cable channels, all of which showed films he'd seen three or four times. Well, perhaps he could find a station that showed naked vulvae. But before he could grow interested in anything, he dozed off with the TV on. He dozed soundly through the night and well into the morning, despite his memories of having hurt a young woman in a city up north.

In the morning, Pineda went up the hall to wash, came back, and resumed watching TV. Nearly all of Pineda's interactions in the last twelve hours had been with cashiers at drive-throughs or gas station hands. When the cleaning lady came into the room, he found his own reaction humiliating. She was a Guatemalan or maybe a Salvadoran. He gaped at the nineteen-year-old brunette with hair tied in a bun and lips that curved so markedly that contact with another pair of lips would make itself felt most distinctly. Her uniform, dark blue but for the apron, covered all but her head and her tiny soft hands. Unsure how to convey to him that the convention was for the guest not to linger while she went about her duties, the maid performed them in an embarrassed silence. He was about to proffer a tip when his thoughts circled back to his finances. The girl finished up, pretended not to notice as he followed the progress of her bouncing buttocks out of this room and down the long hall.

How long before the next young woman appeared before him? Even now, he was devoting inordinate attention to the features, tics, and quirks of every female he encountered, unable to think of any priority or obligation, anything beyond the feminine presence before him. But he never forgot the danger he was in.

Pineda watched cable for about three hours before he chanced to look at his watch. He'd been lounging here for so long, not wanting to part the blinds and look out at the grim distances, the gaudily colored cars moving beneath billboards and golden arches, too lethargic even to reflect on his state and acknowledge that this was what people call depression. He thought he must, *must* have the company of bright smiling faces. If some or all of them were female, so much the better. After changing into a maroon button-down shirt and dousing his torso with Axe deodorant, Pineda grabbed his wallet and key and strode out into the hall. Then, as he was passing room 207 on his left, he heard a voice call out.

"Hey . . . excuse me, sir!"

Pineda paused. Here in the doorway of 207 was one of the most pitiful sights he had ever seen. It was a man in his late forties, not obese but overweight, with bleary eyes, stubble, and hair of a dead gray hue, like a younger Newt Gingrich gone to seed. He looked emotionally exhausted, as if he'd been arguing for five hours. He wore gray shorts and a dull orange short-sleeved shirt with a drooping neckline exposing a thicket of chest hair.

"You're not headed down to the bar by any chance, are you?" the man inquired.

"I am."

"Could you do me a favor, buddy? I, ah, can't really leave here right now."

Pineda couldn't suppress a chuckle. So this stranger had Charlize Theron in his room, or he was on the phone with all the Middle Eastern heads of state, negotiating an end to millennia of conflict. But the humor of the situation went only so far. Pineda sensed right away that this man had done something rotten. Even so, he felt pity for the haggard beaten oddball.

"Uh, okay."

"Here's twenty. I like light beers and I'll take however many that can buy. Thank you so much, pal."

"I may not be back for a while. I mean, like, a couple hours."

"That's okay. Have good time. Just don't forget, okay?"

Ignoring the condescension in that last question, Pineda took the bill and continued down the hall to the stairs.

When he got to the bar, he had already forgotten the middle-aged weirdo who didn't want to leave his room. Here was a garish rectangle of space with the counter running along the edge of the room closer to the interstate. Behind the bar was a man in his thirties with brown hair and a set of bold features like a daytime soap star. The man was chatting with a woman seated at the counter with a cigarette in hand and a black ashtray before her. Their talk went on for a while as Pineda sat there, bored. When the man noticed him, he ordered a Corona. He sat there drinking as the man busied himself over the screen of the electronic register. Now Pineda really noticed the woman. She had a couple of years on him, she had faintly olive skin, and her blond hair had the serrated, dorsal-fin look that some Middle American women do to perfection. He guessed she was a fairly regular smoker and drinker and had said goodbye to her virginity when other girls were learning to drive, yet she was not undesirable by any means. Her clothes were nice and in her eyes he detected flickers of intelligence. She had a glass of something fairly potent in front of her. Somewhere, within a few miles of here, Pineda imagined a house full of bare airy spaces, with polished boards on which nothing much ever accumulated, tasteful prints of rural scenes on the walls, and at Halloween, a pumpkin that cackled, its eyes flickering madly, when you went near it.

Now he noticed the woman noticing him.

"People are easiest to relate to when they're between two places," was what he came out with.

The woman considered this.

"I suppose so. I can tell certain things about you by looking at you. I'm Janice, by the way."

"Rick," he said, pleased at her responsiveness.

"Nice to meet you."

"What can you tell about me?"

"You're cute, for one thing, but there's more. I can tell you're not from here but you have some kind of past connection to this place, and you've been pent up in that room of yours for a while now, for far too long, and you're getting a hard-on just sitting there looking at me," she replied.

At a loss for words, Pineda sat there gaping at her. Then she laughed.

"I was kidding about the last part, Rick. Or at least it's fine for you to think I was."

Pineda felt both bewildered, and encouraged by her non-chalance.

"Well, it is nice to lay eyes on you. I've been, uh, sort of without company for a while."

"What did you leave behind?"

"Oh, never mind."

"Do you want to talk about it?"

"It's really not all that interesting, Janice. I'm just in sort of a transitional time. That's not at all a bad way to be. I'm ready for new faces."

"Are you really?"

"Why wouldn't I be?"

"Every scoundrel you've ever known was a new face at some point."

The thirty-something man was still busy over the register, his back turned, and it was impossible to tell whether he was listening. Now irritation crept into Pineda's voice.

"This isn't a child you're talking to, Janice. I think I have pretty good judgment about strangers."

"Look, I'm not saying you should necessarily avoid strangers. It's in the seemingly random interplay of strangers that tricky questions get answered and karmic justice gets dispensed."

"*What* gets dispensed?"

"Forget about that part for now, Rick. Tell me: is it worse to lie, or to hurt another person intentionally?"

"Some people deserve to be hurt. In my opinion, it's worse to lie."

"Do you know lies when you hear them?"

"I'd like you to know I have good judgment about strangers."

"That wasn't the question."

Pineda could not suppress a grin.

"You did bring up stranger-danger."

"Have you ever been kidnapped, Rick?"

"No."

"Has anyone you know?"

"Uh-uh."

"Did someone abuse you as a child?"

"That's another, what do you call it, *non sequitur*."

"No. Kids get pulled in a lot of directions. I'm wondering why you seem so broken."

"You're quite right. Look, I'm not really thinking very clearly about my past right now. I've spent a lot of time in my room, and I have appetites I can't ignore."

Immediately he wondered whether he ought to have said that. Fortunately, the bartender was turning his attentions now to a middle-aged couple who'd wandered in and sat down on Pineda's other side, near the door.

"You know, I gave you this spiel about strangers for your sake."

"Could you make a little more sense?"

"Out of kindness, I gave you a chance to explain, to justify your staring at me. But look, let's be clear. I think you get the difference between real passions and plain old stupid horniness."

"Hey—it's not like that at all. I swear, Janice. Can I buy you a drink?"

Before he had gotten the last question out, the woman rose and walked toward the door. On her way out, she said, "You, sir, can't tell a *thing* about strangers!"

Pineda covered his face with his hands. He knew the middle-aged couple to his right were exchanging whispers. When he dropped his hands and looked up, the bartender was leaning across the counter toward him.

"Everything okay?"

"Ah . . . sure. Could I have another?"

Pineda fingered the bills in his wallet. Most of them were crisp bills from an ATM at a nearly Shell. The odd man out was a crinkly twenty, the one that weirdo upstairs had pressed into his hand. When the bartender came back with another Corona, Pineda sprang a question.

"I say, did you recently see a chubby guy with gray hair?"

The bartender nodded.

"Unfortunately, yes."

"Unfortunately?"

The bartender elaborated.

"Last night was pretty busy, man. Not at all like now. There was a bachelorette party going on, and a lot of regulars were here. So, I'm busting my ass, and this dude wanders in and sits down right next to a girl. And I can tell from the way she's looking at me, and at her friends, that she thinks he's weird. She doesn't like his breath, or the smell of him. But the guy can't take a hint. He's breathing all over her, then putting his hand on her leg, her shoulder, as if that's exactly what she wants him to do. As if he's, like, responding to an obvious wish. This goes on for a few minutes, and people are carrying on all around, laughing, and then the girl cries out. I thought it would shatter every fucking glass in the place. All the chatter stops and everyone's staring at this girl and this man more than twice her age. I know this guy's just shit his khaki trousers. He gets up and throws some bills at me and *runs* out of here."

On hearing this account, Pineda felt marginally better. Others were far more inept than he was. Even now it wasn't clear that the woman he'd talked to in here had rejected him, had declined ever to see him again. Pineda thought, with flutterings of pity, of that wreck who'd accosted him in the hall.

On finishing his drink, Pineda asked the bartender for three more Coronas.

A few minutes later, Pineda knocked on the door of 207 with the three beers in the crook of his arm. When the door opened, the face that greeted Pineda was even wearier and more haggard than before. The man had been in a state where neither sleep nor activity is viable. But upon seeing Pineda with the three bottles, he brightened up just a bit.

"Why, that's awfully kind of you. Would you like to come in and have one with me?"

"Another time."

"Hah. Like there'll be plenty of other times. What's your name, friend?"

"Rick Pineda."

"George Tanner. Thanks for your kindness to a stranger, Rick."

"You'll repay me. Don't laugh. The world's not that huge a place."

"If I laugh, it'll be because you expressed yourself in a cliché," Tanner replied.

"Huh?"

"Never mind. See you around, Rick."

But Pineda did not let the exchange end just yet.

"Is there anything you want to share with me, George? I mean, like, in strictest confidence?"

"Funny, I was going to ask you that. You asked first, so you want to talk first?"

"No, sir. Tell me why you're here by yourself. Then I'll decide whether I feel like sharing anything with you."

A quality almost like mirth flickered in Tanner's eyes.

"I wrote a really nasty review of a guy's first novel. He's so devastated he says he wants to track me down and kill me."

"That's ludicrous. I can tell right away you're a businessman, not some literary snob. This is too silly. I'd better call it a night now, George."

"All right, then," said George, in a voice acknowledging that he *had* said something pretty silly.

Back in 211, Pineda thought, *What a poor slob. I'll bet the investors in his hedge fund are suing and he's fucking terrified to show his face to the world. How comical and pathetic, a man his age having someone buy booze for him like he's fifteen.*

Pineda stripped naked and climbed into bed. During the night, Pineda dreamed of the house near the Pine Mountains of New Hampshire to which his parents had taken him as a boy. The entrance to the property was on a remote county road. You moved in through a gap in a row of fir trees and drove fifty yards to a dirt lot outside a house, long but with only one story, and with a wooden porch facing the mountains. The house practically seemed made for filming ads for maple syrup you put on your flapjacks on Sunday morning. It was a long drive from Boston but they went there every August for years, occasionally bringing along a friend named Matthew, a kid with black frizzy hair. In the dream Pineda woke up in his room in the country house, in the dark. There was light somewhere in the hall leading to the porch, and Pineda could hear Matthew crying out, calling his name in distress. It sounded as if Matthew was in an attic that Pineda had never known about. Pineda tried to rouse himself, stuck out his palms toward the darkness, only to see the luminous outlines of another pair of palms rise to meet his, as simultaneously as if he were before a mirror. Matthew kept calling and wailing.

Pineda woke. The rain outside room 211's window gathered force as seven clock rolled around. When Pineda swept the ugly beige curtains apart, he had the same uninspiring view of the parking lot, the sodden knoll with a cluster of elm trees where nobody ever went, and the freeway in the background. Perhaps he might run into the attractive, saucy lady he'd met yesterday if he ventured down to the cafeteria where guests must be eating cereal and watching CNN. He showered and got ready. As he was dressing, he heard an odd noise, like a scratching, at the wall of the next room, 213.

As soon as the door of 211 snapped shut behind him, he heard Tanner's voice again from 207.

"Rick, would you come here, please?"

It was the voice of a man quite used to being obeyed within his petty domain, a voice Pineda didn't like one bit.

"What is it?"

"*Come here!*"

With trepidation, Pineda moved into Tanner's room. At once there came odors of rancid socks, cheap deodorant, and fumes from three nearly drained bottles on the dresser. The aggregate of these odors was a stench of male decline. Tanner was crouching at the window, gazing out at the strip of parking lot that flanked the hotel, at a point Pineda could not have seen from his own room. Whatever was out there, it fixated Tanner as a centerfold does a thirteen-year-old. Outside, the drizzle continued, drops obscuring parts of the glass just inches from Tanner's heaving unshaven face.

Reluctantly, Pineda made his way across the dingy floor to the window. Tanner had been staring at a dark green Pontiac parked on the far side of the pavement, perpendicular to the hotel.

"Do you dream of having a car like that, George? I'd have thought it's within your means."

"Shut up! That car's been there at least an hour, Rick! I haven't seen anyone get in or out since it parked."

"So?"

"*So?* What the fuck do you think the driver's doing, sitting there in a drizzly parking lot? It's freaking me the fuck out!"

Pineda didn't question the last part. Tanner was terrified. Pineda tried to take the situation a bit more seriously.

"Are you sure you've been watching it since it moved in there?"

"Oh, I don't know. I'm pretty sure. Maybe I went to take a piss at some point."

It was unfathomable, but there it was. The man was so shaken he couldn't clearly reconstruct the past hour.

"Would you, uh . . . "

"Would I what?"

"Do you think you could go out there and see who it is and what he wants?"

"George, you're not thinking clearly. You want me to go down there, rap on the window, and ask a stranger what he's doing?"

"I don't know, invent some fucking pretext! Tell him you lost your cell phone, will he dial the number to make it ring. I don't know, just think of something to get him to talk. Find out what he's doing here. Then come and tell me. *I'll* be the judge of how credible it is."

Pineda could barely avoid laughing in Tanner's face.

"No, George. You go and do it."

"I can't! Please, Rick."

"I said no."

"I'll give you a hundred dollars."

Pineda wondered whether he had ever met anyone as determined, as desperate, as this gracelessly aging man.

"Well, all right. But I want it in advance."

Tanner got up, reached into a satchel on the bed, pulled out a hundred-dollar bill, and thrust it at the younger man.

Unlike the twenty Tanner had given him earlier, this bill was as crisp as they come.

"Take this seriously, you bastard."

After accepting the bill, Pineda made his way through the hall, down the stairs, and out of the hotel. The lot out in front was not even half full, so one might wonder why a driver would swing around to the side of the hotel, but Pineda couldn't really bring himself to care. The information was like a plot point in one of the sequels in an also-ran teen horror franchise. Even so, he couldn't help wondering about Tanner as he ambled around to the flank of the hotel in the drizzle. The dark green car was still there. Pineda's shoes squished on the concrete as he awkwardly advanced. When he was a dozen feet away, he fell to his knees as if to tie a lace and peered through the rain at the car's dark and empty interior.

A minute later he was back upstairs in Tanner's room, where Tanner sat on the bed.

"Nothing to report, George. No one there."

The release Tanner experienced now was childish, almost comical.

"Oh my God, thanks, Rick. I really can't tell you . . . do you want to have a round of drinks on me?"

Pineda's voice was firm.

"We'll do the 8:30 a.m. drinks another time. Right now, I'd really like you to tell me what you did and who's after you."

Tanner sighed, his position on the bed stiffening noticeably.

"No you wouldn't. What do you care?"

"You might as well tell me. I'm going to be out of here by checkout time anyway, and you'll never see or hear from me again. There's nothing I could do with the information that could possibly hurt you. I—"

As Pineda was speaking, Tanner's eyes inflated grotesquely and he clutched the sheet with both hands.

"No, Rick. Please don't leave. I'm—I'm at a bad pass right now and I really need company."

"So I've heard," Pineda replied, and now a grin was irrepressible.

"What?"

"Never mind."

"Look, Rick, please don't cut out of here."

"You need someone to get you drinks because they won't serve you down there."

"I need company. A person to talk to. Is that so hard to understand?"

"Someone's after you and you need me to check out strange cars. That's the real motive," Pineda maintained.

"No. That's not the case at all."

"Tell me what you've done, George, or I'll cut out of here right now, not in three hours."

Tanner sighed again, in acknowledgment that Pineda wasn't bluffing. He began to give an account of his relations with a couple of aggressive but not particularly successful fellow businessmen. Tanner's pals were mid-level executives of Conex, one of the securities exchanges that had been struggling in recent years. Hence they were among the first people to learn about plans for Conex to merge with a larger, German-owned exchange. They knew Conex's share value would soar as soon as news of the merger hit the market, but they also knew "fucking well," as Tanner put it, how much attention they'd call to themselves if they were to buy huge blocks of shares so soon before the merger. So, they made a plan with their buddy, George Tanner, whose connection to them and to Conex would—they thought—be quite hard to prove.

He'd buy as much Conex stock as he could afford, and then, a reasonable while after the stock soared, he'd sell off all his shares and give his pals portions of the total value in cash. Tanner promised them, up and down, that it was against his nature to betray friends, that he'd never ripped anyone off in his life and wasn't about to start. It sounded like a plan. No one expected the CFTC's investigators to discover an e-mail exchange between Tanner and one of his pals in which they discussed the scheme in heavily coded terms that nevertheless failed to fool the investigators. Surprise was even greater when the U.S. Attorney's office and the CFTC announced respective actions against the inside traders. But Tanner moved fast. He was able to sell off all the shares even before the investigators made their find. He fled his suburban home with a satchel full of cash before the government could even indict anyone. It was clear that fleeing with the cash had been Tanner's plan all along, irrespective of the government's actions, which added injury to injury for Tanner's two pals.

Pineda could barely believe that Tanner and one of the other plotters had been dumb enough to discuss their plan via e-mail, even in code. Then again, maybe Tanner hadn't been stupid at all. He'd admitted his propensity for lying and mis-leading. Maybe Tanner initiated the exchange with a view to ensnaring his "friends" while he fled with the cash.

"Sounds like you're an awfully smooth liar," Pineda said.

"I've always thought that all stock market activity is insider trading. But I acknowledge the centrality of lying to my be-havior. I just don't think liars are on the bottom circle of hell," Tanner said in an oddly breezy voice that made Pineda think perhaps telling the tale had already had a therapeutic effect.

Never having read Dante, Pineda could neither affirm nor contradict Tanner's view about liars.

Now came Pineda's turn. He began to speak with as much as detachment as he could achieve about his brief relationship with a woman named Nicole in a state he'd left behind. Nicole, whom he'd met in a café one afternoon, was an attractive young lady with rich dark hair and skin the color of diluted marmalade. She was as warm and as kind as any woman Pineda could have hoped to meet, and almost from the beginning of their acquaintance, she had compounded the pleasure of her kisses with gifts meant to woo him, from flowers to chocolates to elegant marble balls painted with Mandarin characters and with bells inside them. He liked her, and not just for her unfeigned kindness. Nicole was brighter and more cultivated than a lot of women he'd fucked. Sadly, she also had an affliction, Lyme disease, as the result of a tick bite when she was a girl. Nicole was in almost indescribable pain nearly every day, and did not like to take drugs for the pain because they rendered her practically comatose. With the pain came depression, and eating habits that bloated her belly, a condition she tried to conceal by wearing clothes a few sizes too big for her.

In hindsight, Pineda knew that he should have been quite frank with Nicole at the outset and told her that he liked her in ways but did not think a relationship was possible. Instead, he strung Nicole along for a few months, alternately enjoying and getting fed up with her company, until one night when he screamed at her for being fat and ditched her. His final words to Nicole were that she was hideous and deserved to die, and he never wanted to see her again. A few weeks after that incident, Pineda had learned from denizens of the café where he'd met Nicole that she was now a virtual invalid and a former boyfriend of hers, one Marco Mendez, felt a fury toward Rick Pineda such as few mortals had ever experienced.

"Well, her flaws aside, it sounds like Nicole was a wonderful lady. I can't understand leaving her for the reasons you've given," Tanner said at the end of this account.

That wasn't hard to believe, because Pineda was quite incredulous when recalling the conduct of a younger version of himself. He'd been a stupid partier, obsessed with the moment. Now, for no reason at all, he recalled once having told Nicole that he'd visited this very hotel years ago, on his way home from a weekend of partying in Florida, and that he'd always meant to come back.

Pineda felt a kind of morbid curiosity.

"What's your most recent experience?" he asked, though he thought he knew the answer.

Having already debased himself, Tanner didn't wince at the question, but his answer struck the younger man as quite odd.

"Ah, well, I was in the bar downstairs the other night, you know. And I saw this really pretty girl, and I tried to talk to her, just basic questions, you know, like where'd you grow up and what do your parents do and what teams do you like and who was your worst boss ever. And I guess she'd met a lot of jerks and she didn't trust my motives at all. She freaked out and made a scene, and now I can't go back to that bar."

"That's bullshit! I happen to know that she slapped you when you felt her up," Pineda said, not without satisfaction.

Tanner's face crumpled inward a bit, in disappointment at the thinness of his lies. He was used to telling sturdier ones, Pineda saw.

"Okay. Maybe so. But damn it, Rick, those *are* questions I would ask a woman!"

"Are they really?"

"Yes. When you're lonely, there are no trivial facts about another person. Every detail is a point to build on. The name of a girl's cat or the number of socks in her closet or a poem she wrote in the seventh grade or the kind of cookies her mom liked to bake for her to take with her to college, any one of these things is part of a person's identity and it fucking *glows* with emotional residue for me. I'd kill to be able to talk to a young woman about anything!"

"Well, then, why didn't you stick to that stuff in the bar the other night? Why'd you feel that girl up, George?"

"She told me a little bit about herself and then she shut up. I kept buying her drinks and she just stared at me. I needed connections to keep building one way or another," Tanner said.

"You sick fuck."

"I may be ill, but I didn't hurt that girl and I'm not convinced as to which of us is on the lower circle of hell."

Pineda decided his acquaintance wasn't about to become any more coherent and there was no point in talk. One thing rankled, though. He had more in common with Tanner than he wanted to admit. They were both desperate for female companionship. He told himself that didn't matter in the face of the reality of Tanner being an egregious liar and a far more horrible person at least in that regard.

"If you want me to stick around another day, I'll need three hundred dollars."

He expected an argument. But Tanner got up, reached into the satchel on the bed, and pressed three more crisp bills into the younger man's hand. Pineda felt ready to celebrate. As he left, Tanner was muttering about calling his sister who lived in another state, but Pineda thought even George Tanner wouldn't be dumb enough to do that. Pineda was no trained covert operative, but he'd been careful not to leave any clues, unless you considered a reference to having once visited this place years ago a clue.

When Pineda walked into the bar, he overheard a bit of conversation. The thirty-something bartender was telling a teenaged porter to bring a green flask filled with translucent liquid up to the "foxy young thing" in room 234, and to present it compliments of the house. The porter took the flask, wrapped in a frilly pink ribbon, slid past Pineda and out of the bar.

The place wasn't packed, but business was way up compared to last night. Pineda got himself a glass of the house red and found a place to stand a few feet from the counter, two-thirds of the way down the floor. He looked around, awkward yet expectant. Perhaps the maid who'd entered his room just after his arrival liked to hang out here when a shift was over. He wouldn't mind meeting her. The faces in this darkened space appeared friendly yet coy. In general the folks here were enjoying their warm cocoons of chatter and intoxication. Pineda felt a rush of excitement when a woman's head a few feet away bobbed backward as she laughed and he saw that the woman was Janice. She had a female friend with her. Pineda moved up behind Janice and touched her shoulder. As she turned around, Pineda saw he'd been wrong, the woman Janice had been talking to wasn't a friend, just a stranger who'd said something funny. For that stranger moved off, leaving Pineda with Janice's undivided attention.

"How're you making out, Rick?"

"Fine. I've been wondering about what you said the other night, about 'karmic justice.' I'd like to understand it better."

Janice grinned.

"No you wouldn't. You'd like to fuck me and you're grasping for anything you can say to make that happen!"

Pineda was taken aback yet he couldn't help noticing a light playful quality in her tone, implying she wasn't averse to the concept of them fucking. He moved a step closer to her.

Once again he found himself admiring her eyes, in which it was impossible not to detect flickers of intelligence that distinguished Janice from young people in Middle America who talked and breathed but in many respects weren't really alive. Her perfume made him think of a nude woman lying face up in a bed of dahlias, a vivid manifestation of her fertility and her longing.

When he began to move his mouth again, Janice preempted him.

"This is Mike. You really don't want to know what he can be like in certain moods."

The guy who moved up beside Janice as she spoke these words was burly and intimidating, nearly two hundred pounds of muscle and sinew packed into jeans and a red and black flannel shirt, full without being fat. His face was almost too young and too fresh, his trim brown hair thicker than Pineda's black hair. In humiliation, Pineda turned and sauntered away from Mike and Janice, out of the bar. It wasn't right at all, he thought as he mounted the stairs. She was toying with him but he had no doubt she desired his attentions later. He felt furious at her. He wondered how anyone could behave that way, could be so cavalier about another human being's needs or emotions. But he wondered what chance there could be of encountering Janice again in the time that remained to him at this hotel.

Then he emerged from the stairwell and saw the porter up ahead in the corridor, the teen in a white blazer, the only porter in this none too distinguished hotel.

"Hey, man!" Pineda called.

The porter turned around.

"Can you help me? You know that woman with the spiky blond hair in the bar down there. I'm wondering what room she's staying in."

The porter shook his head. Pineda reached into his pocket and held out one of the hundred dollar bills. The porter's eyes rested on it for a few seconds. Then the teen gestured to indicate a two, a four, and another four, and he grabbed the bill and took off down the hall.

Pineda retreated to his room and lay slumped in front of the TV for two hours. He thought he must catch Janice without that pig, Mike. She really should know how it feels to have someone toy with your emotions and then dump you, he felt. He wondered with indignation how anyone could behave that way. He'd felt he'd seduce her yet.

Pineda walked down the long hall parallel with the freeway until he reached a hall running back toward the front of the hotel. As he moved up this new corridor, he passed 234 without paying it any mind. He reached yet another juncture and walked along the hall behind the hotel's façade until he stood before 244. Pineda pressed his ear to the door, careful to stay below the peephole. Janice's was the only voice he could hear, but she was definitely not alone. The timing of her speech, the nuances of her voice indicated she was acknowledging another presence in the room, responding coyly to faces and gestures.

"Oh, I know there are some strange specimens in our midst. Be civil. What? Oh, no, I don't think we need to . . . Oh? Hey, stop it, we'll get to that soon. Promise. Stop it. Now look, some people are so dense you've got to talk about the celestial design in kind of silly terms. Karmic justice, crap like that. You have to. I can't imagine how the dumb and direction-less will swallow *Malebolge*. No, stop it, I said we'll get to that. Be patient. Others wish they had half as much time to play."

Pineda could not begin to make sense out of what he was hearing. He fled back the way he'd come, slammed his door, and turned on the TV again.

An hour later, as he was watching Tim Robbins act in a film he'd seen so many times he knew what the characters had to say before they opened their mouths, a knock came on the door. He thought, *I knew she'd come around sooner or later.* But when he got to the peephole, he saw to his astonishment that it was not Janice, but a lass he'd never seen, or at least, whose presence had never registered. He opened the door. She was about twenty and had prominent lips the color of rubies, contrasting sharply with her face, which looked like parchment that time had given just a trace of pink, disdaining yellow. She'd pushed her black hair straight back and tied its extremities in a bun high up on her delicate scalp. Her lips were primed for a kiss, her eyes for far more.

She said, "I'm sorry to bother you, sir, but I saw you storm down the hall a while ago, and you looked *so* upset. I'm just wondering whether you need some company."

She advanced into the room. He produced another $100 bill, and for the next two hours, forgot all about his resentment toward Janice for having been so cavalier about another person's deepest needs.

"You can't leave," was the first thing Pineda heard upon emerging from his room at 7:12 the next morning.

"Excuse me?" Pineda said, turning toward the open rectangle of space to his left.

"You can't. Please. Please don't walk out of this hotel, or I'll cut my fucking wrists."

The man sitting on the bed inside room 207 was paler, far closer to a zombie state, than the woman who'd visited him the night before, but with no redeeming beauty. Tanner still hadn't bathed since maybe the Clinton administration, and his hands were clutching the sheet so savagely that if it had been a living thing it would have choked and died. Pineda stood there for a minute, not responding, just relishing the most pitiful sight he'd ever come across. Here was a member of an aristocracy to which Pineda could never aspire. He'd fallen so far, through social strata, through layers of circumstance, that he was begging for Rick Pineda's charity.

"Well, George. I was going to check out right now and call a cab, but I might just be prevailed upon to extend my stay. But if I do, I'll need you to stop being such a stingy bastard and think about the needs of others and how your behavior affects others for once in your life. Do you think you can do that, George?"

"Please, Rick. I'll do it. Please!"

"Very good, man. Now, I want a hundred dollars for every minute I'm going to stick around here."

"*Done!*"

The overweight middle-aged man reached into the satchel, grabbed a pile of bills, and thrust them into his acquaintance's hands. Pineda began to even out the stack in his hands, thinking *I didn't even realize what a shitload of money is in there.*

"Maybe you've at least learned your lesson, George. You shouldn't lie to people," Pineda said with all the weight of moral authority.

Tanner put his face in his hands and began to weep. Pineda glanced past Tanner, out the window, at the grounds where the drizzle hadn't let up. The world was as gray and dull as ever. Pineda looked out at a strip of freeway, a smaller portion than he could view from his own room. Nevertheless the view encouraged him to meditate on the passage of cars and the anonymity, from the viewer's perspective, of the souls encased in those vessels racing through the dank gray and spraying the side of the road with water as they skirted over elongated puddles. So relentless was the drizzle than an observer might feel tempted to get down and beg for something to emerge, for a person to break through to this dry warm place, no matter what visage the stranger might present to those who'd already taken refuge here. Pineda looked out at the cars and wondered who might turn in here. He imagined Tanner filling hours with no activity other than looking out there, trembling, shuddering, following the progress of a car on that road and thinking *Stranger, stranger, who are you and what will you come to mean to me?*

Pineda went back downstairs to the bar, but patrons were disappointingly sparse. On one stool was a burly trucker brooding over a whiskey, on another, an aging lady with a coarse face, a gaudy curtain of yellow hair, and a lascivious manner, whom he decided he'd rather not get to know. He had one drink and went back up to his room. As he turned the TV on, he was already growing a little afraid of what he might do in his boredom. He watched yet another insipid mainstream film, this one starring Tom Cruise, for nearly two hours before he happened to turn his head to the left and notice the note under his door.

He got up, picked up the piece of yellow hotel stationery, and read three words scrawled in pencil: COME SEE ME.

His first thought was that some whores have too much capitalist ethos for their own good. That "foxy guest" in 234 wanted more money. Well, she wasn't going to get it. Then again, maybe the note was from Janice. She'd caught him spying, or someone, the porter perhaps, had told her he'd been trying to connect, or it had been obvious to her all along. But she clearly wasn't going to give him what he was after. Like so many others, she underestimated Rick Pineda's intelligence and sought to lure him into a trap, he thought. Yet again, the scrawled characters on the piece of stationery were, to his mind, insufficiently feminine in appearance for either thesis to be too likely. So, Tanner had grown so desperate he'd made this pitiful gesture. The liar wasn't even brave enough to make his presumptuous request in person. If he wanted Pineda to stick around, he was going to part with another fistful of hundred dollar bills, Pineda resolved.

He went out into the hall, flung open the door of 207, and moved inside. He was so eager to confront Tanner that he didn't even have time to react to what he saw and turn around.

Two strangers in expensive suits were in the room. A man with a stout build and the cruddy matted hair of a short-order cook sat on the bed beside Tanner, holding the tip of a .45 to Tanner's temple. The second well-dressed stranger, a younger and thinner guy with trim red hair, stood to Pineda's left, almost out of sight until you were in the room. As soon as Pineda entered, the one on the bed turned the gun on him. Now Pineda noticed that the younger stranger standing near him had black gloves on his hands, and a pair of brass knuckles on his right fingers. Before Pineda even had time to process the scene, the younger man slid around him, shut the door, and pressed a button in the knob.

"Glad you could join us," said this polite *homme d'affaires*, making a darting motion with his eyes to indicate that Pineda wouldn't have time to run out of the room before the man on the bed shot him and Tanner both.

Tanner's eyes were hemorrhaging tears. Those poor dejected orbs rotated upward in their sockets until making contact with Pineda's eyes. Pineda didn't care about Tanner, but that gun was pointed at his face. Even if he could get the door open, he wouldn't get outside quickly enough, a bullet would strike him in the spine or the back of his head.

So here were the men Tanner had ripped off. Tanner had brought them here through an elementary mistake, calling his sister and letting slip details about where he was.

The man on the bed said, "How much have you given this greaseball?"

Tanner swallowed and wiped his eyes with his fingers.

"Nothing. He's just this guy I've been hanging out with. Let him go."

The two men in suits looked across the room at each other. A bit of mirth entered their faces.

"At least you're totally reliable in one way," the standing man said.

Pineda silently agreed. When lying became pathological, it assumed its own kind of clarity, a certain inverse relationship to the truth.

Now Pineda began to reach into his right front pocket. His fingers had closed around a cluster of bills when the man on the bed stood up and trained the .45 on him. When the man took a step closer, sizing him up, alert to his every breath, to every quiver of his muscles, Pineda guessed that the man was getting into position to shoot him execution-style.

The four men in 207 heard a noise, like a female cat re-acting to the appearance of a predatory male on the far side of a glass door. It was a shriek rising steadily, inexorably in pitch. It fell, rose, fell again, and rose once more. At its lower volumes it had an odd wheezing quality, as if getting it out had begun to kill the source's lungs. The shriek was eloquent in its anguish yet totally primal. The man who'd been standing when Pineda came into the room removed the brass knuckles, withdrew a folding knife with a brown-green checkered grip from a breast pocket of his sports jacket, then slipped past Pineda and out of the room.

Pineda had already realized what went down. He'd heard the sound before. The guest in room 213, the room next to his, was someone he knew quite well. She'd been sitting cross-legged on the bed when her pain, which had been testing and teasing her for hours, became so acute she could not hold back. Nicole had barely had the strength to write a three-page note and ask a maid to slide it under Pineda's door. Now, whether in protest or in surrender, Nicole had to give voice to her agony.

Two minutes later, the thin man came back into the room.

"I didn't cut the bitch, but I made sure she got a good look at this," he said, brandishing the knife.

All four men were utterly astonished as the door, which the thin man had carelessly swung toward its frame as he moved into the room, swished wide open and three men followed him inside. Here was a trio of young guys in black leather jackets, one of whom, a tough-looking dude with Peter Weller cheekbones, was easily recognizable to Pineda. He was looking, with knowledge, at Marco Mendez, Nicole's one-time boyfriend. The three intruders carried Beretta pistols with silencers attached. In a motion so fast no one saw it, the man on Marco's left raised his arm and fired, and the tall red-headed man collapsed on the floor with a neat hole in his forehead. When the guy on Marco's other side fired, the result was not so neat. The older fatter businessman jerked back on the bed as the bullet sheared off the top fifth of his head, spraying the dull yellow wall with blood and brain tissue. Then the three turned to their real target.

As they began punching Pineda, and kicking with him their steel-tipped boots, and he collapsed into a ball on the floor, he heard Tanner talking calmly from that same position on the bed.

"Ha, ha. You thought I'm the worst specimen of humanity, Rick, because I've lied. No, sir, you've got it quite wrong. I may have lied, but believe me when I say the two men who just died in here were the most wicked thieving bastards you'd ever meet. They never met their reporting obligations, and in stealing from them, I was repaying them in kind. I never hurt anyone who didn't deserve it, Rick! *Your* case is a little different. You did the worst thing a person can do. You didn't lie but you got that poor girl Nicole to trust you, and then you were so deliberately hurtful she tried to cut her wrists, as if the Lyme disease wasn't causing her so much pain every day she wanted to cry and throw up on that account alone. Yes, Rick, she tried to slash her wrists. I don't know whether you knew that. Liars are not on the lowest circle of hell, my classically untrained friend, but on *Malebolge*, the penultimate circle. You're on the ninth circle. But don't worry, we can really only take this analogy so far, because you won't have eternity to contemplate what you've done wrong. Oh no, Rick. I will make it out of this hell and up into Purgatory. You, on the other hand, are turning to bloody mulch right now before my eyes and *I'm enjoying it to death!*"

Where History Lives and Breathes

In the off season, the port of Yorktown, Virginia, has a haunted air, but not in the sense of a Poe story. There is no fear in the visitor's mind, no sense of spirits lurking in the belfries or goblins peering from the windows of the desolate buildings on the York River. It's a place where the visitor feels the absence of things acutely. You just stand there and hear cars hissing over the suspension bridge, and you look around and remind yourself that important events happened in this lonely place, and there is a genuine sadness about it. This is not a town people would give a thought to if it had some other name.

One gray afternoon in January, as the mist rose off the river, Scott Wilson made several wrong turns on the way to a lecture on the early history of Virginia at the visitor's center. The arrows on signs on the roads did not really correspond to the available directions, he found. A cashier in a 7-11 contradicted the signs. Though her directions weren't the clearest, Wilson finally grasped that he needed to keep going straight until the lights right before the bridge. He did so but then he made another wrong turn and wound up in the desolate space directly under the bridge. Knowing that he would be late, he got out and gazed around in frustration. He was ready to turn around and head back to D.C. when he spotted the narrow lane leading up the hill to the facility.

The professor was well into her talk when he strode into the dark auditorium. On the screen behind her was an image of Captain John Smith's map, showing the area and the locations of various tribes, as the map's maker had understood them. An old couple made a racket moving their things aside to let Wilson move through the row and find a seat.

Getting here was worth the effort, he found. The lecture was a lucid analysis of relations with Native Americans, particularly the struggles over territory that had been going on now for four centuries. The Powhatans, the Monocans, the Pamunkeys, the Mattaponis, and many other tribes, including some Wilson had never heard of, had lost land in the armed clashes of 1622 and 1644, and then the Treaty of Middle Plantation had locked them into third-class citizenship on a few reservations. Even without the exodus of Native Americans looking for education and a decent life in other colonies, the power of the tribes would have waned. Quite a few once-mighty tribes now included no more than twenty or thirty members living in anonymity in forgotten corners of the state. On the screen behind the professor, the story played out in images: etchings of the removal of Indians from land they had held for generations, and of the public hanging of upstarts; photos of tribespeople who had moved to Oklahoma in the 1920s and enrolled in colleges in the hope of finding a life not possible in their ancestral land.

Now that Wilson was able to take in the dimensions of the space properly, he thought it was pretty awesome. The college must have a huge endowment and must draw talent from all over the country. Just look at the speaker here tonight. She was the director of a center at one of the local colleges devoted to the history of the area and the remnants of its tribes. Wilson felt a surge of pride and excitement at being able to cover this event. He refused to give up on his goal of becoming a famous journalist. He hung out at conferences and talks, interviewed professors who were changing the direction and content of studies within their field, and sometimes managed to place work in one of the popular historical magazines. The last piece that Wilson produced, an interview with an eighty-eight-year-old former Flying Tiger in a Bethesda nursing home, had made it into *Aviation Past and Present* and Wilson had gotten a check for $300.

After the talk, there came questions from people interested in a CD-Rom put out by one of the professor's colleagues. Wilson made his way through the throng and got the professor's card and her permission to call the next Monday.

He was standing over a sink in the men's room on the lower level, beneath the auditorium, when a hand fell on his shoulder. He turned around.

The face was a few years younger than his own, and the eyes conveyed a manic energy. Black hair poured down on either side and curved like big waves on the shoulders of a blue cotton shirt. Wilson noted that he could not see the young man's ears. Here before him was a member of one of the tribes Wilson had been learning about for the past hour.

"I saw you in there with your notebook, man. Mind if I ask who you're with?"

Wilson smiled politely.

"I'm not with anyone."

"That lady in there, she doesn't know a thing!"

"What do you mean?"

"She doesn't know a *thing*, man. She just throws around all these big words, 'relocation,' 'suppression of indigenous customs,' 'erosion of cultural identity.'"

Wilson wondered where this was going.

"What are you trying to say? Helen Giese is one of the most esteemed scholars in the field."

"She probably is. So what. You ever hear of the Monaki?"

The stranger's black eyes flashed.

"No."

"Neither has she. She said there were eight tribes in the state trying to win recognition from the feds. The eight she named didn't include my people. That's how much she knows."

Wilson thought: *What exactly is left of your tribe, stranger? Twelve people with bloated bellies sitting around drunk and trying to dignify themselves as a tribe and get a check to buy more booze?*

He tried to be tactful.

"How many of you are there? Come on now. If I didn't name Luxembourg as one of the great nations of Europe, you wouldn't call me ignorant."

"Put this in your story, man. We had our tribe wiped out, our genes watered down, and no one gives a damn. No one knows we were once a great nation."

Wilson didn't care at all for this stranger's manner.

"Why are you telling this to someone you don't know in the men's room in a visitor's center? You could get out there and be an advocate for your people."

The stranger chuckled.

"An ancestor of one of my tribal elders was set to take on just such a role, but something rather unpleasant happened to him."

"Sorry to hear it."

"As I said, no one knows we were ever a great nation."

"And you're a living artifact who should get a federal grant. And all the Native Americans were environmentally conscious hunter-gatherers who lived together in harmony. If you'll excuse me, Iron Eyes Cody, I have to get back on the interstate."

Wilson headed for the door. The voice followed him out.

"You're a pig, man. You probably think Parcher was a hero!"

What? Who? Who the fuck was Parcher? But it wasn't worth a fight. To think that he had begun to get intellectual with this freak. Wilson went back upstairs and out of the facility. The parking lot was already empty but for three cars, and a faint sighing came through the rows of desolate trees.

A week later, Wilson positively brimmed with confidence. He'd just had an insightful interview with Professor Giese over the phone, his story was nearing completion, and one of the glossy bimonthlies was interested.

He needed to call the professor again with a follow-up question about her testimony before Congress in favor of recognizing certain Virginia tribes at the federal level. For all his skepticism on this question, Wilson was beginning to see the professor's point of view. Recognition of a tribe affected everything from scholarships to health care. He reached her at her office, and they talked for a while before he made himself say, "In the context of tribal relations, does the name Parcher mean anything to you?"

He'd almost been too afraid to broach the topic, but Professor Giese replied without a moment's hesitation.

"Oh, of course. Edward Parcher. He's one of the heroes of Yorktown."

"I see. A general or something?"

"A colonel. Just like his present-day descendant."

"I didn't know there was a colonel with that name in the present. Who was the historical one, really?"

"The historical Parcher was the scourge of some local tribes. That's just not how mainstream histories typically refer to him."

"I see. Thank you, Professor Giese. I think I'm beginning to make some sense of these things."

That night in his dreams his mind swooped in on a single image. A woman was crying. A squaw with long black hair falling all the way down past her breasts, lightly covered with a beige cloth. She cried and cried but the answer was silence. She sat inside a hut with walls made of branches lashed together by two cords at their extremities and one across the middle. A few of the branches curved out of their parallel arrangement to allow a glimpse of the dark blue universe. A figure stood right outside the hut, looking in, patient, indulgent, expectant.

Wilson did what is commonly described as "putting the finishing touches" on his article and sat at his desk with his finger poised over the send button. He knew that these were not the finishing touches. He always got mad at himself when a piece came out. Some people find writing relaxing, but for him it was a ticket to self-flagellation. At least it had taken his mind off his depressing dream. He forced himself to hit the button.

Later that day, the incumbent Republican president, a septuagenarian who had suffered a heart attack in the middle of a speech on immigration, announced that he would not seek re-election. After the shock over this announcement, speculation ran high for weeks about who would announce a candidacy.

Would Colonel Parcher, the descendant of the hero of Yorktown, jump in?

Though Wilson kept up his productivity, he found he could not quell the dreams. In one of them, a vast troupe of men came toward him in darkness. Fires raging off in the distance, at far points on the plains, threw a detail into relief here or there, a bloody face, an oozing hole where an ear should have been, a head crushed or melted into the likeness of wet clay. They came, driven forever from their ancestral land, angry, silent, humiliated. But it was as if they walked on a treadmill, for they never reached him. They never got near. The maimed were an exhibit, a breathing conscious mess of garb and gore for him to lavish his compassion on across the gulf of centuries and social strata.

Then he dreamt that he lay in pitch darkness in a motel. He could hear people arguing in the next room, though in his vague memories of the motel's exterior, there hadn't appeared to be a room where the sounds were coming from.

"What did you bring him here for?"

"Look, it's not too late to call this thing off."

"Call it off? I don't know what to say. What did you bring him here for?"

Wilson sat up and reached out with both hands and saw another pair of hands reach forward in the dark, the vertical palms aligned exactly with his own.

The squaw was crying. She pulled back a blanket covering a small form. She paused, as if she knew that a shock was coming, and then jerked back the blanket all the way. Laughter came from just outside the bark and woven mats enclosing the squaw and the exposed form on her lap. The noise grew until you could imagine a deity's laugher resounded through the universe.

Exploring various quarters of the web, he found only basic information about Colonel Parcher, much of it detailing his moves and maneuvers on October 19, 1781. A quick bold attack on the flanks of counterattacking redcoats had prevented an enemy breakout while enabling Rochambeau's forces to launch a devastating pincer move. Cornwallis had no avenue of escape. None of this information was of much interest. Wilson decided on a trip to the library.

Most of the material on Parcher in books about the colonial period proved as sketchy as what he'd found online but a thin volume written by a professor at the University of Hawaii offered a bit more. It reprinted parts of a document that Parcher had signed, establishing zones of non-interaction between whites and Indians and apportioning slivers of land for reservations. The tone and language of the document were neutral and legalistic, without the references to savages or scum that Wilson had expected.

Wilson's editor found the article that Wilson finally turned in to be an engaging account of how the center at Professor Giese's college was using oral history to build a case for the uniqueness of each tribe craving federal recognition. When the story came out, Wilson made dozens of copies.

On the following day, U.S. Army Colonel James Edward Parcher declared his entry into the race for the White House. He made the announcement to the world's media with much rhetoric about America's role as global leader and the need to make the world great.

At once Wilson's nightmares became more frequent. He saw ditches full of dismembered bodies, and tall fences splayed with intestines and limbs. In the morning, as he sat on the edge of his bed with his face in his hands, cursing and weeping, the visage of the stranger in the visitor's center recurred to him, and the images from his dreams, and the sound of the young squaw weeping.

Turning on his radio or TV at odd intervals, Wilson caught little bits of the round-the-clock coverage of this outsider's entry into the race. He watched part of an interview that Katie Couric conducted.

"It seems that your campaign is largely predicated on hostility to what you've termed the 'intellectual elite,'" the host said.

"Well, you know, Katie, Susan Sontag once referred to the white race as the cancer of human history. I don't think she had it quite right," the candidate said in his genial Midwestern uncle's voice.

Later in the interview, the candidate said, "They're circling the wagons, they're sharpening their blades, and we have to look at *all of our options.*"

Later still in the same interview: "You can have a Democrat candidate who's very politically correct and mouths the approved liberal sentiments and has lots of friends in the mainstream media, but I wonder what he'll actually get done."

Even later: "We have weapons that can jam and neutralize the enemy's nukes and clear the way for a preemptive strike. Annihilation for them, zero loss to us!"

It didn't take journalists and reporters long to find out about the new candidate's pedigree. When Wilson snapped on the radio, he heard an announcement about a rally coming up next week for Colonel Parcher, the direct descendant of one of the heroes of Yorktown, and the candidate running on an independent ticket to replace the ailing president.

When the night came, he didn't want to see what was going on in that auditorium downtown. But if the event gave just a bit of clarity and specificity to the candidate's identity and motives, then maybe the nightmares would end.

He turned on the TV. Even at this remove, he could feel the tension inside the auditorium. Guards flanking the stage gazed like angry statues at the eager mass of heads and shoulders visible over the tops of the seats. At the first whisper of trouble, uniformed statues would descend from all sides to pull someone apart. When Parcher strode onto the stage, he had the physical presence almost of a Roman deity. Here was a warrior-statesman with a powerful intellect at work within his hard nearly bald scalp.

"Good evening, my fellow Americans. I am speaking to you at a unique juncture in history. In recent years, you have heard all about the need and the imperative to make America great again. While it is hard not to agree in principle with that goal, I have always felt that the rhetoric fell short. We are the world's leading superpower, and it seems to me that our task, our manifest destiny, is to make the *world* great, leading by example."

What followed was not as explicit as Wilson had hoped and expected. Parcher spoke briefly about the need to combat terrorism, handle rogue states, and restore an international balance of power where Russia and China respected America and her leadership. Then, to Wilson's annoyance, the candidate spoke for half an hour on bland topics like taxes and healthcare. Wilson sensed that here was an elaborate diversion, an effort to build straw men to preoccupy those who might otherwise ask pointed and probing questions.

So Wilson must do it himself. He walked out of his building, got into his car, and drove down to the hall on K Street with the image of the crying squaw, and a vague presence outside the hut, recurring again and again in his mind. There was little traffic, and he ran six red lights in his urge to close the distance. He parked behind the auditorium and sat waiting until the back door flew open and Parcher's entourage began to emerge. Then came the candidate himself.

Wilson got out and dashed toward the little party. Two of Parcher's bodyguards stepped forward and grabbed Wilson by the elbows with such force that he screamed. But then Parcher came up and gestured at the guards. The grips eased, perceptibly enough though not fully.

"Is everything okay, young fellow?" Parcher asked in a voice like an imitation of someone's genial Midwestern uncle.

"Fine, sir. Everything's fine. I just hoped that we could talk. I've been having these incredible nightmares."

"Well, then, everything's not fine. What's your name, son?"

"Scott Wilson."

Parcher smiled. "Didn't I read something of yours in *Aviation Past and Present*?"

What were the odds of Parcher reading Wilson's piece in that niche publication and remembering the author's name?

"Well, ah, that's not my most recent publication, sir. I'm really interested in your policy toward indigenous Americans. Can we talk?"

The grips on his elbows were still painful.

"You should have been at the rally, son. There was a Q&A and journalists were free to ask me anything. I have to go now. You should go and get some help."

"Listen, sir. Most of what you said tonight has nothing to do with your agenda. It's smoke."

The candidate stood listening. Even now his manner was patient, indulgent.

Wilson continued to press him.

"We've all heard about America first and making America great and all that. Now you're talking about making the world great. Tell me what you think, what you really think, about all of the *others*."

"The who?"

"The others. Those who aren't like us. All the non-western and non-white races with which we share this planet."

Parcher laughed. He looked quickly around the lot, as if encouraging his entourage to join him in laughing. Then again, maybe he wanted to make sure that what he said now wouldn't end up on YouTube in a matter of seconds.

"Okay, I'll tell you. But I think you already know. They're circling the wagons, boy. And it's getting to a point where we can't put *anything* off the table. Now if you'll excuse me, I need to get back to reading *The Turner Diaries*."

Apparently Parcher meant this as a joke. The smile on the candidate's wrinkled face was broad and kind. Now he moved on. The guards held onto Wilson until Parcher and the rest of the entourage had gotten into a black van. Then they gave him a hard shove and climbed into the van, which glided off into the evening.

Wilson sat at his desk, thinking of the puerile tourist brochures that had invited him to come and explore the ancient towns of southeast Virginia, where history lives and breathes. He thought of the freak in the visitor's center, of the professor, of the weeping squaw in his dreams, of the historical and the contemporary Colonel Parcher. His mind returned again and again to the quip—or was it a quip?—that the candidate had made about reading *The Turner Diaries*, the white supremacist fantasy depicting the mass killings of nonwhites within and ultimately beyond America's borders. Wilson had read *The Turner Diaries*. Normally, upon finishing a book, he'd place the book on one of his shelves, because he liked to see all the books he had read lined up spine by spine, rather in the way that a bricklayer relishes taking in the end result of a day of hard work. But *The Turner Diaries* wasn't just a work he didn't agree with. It was a deeply savage book, a psychotic book, a book that reeked of contempt for the value of human life. He'd thrown it out. Now, sitting at his desk, he wondered whether Parcher could seriously have adopted *The Turner Diaries* as his bible.

The phone on the desk rang. He recognized the voice on the other end at once.

"Hello, sir. I see you didn't take any of what I said into consideration when you wrote your article."

"You obviously know my name and a few more things about me. Are you going to tell me yours?"

Wilson heard a little laugh.

"You'd never pronounce my name. So I'll give you an easy one to use. Call me Matthew."

"Well, Matthew, I've been having awful dreams ever since you touched me on the shoulder in the men's room at the visitor's center."

"Oh. Poor boy. Did it occur to you that when you see something real, it's not a nightmare at all?"

"The things I'm seeing can't be real, in the sense of existing now in the world. Anyway I don't want to see them anymore, and I've got to think about my options and about how to respond to the person who made this happen to me."

These words carried insinuations of a lawsuit, though that was absurd.

Matthew said: "Let's meet."

The visage of the stranger was four feet away, at the other end of the bench. A few kids played in the damp air over the acres of green scored by concrete paths wending from the pavilion abutting the busy avenue. Not for the first time, Wilson reflected on the oddness of encountering the face of this sorcerer, this elder of temporal bounds, this emissary of unfathomable weirdness, in a mundane setting. He wondered what he might say if one of the children chased a ball over here. *Hey, little kid. You have no idea of the subterranean tunnels of the history over which these fields and paths are a pitifully thin stratum. If you don't want to wake up at night terrified of every shred of light coming through every crack in your room and of every little noise you hear, don't let this freak touch you.*

Now the stranger who had deigned to render his unpronounceable name as Matthew reached out and grabbed Wilson's left wrist. In that moment, the mundane setting fell away and he saw darkness all around, but as his eyes adjusted the darkness retreated to the spaces around a stage he had seen before. He was sitting in the auditorium at the visitor's center. Here before him on the stage, in a narrow cone of light, stood a professor loosed at last from all constraints on thought and speech. Behind the figure was a vast map, not the famous explorer's, but a map of the planet that a controversial candidate had promised to make great, aping the outgoing president's rhetoric while taking it to unsuspected levels.

The outgoing president had aroused his fair share of concern among those who couldn't imagine him getting access to the nuclear codes. In the scene that Wilson witnessed now, it was impossible not to understand what Colonel Parcher had in mind. The regions of the world that he glimpsed at odd points in the murk behind the stage, on all sides of the map, corresponded clearly enough to countries whose borders did not appear on the map but whose contours every educated person knew. The mushroom clouds over China bloomed for miles and miles, each one a startling mélange of orange and yellow and unnamable hues where one region of heat and fury bled into another, the sky on the periphery a zone of dark tinted with the blood colors, the bits of earth around the blasts, the fields and river beds and hills and mountains, the widely dispersed fences and the occasional huts, shrinking until they crisscrossed the country at increasingly rare intervals and finally disappeared.

Now Wilson saw what Parcher had in store for India. Making the world great involved a strategic use of neutron bombs on the cities followed by a rain of toxic chemicals throughout the valleys and basis where the multitudes of wretched poor were not even worth the expenditure of big mighty weapons that the president might need to keep Russia in check. In these remote provinces of India, men, women, and children in rags staggered out into the fields in their hundreds and thousands and tens of thousands and millions, gasping and crying, their faces oozing from multiplying fissures and bursting forth in sprays of blood and tissue and bone as the chemicals worked their way up through every traumatized physique. Their polluted quivering bodies fell in heaps in the mud and rendered river beds invisible as they gasped and died. The use of neutron bombs was still more selective on the coastal lowlands, the outer reaches of Korea and Vietnam and other countries the president destroyed almost as an afterthought in his drive to make not just the country but the world great.

Wilson's vision turned inward, to the scenes that had bloomed in his mind as he lay in his bed in a semi-conscious state he could not avoid even as he came to dread it more than death. Here the universe was blue, the radii of mushroom clouds were nowhere in sight, but the squaw in the hut was crying. How she had dreamed of educating her offspring, inspiring her boy to grow up to be an eloquent champion of the dispossessed indigenous peoples of the great continent. The figure outside the hut laughed as the woman pulled the blanket away from the form on her lap and a look of horror and revulsion contorted her pretty features. The U.S. Army colonel in a crisp modern uniform replete with medals and epaulettes stepped out of the blue, into the hut, and opened his right palm, revealing a pair of tiny ears.

Sitting on the park bench, Wilson understood the depth of his need to believe that the races of the world could get along with and even love each other. The stranger, Matthew, was of a less sanguine and more pragmatic cast of mind. He gave Wilson to understand that there was no exact equivalent in English for Wilson's appointed role.

"For want of a better phrase, I am deputizing you. Maybe, for the first time in human history, a journalist will actually do something useful."

He shared what Wilson must do to open a dimensional portal.

On the day after the election, the teeming streets had levels of noise, the chatter of the crowds just audible under the blare of the music from the speakers which was itself just audible within the roar of the coming convoy. Confetti and scraps of paper drifted through the air and over the throngs pressing against the barricades all along the avenue. Stiffening his back ever so faintly, Wilson could feel the power and immensity of the human wave behind him, an elemental force like the mobs in *A Tale of Two Cities*. He feared for what might happen if the gun in his jacket went off by accident.

The crowds pressed harder and harder against him. Across the street, it was the same kind of scene. A middle-aged woman in sunglasses was looking at him and smiling at the predicament they shared on their respective sides. Wilson thought of those soccer games over in Europe where dozens of people die in some of the most horrible ways imaginable.

He had to stay in his excruciating position. The motorcade was coming into view, three rows of cops on cycles followed by a trio of long sleek black cars and three more rows of cops. He could hear himself panting now. It was difficult to move. The edge of someone's belt buckle dug into his thigh. Even now the woman across the street was watching him and smiling, though maybe more out of spite than amity.

The rumbling of the motorcade began to drown out the smaller noises. The helmeted statues on their big bikes gazed right ahead, the vanguard of an order hardly anyone dared question or oppose. The buckle kept digging into Wilson's side, and when he tried to pivot his body he only made the pain worse. All around the noise was relentless, terrifying.

He, and only he, knew what was behind the tinted windows of the middle car, or so he imagined. The fate of the world was up to a third-rate journalist. Now to his dismay he found that he couldn't see in a direct line across the avenue. The realization that he might not be able to climb out from behind the barrier in time finally came.

The cops rolled past, and now the first car, and if he waited another second, he'd end up chasing the president-elect up the street. When he tried to move, the masses enclosing him were as tight as ever. His left foot felt like a rubber appendage. It felt paralyzed. The agony in his side made him want to scream. Perhaps the president-elect was going to get away and commence the nuclear annihilation of all those who, in Parcher's mind, denied humanity's potential, kept the world from being great.

What happened now took several seconds for his brain to process and understand. A quartet of warriors, clad from head to toe in hardened leather and bright woven feathers, and bearing axes, machetes, pistols, and shotguns, leapt out from a point on the far side of the avenue that Wilson had overlooked.

Ignoring the cries and warnings from the mounted cops, they charged down the avenue until they were close enough to attack the middle car. Just as they got there, all four doors of the front car swung open and men in suits clutching MAC-10 machine pistols leapt out. Under a touchingly quaint concept of combat, the native warriors raised their mostly non-mechanized weapons. The security force opened fire in unison, causing feathers, blood, and tissue to coat the crowds and the pavement. People screamed and cried and took off every which way. At last Wilson felt the buckle withdraw, and sensed an easing of the pressure pinning him to the barrier. The four warriors fell in pieces on the street. Wilson knew that as soon as he tried to jump the barrier, he'd draw the attention of the men with MAC-10s. He would die before getting anywhere near the president-elect.

Now things got odder still. Wilson could just make out a bit of motion, perhaps a side door opening, not too far from the opposite curb. Then an unmistakable personage stood out in the open on the street. President-elect Parcher stood grinning at the aftermath of the doomed attempt on his life. Much like the Nazi official Heydrich in Prague in 1942, he was so brash and so contemptuous of his attackers that he engaged directly with the situation rather than tell his driver to floor it. In contrast to Heydrich, it appeared that Parcher would go totally unscathed. He was there, in the sun, for eight seconds before half a dozen security men formed a circle around him. Wilson thought that Parcher would address the crowds now, would decry the violence and perhaps even offer words of sympathy for the attackers, who now would never get the help they needed. But it was a new age in America. Parcher was a different kind of politician. He appeared to relish the moment too much even for such empty gestures.

The cops paused on their bikes. Citizens all over gasped and pointed and took photos. The weight in Wilson's jacket made itself felt against the tender space around his heart. He didn't have a clear line of fire, or even close to one. But now Parcher and his detail began to walk around to the space between his vehicle and the front one. If Wilson didn't draw the gun now, the moment might vanish forever. Hoping desperately that Parcher would come further toward his side of the avenue, he reached into his jacket. It was logical that Parcher should keep coming, Wilson thought. Emergency personnel needed space to deal with the fallen attackers, and for propriety's sake Parcher needed an area free of blood and garb if he did elect to make a proclamation.

Parcher took another step, and another, and another, followed closely by the security detail. Wilson reached until his fingers found the handle of his .38. Parcher's legs ceased to move but his head rotated until Wilson knew the horror and fear of a voyeur caught gazing through a window. He felt certain that Parcher was making eye contact with him.

Four more men in elaborate feathered garb leapt into the street, this time from Wilson's side. They ran desperately toward the grinning man between the two cars. More screams filled the air until the roar of the MAC-10s once again supplanted other noises. Now this side of the avenue was as bloody and slippery as the other. Whether the attackers had made a studied diversionary move to help him, or whether they made their futile sacrifice without knowledge of his existence, Wilson never learned.

One of the security men moved forward and raked the bodies of the second wave of attackers with MAC-10 fire, as if to drive home that no one else should be so stupid. Wilson withdrew his .38, leapt over the barrier, and shot the man in the head. He whirled and shot two more strangers who stood between him and the president-elect. Parcher definitely saw him, but even now the grin stayed in place. Wilson ran toward him, trying to align the gun's barrel with the grinning face. He fired twice and missed. He closed the distance to twenty feet.

Now fire came from a couple of directions and bullets blew chunks out of both his legs. He toppled onto his belly. The pavement greeted him with awful force. He shot two more security men before another bullet, perhaps from one of the cops, grazed his head and made him scream. As he crawled, still firing his weapon, he realized that the president-elect stood alone now in the middle of the street. He fired toward the cops. For the moment they seemed afraid to move out from behind their bikes. More bullets tore flesh from his back and buttocks and another one shredded his left foot but he managed to crawl further. Gasping, spitting blood, he looked directly up into the grinning face. With almost his last bit of strength, he raised the weapon, pulled the trigger, and heard a click.

Parcher laughed.

"Boy. It's a shame you won't be around to witness the blooming of all my nuclear dreams. We are going to make the world great. No more global tensions, no more p.c. histrionics. Can you even imagine it?"

The president-elect laughed again. In his peripheral vision, Wilson saw a mob of uniformed bodies running toward him. He thought he had seconds to live. He dropped the gun and found the strength to reach out and clutch Parcher's left ankle.

In that moment the portal opened. Filling the sky above the chaos, blood, and gore was a cosmic wilderness that assimilated all moments of history, a region where Parcher and his enemies existed at every age they had been or would be, yet where it was possible to decide ancient conflicts forever. The moment was here.

In the sky above the bloody street, a shaman, tall and muscular but with scars where his ears should have been, and clad in a simple cloth from his waist to his knees, moved across the horizon and stood face to face with the colonial officer in full regalia. At once the titans engaged. In a motion too quick to see, the shaman put his hands around the commander's throat. The officer fought back, punching the shaman in the face and chest with both fists, but the shaman clutched harder and harder, adrenalin raging at the fate of the incinerated billions throughout the world. The officer cried out, then was able only to produce gasps and clucks from his constricting throat. The blows stopped, but Parcher's hands did not fall limp. He reached into an ivory scabbard at his belt, withdrew a dagger, and thrust it into the shaman's bare chest. Then, using both hands, he began to twist the instrument, causing blood to flow all over the shaman's torso and down onto the loincloth. But the cries of the dead billions gave the shaman such power that he managed to crunch the officer's neck to a fraction of its proper width. The commander let go of the dagger, screamed, cried, gave a final gasp, and then fell completely limp in the shaman's grasp. The hero of Yorktown was dead.

On the ground, above Wilson's prone bleeding form, the president-elect wheezed, cried, and emitted a clucking noise for several seconds. Then a corona of blue flame enveloped him, melting his clothes, and his body turned to a heap of ash before Wilson's eyes. It was the last thing Wilson saw. Behind him, on the other side of the very barrier he'd jumped, a young man with striking locks of black hair and alert intelligent eyes took in the scene with a look of something like respect.

The Colossus

Reed Blackburn maneuvered among the guests, trying not to spill his wine onto the floorboards of the old gallery. He was grateful for a chance to attend one final show before the Klaubers, the gallery's elderly owners, said goodbye to their adopted homeland forever and went back to their village in Moravia. Lots of people would miss the Klaubers, not to mention all the odd art that graced the walls of this dusty gallery above a disused warehouse. Reed loved the old place. But tonight it was packed and most of the guests were much older than Reed.

He swerved, wheeled, slid, pivoted, and moved again amid the guests, many of whom he surmised had little use for twenty-somethings. They seemed bent on ignoring a representative of the hip youngsters who'd partly taken over the neighborhood. Maybe they assumed that Reed had little use for people who'd never used Facebook, Twitter, or Snapchat, and they were happy to reciprocate his contempt.

Harry was somewhere near the front of the gallery, in the midst of one of the crowds, taking questions. The paintings and etchings captured street scenes in Prague and Budapest, the façades of little butcher shops and bakeries, dense skies about to let loose, valleys and meadows where sheep or cows grazed against a backdrop of jagged snow-capped peaks. Then there were profiles of obscure writers of the middle and early years of the last century. One of the artists had rendered monsters with oval bodies except for their bony arms and legs, kind like an owl crossed with a Tyrannosaurus.

Reed took in the art with admiration. He gave up on getting close enough to Harry to chat. Guests of the same generation as Harry and Esther seemed so jealous of their time with the couple. Part of the issue was that Harry was quite hard of hearing, and sometimes did not follow what he did hear or reply clearly, and in order to have any kind of conversation with him, you had to engage for a long time, repeating phrases loudly, parsing Harry's replies, getting him to repeat them many times.

Standing on his heels, gazing over shoulders, Reed at last caught a glimpse of the thin, wizened, white-haired man. Harry stood there, a glass of wine in hand, grinning and laughing. Reed doubted that Harry followed a tenth of what people were saying to him. Maybe when you're really old, when your body and mind are giving up, one of the last things you keep is your sense of when to laugh, Reed thought. He wanted to believe that there might yet come a moment when all obstacles vanished and he could engage with the old collector and talk about Rodchenko, Mondrian, De Chirico, Bacon, Picasso, all the others whose named evoked realms of such breathless experience you could black out. Not that Reed found all of those artists to be great. But they were all, unmistakably, artists. They practiced their craft in the full awareness that one day people might walk around in t-shirts blaring things like "Picasso Sucks."

Reed moved out of the room and into the gallery's rear chamber. Rotating his body, he took in a bit of the art on the walls. The work on one wall was abstract, a mélange of purples and blues. On another wall, the paintings conveyed an aesthete's love of sunlit rural landscapes. None of these canvases were of much interest to Reed. He moved to the back of the room, the furthest point from Harry.

There was lots more art down here, in this neglected corner. Here were paintings and drawings of plain objects such as levers, pipes, plinths, chains, pulleys, and turrets, in no discernible relation to anything else. These things, in their grainy simplicity, were the objects of an artist's obsession. In other parts of this corner, rustic scenes lured the viewer to abandon and foreswear all sights and noises that did not belong to a particular place and time in Europe's past. Here were rickety huts flanking muddy roads, carts pulled by mares with dark pearls peering above thick manes, houses and churches that looked as if they could barely stand upright under the rain. A few of the paintings depicted workers in fields, men and women bent in devotion to their role in ancient cycles, indifferent to the artist or any other observer.

In the midst of all these images, Reed found a unique work of art. He was looking at a titan, a colossus, or so the subject of the painting first appeared. Upon further scrutiny, Reed decided that the figure could have been of more or less normal height, but the bulk of its muscles gave an impression that everything about it must defy normal proportions. The figure stood in a setting as humble as Reed could imagine, a muddy lane with a rusted wheelbarrow and a pile of sandbags in the background, but the intensity in the figure's dark eyes conveyed an intelligence and refinement that belonged to civilized settings. Reading the brief caption, Reed found one of the oddest words he'd ever encountered. He began to pronounce it to himself.

A hand fell on Reed's shoulder. Turning around, he gazed into the face of a young man in a black turtleneck. Here was

Len Pilger, the manager of the new gallery two blocks away, the trendy place that drew no small part of its allure from its location in a grimy industrial part of the city where kids still got hit by bullets in broad daylight. Recalling a bit of what Harry, in a moment of lucidity, had said about that new place, Reed felt kind of reluctant to talk to Len. In his oblique mumbling manner, Harry had suggested that the owners of the new gallery were made men who used it as a shell company in order to launder money from the sale of drugs and guns. Cash went to buy paintings that were ostensibly of cultural import but held no more than a fleeting position in the trendy new gallery. At any moment, the owners would liquidate one of the assets that they'd installed with much pomp days before.

Reed knew that unless he wanted to be rude, downright insulting, he had to talk to Len.

"Reed, man. Why are you wasting your time here?"

"I was actually kind of enjoying myself."

"You call this stuff *art*?"

"It's close enough. Your low opinion of this place isn't exactly a surprise to me, Len."

"But your estimation of it is a total surprise to me. I'd like to know what you see in this maudlin pseudo-déclassé crap."

"I don't know, they've got something here."

"Oh, like, a window into another world, or something?"

"Do you have any specific criticisms? Or is this just a newcomer's feeling for a more established place?"

Len laughed.

"My you speak boldly, Reed. It's like you have no concept of the hierarchies in this world, man. Don't you get it? My gallery is an attraction for all kinds of talent, and places like this, and this one in particular, are a drain on the venues that could actually sustain this neighborhood."

Reed pondered how to respond. His eyes shifted vainly for an escape.

"You're so hip and you don't imagine that you could ever be hidebound. But there's more than an odor of arrogance when you talk, Len. And I say this with respect."

Len looked around the crowded galley, taking in the art on the walls with contemptuous eyes.

"Reed, buddy. You'll come to reject all this crap. You want to see the future of art, come to my gallery the day after tomorrow."

So he did.

Here was a place Reed had never seen or imagined. In this bright new gallery, the perpetrators of abstract and precious bizarrerie had far greater space than in Harry Klauber's loft. As Reed wandered about the big rooms, he paused only briefly to study the contours of the blue suns, the orange worlds, the yellow whirls of cosmic radiance. Here and there, a crude imitation of a ragged Giacometti figure, with only a bit of the ominous portent of the master's work, peered at Reed from the top of a thin plinth. Wherever Reed wandered in this gallery, he found himself looking at the backs of well-dressed guests. He approached a table draped with a stylish blue cloth on which Chardonnay glittered within three dozen thin glasses. With a grin at the blonde behind the table, he took a glass and moved again amid the strangers.

Now he heard a voice, and regretted that not everyone here was a stranger. He had no desire to talk to his acquaintance Keith Dewar, but he turned around.

"Hi, Keith."

"Reed! Hey, man. This gallery's going to knock the others clean of the market. I haven't seen a show like this since we went to SoHo that time."

Reed thought, *You mean since you invited yourself on an outing I took with the one girl I've had a serious interest in within the last three years.*

"Oh, I don't know, Keith."

"What, is this place too pretentious for you?"

"It's all a bit of a jumble. There's a missing element here. Call it thematic integrity."

"I see. I thought you were going to say something about the owner."

"You mean Len?"

"No, Len's just one of the managers."

"Oh, yeah. So who's the owner? An alien who witnessed all this cosmic crap and decided to ruin some perfectly good canvases?"

Keith looked around.

"You might want to keep your voice down, Reed."

Reed thought, *How dare you say that after you said something with the clear intent to provoke me?*

"If you want me to withhold my opinion, Keith, then maybe you shouldn't ask for it so boldly."

Keith grinned.

"Reed Blackburn. A man who says exactly what he means."

"Let's hook up a little later, okay, Keith? I need to go talk to Len for a minute."

"Sure, man. Emily's here and we're going over to Peter's later. You should come."

He really would rather not encounter Len or Len's boss, but at least he got away from Keith. Taking care to avoid the clusters of people, he swerved through an adjoining room, and then made a left turn into a smaller room whose walls held a couple dozen abstract paintings mingled with semi-abstract Escher imitations and a few images of nude women touching themselves.

Before he got anywhere near the back of the room, he saw it. The colossus with the big smooth muscles and perfectly symmetrical features gazed out at him from inside its metal frame. The figure looked as if it yearned to break out of its confines, and was quite strong enough to do so. Reed recalled what Harry Klauber had told him just days before. The old man wanted to put his art on display, at the humble gallery above the disused warehouse, and then take it all back to the town in Moravia where he and his wife could die surrounded by it. There'd be no further sales from Harry's collection, not one. Yet here before Reed now was, arguably, the most prized work of art that the old man owned, or had owned.

Reed looked around. No one was watching him. He thought hard about whether to call the police, but decided the police wouldn't do much in the absence of any kind of evidence of a theft. It would be necessary to involve Harry, and the old man much of the time could barely make himself clear to people he knew, let alone to strangers whose presence would upset him. Reed doubted that Harry's wife could help much here either.

He walked out of the gallery in disgust, ambled to a café a few blocks away, drank four glasses of Schiava, and then, still feeling furious, retraced him steps. Outside Len's gallery, clusters of people stood talking, and Len leaned against a wall, smoking. In the drizzle, the puddles in the lamplight rippled continuously, their little furrows lasting just long enough to catch the viewer's attention.

"Hello again," Reed said in a casual voice.

"Reed. Delighted you could make it out tonight."

"I think I left my cell phone up there, Len."

"No problem. Come with me."

They climbed the stairs and entered the new gallery. Reed wasn't sure what he wanted to do or could do. If Len offered to dial Reed's number, Reed would say he'd left his cell phone on vibrate, so calling wouldn't help locate it. But upon entering the gallery, Len didn't say a word to Reed, he just flicked on the lights and vanished into the restroom. Reed moved through the middle room and into the small room, took the painting off its hook on the rear wall, lifted the back of his windbreaker, pushed the painting down between his belt and his spine, and pulled the windbreaker's flap carefully down. Then he took his cell phone from a pocket of the windbreaker, where it had been the whole evening, and walked back to the front room.

"That was fast, buddy," Len said.

"As soon as we came in, I remembered where I left it."

They went back down to the damp sidewalk. Len seemed to want to hear Reed's thoughts about the evening, but as soon as they were outside, Reed turned and walked back to his apartment through the drizzle.

Sandra was obviously happy to be with her boyfriend, and Reed hoped to parlay this emotion into something rather more significant. She was a beautiful young woman who'd moved out here from Chicago. They sat in the little living room of her flat, drinking wine, talking, listening to the rain. Reed acted as if his taste for the merlot that Sandra kept in her fridge had grown to the point where he was not content with his customary two or three glasses. He was happy to sit here with her for hours, drinking and allowing the tones of his girlfriend's voice to lull him. Its susurrant qualities rivaled those of the rain, or so Reed would have her believe. He didn't think she'd ever find the painting he'd hidden in one of her closets.

Sandra was talking about the instructor in her fiction workshop, a feminist who launched into harsh critiques of the work handed in by young writers. It was now the small hours of the morning, and though the rain had not relented, someone had to acknowledge what they both knew, that it was not the custom for Reed to sleep in Sandra's bed when she had an early shift at work ahead of her. Reed knew that Sandra must be wondering why he hadn't left. He decided to pre-empt her.

"I wonder whether you can imagine us leaning a radically different life from the one we have now."

Sandra set down her glass.

"I'm intrigued with the way that 'we' figures in your sentence."

"I mean it, Sandra. A totally different life."

"Reed. I can't believe you're saying these things to me. You've been avoiding me the last few evenings."

"Of course I haven't been avoiding you. I had some openings to attend."

"The art was so much more thrilling than my company could have been."

"You're being childish! They're not mutually exclusive. I happen to believe in the cathartic powers of really good art. And I really love your company."

"I enjoy yours, Reed. But we're not at the right stage to have a discussion like this."

"I'm not necessarily even talking about the relationship itself."

"Could you try to make a bit of sense?"

Reed paused. The rain drilled seemingly with great purpose on the roof.

"Stop and consider your life. Ask whether you're living in this city because it meets all your needs, or because it's a default place for stylish young people."

Sandra picked up her glass again and sipped her wine, perhaps to have a reason not to talk. Reed prompted her again.

"Maybe you don't need to envision a different life just yet. Maybe we could go away for a while. Try a different life, in order to, you know, broaden our perspectives. We could move to Texas for a few months, and I could get a job, and you could Skype with your nasty instructor if you wanted."

"Oh, how very considerate, Reed."

"I'm trying to be considerate while telling you exactly what I'm thinking."

"I didn't imagine that you'd come over this evening and start an argument and I'd get really upset."

"Okay, I'll just lie."

"Don't lie. Say exactly what you're thinking."

"I encountered a really strange word the other day. Do you know what a golem is?"

"I need to get up early, Reed. I have to ask you to leave."

Reed got soaked on the way to the writers' space to which he paid $200 a month for his membership. He went in as quietly as possible, felt relief that there was hardly anyone here, and stretched out on the couch between two rows of cubicles, looking at the ceiling.

In Reed's dream, the lanes of the village are just wide enough, the mud of just sufficient consistency, to permit the passage of several horses with carts hitched behind them, moving in the direction of the market at the base of the hills with their jagged configurations of trunks and branches and shrub, and clusters of red poppies that have outlived the frost. Notwithstanding their age, the carts bear their cargo of maize and barley with few creaks and groans. A few kids stand in the mud watching the carts though it is a sight as dull and regular as death. The carts move on into the market. The horses break into a half-circle and stop in the mud outside the merchants' and exporters' shops.

The rain is gathering, but rather than obscuring the windows of the village, it lends an entrancing quality to those with lights on behind them. If you are in one of those intimate spaces and a window is your means of taking in the outside, you will witness a fluid tableau, a number of figures who weave and dance and whirl again and move closer to the window, just near enough for you to begin to make out their features, then withdraw to points far off in the damp and cool. They might return, or your sense of them might remain as vague as ever. Anyway, even if you stay inside the house, you cannot fail to notice what is happening now.

The armored column moves into the village preceded by a phalanx of troops whose helmets protect their scalps from the rain. The noise of the half-track is bad, but not so severe as to cover up the oaths and threats coming from the mouths beneath the rims of those gray helmets. Not all of the invaders are profane. Some of them yell praises to their leader, a dictator in a distant city, as they advance. They reach the square, where all of the carts lie still. They bellow orders, make threats, and begin to coerce people into a circumference of a few yards in the middle of the area.

Even at this distance from the brightness of the sun, the barrels of the Schmeisser MP-40s appear imbued with a kind of radiance. The soldiers in gray helmets with cruel sleek curves ostensibly belong to a martial tradition in which one does not use Schmeisser MP-40s and Machinengewehr-42 to menace kids and their mothers. But the gray helmets spread out now in a pincer move, making the crowds draw back though they already press hard against the boundaries of the market. The people of the village know they've wasted far too much time in recent weeks quarreling about how to meet the threat, and about petty personal things.

Inside one of the houses, a frame on a wall contains a figure that until recently occupied a spot in a house way up on one of the hills around the village. The frame shimmers and then the figure bursts forth. The figure that moves now into the square is not a monster or a demon. It does not care what the ignorant or the cowardly call it or whisper about it. Here is a golem. The golem advances to a point in the center of the space framed by the retreating civilians and the gray helmets and guns. It ignores the bullets that slam its torso. A number of the rounds ricochet and find their way right back to those who fired them. Uniformed bodies crumple. Invaders cry out. The golem's fists close around gray helmets and crush their contents. It grabs the troops by the neck, by the waist, and by the ankles, and flings them over the roofs of the village and onto the muddy banks of the hills. The golem advances, with contempt for the puny weapons, trampling on corpses and terrifying the remnants into flight. Blood flows from dozens of sources, currents and rivulets mingle and form morphing masses of viscous red beauty from which in turn new streams issue, flowing every which way over the mud at the base of the frosty hills. The liquid seeps and runs to the base of every doorstep of a shop or station, and grows so dense that the people of the village can rejoice at a new, susurrant flow more pleasing than even the patter of spring rain.

It was absurd to be afraid to go home. Ludicrous, preposterous, outlandish. Len could have no way of knowing that Reed took the painting. The new gallery had been so crowded that night, and people swipe art in far easier circumstances. Reed was still thinking about how to approach Len, about how to frame his awe for the show, for its rich display of new talent, in a manner that would highlight Reed's innocent relationship to the event, his unawareness that a work of art had gone missing. He wondered what Len must think about the matter anyway. It wasn't as if Len or Len's associates had made huge sacrifices for the image of the golem.

Walking amid swirls of ochre leaves on a blustery afternoon in the city, Reed chided himself for his panicked reaction to his own act of rescue. He had the painting and he needed to return it to Klauber, somehow. Surely it was crazy to imagine that Len Pilger, the young guy who wore turtlenecks and said "like" and "man" and "dude," would take any kind of action that might endanger Reed or people he cared about.

Reed stopped at a distribution box for one of the little community papers, pulled out a copy, and found three hundred words about the closing of Klauber's gallery. The item noted that a few of the artists on display there over the years, including one Max G., had a mystical and occult bent.

When he reached his flat on the third floor of a dusty brownstone, Reed realized he'd been neglecting his duty to go down to the apartment directly below his and feed Natalie, the cat belonging to the young tenant, Claire, who was off in Greece. He went downstairs and petted the cat effusively and fed it. Standing there, watching the cat eat, he was acutely aware of the absence of rain. Looking out the window at the bleak day, with its tepidly shifting light and random gusts, he wondered when the susurrance, the beloved rhythms, would resume.

He entered his own apartment just in time to pick up his ringing phone.

"Hello?"

"Reed. Hey, man!"

It was Keith. Only now did Reed remember that he'd made plans for this evening. Though he had no wish to hang out with Keith, he valued the company of Peter Forsyth and

Emily Williams, a couple he knew through Keith. Reed felt that knowing Peter and Emily, having them in his life, bolstered him in Sandra's eyes. He could have them all over, or risk seeing much less of any of them.

"Yeah, seven still works. Pick up some white zinfandel on the way. I'll reimburse you."

"See you soon."

That left him an hour and a half of privacy. He relished the chance to rehearse lines he could use in the company of that bright desirable couple.

At seven, he greeted Peter and Emily at the door. Keith was late with the wine. Sandra arrived a minute before Keith.

Here they were in his apartment, his friends. Peter, Emily, and Keith sat down on the couch while Sandra took the frayed love chair where Peter liked to sit with a book and a glass of wine on evenings when it did not rain. The accumulation of beautifully written passages could have a cathartic effect on Reed.

Of the friends filling the space now, Keith acted the most brash, as if he knew he'd be the last to leave if Reed had to pare down the company.

Reed looked at Sandra. She'd barely moved her gaze from him since easing into the comfy old chair. He raised his right arm, with his glass of zinfandel in hand, paused, then lifted the glass straight upward. She smiled but did not join in the toast.

Peter and Emily were talking about music. Peter had taken her to a really impressive number of concerts in the months they'd been dating, the total was around forty or fifty, and he always tried to engage her in discussions of the relative merits of the bands. But now Keith broke in.

"So I finally caught up with Reed here at the new gallery. I was beginning to think Reed didn't give a fuck about the art market in our borough."

Reed wanted to let this dumb comment pass.

"Well, Keith, my gallery attendance hasn't been bad at all. I just don't happen to share your zest for the new gallery."

"I see. So you've been taking in the rarified air of some other gallery I've never heard of."

"Just possibly, I have."

Keith grinned, looking doltish.

"You don't want to tell us which. Maybe you've got a little souvenir from that place in your possession."

"Maybe I do."

"Thief!" Keith said, and reached for the half-empty bottle.

Emily spoke.

"Reed here is always telling us to go and see art! It makes Peter here furious. 'Are you sure you want to hang out with Reed?'"

Peter looked anxiously at the host.

"Emily—" he began.

"Look, there are tons of lovely galleries. But if you hit them all regularly, you're going to miss lots of concerts," Emily said.

Reed tried to look interested. Sandra still watched him coolly from the chair.

"Really. Tell us what you've seen lately."

Reed's interest clearly flattered Emily.

"Oh, so many wonderful shows. There was Donovan Green at the Odeon, and June Moon at the Holland Club."

As she said these words, Peter looked perturbed.

"Ah, no, Emily. It was June Moon at the Odeon, and Donovan Green at the Cliff's Edge. The Holland Club closed three years ago."

Emily kept up her polite front.

"I'm terribly sorry, Peter. Those shows were really—"

"Unforgettable? That's why your memory is so clear."

"It's the magic of the shows I really recall, Peter. That's the important thing. The art."

"Emily, I will say, you've seemed pretty distracted these last few days. Honestly I'm not sure you value the music more than Reed does. You just want me to think you do!"

The others couldn't believe Peter and Emily were saying these things to each other, in their presence, and their experience contained no precedent. Emily was clearly nervous, her eyes darting around the room as if to convey to Peter that surely they shouldn't be having this talk here, now.

"Well, in truth I have been distracted. I'm awfully sorry."

"It's the lawsuit."

"It is not the lawsuit!"

With egregious timing, Keith broke in.

"What lawsuit?"

"Shut up, Keith!" said Peter, his tone implying Keith was lucky Emily sat between them, although everyone had reason to doubt this, given the undisclosed nature of Emily's legal troubles.

Still Sandra looked at Reed intently. Reed knew he'd better say something. But now his cell phone rang. Without regard for the etiquette that he usually observed ("Should I take this?"), Reed reached into his front pocket, brought his phone to his ear, and retreated to his little bedroom.

In the tight space he heard a familiar voice speak from some point in the city, in the blustery day.

"Hello, Len," Reed said.

"Reed, my friend. Am I catching you at a good moment?"

"Not particularly."

"Love your candor, buddy."

"I'm sorry, Len."

"No, no. I really wanted to ask you what you thought of the show the other night, but you took off before I got the chance, and I was stuck talking to this guy who thought it was so cool that he met Francis Bacon in Paris once. Or he claimed to have. I was a little skeptical."

"You and I do see things much the same way."

"Do we, Reed? Give me your assessment of the show."

"Ah, well. From a technical standpoint, the work was fine, but the work really wasn't what I'm into. It was, I don't know, too precious, too infatuated with its own cleverness, for my taste."

"Reed. What's your favorite color?"

"Excuse me?!?"

"What's your favorite color?"

"Please explain your non sequitur, Len."

"The question suggests certain things, doesn't it? That you're free to experience what you like, to go in any direction you please."

"I don't have a favorite color."

"Do you want to know mine, Reed?"

"Not particularly, Len."

"Well, Reed. I'm sorry you didn't like the show at my gallery, and yet I'm not sorry. I asked you for your honest assessment and you gave it to me. I just want to know, and I'm not asking you to lie, whether anything at the show interested you. Anything at all."

"Nothing, Len."

"There was no item that you wanted to take home and keep forever. Or give to someone else."

"Nothing at all."

"Well, in view of your admirable concern for candor, and transparency, I'm sure you won't object if you get a visit in the next few days. Or the next few minutes. Take care."

Len hung up. Reed walked quickly into the modest living room where the guests were talking about a mishap at the

Oscars ceremony. He had little doubt the talk was a contrivance, a distraction from the lawsuit that had so complicated Emily's life. Of course the others were curious as to how Peter could ever have come to hold such an exalted idea of the influence of his own devotion to concerts. Here, obviously, was a conceited young man, but despite Peter's arrogance, his lack of any sense of others, the guests clearly held out hope that they might all gather on a blanket in a peaceful place where the powerful susurrant waves of a vast luminous ocean assailed the shore.

"Okay, this wasn't the best idea I've ever had. Let's head out to Farrell's Tavern. I'll get the first round," Reed said.

"What?"

"No!"

"Not now, Reed!"

He found a firmer tone.

"You *can't* stay here."

All the guests preceded their host through the door, down the stairs, and out onto the avenue. They walked to the pub with a sullen air, but once they arrived in the bright noisy space, Peter, Emily, and Keith got busy drinking beer and exchanging opinions about one of the teams on the screens above the bar. At last Reed had a chance to face Sandra and talk to her without unwanted attention.

"Sandra. I'm so deeply sorry. I had to do something to bring us all into a different context. I couldn't get out what I wanted to say before, and I don't just mean tonight, but I wish you'd consider the potential for what can develop between us. It will wither if we keep sleeping apart all the time. I'd rather cut my wrists. You are not just the most important person in my life, you are *necessary* to me, Sandra. You came out here from Chicago, from all the storied American centuries, and you are effortlessly charming and intelligent."

Sandra raised her glass of beer, took a draught, set it down, and considered Reed's words. Then at last she smiled.

Reed walked through the streets of a part of the neighborhood where the private equity shops were buying up a lot of the larger properties. The area was losing its so-called authentic blue-collar character, but that in itself was a pretty nauseating cliché. The change didn't really endanger any working-class Poles or Italians as far as Reed knew. He could not help thinking about Sandra and the course of their relationship.

Now as he walked amid powerful gusts of wind he realized he'd never said goodbye to Klauber, it was too late, the old man and his wife had flown back to the Czech Republic, and trying to connect with Harry now, much less explain what had happened to the item from the old man's collection, would be tricky in the extreme. Reed had taken the painting precisely out of concern for Harry. He must resolve the issue. But he had Sandra to think about. He needed to live with her, at least for now, and in obtaining her consent to this he had finally said words that eased them both into a state where the plan almost kind of made sense. He thought of Sandra's ochre hair and her sensitive intelligent eyes and wondered when he'd ever desired her more.

A dull green Saturn moved with peculiar slowness down the street behind Reed. Maybe the driver was trying to pinpoint an address. Or maybe not.

Reed quickened his pace and made a sharp right onto the perpendicular street, and then another right, walking in the opposite direction to the one in which he and the car had been going. Seconds later, the car appeared around the last corner Reed had turned. Reed ran two blocks, turned right, ran three blocks, and stood panting on the sidewalk. Of course Sandra's flat was the one place he must not go. He hurried along several more blocks and climbed the front stoop of his building. As he was fishing out his keys, he felt the impact of raindrops. Feeling almost smug about his wisdom in giving Sandra's place a wide berth, he moved inside, walked up to the second floor, and entered Claire's dark desolate apartment. The cat was hiding. When he lay down on the couch, looking at the ceiling, he felt he could hear nearly any noise in the building, and he was in an ideal spot to appreciate the aural qualities of the rain. He lay there, wondering how many of his ideas and emotions over the last four days were pure paranoia.

Directly above him was his apartment, a space in which nothing moved. It was a serene place where no one struggled to find the right words to say to a friend whose status as a friend was tenuous or to an acquaintance who maybe had the potential to be a friend but kept lapsing into crude conduct. When people are divided, they are hopeless against external threats. They need saviors.

The apartment above him now had a kind of innocence, almost sweetness, about it. If you walked in there and saw all of Reed's books on shelves that he'd found on the street, you might imagine that the occupant was secure within a cultural and intellectual niche.

The rain was gathering. He wanted to savor memories of Sandra. With a glance at the streaming pane twelve feet from where he lay, he wondered what figures might emerge from out of the rain. The idea bloomed that the obstacle to having more harmonious relations with people in his life was simply that he had no idea who they were. He'd been hoping intensely, though maybe not fully consciously, that struggling through awkward situations would lead to a moment of triumph, of catharsis. Now, as the noises lulled him, he took pleasure in imagining that there were not buildings, cities, civilizations, and missile silos out there, just intimate moments encircled by rain.

The ceiling above him seemed vaguely hostile, the way that inanimate things do when you are drunk and you realize your awful giddiness does not extend beyond yourself. The rain grew louder, more insistent.

Reed heard the door downstairs open and close. There were steps in the stairwell, and then somebody passed through the second floor landing not ten feet from Reed's head and mounted the stairs to the third floor. Something rattled in the keyhole of Reed's door, and then the invader walked on the floor of Reed's apartment. He heard the intruder move around, in and out of the little rooms, opening and closing drawers and closet doors. Then the steps moved off to the edge of the building furthest from the stairwell. The visitor wanted to check out the little study where Reed sat writing some evenings. Reed entertained the idea that just maybe it wasn't a hostile intruder, it was one of his friends who'd come by in the hope of really coming to know Reed Blackburn.

The tenant's cat jumped onto his chest, purring. The visitor finally left. The rain went on all night.

Reed sat in his usual chair in Sandra's flat, drinking wine, talking with his girlfriend and their three friends.

"So I looked in the local paper today. Some guy is buying up a loft in the neighborhood in order to open a gallery. It's kind of a strange location for a gallery, in my view," said Keith.

"Who's the buyer?" Reed asked.

"A friend of the former owner, an old man who went home to the Czech Republic just a few days ago."

"Well then maybe we'll have some decent art to look at here in the neighborhood after all," Reed replied.

Keith considered this.

"There was a time when I would have laughed in your face, Reed. But I guess I'm feeling a little more charitable toward certain kinds of art."

"I don't know how you ever could have valued the precious crap in Len Pilger's gallery."

On the other side of the tiny living room, Sandra's eyes said, *Please, Reed.*

"I realize now I was too harsh on old Harry Klauber," Keith said.

Reed began to think that maybe his judgment of Keith had been as obnoxious, in its way, as any of the things he'd mentally accused Keith of doing for so long.

Peter moved around the little space, filling people's glasses with the white zinfandel from one of two bottles he'd brought over. Whatever tensions might exist between him and Emily were not in the open now, at this moment on a brisk late September evening. Keith kept talking.

"Oh, believe me, this shift in my attitude hasn't been painless. Of course there are valid commercial considerations. I've had arguments with Len Pilger about how receptive the market here should be toward different genres and styles of art. He asked me how I could ever defend and justify another gallery that will bring very few buyers to the neighborhood opening up in the same space as old Klauber's."

"So what did you say?" Peter asked, pausing with the wine.

"I told him I'd ask Reed and Sandra when I saw them tonight."

Reed looked out the window to his left. The faded brick building across the street was desolate, with no lights behind its grimy windows. A breeze carried bits of rubbish through the early dusk.

"All of our conversations are so profound. I've always thought that," Peter said with a glance at Emily, who looked quite lovely with her hair in a bun.

Reed said to his friends, "Let's all go out to Farrell's right now."

"What?"

"No!"

"Our dear friend Peter has it totally wrong. Beer, not wine, is the basis for intelligent socialization. I'll get the first round."

Reed stood up, with a look conveying his expectation that everyone else would quickly follow.

A knock came the door of the flat. Reed looked at Sandra. "Expecting anyone?"

She got up, moved to the door, and opened it. Two young men with trim dark hair pushed their way inside, followed by Len Pilger. The two strangers pulled .45 pistols from their coats.

Reed thought of the painting in the closet. Reflecting on the distinct lack of cohesion in a rainy village in a distant part of the world years ago, he thought that the moment to try to resist was not now, not just now.

The others in the flat were afraid to speak. On seeing the guns, both Keith and Emily threw up.

Now a silver-haired man in a dark suit and overcoat followed the three intruders into the flat and stood looking at the young friends expectantly.

Len addressed Reed.

"Where is it?"

Reed moved into the tiny guest bedroom, reached into the closet, and came back holding the image of the golem. Sandra looked at Reed as if he'd murdered her parents. Len took the image and studied it.

"You assumed that this was an idea of marginal value and we'd barely notice its loss."

The young clean-cut thugs with guns made gestures. They moved the five friends out of the flat and into a van on the street right outside the building. The van rumbled through the dimming streets until it reached the steel door of a big warehouse with walls of dark brown stone. The door slid upward into its frame, allowing the van to roll into the warehouse.

Len, the silver-haired man, and the two young thugs forced the others out. On the far side of the space was a dull green Saturn that Reed recognized. As the men with guns pushed the five friends into the center of the desolate space, Len appeared to guess what Reed was thinking.

"Yes, Reed. You know exactly where you are. Why should I keep anything from someone who's about to die? You're right below the loft that old Klauber's gallery used to occupy."

Reed nodded. Len went on.

"You didn't seriously think that the old codger and his wife left because they felt homesick? They *loved* this neighborhood! But we convinced the landlord that the rent here wasn't nearly market."

Reed looked at his friends. Keith and Emily even now had puke on their faces and clothes. Peter looked too terrified to speak. Sandra seemed cool, but Reed wondered what she might be wishing on him at this moment.

Looking at the image in Len's hands, Reed thought that even now, there was still a bit of cohesion among his friends. Hence this wasn't the moment. Len stepped forward.

"Maybe we can have a bit of fun here. Surely you don't all deserve to die. So help us be a little selective."

Now Peter managed to speak.

"Don't listen! There's no way he'll let any of us live to talk! He's—"

One of the two young clean-cut thugs calmly extended his arm and fired his .45. Peter grabbed his abdomen and collapsed with a cry on the dirty floor.

"Come on. Some of you deserve it more than others. Convince me and I'll let one or two of you live," Len said.

Emily pointed at Peter.

"You should have aimed for his forehead. This man is like a partner on a cross-country road trip who says it's got to be his tunes or you can get out and walk. No Peter in my life, no money, no VIP entry to exclusive events around the city," Emily said.

"Bullshit!" Peter cried, spittle mingling with blood on the ground.

"Don't listen to that bitch!" Keith said.

Everyone turned to Keith. He continued.

"Emily here had people fooled with her manners and her smile. But I found out about the lawsuit that keeps her in need of Peter's money!"

Sandra gasped. Emily looked at Keith with horror and incredulity. Peter wheezed and spat blood.

"Oh, she's got people fooled. This nice girl here bankrupted her family with legal costs after she put a pencil through another girl's eye. A girl in Emily's senior high school class who wouldn't repeat the party line about Emily Williams!"

Emily took a step toward Keith, then stopped as one of the guns shifted toward her. Peter spoke up.

"You know what? Kill Keith. He's not just a little annoying. He's a social parasite! A groupie who defines himself through his knowledge of other lives!"

These words didn't appear to faze Keith a bit. Len and the others turned to Sandra expectantly. She looked at Reed.

"Oh for fuck's sake, kill my boyfriend! It's one thing if he wanted to die for art's sake. He's made us all into satellites of his own vanity. I could kill him myself!" Sandra screamed.

Reed spoke up.

"This game is bullshit. I'll be candid. None of us deserve to live."

With these words, he knew that the moment of supreme division and utter vulnerability had arrived.

Something happened inside the frame in Len's hands that made him shriek and drop it on the ground. Len looked up at Reed in shock, as if, even now, Len had the right to expect Reed not to mislead him and his associates.

The golem climbed out of the frame and stood on the cold concrete, seven feet of awesome gray muscle and sinew. It appraised the scene with its glinting black orbs, not flinching when the two young thugs raised their guns. They fired desperately, furiously, filling the space with the odor of gunpowder. Len cried out as the crotch of his khaki trousers grew damp.

The golem seized Len by the neck and flung him at the two thugs. The older mobster took his pistol out of his overcoat and trained it on the captives. The golem moved in front of them just in time to block the bullets, which bounced wailing and shrieking in haphazard paths off the golem's torso. Having emptied his weapon, the old mobster ran across the floor and got into the green Saturn. Meanwhile, the two young thugs picked themselves up and began changing the clips in their guns. The golem strode up to them and rammed their heads together so hard their skulls split and bright bursts of red relieved the monotony of the dank backdrop.

The Saturn shot across the room and slammed right into the golem. But the golem did not budge. The car whirled across the room. Reed grabbed Sandra and pulled her out of the spinning vehicle's path. As soon as it stopped, he gestured for all his friends to move behind it, and he joined them there, crouching and panting. The driver was dead.

Now four men with TEC-9 pistols ran into the wide space from an adjoining office. The roar of automatic fire filled the space, overwhelming every other sound. The golem strode up to the men and began grabbing and pulling limbs. Blood spurted dozens of feet, drenching the ceiling and the far corners of the warehouse, forming streams that quickly passed under the wrecked car and stained the knees and hands of the huddling party. Cries and wails rose, then ended abruptly. Reed peeked over the hood of the car just in time to see the golem move up to Len, who was staggering toward the office door, grab him by each arm, and pull him apart. The golem flung Len's head across the warehouse. It landed and partly sank in an ocean of blood.

Now the golem slid back into the frame of the painting, ready to take up its old position in the loft upstairs.

Reed looked at the others. For Reed and his companions, the feeling of release, of catharsis, was so strong it made talk an impertinence.

For now.

The Flock

To the north there was a huge plain under a white sky. To the south lay the approaches to a cliff high above a shore covered with sharp rocks and rough sand. On the eastern and western flanks lay uneven, barren terrain. The surest way out of here should have been to take a northerly route, and that was what a number of the men crouching by me behind the big rock were ready to do. I told them they couldn't just up and run. I was working out a plan and they'd better wait. How I'd warned these men, over the past few hours, but a few of them were past the point of listening. The catalyst for the trouble was an intense youth named Miles who'd always been quick to question or belittle me despite my knowledge of the land and my feel for how much time it took to go from one point to another.

"Look, we *can't* stay here. They're going to come swarming over those fields. Let's go, let's move out now while we have a chance," Miles said.

A couple of the other men, Pitcairn and Morehouse, were listening attentively. They did not make eye contact with me, as most of the others did, when I contradicted Miles. But in my role as officer of a consular mission of the world's greatest empire, I had to try.

"Listen, guys. I do know how ravenous you all are. It's been, what, forty-eight hours now."

"Correct, sir!" Miles said, his face pasty and damp.

"Which brings me to my point. It's unthinkable that you could spend so much time only to do something dumb and make the whole investment of time pointless. Now, I know that this rock isn't the loveliest thing in the world. But you need to stay here a bit longer. Let's think. To act now is totally premature."

"That's what you told us yesterday," said Miles.

"Yeah, that's exactly how you phrased it. Don't act prematurely, just wait a bit longer, soon they'll send in the copters," said Pitcairn.

Two of the other men, Carter and Jewell, looked at me as if their willingness to listen to me depended on what I said now. But I saw that I wasn't going to win.

"I've said what I had to say, Miles."

"All right, then. Don't try to hold me up any longer, Colby."

We crouched there, panting. The sky was pale, and the air had a quality of mocking dampness. We were aware of the contrast between our sweat and a moisture that was nice, fragrant. The grass all around was damp enough to make you slip if you got even a bit careless, and the clusters of rocks were so far apart it was as if people had deliberately resettled them.

I reconsidered my decision. I thought I had to try at least once more.

"In about five hours, it will be dark."

Miles spoke up.

"It's the summer solstice. The dark hardly lasts at all. Anyway, I'll bet they don't play around at night like they're doing now. We'll probably walk right into their interlocking fields of fire. I think we really have one course here."

I wanted to protest, but I honestly couldn't say that movement was any safer in the dark. To resolve the dilemma, I'd have to look into a part of myself where I knew cowardly impulses flickered. I said nothing. All around us there was total quiet, and this added to the sacred quality of the rolling green.

Miles, Morehouse, and Pitcairn got up, leapt over the rock, and ran in zigzagging fashion toward the plains off to the northeast. Confident that their actions provided enough of a distraction, I peeked over the jagged top of the rock. They got about thirty yards before we all heard it. The blast resonated across all the plains, rocks, and grass with clarity, like an unanswerable judgment of a man's life and character. The man in this case was Morehouse. His scalp shot fifty feet into the sky, brain and blood filled the air around his head in a shroud, and he pitched forward and slid nearly ten yards on the wet grass. The next shot made Pitcairn spin and whirl crazily before he fell into a heap twenty feet from the first corpse. That left Miles, the instigator, who ran faster and with ever wider swerves until he slipped and landed on his belly. He picked himself up clumsily and got a few more feet before the third shot. I watched the young man's right temple burst open as the long bullet that had entered on the other side made its exit. He cried out briefly, fell, and then all was still and quiet again in the mild wet afternoon.

Though it was just the result I'd predicted, no one seemed to grant me any more respect than before. The men fell to discussing and arguing over their options. Jewell said he had an idea. The cliffs were sheer, there was no way to climb down, but we could make a really long rope out of our clothes. A few men liked the idea but Carter said it was a poor one. The ships were out in force and they'd spot us as soon as or even before we began to shimmy down the cliff's face.

I tried to think about the logistics from the enemy's point of view. They had expert marksmen and high-powered rifles that could blow heads open from literally a mile away. My sense was that they were subjecting us to all of this in a spirit of fun. If they sent out overwhelming numbers, killing us would just be too easy.

The men were pretty hard to look at now. Their fear and anxiety were not the kind you can assuage through pep talks and appeals to man up. As I studied their sickly, sweaty faces, I tried to make out any hint of further conspiracy. I was beginning to develop an idea for a plan that just might save us, but it depended on the others not doing anything crazy, at least not at this point.

The faces of the men were distinct in so many ways, but they all betrayed terror, desperation. I gazed at them. Carter. Jewell. Thorburn. Prager. Stevens. Wilson. Kowalski. Burgess. Campion. It had been so long now since we had come here, unarmed, wishing to avoid even the hint of a provocation as we tried to establish relations with citizens who'd not yet declared their fealty to either of the powers vying for control of the region. We'd had an idealistic faith in the potential of diplomatic and cultural missions. We just needed a bit of time. Little did we grasp that two of the mightiest forces in the world were moving toward war. We'd occupied our discrete little part of the universe with no idea of how vulnerable we were.

"Listen, now. If you try to flee, your brains will be all over this beautiful green earth. You must pay attention to me and do exactly as I command if you want to see your families again."

A few of the men nodded. Jewell gazed at me with, I sensed, a hard emotion somewhere between anger and spite. It was as if, in making them acknowledge the reality of the situation, I had brought it upon them.

The air around us was clear though the sky was still a pure dull white. I, and maybe not a few of the men, could not help thinking that perhaps not two miles from here, a family lay on a big blanket on a knoll, and the bare-chested father got up, extended his limbs, and took in the acres of lush damp grass, exulting in his status as a member of the hyper-connected *parvenu* class that could humble its counterparts in other nations through its quality of life and ability to spend. On a semi-conscious level, that father I imagined might have thought that his view was limitless, that he could take in all the oceans, canyons, hills, knolls, ravines, and mountains of the world, that here was his domain, that he had a guarantee to it all thanks to the junta that had seized power in this country. There was so much wealth here, there were so many resources inviting the bold to tap into them, and in a land such as this one, little foibles, such as a lack of experience in or familiarity with the global markets, faded into irrelevance as the *parvenu* classes surged.

Here we were. Once again I took in the sad, desperate looks of the men huddled with me behind this rock. Jewell, the rugged Edinburgh bloke, looked angry and vengeful. The tall and gangly Thorburn appeared not to know he was drooling as his head lay against the folds and curves of the rock. I wondered who among them might try to kill me if I did not relent in my role as enforcer of a reality. The talks that needed to happen now weren't ones I wanted to engage in, and not just for the obvious reasons. There was something pure and holy about the whiteness of the sky that made me want to drop everything and kneel in prayer.

"All right, Jewell. Let's see that radio again."

His look was as insolent as ever. He didn't want to obey me, but all the others were looking at him expectantly. For form's sake, if for no other reason, he set out the little device on a patch of grass behind the rock and played with a few of the dials and switches. We sat in a circle, listening intently. We heard static. I made several appeals.

"Hello, anyone listening?"

More static came. The men were still, their faces looked as weary and hopeless as ever.

At least a voice broke through the static.

"Come in, consular party . . . Come in, consular party."

"Colby here."

"You're awfully persistent, Colby. This is Field Marshal Douglas."

"Hello, sir. We will have to talk about the wisdom of this little expedition. In the meantime there is a more immediate issue. Do you have any sense of our coordinates?"

"Only the vaguest, I'm afraid. You are somewhere on the coast of the lower peninsula, if I'm not mistaken."

"That's right, sir. We can't go south. It's a sheer drop. And we can't go north either. They've got the whole space covered."

Static. A long pause.

"You're all strong capable men. Be decisive. Take action. Uphold the Five Principles of the government and crown..."

Static hid the officer's voice. We all looked at each other, anxiously, nervously, but with a sense of having something critically important in common. The voice came and went as the static wavered.

". . . to explain that in the current international order, there are certain conventions and protocols when it comes to the treatment of diplomatic corps, whether or not the other party recognizes you as such. . . "

"Sir!" I called out, but the voice went right on.

"The international community has recognized and ratified a protocol for the treatment of such personnel. They have an obligation to respect certain rights and liberties for as long as you are within their borders."

A few of the men appeared to be listening with interest. I looked at Jewell. He wasn't looking at me. No matter what seditious thoughts might be growing in his head, he appeared to be listening to our senior officer as intently as the others.

I stood up, though I knew my scalp was just visible over the top of the rock.

"Jewell, turn that off right now."

He went on looking at the radio.

"Jewell, I just gave you an order."

He went on ignoring me. But now once again, a bit of the old dynamic began to reassert itself. All the others were watching him. He could no longer act as if he was out here, in a Hobbesian state, with no one of a higher rank overseeing him. Warily, with infinite reluctance, his small black eyes rotated upward in my direction.

"Jewell."

"All right, sir."

He reached for a switch on the radio. The last thing we heard was from it was a curt pronouncement.

"But don't ever lose sight of the values for which you are fighting—"

They were all aghast.

"Why'd you give that order, sir?" asked Carter, in a tone conveying the good faith of an honest dissenter.

I steadied myself, expecting a bullet to come whistling over the top of the rock any moment now.

"Don't speak out of turn, Carter."

He grimaced, looked at his knees.

"All of you men know, or you ought to know, when you're not hearing a live person address you. It should be obvious when you're hearing a recording. That's how they handle these touchy situations when they can't commit for or against a course of action. You heard the field marshal speak for about three seconds there, and then he switched on the recording."

There were nods, sullen looks. I guessed that they knew what I said was true and there was little point in listening to a kind of generic encouragement. They saw the truth now. Or so I thought.

Stevens, the Manchester lad, had always seemed like the obedient type. When someone has such a common name, it's easy to assume the individual in question has an ordinary, prosaic, manageable character. He had so rarely complained about anything. In truth he'd spoken little to me in the entire time he'd been with me.

Now he stood up and pointed his finger.

"Listen, blokes. This man here, Colby, gave our coordinates to the enemy! He comes across as so professional, but I've noticed the way he looks at all of you when he's walking behind you. That's not what he should be doing. You do know that? Colby's the leader. He should be walking out in front of you, the first to speak for us, the first to give his life if it comes to that."

A few of the men stirred. Carter and Thorburn made little gestures as if to urge him to shut up. This appeared to have the opposite effect. Stevens cried out even louder, moving his limbs all over desperately, as if trying to shake off ants.

"This man, Colby, is not fit to be an officer! I've noticed the movements of his hips. It's a reflection of moral weakness. This man is Judas and you are the poor deluded flock!"

The bullet sheared off a neat column of his scalp, loosing blood that got onto a few of the men. Stevens let out a startled, anguished cry as he flipped backward onto the grass. I couldn't help admiring the enemy's talent. Someone way over on the far side of that rock had detected a bit of brown hair moving behind the rock and had aligned the barrel of the rifle with such skill you might have thought he and his victim had rehearsed together for weeks.

When everyone had calmed down, I ordered Carter and Thorburn to grab the body by either hand and drag it to a point a few dozen yards to the southwest. They carried out their task with grim resolve, turning and looking back to be sure that the rock hid their progress. Finally they released the body on a patch of damp grass, turned, and moved back to the space just behind the rock. We huddled there, wanting to look strong, to affect indifference or contempt to the forces out there in the white day. The shot that felled Stevens, like the earlier ones, had such a terrifying finality to it that I thought we could have stayed huddled here for days, no matter how hungry we got.

In the early hours of the morning, we were still there, shivering with our hands joined just above our feet. I turned my gaze to the south, toward the cliffs I could not see. Perhaps in my mind the scene down there had an obligation to fulfill a preconceived romantic idea, it had to take on the properties of a Turner painting, but the motionless dark prevailed for now. I dozed off with my head lolling against the white and silver swells, crags, and crevices of the rock. When I woke up, the earth was still dark but the outlines of hills and rocks were more distinct. I wondered about the identity of the man who'd killed four members of our party in the last few hours. Of course I ought not to have assumed that one man fired all four rounds, but that was the way my poet's sense had it.

I imagined finding the courage not just to stand up, but to run out into the white afternoon without pausing to justify my decision to anyone. The country was so pretty, so inviting, it seemed criminal that only people on one side of something so arbitrary and artificial as a military and political divide could get to enjoy it. That was not the way of the trees I could see, far off, it was not the way of the gently curving green plains on either side. Now I imagined running, as lithely as I could, minimizing my contact with the wet grass, darting out into the pale afternoon, looking up at intervals, looking in the only direction from which I welcomed any decision, any judgment. Maybe it would rain, and the turf would grow still more slippery, but I would welcome the independent character of this place where nature did what it must do. *Sky, rain, trees, grass.* I'd breathe deeply of their aromas as I streaked through this lush remote part of the world.

These thoughts came to me before night had fully yielded. But soon enough I was once again crouching in pale light behind the big rock, with all the men looking at me expectantly, in need of a way forward. At least that was what most of them wanted.

Wilson stood up. He fixed me with his cold gray eyes. At least he did not point, the way Stevens had. But, looking into the eyes of this slender handsome young man, I knew that certain processes had run their course in his head and he thought he saw things about me that he'd ignored up to now. Well, I felt I must let him talk.

"Have you got something to say, Wilson?"

"Oh, yes. Listen up, everyone. I've got a little announcement to make to our party," he said, laying ironic weight on *announcement.*

"Let's hear it."

"The only appropriate course is surrender. That's the only way to save our lives."

There came cries, gasps.

"No. They'll cut us down if we try to approach them," said Thorburn.

"No one has recognized you," one of the other men, it might have been Jewell, said to Thorburn.

"You all better recognize me," Wilson said, seemingly indifferent to whether a bullet might come over the rock, though he was supposedly speaking now out of a concern for all our lives.

The men looked at him.

"Look at the position that Colby here has put us in! Here's an officer who can't be honest about anything. You're deeply deluded about why you're here in the first place. This is not, and has never had any convincing pretense to being, a diplomatic mission."

There were more gasps and cries. He went on.

"Look around you, look at each other. Have you ever tried to get an idea of one another's diplomatic credentials?"

The men looked around, viewing each other with a scrutiny to which I knew they felt entirely unaccustomed. How they'd laughed and joked in the hours when we set out.

"Do you wonder why there are no women or old people in this mission? A bit odd, I'd say. It's not a consular mission by any means. No, guys. It's a military mission. Colby here was bringing us to a village where we'd terrify the populace into giving up their space so we could use it as a base, or maybe we'd provoke them into doing something that would give us a pretext to nuke this little country."

The cries were shriller now, and I wondered how much time I had before they'd jump me and throttle me to death.

But I was wrong to believe that about the men, as wrong as I wanted them to believe Wilson was about me.

"Never surrender!" said Jewell.

"They'll cut us down if we so much as show our faces out there. Wilson's trying to get us all killed!" Prager added.

"Bless the Crown! Remember the Five Principles!" Carter said.

Before I even registered what was happening, another of the men, it might have been Kowalski, had gotten behind Wilson. He held the upstart by both elbows. Then Carter picked up the radio in both hands, stepped forward, and slammed it on Wilson's forehead. He repeated the act five times. Wilson kicked and cried out as blood sprayed.

"Kill him!" someone yelled.

Ignoring Wilson's kicks to his shins and knees, Carter brought the radio down again, harder than ever, loosing flecks of skull and chunks of red mulch. Kowalski let go and Wilson fell to the ground. Carter dropped the bloodied radio. At least it had been useful for something.

I had to address the matter of our survival. I'd had it with dreamy, self-indulgent states where I'd envisioned running out onto the plains in a state of total freedom, or at least total indifference to what might happen.

"If you men want to see your families again, then listen carefully."

They appeared to listen intently, though I detected a certain ease in their manner, now that there was no more question of disloyalty.

"They aren't going to let us leave, and they sure won't allow us to surrender. Now it's really tempting just to wait here, behind this rock. But if we stay here, we die. They longer we wait here, the hungrier and weaker we get. There's no point in waiting for dark because they've got laser sights. We *have* to move. Soon there'll be no question of dodging bullets or getting out of range of their rifles."

I almost said *We shouldn't have waited this long,* but that would highlight my earlier errors in judgment.

"Not all of us are going to get home."

The men nodded somberly.

We broke up into four pairs. At my signal, each pair would take off in one of four directions. The sharpshooter would shoot at one member of one of the pairs. Whether he hit or missed, the other member would get a warning and could step up his evasive moves. I found it unlikely that the sharpshooter would let the other member go before starting all over again and trying to get a bead on one of the other pairs. Three of the four pairs would have a decent bit of time to run. The best case scenario, as I saw it, was a bad deal for at least one member of one of the pairs, while the other pairs had a chance of getting to a tree or boulder if we moved really fast.

"Now, remember. This is our only chance. Our beloved field marshal has absolutely no intention of risking more lives to try to get us out of here."

Prager spoke up.

"From his point of view, it probably would be much simpler if the enemy had just killed us all."

"I don't understand why they haven't come and done it. They've got more time-efficient methods," said Thorburn.

"You can't deny people their fun," I replied.

"I thought these people had, you know, proud military traditions. They're picking us off from a distance, like cowards," Prager said.

"Don't talk about it in the present tense, like it's going on now. They did kill some of us. But we're going to get away."

Again the men nodded solemnly. I ordered them into pairs. Carter and Jewell. Thorburn and Kowalski. Burgess and Campion. Those last two looked almost absurdly young for members of an official mission. Finally, Prager and myself. We got into position at the edges of the rock. Without ceremony, without pausing to say anything profound, I gave the sign. We moved around the edges of the rock and dashed out into the expanse of wet grass. All around was a miraculous quiet. I heard only the squish-squish of my feet on the grass, and Prager's footfalls a number of yards behind me. Something in his exhalations conveyed an astonished relief. My timing had been so impeccable, or we were so lucky, that we'd run out onto the fields at just the moment when the sharpshooter was off taking a piss. We charged, weaved, and scampered over the grass.

The blast had a terrifying clarity. It was just like the earlier ones, except that the delay before we heard it suggested an even more exact calibration of time and distance. I heard a man cry out. From such a distance, I couldn't be sure, but I thought it sounded like Carter. Then there came a second blast, and another yell, not from the same throat. Two men were down, but six others had time to get away from the rock and closer to new shelter. I wheezed and panted, looking at a cluster of trees far ahead on the plain. For all my warnings about the need to zigzag, I could really think of little more than the imperative of speed. The trees appeared to be mocking me. It was as if they pulled away with every footfall. This impression made me still more desperate, I ran even more frantically, and soon I found myself growing winded. I thought of diving and hugging the grass in order to catch my breath. That might have been sacrificing my life for a moment's comfort. I head another blast, another cry. At this point, I thought I knew exactly what was happening. The enemy was lying in the back of pickup or on the slope of a hill, honing his aim in a leisurely way. He fired a fourth time, and I heard Thorburn shriek. I ran even harder. It was almost intellectually interesting to guess who was next.

Still the trees seemed to be pulling away from me, to mock my frantic efforts in the face of mortality. The sky was as gray and dreary as on the day of a graduation, a birthday, a wedding, or any of the other occasions in our brief sad lives.

I ran with renewed determination, thinking those mocking trees must not be the last thing I saw. I heard another blast. To my amazement, I still ran, completely unhurt. Even more incredible was that I could still hear Prager running behind me. The enemy must have missed both of us. Such was the cunning of my plan that what had seemed an unerring, Olympian force had plainly failed. Prager and I were alive, and maybe those boys, Burgess and Campion, were too. The trees were closer now. I ran and ran. Then I heard two more blasts, and Prager cried out both times. I no longer heard him behind me. I reached the trees and hid myself behind one of the thicker trunks, facing the cliffs way off to the south. I stood there, breathing heavily, then more evenly, for maybe an hour.

If no one back there was alive, then I had nothing to apologize for if I fled up the coast without a look back. Maybe, if I got far enough, I could make contact with a vessel from a nonaligned nation. I imagined lying on the deck of a ship in the sun, having beers and singing songs with a crew. But clearly in the intoxication of my one modest success, I was assuming far too much. The gaggle of trees around me gave temporary shelter. According to the logic I'd set forth before we left the rock, I could not stay here, and there was vast empty space all around. If the enemy was riding in a pickup, then once I tried to move again, I might be an ever easier target than before.

I thought of walking on the very edge of the cliff and hiding on its face at signs of trouble. But that was silly. The drop was sheer, there was nothing to hold onto. The only way was up the coast on a slightly inland route. I'd gotten my rest.

I set out on the route I'd been going before I got to the trees. I ran, but I paced myself, hoping the enemy was in a state of at least temporary confusion as to where I was. Indeed he seemed to be. I dashed across the field, listening for that familiar report, but it never came. The enemy really was oblivious, or he was crueler than I'd guessed and was giving me a crumb of false hope. I ran on under the gradually brightening sky. The grass felt just a bit tougher and less slippery.

Far off to the north, I thought I made out the outlines of a house. I ran faster, zigzagging to convince myself that I was skillful and wise after all when it came to survival. I dropped, lay prone, caught my breath, and resumed running again. It felt warmer now. The sky was definitely brighter. But something about the air, the light, felt deeply odd.

I paused and turned around.

Prager was running after me on two bloody stumps.

Cursing myself for pausing, I ran faster than ever. Then I heard it, a loud clear blast, it seemed the enemy's way of saying *Yes, I've been here all the while, and I've been having a good bit of fun.* I didn't turn again to look back at Prager's body.

The shooter must have seen that house up ahead. He must have known I was going to be there in a couple of minutes. Maybe he meant to consummate his pleasure by letting me get right to the door before he pulled the trigger. Running hard, zigzagging again, I closed the distance. If I quit running and weaving, if I just walked the rest of the way, were my chances any different? The thought was too disturbing to entertain. I was an envoy of the noblest class of a great nation. I was bold, decisive, courageous.

I ran over the grass until I was on top of a knoll, looking across thirty yards of grass at another knoll right before the house. A wooden flight of stairs ran from a bare little porch to a patch of dirt and grass on the house's southern flank. I could be there in twelve seconds, if nothing interceded. I looked up at the brightening sky, turned to the west, and took in the rises and falls of the land, a line of trees far off on the other side of the killer's position, and the vast white peaks of the mountains in the far distance. Maybe there was no truck. Maybe the expert marksman was lying somewhere, in the flowers, enjoying his pastoral experience in the steadily improving day even as he relished killing us off one by one. There was no tactical reason for this to have gone on so long or for me to be alive right now. He must have been a pure sadist. Or maybe he was off taking a piss.

I charged down the side of the knoll, ran across a stretch of moderately damp grass, and raced up the side of the little hill abutting the house. Within seconds I was up on the porch. I placed my hand on the knob of a white wooden door. I entered the house. Here was a bare wooden hall with a couple of openings on my right. I walked down the hall a few steps and turned into the first room.

The man and woman were in their early sixties. They both sprawled on antique chairs, and they shared a refined but absent expression. The woman was looking at a bookcase across from her, to my left as I entered the room. The man was watching a shadow or a spot of dust on the ceiling, or maybe nothing at all. I stood there in the expectation that they'd cry out and maybe one or both of them would come at me, but my presence seemed not to register at all. In my bewilderment, I took note of a few more features of the room. The home of these aging people wasn't really such a humble place after all. The carpet was of rich scarlet and black fur, and an antique lamp on a table, a few feet from the man's head, could provide light to read one of the musty volumes from the bookcase. But

I wondered how long it had been since the man or his wife had been equal even to a task such as that one. They appeared to breathe in the quiet and motionlessness around them as if it nurtured and comforted them, made them feel they belonged right here doing what they were doing.

Hearing noises from elsewhere in the house, I turned. Before I could leave the room, a young man with long dark hair came in, clutching a large pistol. A muscular physique lay behind his white tank top and black trousers. He leered as if seeing me had confirmed a suspicion. He'd had an idea, upon growing aware of a stranger's presence in the house, of what he might find. Now here I was, a once-proud officer who had run and hid in desperation.

"You can't stay here," the young man said in a thick accent.

I felt total astonishment that he said such banal words, rather than shooting me right here. The only explanation that came to mind was that his two elderly parents were proud of their nonalignment in the gathering conflict, they depended on it, and there were reasons why their son couldn't deviate from this model. Tranquility must prevail in this house.

"I guess your folks would be pretty upset if you shot me."

"They're decent people. I can't shoot you just for being in this room. But if you refuse to leave, I think they will understand."

"If I go out there, I'll die. You do know that."

He sneered.

"You already passed the threshold when you came to this country on some false pretext. There was never any question of you getting out. What happens now is just a sorting of details."

He spoke my language rather well, even if his accent had encroached over his English over many months of infrequent use.

At least this young man did not have the right to con-
travene his parents' nonaligned stance in the international
conflict. That was the only reason the sorting of details, the
working out of the circumstances of my death, must take just
a bit longer.

"All right, then. Please don't point that at my face."

I walked back into the hall, but I didn't retrace my steps
all the way. I walked to a door on the other side of the house,
the north side. Through the window, I saw a larger porch and
steps leading down to yet another field. The sky had brightened, but there was still that old passive dullness all around.
The window was too narrow for me to gain an inkling of what
lay off in the distances to the west. Maybe the question was
academic, maybe a bullet would fell me before I even got off
the porch. I really was beginning to believe the young man's
terse words about my time in this bleak white land.

I threw open the door, ran out, dashed off the porch, and
took off. I listened for a blast. All I heard was my panting and
the squishes of my feet on the grass. Notwithstanding the brief
respite, my body was exhausted. Running felt utterly pointless
in light of the change in my philosophical perceptions.

But I ran and ran. I did not once look to the west. It was
as if the shooter and I had a kind of parley at the moment.
About a mile ahead, I could see the outlines of another house.

Right then a blast came out of the stillness and silence.
So familiar was the noise that I knew immediately what to
do. I dropped onto my belly, feeling a parting of the air right
above my neck as I fell. Then I got up and resumed running
in the wildest fashion. Three more rounds went past me. He
was getting tired now, or he was really far away. I ran until I
reached the little house, whose rear door rested snugly in its
frame over a patch of mud. This door was locked. I punched

a glass panel above the handle, reached in, unlocked the door, and went inside. Even now, the populace appeared to believe that consular missions were more likely than hostile military ones. Even now, security at houses in the region was minimal to nonexistent.

Here was a modest house with a similar design to the one I'd barged in on earlier, though everything was humble, pared down, in comparison. Moving up the hall from the back door, I passed a kitchen and dining room filling most of the rear half of the house. Taking up the better part of the front half was a faintly lit chamber with red velvet chairs, an oak desk with a swivel chair, and a bookshelf spanning the entire east wall. In one of the chairs, a man sat calmly. He was thin, and of modest height, with hair the color of a sheet that no one has changed in a few months. Standing in the doorway, I wondered what he'd been doing in the moments before I broke in, and I decided that in all likelihood he'd just been sitting there brooding.

Then my eyes roamed over the room again, and I noticed all the things I'd missed the first time. On a narrow table beside the desk, a radio rested. It had all manner of dials and knobs and a cord leading to a transmitter hanging from a clasp on the radio's side. Above the desk, an array of framed certificates and medals decorated the wall. Beside the desk, an old rifle with a long sleek black barrel leaned against the wall. The house of this important personage looked inconspicuous from the outside. Maybe he didn't really matter.

No. That impression was crazy. My mind was such a jumble that I couldn't make logical deductions, simple associations. The radio had a purpose. People listened to what this man had to say. It hadn't been hard to break in, but that was as the man wished. He wasn't afraid of anyone. I felt utterly intrigued. I moved the empty chair to a spot directly in front of his chair, and I sat down facing him.

"You're wondering how it could be so easy to break in here, if I'm somebody important," he said.

"Honestly, I was a little curious about that."

"Impudent foreigner, I could kill you with a look."

"I see."

"Do you doubt it, young man?"

"Yes. I mean, no. I'm sure you're speaking figuratively."

"Now there's a distinction without a difference. For you, anyway."

"I believe you."

"Do you want to live, young man? Do you think you deserve to live?"

"Well, now. I've been running desperately and dodging bullets for many miles. I'd like to think that after all the terror and death, there's some reward waiting for me."

Now he looked downright cross.

"The planet's most obnoxious imperial power decides it's entitled to land down here on the other side of the world. So here you come. Here you come, the head of a so-called consular mission whose real purpose is not cultural at all."

I nodded.

"You're right. I can't make the effort to lie just now. You are so completely right! I brought all these men here to conduct reconnaissance, although I kept our purpose mostly a secret even from them. I was going to reveal it, and then we all began dying."

He laughed.

"You really think that you deserve to live!"

He took on an air now. He was like a professor relishing the sight of an undergrad squirming, groping to explain why he should squeak by. Plumbing my memory, my patchy knowledge of history, I thought of the name Alcibiades.

"What can I say, stranger? I wonder what I can tell you that might stir some reflections. But let me try."

He listened with a wry look.

"If this experience is to have any sort of conventional narrative arc, if it is to be the least bit dramatically satisfying, if it is a story that I hope someday to relate to others, then it is obvious what must happen now. Oh, it's clear what I must do. I've got to take that gun, go out there into the fields west of here, have a dramatic showdown with the sharpshooter, and blow his brains all over the grass. My story can't exist as a story unless I do that.

"But I do not choose that course, I will not choose it. If I were an Athenian general at the height of the most brutal conflict in the world to date, I'd burn with the need to go out there and prove my devotion to the *polis*, the city, the state, the country to which I belong. But, you see, I have proved it. I led all those men. I inspired them. Maybe most of them are dead, but they died believing in my resolve and my ability to formulate a plan and give them, if not a guarantee of freedom, at least a chance to try for it.

"Did all of them perish? I don't know. I'm holding out hope that one or two made it out, in spite of the shooter's ability to blow heads apart from a mile away. The fact is that *I inspired them*, rather in the way that you yourself have influenced people to do and act in a given way. I won't lie! I won't deny that for much of this ordeal my spirit has cried out for a way to strike at that anonymous, invisible bastard who has killed so many men before my eyes. But I posit that that isn't the only kind of fulfillment that's available to us. That isn't the only way to meet our obligations to the *polis*, and our higher duties."

The man listened, as nonchalant as ever, yet with a flicker of interest in his amber eyes. I continued.

"I accept that I won't have a chance to get even. I accept it. My story will provide no conventional payoff. I'm really okay with that. I ask you not to be blind to who I am and what I've accomplished. Maybe we're on opposite sides of a geopolitical divide, old man. But, damn it, this is such a fleeting and arbitrary divide that I can't believe it would keep you from recognizing traits that you see in yourself! If I'm a member of a *polis*, and I carry out my duty in the face of such danger, and I achieve a modest victory, not the kind the masses yearn for but a victory nonetheless, I've proven something, I've demonstrated traits that have a place in the celestial order. I know you can see the truth of what I'm laying on you here."

The man nodded slowly, but then he looked at me as if I were taking up time he could be spending with a book from the huge shelf. In his look there was infinite condescension, but also, I thought, something close to pity.

I got up and exited the house through the front door, going north. I can't know what he did with all the dials and knobs or the transmitter.

All around me the day was as dull as ever. There was not even a hint of grandeur. I grew winded and felt a distinct pain in my right foot, where the sole of my shoe was in ruins. I wondered how much more dead space was out there to receive me. Keeping my eyes on the barren fields up ahead, to the north, slightly inland from the coast, I summoned every last bit of power in my numbing limbs, I panted, I cursed, I pushed myself, I ran.

My Art or Yours?

So what kind of place is New York today, and what's the right attitude toward strangers? The place has changed under the last few mayors—hasn't it? I think I can offer insight here, but we'll have to back up for a minute.

People keep asking me to clarify the role I played in the downfall of the great Nicholas Behrens, so I'll take this opportunity. I do feel sorry for the man. When one falls from the top of the art world, it's a long way down indeed.

I met Behrens one evening at an opening at his gallery in Chelsea. The buzz in the art magazines and the chatter in cafés had led me to expect a nasty experience when I met this celebrity in person. Reporters threw around words like "discerning," "patrician," and "aloof," and habitués of the art world affirmed that Behrens was a pretentious cad. I believed them. I doubted that a trust-funder, who owned a Chelsea gallery and a West Village café, and flitted back and forth between Manhattan and his parents' home outside Nijmegen in Holland, could be other than a toff who prattled about art in a voice that made you want to forswear art forever.

The rumors weren't just gossip. Nicholas Behrens proved to be quite an odd and difficult person as my acquaintance with him developed. But the art he liked wasn't bad at all. On this night in September, the gallery on West Twentieth Street was full of abstract expressionist canvases by an up-and-comer who'd attended Cooper Union and Bennington and now lived in Greenpoint. The bursts, splotches, and cascades of yellow and red on the canvases might make you think of the Earth in collision with a star, a ghastly yet bracing moment when there can be no limit to energy or ambition. I was hoping to milk the opening for a story and sell what I wrote to one of the art journals. But upon arriving, I just milled around, drinking pinot grigio, until a twenty-something woman in a light blouse with a floral design smiled at me. She introduced herself as Claire. She said she was taking art history classes at the New School, and knew tonight's artist personally.

Then, quite abruptly, Sally Forbes, an editor for one of the glossies, pulled me away from Claire and brought me to a point in the middle of the gallery where none other than Nicholas Behrens stood amid a cluster of men and women clad in black. I felt no small anxiety. The circle parted to give me a full view of Behrens, a fortyish man with a thick dark beard and the hint of a paunch, wearing a black blazer over a black cotton shirt, blue jeans, and loafers. As Behrens made eye contact with me, his look was confident rather than arrogant, with a flicker of wit in his deep brown eyes.

"Nicholas, this is Alan Worth. He writes for the art publications. You may have seen his byline here and there. I'm sure he'd be grateful for an introduction to the artist, David Peterson," Sally Forbes said.

Behrens nodded.

"It's a pleasure to meet you, Alan. We'll try to track down David a little later. Five of us should be sufficient to corner him, and if that doesn't work I'll tackle him for you," Behrens said, to chuckles.

"I can't fault your taste, sir. I admire what I've seen of this guy's work," I said.

"How's the freelancing going?"

"Could be better."

"How?"

Just as I began to answer, Behrens spoke again.

"I should never put you in the position of having to answer a question when the answer's built into it. Your income's directly related to the number of shows like this."

Just now I noticed the ring on his left hand. I recalled hearing about a troubled marriage. If his wife was milling around here tonight, it had escaped my notice. I was curious about his partner, about the tastes, skills, refinements that complemented the eccentric nature of this man. But Behrens was still a stranger and I didn't trust him.

"Will I get to meet your wife tonight?"

People all around us were quiet, embarrassed at this breach of etiquette. Then Behrens gave an indulgent, faintly sad smile.

"I think Janice is around here somewhere. She did handle the logistical side of the show. But she and I have an etiquette about introducing acquaintances. We like to be able to vet people in advance rather than have them foisted on us without warning."

"Thanks anyway."

Now Claire, the young lady I'd flirted with, beckoned me over to an area of the gallery I'd overlooked. In a corner to your right as you came in, there was a kind of annex to the show, with maybe twelve paintings. The canvases were on wooden easels that looked too déclassé for this gallery to have provided. I was instantly curious about the work here. Maybe the cluster of admirers had found relief from the preciousness, the pretentiousness, of so much of the art filling this chamber. I planted myself beside Claire, who looked mesmerized by one canvas. Here was a rendering, in bright watercolors, of a hut fashioned of long, rough but symmetrical logs, with a dark thatch roof, on a hill overlooking a beach the color of diluted clay. The beach was a setting where you might expect to find throngs of nearly nude people having fun, but it was barren. As for the hut, it had an intimidating somberness about it. You had to wonder about the punishments meted out there. The title of this painting, appearing on a card on a rung of the easel, was *The Overseer's Hut*.

Beside it stood a work of equally striking contrasts. On this wide canvas, one found a large number of well-fed people in Club Med attire, lounging at tables or leaning against the rail of the deck of an elegant restaurant, drinks in hand. Behind and to the left of the deck, a score of islanders walked in single file, their necks joined by chains. They didn't look at the revelers, nor the latter at them. The title of this work was *Guests*. The artist was Marcus Eden, an Afro-Caribbean artist living in Brooklyn.

Just as I turned to a third canvas, depicting the aftermath of a native's rape, something altogether unexpected happened. A blonde, conventionally pretty, dressed in a taffeta blouse, pants the color of a Yukon tundra, and shiny black shoes embellished with stardust, approached our cluster. I was looking at Janice Behrens, socialite, art aficionado, and *de facto* ambassador for artists craving recognition.

"Janice! Alan Worth. You may've seen my byline in the alt weeklies," I said, extending a hand.

"Alan. I've been meaning to reach out to you ever since I read your piece on the Cornell retrospective."

"Why, thank you."

"In fact, there are three other pieces of yours that I really like," she added.

Too many good things had happened to me in a night for a terrible event not to occur now. Behrens spotted his wife from across the floor and dashed over to the makeshift annex. The man looked so astounded and flabbergasted I was briefly afraid for my and Claire's safety. He looked pale, almost pasty, and you would've needed hooks to keep his lips together. He'd quite obviously had no idea that his wife, whom he'd trusted to organize the show, had allowed Marcus Eden's work onto the floor. He moved up to Janice and half-coaxed, half-tugged her away from the annex to a spot near the back wall. This served little purpose, for not a word was lost on us. His position was that his wife of three years was "a scheming, ungrateful bitch." To hear her tell it, Nicholas Behrens was increasingly the butt of jokes, and the cause of dwindling sales, thanks to his rectitude, his anachronistic habits of thought, his unwillingness even to consider certain types of artists. The argument devolved into a screaming match before two embarrassed young men in dark outfits ushered the two of them toward a back room.

I planned to visit the gallery again before long. In the meantime, I got an incredible surprise. I was home in my apartment drinking Zinfandel, way too tired to go out, when I glanced outside and noticed the rain had let up. I climbed out onto the fire escape, sat down, lit a cigarette, looked out on the cozy domestic scenes visible through rear windows of six buildings on the other side of the block. In one of the apartments over there, I could see a female couple, standing in their kitchen and talking. In another apartment, a muscular young man in a tank top sat with his girlfriend on a couch watching a movie, his arm around her. The lights were off and I saw them in the flickering emanations from the screen. In their respective ways, people were enjoying the evening as much as I was. It was so comfortable out here, even with drops spattering my hair and face. I got through two cigarettes before the phone beside my bed rang. With delight I thought it must be Claire. I went back inside, grabbed the phone, returned to the fire escape.

"Hello?"

"Alan? It's Janice Behrens."

"Oh! Hi there, Janice."

"Alan, I wanted to say I'm quite sorry for the scene the other evening. I know you were pretty psyched about coming to the gallery and that wasn't at all what you expected."

She was certainly right about that.

"Well, ah, thanks, Janice. Look, I hope you're not worried that this is going to turn into negative publicity or anything," I said, neglecting to add that I could hardly imagine why else she'd call a virtual stranger.

Janice clarified the matter.

"I really couldn't give a damn about publicity, good or bad—the distinction stops mattering after awhile—it's just that I don't want you to feel put off and decide you shouldn't pursue covering the gallery," she said.

"I do appreciate that."

"Obviously, I'm not in agreement with my husband about the direction of the gallery. We're going through a really rough time in our marriage. He's been so unhappy for so long that I'm a bit worried."

"I'm quite sorry, Janice. I'm sure it'll get better. You know what they say you should do. You can, you know, make lists of what you value about each other and read them out loud, or something."

"Oh, we've tried things like that. But we keep fighting, and it always comes down to this question. *My art or yours?* It's a bigger issue than you realize, Alan. Because, you see, what's behind my husband's aesthetic elitism is *social* snobbery. He quite literally doesn't want to let people wander into his gallery off the street. If they haven't got the 'formal training'—if they haven't gone to the most exclusive schools and bought into the system—then they're unworthy."

I fumbled. I began to formulate sentences and tried to go back and re-formulate them and gave up. The rain dampened my hair.

Finally, I said: "Maybe we don't read the same publications. Nicholas Behrens is known for showing some fairly edgy stuff."

"Oh, he likes to think so, but his edginess has its limits, Alan. The darkness in the work you'll see in that gallery is so generalized it's just an empty pose. Now, take someone like Marcus Eden, who's really seen awful things in his life. You saw how my husband reacted to that artist. Never mind most performance art."

"Well, that was because he wasn't expecting to see Eden's work there—"

"You don't need to make a half-hearted defense of my husband to me, Alan. I do know him a bit better than you."

"Point taken."

"We've been having the same argument for a while. This week it's about Marcus Eden. A couple of weeks ago it was about Sam Grohl."

"Who?"

"A figure painter. He does a lot of nudes. I think he's immensely gifted, but of course my husband won't be in the same room with him or his art," said Janice.

"Any reason why?"

"Sam Grohl has a conviction for statutory rape. He was also accused of pedophilia, a number of years ago, but there wasn't enough evidence to indict him."

"Well, you know, talent's what matters," I said, but I don't know how much conviction my voice carried.

"Anyway, I just wanted to call and say that on one level my husband is a very enterprising man and being married to him is an adventure, but on another level, he's an egotistical bastard who looks down on too many people. Sweet dreams, Alan."

I climbed back inside, wiped droplets off the phone, finished the wine, and went to bed.

I met Nicholas and Janice Behrens, along with Sally Forbes, at the café in the West Village. It was nearly empty at a few minutes past 7:00 p.m., but things were likely to pick up as shows let out at the indie cinema a block and a half away. Sally sat across a table from the couple, sipping a latté and talking energetically. My eyes wandered over the bare wooden tables, the open doorway in the middle of the east wall, and beyond it the staircase leading up to the owner's apartment. Then I walked boldly to their table.

"Alan! Nice you could join us," said Nicholas, rising and extending a hand.

"Alan here's a wonderful conversationalist," Janice said to Sally.

We went outside, walked up Houston Street to the corner of Sixth Avenue, and began going south. Our pace was leisurely. It was one of those evenings that make permanent New Yorkers out of people. The air was so fresh and moist you wanted to breathe it in for hours, to ingest purity and innocence into your soul. The sound of water, the relic of two days of rain, coursing through drainpipes was ineffably soothing. I felt so much goodwill toward the people I was with that I wished Manhattan extended south along the eastern face of the continent so we could keep walking and walking in this air.

But after a few minutes we came to the door of an apartment building. Sally was mysterious about who our host might be.

As we progressed into the building, I felt trepidation at the sight of the staircase, with its metal banister painted a dull institutional green, wending its way up through floors populated with artists and writers of unknown provenance. At first I didn't notice the lift directly beside the stairs. As soon as Sally pressed a button, the doors slid apart, revealing a compartment so narrow I was afraid to step inside. The lift took us up to the fifth floor and we moved out into a dark room with a staircase leading to a rectangle of open space through which we could see stars amid the dissipating clouds.

"Do you want to lead the way, Alan?" Sally said.

I didn't, but I led the others up the stairs and we all stepped out onto the roof. Up here, about thirty guests milled around clutching Coronas or mixed drinks. Many of them wore multicolored short-sleeved shirts, defying the cool, and khaki trousers or jeans. Complementing the beach club style, Bob Marley's voice came from speakers at either end of the roof, singing about emancipation. I have mentioned the stars. The air had cleared up without losing its seductive softness, its delicious quality. The densest cluster of guests was in front of a replica of a wooden hut with a thatch roof. A rotund man with thinning black hair leaned on the sill of a swing door, doling out spiked punch and pomegranate juice. When I saw that purple liquid swirling in a glass in a guest's hand, I thought that nothing in the world, neither a kiss nor an orgasm nor a view of the Dordogne countryside as a plane deploys its landing gear, could come close to ingesting that liquid.

The four of us began to move in a cluster toward the hut. When we'd gotten halfway there, we all started at a voice, leisured but with a latent power.

"Welcome, friends! Delighted to see you!"

Marcus Eden had stepped out from behind the hut and had begun to approach us. I nearly fell down. Was Behrens going to turn around and bolt? Would I be responsible for leading the party into a trap?

To my immense surprise, the big man's reaction was civil, to the point of banality.

"Hello, sir. Nice party you've got going."

"The people of this island nation welcome you, brother Behrens!" the host said with a grin and a theatrical sweep of his arm, taking in not only the roof, and the happy guests, but all the island on which we'd staked our fortunes, on which hopeful and desperate souls flitted and fluttered in cafés, offices, galleries, studios, spas, and homes.

Then I had a further surprise.

"Alan! Hi!"

Claire, the pretty young woman I'd flirted with at the opening, walked up to me and placed a glass of that pomegranate juice, spiked and fairly glowing, in my hand. As she did so, she leaned forward to plant a kiss on my lips.

"Enjoy your drink, brother Worth," said Marcus, who, I later found out, was familiar with my journalism and had also heard about me from Claire.

Soon we all had drinks in hand. We raised them in a toast. The juice was the perfect complement to the beautiful cool air. Here was the distilled essence of kindness, mercy, humanity.

Nicholas said, "My sincerest thanks for your hospitality, brother Eden."

On Saturday, I had a late lunch with Claire, followed by drinks, at a restaurant on Hudson Street. She entertained and enthralled me with talk about all her odd and funny siblings in

Middle America. Her smile charmed me more than anything. Outside on the pavement, we kissed theatrically for a couple of minutes before she turned south toward Tribeca and I made my way toward West Houston in a mild breeze. I walked for another twenty seconds before I had to stop, just to breathe the delicious air, just to *be*, on this street at this moment, a contented mind in a healthy body on the streets of a vibrant, surging city. I sneezed. Twelve feet ahead on the sidewalk, a bit to my left, a woman in her late twenties, about 5' 6", with curly brown hair down to her shoulders, turned around and said "Bless you!" with a generous, infinitely charming smile. I began to mumble thanks but the words foundered at my realization of just how attractive this stranger was, in a blouse with green and scarlet floral designs on a black background, and in a pair of beige trousers that hugged her slender form. She had faintly olive skin, and coyly arching brows above intelligent eyes. Her moment of communion with me inspired hours of wondering about who she was and where she headed on this cool fresh day.

I found a wine bar and hung out there until it got dark. Then I walked to the café on Houston Street, moved through it, mounted the stairway to the building's second floor, and pressed a buzzer. The face that appeared before me was pleasant but haggard, creased with irritation.

"Excuse me," Behrens said as soon as we were both in the apartment, and disappeared into a restroom where I soon heard water slapping flesh.

He came out again, flicking drops off his beard, and guided me across the polished boards until we stood beside a circular Ikea table, sturdy, adequate, a few notches below elegant. On the table I noticed a printed page beside a Dell computer and a printer in a gray plastic frame. Across from the table sat a plain gray-white couch.

"I've got a bit of a crisis here, Alan. I was sort of hoping you could help me out," he said.

"Of course."

"I'm sorry you have to see me like this. Janice and I had another quarrel. She's really been wanting to try the Superior Hotel—do you know it? She said that everyone who lives in the new New York has to stay there. You know, it's classy, it's chic, it's what the contemporary city is all about, all that non-sense. And I was up for it, until I started reading about all the wild stuff going on there. Exhibitionism, voyeurism, drugs. I don't have time for that. And when this buyer, who's coming over in a few minutes, first suggested meeting tonight, I told Janice to cancel the reservation. I said, there's no way in heaven or hell I'm going to miss this meeting, so cancel. Do I need to go further, Alan?"

"Not really."

"I haven't seen her since she stormed out of here, and she won't answer her cell."

"So now I'm going to help you deal with your marital problems."

"*Please*, Alan. It's humiliating to have to ask. Please help me out this once."

I stood there for a moment, longing to return to the sights and smells of the afternoon that had passed, to Claire's company, her smile, the warmth of a stranger, the sensation of expensive wine entering my mouth. But I felt pity for this man who was so utterly unable to see his wife's point of view.

"If I help you, will you host a Sam Grohl show? Your wife says he's one of the best figure painters around."

"My God! Don't even mention Sam Grohl within these walls. I'm willing to listen to your *general* ideas about my ex-hibits but right now I desperately need you to help me!"

"All right, then."

I picked up the sheet from the table, turned, walked out of the apartment and over to the West Side. Minutes later, I strode across the hotel's pavilion and moved briskly through the lobby, too fast for the clerks who looked like Nordic male and female twins to call out. Soon I stepped off an elevator on the fourth floor.

Referring to the printed sheet, I quickly found room 412. The door was ajar.

"Janice?"

My voice faded and died in a quiet hall. I called out again, and a third time.

Then I heard it. The faintest of sounds. A titter from inside 412.

"Janice, it's Alan Worth. Mind if I come in?"

No reply came. I thought, *Oh, fuck it.* I pushed the door and moved into the room. As soon as I did so, I felt a prick of embarrassment at the thought I'd entered the wrong room. The windows were huge and bare. Beyond them, the lights of the West Village, Tribeca, and the Financial District shone and winked. My eyes took in the computer and modem just before the middle window, the sleek curves of the modish chairs, night table, and tall metal lamp, before alighting on the bed.

Janice had not tied her white bathrobe. She was lying there precariously with her right buttock and leg dangling over the edge. Anyone could have walked through the door. She gazed at me with a grin. I went into the bathroom and used it. Before I left, I noticed that the shower wasn't dripping, in fact there was no water anywhere beyond the sink. This fact stood out in the context of Janice lying there in a bathrobe she hadn't bothered to tie, in a hotel known for certain games on the part of its guests.

I moved to the window nearest the bed, wondering what was out there, in the mist, and what minds, what intelligences, took an interest in the woman in this chic chamber. I turned around.

"Janice. Please tell me that you haven't been flashing people on the street."

She giggled.

"Oh, Alan. I've never had much use for this taboo that people shouldn't see you naked."

I realized she'd probably done a fair bit more than flash. Would the wife of Nicholas Behrens, hotshot gallery owner, be on the front page of the *Post* tomorrow?

"Janice, uh . . . who was looking?"

She giggled again.

"The Boy Scouts. It's an awful long way from Utah!"

"Janice, please be serious."

"I don't know, Alan. Would *you* like a look?"

The robe fell to the floor as she rose.

I slid around the bed, darted out of the room, returned to the ground floor, passed through the revolving doors out into the misty dark. The chairs and tables of the pavilion were empty. Revelers had retreated to the indoor bar as the mist spread. But it was surprisingly mild outside. I crossed the empty pavilion and walked down to the sidewalk running parallel with the south side of the hotel. Down here, you had to navigate the pillars of the Highline. Wending my way among the squat rectangles, I marveled at the night's mildness. I looked up at the windows of her room, half-expecting to see her there, but caught only a penumbra of light from the tall lamp. As soon as I turned around, I spotted a thirty-year-old man in a suit, leaning against a pillar in the driveway of the warehouse across the street. He'd been completely alone down here until my arrival. As I approached him, tentatively, I saw that his suit fit him perfectly and his brown leather shoes had the elegance of a high-end designer.

"Good evening, sir. What a perfect spot to be alone, huh?"

When he spoke, his voice was dry, even, and reassuring.

"Oh, it's awfully pleasant. It helps me, you know. I'm here for my nerves, really, you see."

"Come again?"

"My job gets a little hectic sometimes. I need a place just to relax and breathe at my own pace, someplace where no one recognizes me."

"I understand totally."

"What about you? Just out for a walk?"

I thought at a furious pace.

"My neighbor, this pensioner who lives in the condo down there—" I said with a gesture toward one of the buildings down on the far side of the warehouse.

"Yes?"

"She, uh, said she was upset by something going on in one of the rooms up there," I continued with a gesture at the Superior.

He nodded.

"So, to help calm her down, I said I'd go take a look. So, uh, what about you? Have you seen anything?"

"Quite honestly, it never occurred to me to take a look up there. I wouldn't ever peer into the private space of strangers."

"Well, that's good to hear. If only everyone I met were so polite."

"Yes, good night and get home safely," he replied in a voice so polite I couldn't help thinking of an older New York where everyone took civility for granted.

I made my way back to room 214, where the door to the bathroom was closed and I could hear the shower running. I sat down and watched CNN until Janice emerged from the bathroom in a towel. I did passable job of watching the screen as she dressed. Then she proposed that we go out together for dessert.

Two nights later, I walked through the damp streets to the galley in Chelsea. Maybe it was naïve of me to expect to show up unannounced and gain an audience with the great man right away. Still I felt the slithering grip of annoyance as I lingered there in the middle of the place for nearly half an hour while Behrens talked with the buyer, Hervé Galleon. Behrens was expounding on the virtues of a painter whose work had come to the gallery through a referral and who specialized in landscape paintings. The setting was Ontario or someplace. The landscapes were mostly fields and valleys in winter, over which the sun loomed as if in an effort to rouse the earth from its white inertia. The grass, the boulders, and the creeks stood out distinctly without calling attention to themselves or detracting from the paintings' unity of effect. In this regard the art may have been superior to that of Marcus Eden, whose broad-brush approach sacrificed topographical detail.

Finally the buyer got busy with the calculator on his Smartphone, and I snagged the great man's attention.

"Nicholas! I still haven't briefed you on the other night. I thought you'd be kind of eager since Janice is, you know, your wife."

"She told me she was sleeping when you arrived and then you went out for dessert. Am I missing anything?"

"Janice clearly isn't getting enough attention or respect from you, sir. Janice has a point of view! You've ignored her interests for so long, I'm surprised she didn't pack up for Seattle years ago."

Behrens chuckled.

"I think the Bowery's more to her liking."

"Nicholas, *she has a point of view*. And damn it, the artists she likes, and the social strata they come from, really are important to someone who isn't totally shut up in a world of elite buyers and exclusive shows."

I was nearly breathless when I finished. He fixed me with those alert, yet distant, eyes, and for a moment his lips did not trouble the fringes of his thick dark beard.

"Alan, this quarrel with Janice is a 'tedious argument of insidious intent,' as Eliot put it. It has consumed energies that could have gone toward establishing this gallery as one of the most coveted venues in the city."

"So that's what it's about? You don't have time to debate aesthetic principles while you're trying to gain a commercial edge over other galleries?"

The great man was imperturbable.

"No. That's not wholly or even primarily what our quarrel is about."

"Well then what is it about?"

"Excuse me," Behrens said before turning back to Hervé Galleon, who had finished his calculations and was ready to buy some paintings.

Halloween came. A few minutes past eight p.m., Claire and I walked up to Houston Street and turned west, toward Behrens's café. We'd enjoyed each other's company all evening. Upon entering the café, we found the place quite busy, thanks to the egress of patrons from the cinema nearby. There were interesting films on the bill there, including one about a notorious artist whose name had been synonymous with subversion back in the eighties. But some of these people almost certainly had been at the parade, or had tried to see it before cops drove them off.

We found a table by the wall closest to the river. Across the room, the tables were full on either side of the open doorway giving access to the stairs leading up to two floors of apartments. The tables on both sides of the entrance were also the domains of customers in fervent discussion. I whispered to Claire that this wasn't the salad-and-spring water crowd you'd find at midday. As we talked about Claire's family, her father and brother in Ohio and another brother in Virginia, I couldn't help overhearing bits of the exchanges around us. To my astonishment, I heard a name I'd heard before, Sam Grohl, not once but twice. There was also talk of art schools, shows, catalogs. Clearly we had a number of artists in our midst.

Some of the talk was pointed indeed. At one of the tables at the front of the place, a woman with stringy dark hair spoke the clear measured English of someone who has learned it as a second tongue. She was talking about an experience at her place of work. I gathered that she was what they call an "exotic" dancer, and now that topless, let alone nude, dancing was illegal in New York, she had to go to extraordinary lengths to keep tips coming. Earlier this evening, as she walked the platform at her club, she'd spotted a young guy at a table, drinking beer. She'd called to him, gotten his attention, bent forward, and pulled a flap of her nylon outfit away from the cleft of her buttocks, giving the stranger a nice view of her most private parts. Then, when she turned around and asked for a tip, the guy just sat there staring as if he hadn't heard.

"I'll kill him," the dancer told the young Hispanic man seated across from her. "I'm serious. If I see him outside, he's dead!"

Wow. I hadn't heard such bloodlust in a while. I don't know whether Claire overheard any of that talk, but I'm fairly sure she caught a bit of the exchange two tables down on my left. Here, a twenty-one-year-old woman with dirty blond hair, in the most literal sense of dirty, sat across from a muscular guy the same age with a purple Mohawk. Her t-shirt and wind-breaker were as filthy and ripped as the guy's tank top. She was saying that in the two weeks since she'd stepped off the bus from L.A., she hadn't been able to take a shower. The guy, who mentioned he was from Lansing, Michigan, told her what had happened to him earlier this very day.

"I was punched. It was a yuppie. A fat fuck."

Although Occupy Wall Street was not going on, there were still clusters of "protestors" down there in the Financial District, giving the moneyed classes trouble whenever possible.

"I wonder what that yuppie would look like with his guts tied around his neck!" the guy with the mohawk added.

I didn't catch what either of them said immediately after that, but their discussion moved on to a party the dirty blonde had been to since her arrival. By her account, there were three bags of smack and four bags of dust there. I'd had no idea of angel dust's lasting popularity. I began to imagine the people one might have met at this party she was describing.

At yet another table, between ours and the counter, the talk was no more Christian in spirit. A well-spoken young man with clipped dark hair, in a blue dress shirt, was telling his friend, who resembled a twenty-something Allen Ginsberg, about his wish to kill his boss, who'd repeatedly come down on him in front of others.

"You probably should kill the fucker. I'm amazed in doesn't happen more often!" said the young Ginsberg.

"I just might. I also happen to know where his kid goes to school," said the guy in the blue dress shirt.

Although Claire must have picked up bits and pieces of the talk, she was still chatting away about her father's second marriage in Ohio. I listened calmly, enjoying the sound of her voice.

But other voices surged all around. At one of the tables across the room, to your left as you came in, a sandy-haired kid in a black denim jacket was telling a youngster in jeans and a yellow shirt hanging loosely around his trim waist about how tonight's parade reminded him of an experience at the parade on Puerto Rican Day a few months before. On that earlier occasion, he hadn't even planned on taking part in the parade at all, he'd just been trying to make it to work when he got lost amid hordes and hordes of bodies. Then something awful happened. He grew dizzy and nauseous, his breathing began to get funny, he became terrified about his heart. He felt hot and sick and could barely stand up. People of all races in the crowds pointed and jeered at him. He wanted to cry. At last he spotted a gap between a couple of barriers right below 59th Street and moved desperately toward it. Just as he got there, a grotesquely overweight cop on the other side moved up to the barriers and announced it was time to close up the gap. When the dizzy, nauseas young guy made a plea, and asked how else he could possibly get out of there, the cop said, "I don't know! Not my fucking problem!"

The café patron hearing this anecdote, who reminded me of a Berkeley grad student, said, "Man, don't even get me started on cops. Of course they want control, but it's about a lot more than that. You know, I saw one of those 'Cop Shot' bumper stickers the other day, offering a ten thousand dollar reward. For a moment I wasn't sure whether the reward is for reporting a cop getting shot or doing it yourself. I was behind on my rent. . . . "

Claire wasn't listening to any of this. She'd ceased talking about her father, and was now telling me about the brother in

Virginia. At yet another table, opposite us, between the open interior doorway and the counter, an obese man in his forties, in a dress shirt and trousers, was holding forth to a younger guy, also in semi-formal wear, about a woman he said was disloyal in her personal relationships. At her office, this same woman could be quite aggressive, but she also played the victim and relied on male colleagues to deal with any man who openly disagreed with her. If I understood this slob in the café correctly, the woman he was talking about could be a feminist or a weak woman as the occasion demanded. He went on in this vein for a while before the younger guy at the table responded with his idea of a joke.

"Why do women have two holes so close together?"

"Why?"

"So that when you're done with them, you can pick them up and carry them like a bowling ball!"

The older man laughed long and hard.

I'd had quite enough. Coming to the café tonight was a mistake. I asked Claire to excuse me so I could get up to use the little restroom between the interior doorway and the counter. When I made my way back a few minutes later, I noticed that the room looked slightly different. What was it, exactly? I resumed listening to Claire. After a few minutes, I saw the fat forty-something man get up from his table and disappear through the interior doorway. Right after that, I caught in my peripheral vision someone's passage down the stairs and across the bare space leading to the primary entrance and exit for building's tenants.

I realized what was different was the absence of two or three of the patrons I'd overheard.

I tried to keep focused on Claire, who was talking about her brother's work for a defense contractor, but she saw the extent of my distraction as four more patrons got up and moved through the inner doorway and up the stairs at intervals of a few minutes. As before, there was traffic both ways on those stairs.

"Well, Alan. I'm thrilled that nothing I have to say is remotely as interesting as the other customers in here," said Claire.

"Claire, I'm very sorry. Will you excuse me?"

I got up, slid past her, and followed the people I'd been watching. I dashed up the stairs, pushed open the door of Nicholas Behrens's apartment, and charged inside.

Janice was prone on the gray-white couch, naked, duct tape around her mouth, her wrists and ankles bound by cuffs. The figure standing above her was none other than the guy with the mohawk, in a ripped red tank top. The guy who yearned to strangle yuppies with their intestines. He was trailing the tip of his penis across Janice's bare nipples as she writhed and sobbed. I noted that someone had put out several cigarettes on her face and neck, and somebody had stabbed her forehead and slit both of her cheeks with the bloodied knife a few inches away on the floor. The glistening liquids covering most of her bare skin were spit and cum. I spotted blood between her thighs and guessed one or more of the patrons had already penetrated her.

I groped for words. I wanted to sound really scary to this punk. But Nicholas Behrens moved up through the space between the couch and the table. Just as he did so, I noticed the camcorder on the table.

"Alan! You're here to enjoy some performance art!"

"Uh . . . Nicholas?"

"Oh, you know, Janice and I have had a long-running argument. It comes down to this question: *My art or yours?*

She's called me stuck-up innumerable times! She's said I'm not trusting of people and it's all because of my insufferable snobbery. And she ridiculed me to no end for not liking performance art. Eventually, Alan, I had to begin to wonder whether she'd stand by her ideals. Does she really value radical art? So I told my patrons that for one hour on Halloween, they could come up here and do whatever they please to Janice! Both of us would welcome it! So tell me, how's this for unfettered expression, Alan?" he said with a gesture at his wife, whose terror was so severe the room was now full of the reek of urine.

"*You unbelievable sick fuck!*"

I punched the guy with the mohawk just as he was reaching climax. He staggered backward with a cry and fell on the table, which tilted over far enough for the Dell computer to topple onto the floor. Shards from the Dell's screen nicked my skin. I kicked the guy really hard in the head until I was sure he wouldn't be getting up anytime soon. Then I dashed down to the café, whipped out my cell, and spoke breathlessly to the 911 operator.

After the cops came, I walked through the West Village with Claire in the cool delicious air.

285

The Unraveling

Kara wanted to quit going to the café where Michael was always holding forth about one topic or another. Most of Michael's interests were literary, so his monologues were about who had just published or was about to publish a novel or about the influence of long-dead Europeans on the scene today. The latter topic in particular was one that Kara loathed. Michael idolized Franz Kafka. Why, Kara had it from no less an authority than *Atlantic Monthly* that Kafka was overrated and had an influence way out of proportion to his gifts. She didn't want to hear about Kafka or Dostoyevsky or Dinesen or Krleža or Horvath anymore. It was a new age. Time for others to make their mark.

Kara loathed nothing more than hearing about the pending publication of Michael's debut novel, *The Harlot's Dream*. It was enough that Michael was a year younger and he'd gotten so much further than Kara. Surely Michael knew that once the novel came out, there'd be many opportunities to promote himself, and there was no cause for him to make Kara and others feel even worse than they were already prone to feeling.

One afternoon, Kara raised the point with Michael. She told him how weary she, and others in the café, had grown of hearing him say things that came off as self-congratulatory and, by implication, denigrated those who hadn't come close to Michael's level of recognition. Michael told her that he knew she was struggling and it was normal for her to resent him. Kara resisted the urge to hit him.

One afternoon, a few days after that time in the café, Kara felt really depressed and lonely. She'd been going to the same handful of venues in her free hours. But Kara had heard about a gallery, a thirty-minute walk from her flat, that featured edgy provocative work. The streets were wet, and the air was blustery, but the experience awaiting her promised to be new and bracing.

When Kara arrived at the gallery, she found the art reasonably competent, nothing more. An artist had rendered suns, black holes, supernovas, and galaxies. Kara wandered through the aisles taking in the art for a few minutes before she saw the man in the gray raincoat at the juncture of a couple of aisles. She quickly recognized him. Here was Daniel Clivner, a literary critic, not a celebrity like the *New Yorker*'s James Wood but a moderately successful reviewer. Never having met Clivner, Kara recognized him because one of the papers he wrote for included his pixellated likeness above his byline. Kara had read a number of his reviews and had enjoyed them without exception. For one thing, she thought that Clivner had a gift for seeing books and ideas for what they were without having to situate them within one or another tradition. Sometimes things just existed spontaneously in the world. And he never sounded pompous like Michael.

Kara walked briskly up to him, introduced herself as a local writer, and told him how much she relished his work. She was nervous about how he'd react to the approach of a stranger, but Clivner seemed intrigued with her, so much so that he spared her the awkwardness of having to ask him out. He proposed that they should head off to a wine bar nearby to discuss books, writers, the contemporary scene.

They walked through a drizzle to the wine bar three blocks from the gallery. In this subdued setting, the light in the centers of Clivner's dark brown eyes appeared both mischievous and charming. Listening to Clivner talk about his favorite topics was entirely different from hearing Michael declaim from his place in that café. Clivner illuminated the prophetic qualities of J.G. Ballard, as manifested in that writer's depictions of the alienation and hatred permeating a modern world with citizens divided up into zones of steel and glass. He seemed to enjoy few things as much as talking, but Kara thought she knew what the other things were. She just had to prod the conversation a bit further.

In the course of their second encounter, and their first proper date, Kara raised the issue on her mind with Daniel Clivner. She told him all about Michael's debut novel and said she found it tragic and grotesque that such a pretentious and precious book had caused so much of a buzz. Its release did not reflect well on Michael's publisher, Wisteria Books. Kara wondered aloud whether there were any honest reviewers left in the world, or whether they were all subject to the terms of secret deals between publishing houses and the media. If a reviewer could tell the truth, she might just regain a bit of her faith in the critical establishment. Her date's eyes glittered at her from his place on the far side of the flickering light on their table as she told him that she guessed he, too, had needs.

For a week she did not see Daniel. As she walked through the streets alone, she couldn't help thinking of the face in the shifting light above the candle, and his parting promise to see whether he could apply his acumen to Michael's debut effort.

For all the vividness of her memories, Kara could only wonder, as she walked on the wet pavement, whether Daniel was thinking of her. Surveying the storefronts and the façades of brownstones all around, feeling the light rain on her face, she felt utterly alone in the world and wondered where things would lead.

Finally the universe gave her an answer, and when it did, she wondered why her thoughts had wandered so far from the projected course, from all logical expectations. She walked to a news kiosk and bought a copy of the paper of record. Inside, on page C3, she found Daniel's review of *The Harlot's Dream*. With a feeling of ecstasy, a rising thrill, she scanned the columns of text.

"This debut novel contains words and references that had me rushing to my thesaurus and to Google. That's not to say that Michael Jonas is a precocious writer. On the contrary, his windy and precious prose gives every indication that his literary sensibility has never progressed beyond what it was in his sophomore year at a state university."

"As if the world had not had enough of the likes of Jonathan Safran Foer, here comes a writer so precious it is possible to imagine that his idea of clever is to think of a word, stop writing, pick up a thesaurus, and find the longest variant. And then he expects intelligent readers to marvel at his technique. The author envisions a world without violence or want. Though some will commend his deep aversion to violence and belligerence, the author is the most annoying kind of left-wing intellectual."

"The plot of this novel is barely worth summarizing. It is as if Michael Jonas is so convinced of the freshness and audacity of his vision that he inserted a plot almost as an afterthought. Some people detest the author for his attitudes about war and aggression which seem reminiscent of Dalton Trumbo and

1930s communism. I object to his book on entirely different grounds."

Only when she had touched herself recently, lying in bed after her first proper date with Daniel, had Kara known a more pleasurable feeling than the sensations that came to her now.

She called Daniel the following morning. In this conversation, he sounded a trifle diffident, as if not quite sure what she wanted. Kara reminded herself that Daniel was sitting in an office where people could easily overhear him, so naturally he didn't want to appear to be at either end of an undefined quid pro quo. Despite his manner, his seeming uncertainty as to the purpose of her call, Daniel agreed to meet with her in a suite of a hotel downtown on the following evening.

Kara greeted Daniel at the door of the suite on the third floor. In his beige blazer and tan trousers with a sleek black tie scoring the blue of his dress shirt, he looked stupendously handsome. He'd slicked back his acorn-hued hair. The scent on his body seemed calculated to drive her into heat. It suggested a male wildness and a temporarily tamed libido. As Daniel advanced into the room, Kara thought he'd quickly notice the $300 bottle of zinfandel she had propped before the big mirror on the table across from the bed.

The door closed.

He turned to face her.

"Kara, will you *please* explain what you needed to see me about?"

She didn't want to have heard him correctly, but his voice was dry and precise.

"Oh, I've been thinking about you all week, Daniel."

"Why?"

"Why do you imagine? I loved your latest review. I've been so excited about seeing you again."

"We only just met. We're strangers as far as I'm concerned."

"Are you saying you didn't enjoy our two dates?"

"I've met twelve-year-olds who know more about literature, Kara."

She had an impulse to seize the $300 bottle and break it over Daniel's head.

"I thought we had a certain understanding."

"About what, exactly?"

"I'll say it again, Daniel. I *loved* your review. I feel like you've done me a service and I need to do something . . . "

Her voice trailed off. In spite of her earlier impulse, she advanced toward the handsome man and extended her face until her lips were millimeters from his fragrant right cheek.

Daniel shoved her so hard she staggered backward into the table and the bottle flopped on its side, but fortunately did not break.

"Hitting on me! You dumb little slut! And for a moment I was deluded enough to think you were curious about literature!"

"*Daniel!*"

He pivoted and walked out of the room.

Tears came hard now as she listened to the tramp of his feet toward the elevator.

Kara spent the next week crying in a fetal position on the floor of her apartment. The burst of dialogue in the hotel suite was so bright, so vivid, so painful, that she grew desperate to forget it. When Kara finally managed to get up and walk the streets and engage with people again, she tried to mute the sounds of their words before she'd fully heard them, to retain only their general sense.

Kara had little doubt that Daniel was a regular of the wine bar where they'd sat and talked and that he took people there for one purpose or another, personal, professional, or a mix thereof. Maybe she could reinvent herself and take on an assignment for one of the glossies as a journalist whose duty was to interview members of the critical establishment. Suppose she cut her hair short, put on tons of lipstick and makeup, and set up an interview with Daniel three months from now. She wondered whether he'd recognize the pale cheeks and scarlet lips on the far side of the flickering light.

All around were the sounds of an unsettled universe. Rains of unpredictable and rapidly shifting force, and the cries of children ignored by their patents. The heavy rain didn't keep Kara from strolling throughout the neighborhood and glancing from time to time through the broad front window of the wine bar.

One evening, she paused on the wet pavement and turned her gaze to the place's interior. Sure enough, Daniel was at the same table where he'd sat with her, in the company of a man Kara recognized. There on the opposite side of the flickering candle sat Oliver Rance, the head of an independent publishing house, River Bend Press, that competed directly with Michael's publisher, Wisteria Books, as a vehicle for midlist literary fiction. Now Kara understood why Daniel had savaged Michael's novel. Without a pause she pulled out her phone, activated the camera, and pressed the button.

Kara had evidence that could hurt Daniel. The question was how best to use it. She looked up the e-mail addresses for op-ed submissions to all the major newspapers, and sent them her photo along with a cover letter making nasty insinuations. Then she returned to her lonely flat and spent many hours curled up in anticipation of a reply that never came.

So something in this corner of the universe was profoundly out of whack, but the big papers didn't care.

Kara knew where to turn now. It was easy, almost too easy, to arrange a meeting with Andy Nolan, the editor of the *Searchlight*, an alternative weekly. Nolan rarely passed up a chance to provoke and embarrass prominent people.

They met on a bench on an overcast day. Kara explained what she knew and, feeling that a bit of hyperbole never hurts, outlined her plan to help make the *Searchlight* the most respected and feared adversarial news organ in the world. So profuse were Andy Nolan's thanks that she wondered how the meeting could have ended on better terms.

Kara came out of her depression and lethargy often enough to visit distribution boxes for the *Searchlight* every Thursday for four weeks. Surely the article, the exposé, should be out by now. Kara called the offices of the weekly but could not get Nolan on the other end of the line. Scanning the pages of the *Searchlight*, Kara found the e-mail addresses of several contributors. Kara thought about writing to them to express her shock over Nolan's apparent gutlessness. But she realized that she might not really know why the exposé had failed to run. She told herself she must never underestimate the degree to which seemingly quite different media entities collude.

Kara recalled the name of a writer, Gil Slater, who'd been a regular at the café until Michael's presence there became unbearable. This writer had once gotten a book contract with Wisteria, the very publisher that had just put out Michael's novel. Then the publisher quite unexpectedly killed the deal for Gil's book. Kara didn't know whether this had to do with Gil's having tried to kill himself a couple of times. She still had his e-mail address.

The message she received from Gil was short and to the point. He guessed that Andy Nolan had initially liked Kara's idea for an exposé, but had then gone home and said something about it to his wife, Margo Katchadourian. Andy's wife, who was Armenian, had voiced utter dismay at the idea of running a piece that would hurt River Bend Press, a rival of Michael's publisher, Wisteria, and would thereby help the latter. Kara wrote back to Gil, saying she could not guess why Margo Katchadourian hated Wisteria. Gil's reply was a single sentence, noting that Wisteria had published the work of a Turkish nationalist writer, Emil Arcep, who denied Turkey's responsibility for, and some said tacitly justified, the Armenian Genocide.

So Kara had teased out another strand. Not only was Wisteria the publisher of Michael's work, it also had the condoning of genocide on its conscience. Kara thought that to know something about the workings of the universe was worth any amount of pain. But it was Michael she really loathed, and for the moment she could rejoice in the belief that she had hurt him. There remained only to confirm her belief.

She walked into the café with a brash air. Not since the end of the initial meeting with Daniel all those weeks ago, before he knew how slimy Daniel was, had she felt so confident. For all the awfulness and despair that filled the intervening weeks, it still gave Kara pleasure to recall lines from Daniel's review of *The Harlot's Dream*, to repeat them to herself like charms.

Just as she expected, Michael was in his usual place at the back, with a black notebook and a few books on the table in front of him. Michael had set aside a Chekhov paperback and was sipping coffee. When he saw her, he set his mug down with a look of mild surprise. To her astonishment, he greeted her and said with all apparent honesty that he'd wondered why she'd been absent from the café for so long. Kara told him that she'd been busy with literary projects. Studying his features eagerly, she told him she was truly sorry that a review by one of the leading critics had been so savage, and she hoped he hadn't taken any of it personally.

Michael asked, again with apparent sincerity, which review she meant.

Kara found she couldn't mute the words that were coming now, they were as bright and vivid as in her exchange with Daniel in the hotel.

"Surely you know the one I'm talking about, Michael. The review by Daniel Clivner that came out nine or ten weeks ago."

Michael's mental effort now was unmistakable. He was actually struggling to recall the review in question. It had been in Kara's mind for all these weeks, and it wasn't even about her. How could *he* not recall it?

At last something changed in Michael's look.

"Oh, yes, I do remember. Yeah, that review wasn't very kind."

Wasn't very kind?

"I hope it didn't upset you too much."

Michael looked perplexed.

"Uh . . . upset me? No. Why, Kara?"

"It must be easy to get really excited when you publish your debut novel, after years of being this person no one has heard of. And then, to have a review like that come out and deflate all your beliefs about the work and about yourself! I can hardly imagine what that feels like."

"I have no idea what it feels like, Kara. Because that's not really what the review accomplished."

Kara gaped at him.

"Well, what *did* it accomplish?"

"It reminded me of the asininity of reviewers. 'Michael uses a lot of big words.' That doesn't sound to me like an astute critic, Kara. That's a high school kid's idea of a clever put-down."

Kara looked at the mug on the table. Maybe the coffee was still hot. She could pour it on him.

"I thought the review was pretty scathing, Michael."

"Then it did accomplish something, at least for you. It's salve for a writer manqué," Michael said.

Again she resisted the urge to hit him.

There came a voice from behind Kara.

"Excuse me."

Kara turned. A woman she'd never seen before indicated that she had an appointment with Michael and needed the chair directly across from him. Kara guessed it was his agent, here to discuss a new book deal.

Daniel Clivner had failed Kara in every conceivable way. But she could hurt him. She applied for a gun permit, and after a background check, received it in the mail. She purchased a Beretta .38.

Kara walked the streets in a drizzle with her .38 deep in her coat. Over the course of a week, she passed the wine bar and peered through the window forty times before she began to wonder seriously about Daniel's whereabouts. At last she resolved to make an inquiry to the big daily newspaper he wrote reviews for. She got a message from an editorial assistant stating that Daniel had answered an appeal from the editor-in-chief of an underground paper in Moscow. The arts and culture reporter for the paper had died in a terrorist attack by Chechen separatists, the last thing anyone had expected, and the paper needed a replacement at once. It was far from clear to Kara why, in this hyperconnected world, the editor required his new reporter to be in the same city. Once again Kara wound up in a fetal position on the floor of her flat.

Kara vowed to return to the café, Michael's little fiefdom. Then she thought, no, maybe the universe would throw something entirely unexpected her way and it was way too soon to do what she envisioned doing. She wrestled with the question as her despair grew and grew.

Three nights after receiving the information about Daniel, Kara strode into the café with the .38 deep in the folds of her coat. Just as she expected, the arrogant young man sat at the back amid his books and papers. When she got seven feet from Michael, she stood still and pulled out the .38. She waited, ready to savor his utter alarm.

Michael's lips began to form a word, but only for a moment. Then, to Kara's astonishment, Michael's right arm made quick darting motions and she was looking right into the barrel of a .44 Magnum, longer and sleeker than the weapon she held. The young man known as a modern-day Dalton Trumbo grinned. She gazed speechless into the depths of the magnificent barrel, from which there now came a flash. With a cry Kara flopped onto her back, in tremendous pain but also with a feeling of elevated awareness like nothing she had ever known.

Though the bullet tore off the right half of Kara's face, it didn't kill her. In her months in the hospital ward of a prison upstate, Kara heard all the details of the threats against Michael that had emerged from the anonymous darkness, and of the left-wing intellectual's consenting to buy a gun and undergo firearms training in order to protect himself from what might emerge from the dark and drizzle.

Lying prone in her bed, full of frustration at the futile efforts of plastic surgeons and physical therapists, Kara thought that Michael's action was the perfect ending, a total surprise but not at all a *deus ex machina*, not in any sense of the phrase. Oh, no, she told herself, it made absolute sense in the context of the life she led and the vast spaces beyond the walls of her little room.

Hearts, Minds, and Spirits

They didn't even have an appointment. The three soldiers had the gall to walk into the Westfield Home for Seniors and demand to see the retired Colonel William Hall, U.S.M.C., right away. Hall lay on a cot in his dingy room watching a football game and sipping lemonade when the knock came.

They were two young men and an officer in his mid-forties. Hall picked himself up and shook their hands. After introductions, everyone sat down, and the eldest of the three visitors reached into a dossier and spread some papers out on the table.

"Colonel Hall, do you remember the inquiry into the deaths of civilians in your sector of Quang Tri province in 1970?" he asked.

"If the Giants don't find a new quarterback. . . . What? *What* did you say?" replied the colonel, sitting up in his cot.

"I believe you were subject to an official inquiry, with the goal of determining the circumstances of the deaths of six people in the area where you served your second tour."

Hall was silent for a moment. Then he said, "I thought you were here because the VFW needs a new board member, or something. Anyway, yes. I and two men under my command had to answer a whole lot of questions, and then they cleared us. I must say, I haven't heard a word about this in more than thirty years."

"Well, sir, you will have to answer some more questions. Recently, a group of Australians were out at the village where those civilians died in 1970, doing an agricultural survey, and one of the locals said he could show them where some bodies—*not* the original six—lay buried. This was less than a mile outside An Binh, but no one had seen these bodies before. And when the excavation was complete, it turned out the bodies were children's."

There was silence the next twelve seconds. Then the colonel said, "I'm not saying another word without a lawyer present."

"We're giving you notice that there will be further inquiries. In fact, the Department of Defense thought it might be wise to pre-empt the media. Unlike the previous case, there may be a trial."

The colonel looked off into space as the visitors left, and then he was lost in memory.

That Private Collins was a joker.

"Would monsieur care to try the *coq au vin*?" Collins asked the Australian captain who had just sat down inside the officers' tent in the camp in Quang Tri. When Collins strolled in here, he wasn't a nineteen-year-old kid from Bay Ridge, he was a servant with perfect diction.

The Australian, whose name was Hawkins, declined to sample the *coq au vin*. Hall sent the private to gather some maps, and then he and the others began talking about the intensified VC action all around them. Every day brought news of a local assemblyman knifed in his sleep, a point man maimed by a mine in an area thought safe, a jeep and the four men in it obliterated by a grenade thrown by a shriveled villager who couldn't outrun a turtle. The troops spoke of fatigue, poor morale, and a growing need to treat every Vietnamese as an enemy.

Hall prided himself on his strength and cool in no matter what surroundings, but some of the tales got to him a bit. The Australian was talking about a journalist named Burchett, who had gone to live among the VC and who had written books and articles in their favor, serving up accounts of what happened to the ARVN in zones they had thought friendly. Entire companies wading in streams got their legs ensnared in spiked coils that grew tighter and tighter and pulled the men into the muck. Spiked globes of bamboo, loosed from the tops of trees by invisible tripwires, smashed into men's faces at fifty miles an hour. But even with the enemy fighting its war of attrition from all sides, the Australian officer called for a careful and rational policy, referring to the methods of Commonwealth forces in Malaysia in the 1950s.

Collins came back into the tent with maps and cans of beer and accompanied by Litchfield, the wire-thin Kansan. He wasn't putting on any airs now, he was just Collins. "One thing, sir, if you take a group photo, put us in so we can impress ah mom and dad."

Everyone smiled. The men drank heavily for the rest of the night.

"Aside from the charges you will face," said the lawyer, "I promise people are going to provoke you. They'll say, 'Hey, baby killer, what's the grand tally?' They'll do anything to make you incriminate or embarrass yourself."

"I know they will," replied the colonel.

"And I know what sort of situation existed in Quang Tri in 1970. Do you still want to deny you ever deviated from the rules of engagement?"

"I categorically deny it."

The country unfolded two hundred feet below the Huey, mile after mile of lush green and brown scored by streams whose source lay in the hills at the edge of the province. Huts lay here and there at the borders of fields where peasants rode water buffalo back and forth to break up the earth in preparation for sowing. Here was life as it had been for centuries. The presence of ancestors in the fields under cultivation today ensured a respect and love for the land, which was one with those who had helped make it fertile.

The men in the Huey were debating whom to kill.

"See that cluster down there on the right, fifty yards from the water," said Corporal Smith, pointing to some huts made of bamboo. "I think they have meetings in there somewhere. Unfortunately, our intelligence doesn't go further than that."

"I say we raze the whole damn place," offered Major Bradford. "Their dead, our dead, just do the fuckin' math."

"I say we send in the SEALs and selectively remove some officials," said the corporal.

"We haven't got enough intelligence to do a thing at this point," argued the Australian.

"You're sitting here talking about the state of our intelligence while our men are walking into traps every goddamn day," the major said.

Suddenly they noticed smoke on the horizon, and they strained to make out its source. They watched the scenery unfolding, the shapes of trees and the contours of land coming into relief, and soon they could make out the carnage to which the enemy had reduced a patrol. A column of black smoke poured from the top of a truck hit by a rocket-propelled grenade, and charred bodies lay about the perimeter, the shells of those who had survived the blast and tried to limp off into the bush. Some of the forms were human only by a generous definition, and in one case, the observers could actually think the lower half of a man's body had tried to run away after the top half's incineration, for twenty yards from the truck lay a smoldering pelvis and two legs.

One of the men in the camp was screaming. The sound ripped through the moist air of the camp near the Laotian border on a particularly sticky night in August 1970. Lying awake in his tent, Hall wondered what kind of man screams like that, and whether the guy had stepped on a slug on his way to the john. He got up and put his belt on and walked out. The cone of light from his bobbing flashlight danced over the tents, the scattered crates and tires, and the jeeps far off at the perimeter where two watchmen were staring out into the dark. Hall moved in the general direction of the sound. The randomness of what he was doing was almost humiliating, until the light fell on the pale face of private Litchfield, who lay in the dirt several yards from the latrine. The private's wide eyes stared into the light for a moment before he picked himself up clumsily.

"I didn't know! Jesus Christ on a— Fuck! I tripped! *Fuck!*"

"What happened, private?"

"Look! *Look right in front of you!*"

Hall turned the beam downward, and then he saw. It was the bloodied body of a young man in a VC regular's uniform. Although there were no bullet holes or any individual wounds at all, something had knocked the life right out of this kid. *I didn't hear any shots,* thought Hall, *and there are no traps around here, but I did hear the drone of a plane overhead a half-hour ago.*

"It's all right, Litchfield," he said, in the paternal tone he had cultivated when trying to win over potential recruits back in Virginia. "Come on, now, we all have to see this some time."

"Good lord, what happened, colonel?"

"I think he just fell off one of our trucks on its way back to the lot. Come on, now, soldier, go to your tent and take out your Bible and read Leviticus and Matthew."

"You won't discipline me, sir?"

"Nah."

The private ran off in the dark.

The Americans got a spectacular welcome as they rode into An Binh. The toothless man in a dirty white shirt thrust his parallel arms up as if hefting an invisible barbell, while another man with thin white hair and glasses jabbed the air with an American flag on a flimsy stick. Kids leapt up and down, girls and women blew kisses at the men in the jeeps and atop the M48 Pattons. Once it had penetrated the village, the jeep carrying Hall and his fellow officers broke from the convoy and headed for a hut where local officials were waiting. After parking in the mud, the men walked inside and shook hands with the mayor and members of the provincial assembly.

A little girl was kneeling behind one of the 19th-century French chairs, clutching something in her tiny hand. Hall looked at her and flashed his J.F.K. grin.

"What do you have there, little girl?" he asked.

No answer. He tried speaking to her in French, and then used the bit of Vietnamese he knew. Still no reply. The eyes kept watching him while the rest of the face and most of her body stayed hidden behind the chair. Hall seemed to be the only one in the room who had noticed her.

The meeting began. The elders of the village were aware of the crisis facing the Americans. If people anywhere knew the abruptness and shock of loss, they were the heads of a village whose young men walked by the score into deadly traps and fell to the arrows and spears of tribesmen whom they thought disliked the Vietcong. Sharing tales with the officers, the elders voiced their consensus that things had not gone quite this badly in a long time. The Americans agreed. Obstacles or distractions of one kind or another kept diverting American and ARVN forces to a perilous route. It was as if the land, the rivers, the very air conspired to subvert the efforts to save this province.

Hall and the Australian, Captain Hawkins, asked about the strength of the ARVN regiments in the area, and then laid out preliminary plans for a joint attack on VC posts in the mountains lining the border with Laos. Those mountains were an uncontrolled zone where VC reinforcements crept over the border into the communist positions, easily setting up new camps and just as easily slipping back over the border when the need arose.

Again, the officers and the elders shook hands. The Vietnamese seemed pleased with the meeting's outcome, as did most of the Americans, but Hall, at least, was curious about the girl who would not reveal her face. Only weeks later would he hear about the fire that fell from the sky.

"The thing we must focus on," said Hawkins, as he and the colonel, flanked by forty other men, descended a knoll on the fringes of a jungle at the foot of a mountain north of An Binh, "is logistics, ours and the enemy's. If you look back at what Australians did at Long Tan in '66, you can see the case for hitting the enemy's command centers and impairing his ability to coordinate attacks."

"You guys did an o.k. job at Long Tan," replied Colonel Hall, "but I don't know how useful that is as a model. Their command structure isn't always that centralized, they've got so many damn irregulars in the field, you've got to nail them individually, in whatever guise they may appear."

The Australian took umbrage at being corrected. "The details may vary, but not the overall model."

"Oh, it does."

"No, Colonel Hall, I tell you it doesn't."

"I don't see how you can know that, sport. You've only been in country six weeks."

"Sometimes I wonder if you Yanks know your arses from your elbows."

That was when Hall barreled into the Australian like a linebacker in full throttle, sending him sprawling at the foot of the knoll. Though briefly stunned, Hawkins registered the look in the colonel's eyes and followed their gaze to a metal hook nestled in the lush grass right where the Australian had been about to step.

The first bullet from the bush tore off the left cheek of a young radioman and made him spin wildly until the weight of his gear flopped him onto his back. More rounds came as Hall sank reflexively and made hand signals at the other men, some of whom stared vapidly at the tree line, newly alive with a cacophony of shouts and flashes. The men began to take cover behind random rocks and trees, but seven were already down before anyone could return fire.

Then six attackers garbed in black rushed out of the bush, followed quickly by another six. Hall crawled behind the base of a mango tree and slid his .45 out of its holster. Kneeling behind another tree, Hawkins opened up with his L1A1 semiautomatic. The rounds punched through the first wave and then the second, spraying bloody garb over the dense green, but another wave followed even as the first two fell. Hall emptied his .45, hitting one attacker directly between the eyes, flung a grenade at the tree line, then began to crawl toward the fallen radioman.

Caught by a burst from the trees, two more of Hall's men fell screaming. When he turned the radioman over, the radio was so drenched with blood that he doubted it would work. But he was able to raise the provincial headquarters and request immediate backup.

"Yes, Colonel," came the drawling voice at the other end, "we'll have the air cav there ASAP, sir."

The colonel crawled back to his former position. No more attackers came from the trees, and the fire died down, but Hall knew that would change if one of his men ventured out from whatever cover he'd found. At least eight were dead, and another seven or eight could not leave on their own. Hall repeatedly signaled that no one was to move for any reason. They waited, and waited some more, as the heat kept coming down in searing waves and blood and sweat mingled freely. Hall kept expecting the familiar groan of a Huey to penetrate the wet stillness, but there was only silence above the trees ringing the knoll, a silence suggestive of infinite distances all around the trapped men.

After another excruciating five minutes, Hall looked back at the radioman, who had now bled to death, and decided not to risk going back to the radio. Fifteen feet away, Hawkins was lying on the ground, panting and looking at him. After another series of signals by Hall, repeated by others for the benefit of those who couldn't see him, it was clear what he had decided to do.

Without further ado, the men stood up and flung all their remaining grenades at the tree line simultaneously. They followed up with a fusillade that nearly depleted their remaining ammunition, and then there began a crazed dash up the knoll whence they had come. The enemy exploited this chance to pick off a number of the fleeing Americans, in an almost leisurely manner, as they left behind thirty yards strewn with the dead and the moaning wounded.

Later, the radio operator and other support staff at the base faced an incensed superior.

"We acted on your orders immediately, sir."

"Then what held up the rescue and made us abandon wounded men to the enemy?" Hall asked.

"We still don't know, sir. We lost contact with the pilot, and the Huey may have gone down. It's under investigation as we speak. The pilot may have misread the coordinates. In any event, right before we lost contact, he was distracted by something he saw, or thought he saw, on the ground, and when he moved lower, part of the bird may have become ensnared in waving branches."

August 28, 1970. Shouting arose outside the tent that night, and this time it wasn't one kid who'd tripped on a corpse, but a babble of voices rising in pitch. When Hall walked out of his tent, men tore right past him as if he didn't exist, calling for help for the truck that had rolled into the center of the camp. Three more vehicles followed in a storm of diesel fumes and shouts. Hall walked up to one of the men who had leapt off the truck, demanding to know what was going on. The man started talking in a shrill tone, and soon the scene had meaning. Thirty miles outside the camp, a troop transport had taken a direct hit from a mortar, igniting the ammunition aboard, which in turn made the gas tank blow. Sniper fire on both sides of the road tore into the men who had been able to clamber out and who had started rolling on the ground in the hope of minimizing the burns. A few soldiers had hidden themselves by the side of the road, and had called for help. The VC didn't stick around, but the truck and jeeps sent to save the men took *forty-five minutes* to arrive.

Then that very truck, packed with the dead and wounded, hit a mine on the way back, incurring fresh casualties, and went off the road, necessitating yet another rescue.

The next day, everyone in the camp was struggling to put on an upbeat air. *Stars and Stripes* had sent a photographer, a sandy-haired kid in awe of everything military, to write a puff piece about the campaigns in Quang Tri. When the reporter walked into the mess hall, a drab facility adjoining the command center, garage, and hospital, the officers gave him a beer and started fielding all kinds of questions about operations in the province and the chances of driving the VC back over the border for good. It didn't take long to see what kind of story the kid's editors were expecting. The journalist had some morale-boosting lines, and now all he needed was a group photo, so he asked the officers to start organizing themselves in the front of the room.

"*Ohhh,* put *usss* in the picture!" hissed a voice from the partitioned door leading to the garage.

All the men in the room turned quickly around. Collins was gazing through the space where the upper half of the door had been and clinging to the lower half with the one hand of his still recognizable as a hand. The only part of his blackened, singed face that resembled Collins before the ambush was the grin. Behind him were Litchfield and a third burned, vaguely humanoid mass.

"Put *usss* in your picture and make us famous! *Please!*" he said, grinning.

"*Goddamn it! I said only KIAs in there!*" thundered one of the officers to a corporal. "What are they doing there?"

"I thought they were KIAs, sir!" said the corporal.

"Get back in there, damn it!" yelled the major, grabbing the upper half of the metal door. He was furious at the burned men. "Get back in there and—" He slammed the door with enough force to sever Collins's fingers from the rest of him.

"Colonel Hall," intoned the prosecutor, looking directly at him, "after the events related so far in these proceedings, is it fair to say that some officers felt a need for massive retaliation against the Vietcong and their perceived supporters?"

Hall's own lawyer was watching intently from his seat. The colonel's hard face looked down for a moment.

"Yes, sir, that's fair."

"Maybe you can tell us about the nature and extent of the retaliation."

Hall spoke for fifteen minutes, without divulging anything one could not learn from the illustrated *Time/Life* books on the war.

The witnesses questioned by Hall's lawyer were an Australian forensics expert and a professor from a university in Texas whose facilities included a center devoted to Vietnam's history. The forensics expert spoke of the work he'd done after the excavation of the children's bodies. The climate of the underground chamber, he noted, had kept the bodies in something close to their state at the time of death.

The lawyer said, "Please describe any holes, marks, or incisions which might indicate a wound from a gun, knife, or blunt object."

"There were no such marks, sir."

Total silence in the room.

"Tell us how you believe the children died."

"I do not know. But because of the absence of any visible wounds, I would speculate that they died from a lack of breathable air."

Then it was the professor's turn.

"I gather," stated Hall's lawyer, "that you are an expert on the customs, beliefs, and mythology prevalent in the Central Highlands and other regions of Vietnam. Tell us something about the routing of evil spirits."

"That, sir, is a very crude phrase to use. But such 'spirits,' in mythology, have manifold powers and means of inflicting harm. There were, and in some areas there still are, communities where people believe that the propitiation of spirits doing harm to the living requires an act of sacrifice."

The lawyer raised his voice for effect. *"And can these acts of propitiation include burying children alive?"*

"Yes."

Hall was watching football. What a game, he hadn't seen anyone play like this since the Jets in 1969.

His lawyer had told him to avoid dwelling on this case, to let it go, but Hall had had questions after its dismissal.

"Of course, with all that's come out here, they're going to want to revive the other case now, because that's the shoe that fits."

"You're thinking emotionally, Colonel Hall. Anyone can adduce circumstantial evidence for any trial in history, can tell you about the climate people lived in. From a legal point of view, nothing in this trial constitutes fresh evidence that would warrant reopening the old case. Consider yourself well protected."

Those words were a relief, for no one today, no one who wasn't there, could hope to see the rhyme and reason of Colonel William Hall's actions.

"You are part of the very life of the land," Hall said to the Vietnamese boy seated across from him in the hut. "The food that nourished you grows on the land where your great-grandparents lie, and their parents, and so on. And you work that land, and you too will make it fertile some time. There are rhythms here that we have disturbed, and someone or something is very angry. Not all the screams I hear at night come from men.

"I'm telling you, some of the elders around here have taken special steps to reverse the course of events, have made offerings based on their deepest-held beliefs and superstitions. That's well and good, but it's not how I do things. It's not what a man would do. My response to it is to say, 'I'm not afraid of anything or anyone, and I will do whatever I like in this country.'

"But none of this need concern you. You are just a boy thinking about your future. You probably have a vision of what you will become, a handsome young man bringing handmade bamboo gifts to *mama-san* and *papa-san* and working the fields all day with the methods perfected by your ancestors. Your mother brought you into the world, and she expected so much. She thinks of you, and she sees the person you will become. She imagines those beautiful cheeks, that mouth, twenty, thirty years in the future, thinks of your skills developed to perfection. She shares the dream with you, and you, too, long to be that man."

Then Hall put the tip of his .45 to the boy's temple and said one more word before he squeezed the trigger:

"Nah."

An Offer You Can't Refuse

Corrigan left the interstate somewhere south of Richmond and had no plans to get back on it soon. How agreeable he found the thought that now no one in the world, not even he, knew exactly where he was. On occasion he stopped, consuming fried chicken, home fries, and Cokes at shacks by the sides of roads, refueling at family-owned pump stations where men in overalls loitered on benches in the fragrant air of late August. If anyone asked where he was going, Corrigan named a town at random. It might be Miami, or the place people around here called Naw'lins. He knew there were homeless shelters in those towns, but held out hope that he wouldn't end up checking into one.

He wanted to crank up the air conditioner in his Ford, but he knew it would kill the battery, which he could hardly afford to replace just now. With both of the front windows down, he drove on through the back roads in the dusk, fancying himself somewhere on the Eastern Shore of Maryland, between central Virginia and the ocean. To the south were strangers. To the north were people and things Corrigan couldn't bear to think about. The road wended southward, like the tail of a great basilisk. Corrigan noted that the headlights were dimmer than when he'd set out. He now had a quarter tank of gas.

Corrigan thought, *I don't want to drive off without paying for gas, but it's not out of the question anymore. Nothing's out of the question anymore.*

He must get some coffee, or risk dozing off at the wheel. In a half-second before his superego kicked in, his mind wandered back to a room in a little apartment where a woman sat on a couch looking at him intently. He could not think of that right now. *Corrigan,* the wind in the drooping fir trees seemed to be calling. *Oh, Corrigan.*

Corrigan switched on the radio. It would wear the battery down further, but his loneliness might fade ever so slightly. There was static, so he flipped the dial, carelessly, cavalierly, keeping his eyes on the treacherous curves ahead.

"Love your enemies, and pray for those who persecute you."

He did not listen to the host of the tiny, remote station elaborate on the words from the Book of Matthew. He flipped the dial until a throaty, elderly voice said haltingly, as if struggling to connect the words, that listeners had just heard Tchaikovsky's Symphony Number 4 in F Minor. Next the dial alighted on a rock station. Corrigan flipped the dial still further past columns of blaring static. When next he found a clear audible broadcast, it was some kind of evangelical talk program, where a guest spoke about not repaying evil with evil. If the host interjected, it was only to agree or expand on the guest's point. Corrigan scoffed at the gutlessness of this backwoods Donahue. Then he found country music, which opened vistas before him of girls walking in fields, coming of age and defining their attitude toward a young fellow who sat at the wheel of a combine or a tractor, who brooded late into the night over glasses of ale in taverns. The female voices coming over the airwaves lulled Corrigan, beckoning him to step into an Andrew Wyeth canvas. Just as he was starting to enjoy himself a bit, the sounds began to break up and he realized he must be further south than almost anyone who listened to this station. The voices melted into a blur of static until he snapped off the radio again.

After scanning the road in either direction, he pulled over to the dirt shoulder on the right. When confident that not even a bird or snail could spot him, Corrigan relieved himself against the trunk of a tall fir tree, thinking he could kill for a cup of coffee. How long before his vision began to blur and he began to nod off? Back on the road, Corrigan flicked on the radio again, spun the dial like a child unaware of what he was doing. Out here the columns of static were thicker and more frequent. When voices came, they were languid, as if the announcers were talking to themselves in the knowledge that hardly anyone was awake and listening. Corrigan searched for a station where he might discover music so alluring that it made him want to park the car in one of these communities and try to meet a lass so utterly unlike the Italian and Irish girls he'd shacked up with. He allowed the dial to rest on a country station he found, but the music here was fodder, full of insipid musings about horses and whiskey and what I'm gonna do when I see that woman again. The sounds broke up again. He drove stubbornly onward in almost total darkness. He was beginning to think maybe he really must go easy on the battery, he wasn't really that tired, he'd just had a spell of drowsiness back there. Where was he, anyway? He'd stopped paying attention to the signs a while ago, so for all Corrigan knew he was in North Carolina now.

A voice broke through the static.

"There can't be many folks listening out there. Not in these parts, not at this hour."

What on earth was this? It was a man's voice, genial, relaxed, but faintly conspiratorial. If Corrigan had to guess, he'd say the guy was in his thirties, with no more than a high school education. Corrigan turned the volume up a bit.

"If you are passin' through and you're lookin' for an opportunity, listen up, now. I won't tell you what I have to offer, but I can tell you it's something you need real bad, buddy. You'll be in and out of here soon one way or another. What say I help you, you help me, and we go right on with our lives."

Corrigan was listening.

"Once again, I won't divulge details here and now—what say you stop off at the roadhouse on South Street. Take the second right from the turnpike about 120 yards, and you'll see it up on your right."

Corrigan strained his ears, but now a car insurance ad came on. He thought: *Well what the fuck do I have to lose?*

Sure enough, the intersection of South Street and the road he was on loomed before him. He eased his foot on the brake, turned right, pursued South Street until he saw what looked like nothing so much as a barn with a neon Budweiser sign in one of the front windows. In the dirt lot outside were a few pickups, peeling and rusting, and a weathered Datsun with a Confederate flag decal on the rear bumper. Another car, a Pontiac, had mismatched paintwork on its lower third, suggesting it had been in several bang-ups. Corrigan swung into the lot, stopped beside a pickup with an empty gun rack, got out, and stood breathing the sweet air in the moonlight. He walked around to the front of the tavern and stepped inside. In the elongated space where roosters had once strode, a woman sat at the bar with a glass of Woodpecker before her. At a couple of the tables, men in jeans and t-shirts sat drinking beer, listening to a John Fogarty song from the jukebox.

Though Corrigan stood by the entrance longer than he should have, scanning the room, the half-dozen fellows did not appear to notice him. But he realized quickly that the woman was eying him, even as she kept her face parallel with the counter. She was a slender lass with curly blonde hair. Time had not begun to dull the freshness of her thick cheeks. Even if she might have little schooling, there was an alertness about her, an intelligence in her eyes. Taking a seat three stools up from the woman, Corrigan looked expectantly at the bartender, who was leaning over the counter, talking with a burly man in over-alls. Corrigan let his gaze wander back to the woman, who, if he was not mistaken, was tilting her face toward him a bit, with a coy look. For a moment, all context fell away, he forgot why he was here. Just as he was about to say something to the lass, a guy about her age walked out of the restroom near the front of the place and took a seat at one of the tables. She picked herself up and joined him without a look at Corrigan. Still the bartender ignored him. Well, he hadn't come here for a drink of redneck juice, now, had he? Sitting down had just seemed like the thing to do. He fidgeted. He thought, *To hell with it. I shouldn't have stopped here at all. I'll think of something to say on my way out, I'll let them know they're all a bunch of hayseeds with nothing better to do than play pranks on folks from out of town.*

First he must use the john. Deliberately not looking at the woman at the table, he walked into the restroom which had only a sink, a mirror, and a single stall. He moved into the stall, stood over the commode thinking of what his parting shot would be. Twenty seconds later, as Corrigan finished up, he heard the door to the restroom swish open. He assumed that someone had come inside, seen the stall was in use, and left. He fastened his belt and moved toward the door of the stall. It wouldn't give. He shoved it, with no result.

"Okay," Corrigan said.

A long pause. Corrigan berated himself for looking at that slut at the bar as if the scenario had any potential at all. He drew a deep breath, trying to steady his nerves.

"Okay," he repeated.

Then came a voice, calm, measured, the voice of someone who knew what was what and was in no hurry.

"Now thank you for visiting our establishment tonight. A child could look at you and tell you ain't from around here."

The speaker chuckled.

"Okay," Corrigan said a third time, feeling like an idiot.

The voice on the other side scoffed.

"I thought we was the ones with the small vocabulary. Anyhow, pardner, two clicks west of here on South Street, there's a road called Sutter's Lane. If you take it southwest, two and three-tenths of a mile, you'll come to the house of a guy who's made life a livin' hell for a lot of people in these parts for quite a few years now. He's gotten away with it, but folks 'round here don't never forget the good nor the ill done to them."

Corrigan was listening.

"If you stop on the way there—six tenths of a mile down Sutter's Lane, or a shade under—there's a utility box on the right side of the road. Now if someone was to take a look in the bushes behind that box, that person just might discover something long and sleek. If that someone was to take that something to the property of Mr. Jepson, the man tends to sit up in his living room well into the small hours on the weekend with a bottle."

Corrigan started to speak, but checked himself.

"You discharge your duty, you get yourself right back up to South Street, drive east for three miles, turn onto Crawford Street which is a straight shot to the interstate. By the time they can begin to investigate, you'll be in another time zone. They're going to ask me questions, but I'll be back at the radio station, on the other side of town, and I'll be caught on the camera of a gas station on the way there. How's that for an alibi?"

Corrigan thought it *was* pretty damn clever. There could be no record of this exchange, or of the snatch of broadcast he'd caught earlier. Even if someone else had heard it, it was vague and subject to interpretation at best. It could have been an ad for a blow job. Indeed there was someone here who probably provided such services.

"Now, I'll be monitoring the police and EMT radios, so I'll know what's what. If you meet your part of the deal, I'll come on the air for a few seconds with some information. You'll be the only one who'll know the real reason I'm mentioning a location. You stop there, then you continue on to the interstate. I've never seen you before, nor you me. Deal, pardner?"

But I've never seen you in the first place, Corrigan wanted to interject.

"Deal."

"Attaway. One more thing, pardner. You stick straight to the route I gave you. Keep to it like a finger on a clit. Don't you set foot on the farms down there under any circumstances. Got it, mister?"

"I understand."

"Okay then."

"But why?"

"Let's just say, 'cause of the effects of inbreeding."

Now the door to the stall was free again, but Corrigan did not move fast enough to see the shape on the other side dart out of the restroom and lose itself among the figures at the tables. He did not even try to get a look at them as he walked out of the tavern. He started his car and turned out of the lot onto South Street, thinking that it was funny, there was a kind of symmetry here that his life rarely had. If he got onto the interstate with what he thought he was going to have, it would hardly matter who caught up with him. Corrigan drove west on South Street, turned left, and then before he knew it, he was on Sutter's Lane, driving southwest in the moonlight between still fields. *Two and three-tenths of a mile*, he told himself. *Don't fuck this up.* Far off, to the north of the lane, he made out the shape of a scarecrow, tall and ominous. He supposed there could be a few of those hicks out there, watching, pressing their sleeves to their mouths to laugh at him. Or perhaps not.

Soon Corrigan spied it, up there on his right: the utility box. He eased his foot onto the brake, his eyes darting every which way. The fear, the revulsion that crept into his chest now were not the equal of a single thought: *I have nothing at all to lose.* He stepped out of the car, strode out into the field behind the box, where he would have tripped over the object if he hadn't caught a glint of moonlight on its sleek barrel. Corrigan bent down, picked it up with both hands. Here was a Remington .220 rifle with a checkered grip the color of honey and a telescopic sight that swelled at either end. Now, as he caressed it in the moonlight, there came the gentlest of breezes, ruffling his hair. Here was Corrigan, a high school dropout with zero prospects. Almost everything he'd ever touched in his life had turned to shit. Now there was no life he could not take, no social arrangement he could not alter forever. He mused on the cunning of the plan. Nobody in this area whom the police questioned could tell them anything of any substance. Even if they caught Corrigan, it would be virtually impossible to prove he'd ever seen, heard, or spoken to anyone.

It was so cool and peaceful here that Corrigan could not help starting, in bewilderment, at a sound that came to him over the breeze. It was like a cry of anger and embarrassment that comes from a house where people watching a game see the home team do something dumb, but to Corrigan there was a feral element to the noise. He listened but the breeze just ruffled his hair until he grew anxious that a car might pass.

He quickly returned to the Ford, sliding the rifle in front of the back seat. As he hit the road again, a voice came to him, from nowhere, rather like a sniper's bullet: *"I know you'd never lie or steal, Joe."* A voice he quickly recognized: his mother's. The voice sorted, differentiated. The other kids in the neighborhood might do such low things, but not her Joe. . . . Impatiently he pressed his foot on the gas, rehearsing the stranger's directions in his head, leaving the scarecrow and the utility box far behind. Soon, when he got within a quarter of a mile of Jepson's place, he must stop cold. What on earth had this fellow done, anyway? If you encountered him on the porch of a feed store, maybe he'd come across as the most genial, tobacco chewin', knee-slappin' son of a gun in the world, but that could not mask the reality of his having ruthlessly bought up hundreds of acres, shutting other farmers off from their livelihood, if that was the case. Or maybe he'd gotten a corner on cotton or one of the other local export markets, depressing prices so far that the smaller guys, with large families to feed, went bust. Or perhaps it was all about a woman? Well, he'd done something to make people loathe him, Corrigan knew that much. *Mom, if you're up there watching, please don't think less of me.*

The road curved gently toward the south, as Corrigan's heart beat hard and the wind whispered in the open windows on either side. Then he thought maybe this was really just a stupid crime of passion, and maybe Jepson wasn't in the wrong here. Well, damn it, this discussion had gone on too long as it was. He'd let his thoughts wander. He'd—

Oh my God
Oh Christ
Oh good God here it is I should have stopped already!

His foot pounced on the brake, and he guided the car to a spot behind a tall fir tree with a vast drooping canopy of branches. About seventy yards from where he sat, there was a house, not a mansion but a big house with an elongated trailer-like section in front and a back porch with a pair of benches and a grill whose dome gleamed in the moonlight. Upstairs the house was dark, but in the window between the trailer-like section and the room abutting the porch, and also in two of the latter room's windows, there was bright light. Anyone standing in one of the windows must surely have seen the Ford moving down the dirt road. Well, Corrigan could beat a quick retreat if need be. He'd come this far. Corrigan put the car in park, left the keys where they were, took the rifle, and slid out. All he could hear was his panting. He scanned the road in both directions, and the area around the house, before walking at a normal pace into the field adjacent to the porch.

Corrigan picked up his pace as neared one of the trees. The closer you got to the borders of this field, the more trees there were. Here was one in perhaps the right spot. He leaned against the trunk, studied the windows west of his position. He raised the .220, peered through the scope. The three windows of what looked like a parlor were big and close enough together that he could take in most of the room. Almost as soon as Corrigan trained his gaze, a figure moved out of the parlor toward the trailer-like part of the house. Corrigan waited, his heart hammering. The lights in the other parts of the house stayed off.

Oh Christ he must have seen me. But if that were the case, wouldn't Jepson, if that was who it was, have hit the lights on his way out of the parlor? *Fuck, who knows.* He stood there, fearing the sweat on his palms would throw his aim way off. *All right, fuck this, let's forget I ever—*

Now Jepson, if that was who it was, lumbered back into the parlor and sat down on a couch, facing the front of the house, profiled in the room's middle window. The man held what looked, at this distance, like a bottle of Jack Daniels. As the grip of the rifle slid a few millimeters in his moist hand, Corrigan indulged his curiosity, studying the ruddy, pouty features of the fat man, clad in a pair of brown trousers and a gray button-down shirt with short sleeves. On the wall across from the window, Corrigan spied an array of plaques and medals. Jepson, he gathered, was a Vietnam veteran. At once, Corrigan had a vision of Vietcong prisoners, hands tied behind their backs, cowering as the beefy man brandished a 10" knife and threatened to cut off their ears if they didn't tell him X, Y, or Z. Corrigan's finger tensed, tightening around the trigger. His hand was way too damp. He thought, *I'm too far away. If I miss, I don't get another try. No money, no deliverance from the hell I live in.*

About twenty yards up, there was another tree. He made a calculation. As quietly as he could, Corrigan stole toward it, watching the middle window. Without the scope, Jepson was a vague form. But in seconds, he'd be a pulsing, quivering human once again, swearing at the TV, raising the bottle to his salivating lips.

Just let me—

Corrigan slipped and fell on his ass, the rifle flying out of his hands and clattering onto a patch of mud. He hadn't seen the ditch. Christ, Jepson *must* have caught a flurry of motion in his peripheral vision. At least the gun didn't go off. In a cold sweat, Corrigan clumsily picked himself up, not bothering to wipe the mud off his pants before he seized the rifle. *God please tell me nothing got into the bolt or the barrel.* It was too dark to peer into the barrel, and with his luck he'd blow his face off if he tried. He moved to the tree on Jepson's side of the ditch, raised the rifle, and looked. Still the fat man watched the TV, whiskey in hand. *Okay. Okay, now.* Beads of sweat dripped into Corrigan's eyes, tickled the skin on his neck and chest. The back of his shirt was drenched. His palms wouldn't stop running, and the grip felt slippery as an eel in his right hand, the sleek barrel no less so in his left. *One shot, one chance. One shot, one chance. One shot—*

Now, the man on the couch set the bottle down on the table before the TV and that head, that flabby face, rotated toward the window! Corrigan squeezed the trigger. The gun jumped in his hands. At the moment it roared, Jepson leapt from the couch and vanished into a space between the first two windows.

No! I missed! I MISSED! No no no no no no no no

On an impulse, Corrigan fired four times at the wall of the parlor. Even as he did so, he could hear shouts within Jepson's house and also sounds from somewhere else—behind the house, perhaps. They were cries, screams, wails, howls, and screeches like the sounds of animals being tortured. He couldn't be sure. Corrigan was so bewildered he wanted to stay right on the spot, listening, but he turned and sprinted in the direction of the Ford, leaping so high over the ditch that he hurt his right ankle coming down. He charged with renewed desperation towards the Ford. From his left, the area around the house, he could hear voices growing from a babble into something just a bit more orderly. And now large figures were streaming out of a house across the road from Jepson's, coming fast in Corrigan's direction. He reached the Ford, climbed inside, propped the rifle against the passenger's seat, turned the key. The car got out in the middle of the road before Corrigan began to execute a U-turn.

He could not be seeing what he thought he saw. A man nearly seven feet tall, with a beard like a comic-book Zeus, stood in front of the car. The furious man was sliding his hands down to the front bumper. Now Corrigan looked hard, really stared at him in the moonlight. Corrigan was so accustomed to everyone he encountered meeting certain expectations, or assumptions, that through a sort of cognitive dissonance he'd seen features of this stranger without really seeing them. This fellow, Corrigan noticed now, had more than just a beard, he had a mane, running from his face down toward his groin, and fur coated his thick fingers right down to the fringes of his thick gleaming nails. The stranger had paws, Corrigan realized, and a dark shape slithering behind him, presumably from a hole in his pants.

Corrigan had no time to ponder the realization that this sick bastard, Jepson, had been cross-breeding people and animals. He jerked the shift into reverse, backed away 10 feet until the rear bumper hit the curb, and made the U-turn, the engine groaning as he accelerated up Sutter's Lane toward South Street. In the rear view mirror, he saw a cluster of figures joining the huge man in the middle of the road. Some of them were nearly as big as he was. Corrigan cursed and wiped his seeping face with his left palm as his frantic eyes scanned either side of Sutter's Lane. Blessedly, the few houses he passed had no lights on. *Come on, come on, I'm not far from the interstate!* It was the longest two and three-tenths of a mile Corrigan would ever drive, but at last he saw where the road merged with South Street up ahead. Still he couldn't refrain from cursing and punching the dashboard. He turned onto South Street, made a right with the wheel clutched in both hands, and then, almost as an afterthought, switched on the radio. A song came on, a ditty about how a stable full of horses will start to neigh your name if you treat 'em right. How something so utterly ridiculous could get on the air, he could not fathom. Corrigan racked his brain, struggling to check his panic long enough to reconstruct the directions he'd gotten in the stall of that tavern. *Now, South Street goes right to the interstate—No! Damn it, that's not right. No, I go three miles east to Crawford Street, and then—*

A pair of large figures in police uniforms stood seventy yards ahead of him on South Street, both looking in his direction. Now came a sickening revelation. *This lunatic Jepson's got this fucking town in his pocket. Someone wants him gone, well, I'm the fall guy, I'm the drifter who wanted to raid his house for drug money. I'm a PATSY! Christ, I'm dead!* Well, it was a rural place with a tiny police force. They hadn't had time to bring in the state cops, and they couldn't very well block every route with a handful of officers. But in the distances, the man-beasts were screaming. Up ahead on his right, Corrigan spotted a dirt lane leading off to a rugged, barely populated area to the south, and he drove for it immediately. The Ford bounced and jostled as it surmounted the curb and entered the crude lane. He slammed his foot on the gas. Ahead in the distance he could make out farms, clusters of fir trees, a house here or there. In the rear view mirror, moonlight fell on a road without a living thing in sight. *Those men back there—were they men? What in fuck's name were they?* Come on now, of course you can't cross-breed people with wild creatures. Maybe the cross-breeding was in Corrigan's fevered imagination, yes, maybe Jepson was just feeding genetically modified grain to his people to make them tougher and stronger than other farm hands. *Stranger things have—*

Now a toothpaste ad succeeded the corny song on the radio. When it ended, there came the voice of the man he'd heard twice before, but had never seen.

"A good evenin' to anyone who may be listenin'. We just heard 'Show Your Horse Where You Heart Is' by Miles Henshaw, and before that, 'If She Ain't An Angel' by Chuck Godfrey."

Corrigan did something he hadn't done in a while. He laughed.

"Listen up, now, folks, it's three a.m. and this station is shuttin' down for the next four hours. To anyone who may be listenin', my buddy says he spotted a deer, near the middle telegraph pole on Crawford this evening. Y'all drive extra careful and get home safe, now. Good night."

Corrigan switched off the radio. The Ford was still bouncing and jangling. *The road down here is really shit,* he thought.

No, he could see the road in his headlights. It wasn't the road.

They'd placed something at the exit back there—spikes, or caltrops, wasn't that what the devices were called? The tires were shredding!

Fuck. There were clapboard houses on either side of the road up ahead, and the car was making a ruckus to wake Confederate corpses deep in the earth. Corrigan made a decision. He eased the Ford to the right, and parked. He sat there feeling his heart rebel against what enclosed it. Then on an impulse, he flicked the radio back on. Maybe, just maybe, he could find out what local authorities knew or didn't know. There was static on the band where he'd heard the sign-off, so he flipped the dial frantically. He was about to give up when he passed over an island of silence amid the static, went back to it.

Corrigan waited a few seconds until a voice he'd never heard, gruff, 60ish, came to him from some remote point out there in the blackness.

I heard a racket out there tonight. I have a fair idea what's afoot. Most people will go to their grave without knowing why some of us here live in fear. I've lived all my days here and I know. And if you should happen to be listening, so will you. One day this man comes home from a faraway war, and he's scarred and broken and lonely as hell. His girl wouldn't wait for him, even if she wasn't inclined to throw bags of dogshit at grunts comin' home. So he's lonely, and he does what lonely men do. He sits around in taverns. He makes drunken passes, gets slapped. This town's always had more than its share of wild, desperate men, some of them a lot more handsome than Jepson, so what chance does he have? What chance at all? But he has no choice. So he sits around, and sits around, until one evening who else should walk into his favorite tavern but a lass with a ripe figure inside a dark gray sweater and jeans. She's got hair the color of an Iowa cornfield and the faintest of dimples on her creamy cheeks, and her eyes are somewhere between the blue of the Gulf of Mexico and the gray of a dying steel town. And she sits down next to him. She smiles. She's rearin' to fuck, and fuck, and fuck, and then, if there's a bit of time left over, to fuck some more. As I said, there are plenty of wild, desperate fellows in these parts, so why does Jepson attract her? Because she doesn't want just any guy. She needs, she craves a man who's licked steaming blood off quivering flesh, who's turned bone and muscle to ash, who's squeezed another man's flesh so hard inside a death-reeking foxhole that garb and innards came gushing out all over both of them. A man who has sweated, bled, killed, damn near died countless times. He's got an edge over just about any other fellow because she's no ordinary tobacco-chewin', cussin' lass, oh no, because Lieutenant Jepson here has got lucky, he has found himself a SUCCUBUS. *And Lord will the two of them breed and beget monsters—*

The screams were coming. He grabbed the rifle, stepped out, and fled down the dirt road. Already it felt like running on sand, exhausting, exasperating, at half speed. To his horror, lights came on nearly simultaneously in two of the white houses he was approaching. With a surge of adrenalin, he dashed right by them, passed a shuttered store, and turned right onto a lane where the drooping branches of the firs on either side concealed the moon. Up ahead was another building, not a house. Corrigan made himself dart even faster until he was standing under a drainpipe running down the south side of what he took to be a disused church. He panted, stroked the barrel of the .220 with the ardor of a fifteen-year-old touching himself. Somewhere to the east of where he stood, a party carried flashlights, growling and uttering curses. Nothing that had happened tonight seemed quite as improbable as the memory that came now. Corrigan thought of the woman sitting on a couch in a tiny apartment in a city up north, looking into his eyes, yes, the eyes of Corrigan the loser. He'd pleaded with her and had actually persuaded her to give him some of the money she collected from a made man who'd long been her lover, and never to talk to that scumbag again—

They were coming, howling like lions. Corrigan fled to the south, darted through a maze of narrow dirt lanes. All right. He had just one chance to save his life. Thirty yards away there was a dark one-story house with a station wagon in the driveway. He tossed the .220 into the bushes, ran up to the front door, knocked. For a moment nothing happened. He could hear the searchers drawing nearer. Then a light above Corrigan's head came on, and the door opened to reveal a forty-year-old man with a mop of thick black hair, in a pair of trousers and an undershirt. He was barefoot and Corrigan had obviously woken him up. Corrigan stuttered, spat the words out.

"C-can you help me, sir?"

The man eyed him, suspicious but curious, looking like nothing so much as Steve Carell's long-lost cousin.

"Can you help me? These men from up north who I think I stole from them are after me. I didn't do anything. But they'll kill me if they find me."

The stranger listened to the furor in the distance, scanning the road in either direction. Then he beckoned for Corrigan to follow him inside.

To Corrigan's surprise, another man had been sleeping on the couch in this little house. As the door closed behind Corrigan and the owner, the second man, a thirty-year-old with sandy blond hair, sat up rubbing his eyes.

"Please turn the light off," Corrigan said.

The owner did so. He turned to Corrigan with an expectant look.

"They're after me. They're going to rip my heart out. Can you get me out of here? Can you take me—can you take me *to the interstate?*"

Now the owner of the house spoke, in a dry, caustic voice.

"I ain't stupid, mister. Them guys out there ain't from up north."

The young man sitting on the couch watched Corrigan with an accusing look.

"What do you think, Zeke? Think we should turn him over to those guys?"

Zeke considered this but did not rise from the couch.

"Please—please don't."

"Why not?" asked the older stranger.

In the distance there were cries, howls, the sounds of frustration over the quarry having temporarily escaped. There was something about those cries. They were desperate in their own way, furious, shrill, feral.

"Who are these men?" Corrigan asked. "What are they?"

The owner of the house grinned. "They're monsters, mister. Beasts. Ogres."

"Oh get off it, Dan," said Zeke, with something almost like mercy in his tone.

"I'm just runnin' with you, mister. But you must've done something pretty low if those guys want your hide."

"No. No. Look, there's no point to this discussion. Let me make you an offer—"

More cries outside interrupted Corrigan. But the searchers weren't getting any nearer just yet; they were off somewhere in an area to the west.

Dan's ears picked up a bit. "What's that, mister?"

"If you'll take me to Crawford Street—I left my money there. A huge pile of it. You can have it all."

Dan and Zeke exchanged looks. It was total bullshit—the instigator of the plot had probably not left anything out there, and if he had, he must have removed it by now, upon finding out that Jepson was alive and kicking. But Corrigan would do anything, would hack off his right foot, to buy himself a minute more.

Dan grinned. He was not unprepossessing when he grinned.

"How much money, mister?"

"A lot."

"If it's your money, how come you can't tell me how much?"

"Because my brain is so fucking rattled right now. Believe me, it's more money than a hick like you knows what to do with!"

Dan and Zeke both laughed. If Corrigan could actually get them to take him out to Crawford Street, he'd buy himself a chance to flee. *One chance in ten million, maybe, but fuck . . .*

"Okay, mister. Come on."

Dan and Zeke put on their socks and shoes and led Corrigan into the station wagon, where he slid down into the space between the front and back seats. His heart pounded against the rubber mat on the floor of the car even as he was blissfully aware of motion, of the vehicle navigating the narrow spaces around them. The cries in the distance grew fainter, then inaudible. Dan drove the station wagon about 20 miles an hour, not too fast, on the back roads up toward Crawford Street.

"You know you can sit up, now. Whoever it is you're afraid of isn't gonna see you," Zeke prompted him.

"Cops might see me, and they wouldn't understand," said Corrigan.

"There's three cops in this town and they ain't got the most sophisticated scanners," Zeke replied.

"All the same," Corrigan rejoined.

"Who's really after you?" asked Dan.

They were near Crawford Street now. Corrigan made a calculation.

"You ever hear tell of a fellow named Jepson?"

The men up front snorted.

"Ain't he one son of a bitch," said Zeke.

"Damn straight," the man at the wheel added.

"What did he do to you?" Corrigan asked.

"It ain't what he did to us. He ain't no honest entrepreneur, let me tell you. And there's not a pussy in this town that he don't get exclusive rights to when he wants it. If you don't stay away, he and his guys'll ambush you comin' out of a bar, kind of like he did back in the 'Nam, I guess," Zeke explained.

"And that ain't it," Dan said.

"That ain't it by a damn sight," Zeke agreed.

"Bastard used to slit people's throats in front of their families back in the 'Nam," Dan added.

Corrigan picked himself up a bit, looked out the side window. They were turning onto Crawford Street just now. Soon Corrigan would have his chance. But he couldn't help rebuking himself for how wrong he'd been, how susceptible to lunatic fancies. The men after him were all too human and the only monster was the fat, slobbering tyrant he'd tried to assassinate.

Or these two were ignorant.

The car passed a telegraph pole.

"Now at the middle pole we stop?" asked Dan.

"That's right. Then take a look in the fields behind it."

Seconds later the car eased to the shoulder and Dan put it in park. Corrigan got ready to bolt, his muscles tensed. Suddenly Zeke pulled a black revolver from the glove compartment, reached behind his seat, and pressed the tip of the gun to Corrigan's left temple.

"Why don't you just get real cozy for a minute, mister?" Zeke said.

Fuck! In despair, Corrigan let his muscles go limp. Dan opened his door, got out, and moved off into the fields.

"The enemy of my enemy ain't necessarily my friend," Zeke remarked.

Corrigan wanted to cry.

After a few minutes, Dan returned to the car carrying a large beige pouch. He closed the door, sat down, and began to leaf through it.

"Well, damn it. Just damn it," Dan muttered.

"Dan?" said Zeke.

"Damn if there ain't thirty grand here, Zeke."

Zeke withdrew the revolver from Corrigan's temple. Dan held piles of the bills to his nose, sniffing them ecstatically, giving a few to Zeke, who did the same.

"Tell you what, pardner. Tell you what. You can have ten grand. That should see you on your way," said Dan, handing stacks of bills to the passenger.

Corrigan couldn't speak.

"Now git. I don' never wanna see your face again or know your name. Git, mister," said Dan.

Corrigan obeyed. It was still dark. By the time the first rays broke through the clouds, he'd be in North Carolina. Only later would he find a newspaper with a story, buried deep in the local news, about a man who died after a bullet came through his window, ricocheted off a bronze plaque, and lodged in the victim's neck. Until then, Corrigan had time to brood over Dan's parting words:

"Folks 'round here don't never forget the good nor the ill done to them."

Into My Heart an Air That Kills

Kyle Tanner thought: *Am I alive?*

His body was intact, but he was in such a daze he forgot to be grateful. He'd managed something between a crash and an emergency landing out in a remote field after some force, probably a bird, had caused a problem with one of his little jet's turbofans. Kyle had barely pulled himself out of the cockpit when the self-recrimination began. *These tiny planes are so dangerous. You aren't experienced enough to be flying out here by yourself. You don't know the northwest at all. No meeting in Seattle is important enough to justify acting recklessly. And now you're out here all alone in a field in Montana or some damned place. There are more rocks here than you could have imagined and they're mocking you, yes they are, Kyle, they're poking their little faces up above the whispering grass and having fun at the expense of a junior executive who fancied himself a pilot.*

He rubbed his head, which ached badly from having slammed into the cockpit's roof when the plane ceased skidding and bouncing over the rocky grass. He felt in his pockets for his cell phone. Just as he was about to dial an emergency operator, he decided against it. Kyle did not know what was the right thing to tell people about this mishap, or what it might mean for his future at the firm, if he had one. He was in no state to try to recall every policy he'd read and signed. He wanted to have a doctor check for bleeding on the brain, talk to his lawyer, and then go about notifying people of what had happened.

Of course, he was assuming that he was alive. He looked around. A pair of giant white peaks loomed over thousands of firs, unperturbed by events at this low altitude. Trees surrounded the mountains and stretched away for many miles in all directions. Maybe Kyle would happen on a stream, and by following it would come to a settlement. Now he could not help but feel grateful that most of the pain was quite literally in his head, and his legs were fine. He walked over the grass and rocks to the tree line, pushed ahead into the firs, and navigated the wildly varying densities of wood and bush. He had no idea which direction of the compass he was going, but the thing now was to cross this terrain aggressively, and to try not to let the beauty of the surroundings distract him. He recalled A.E. Housman's poem, "A Shropshire Lad," and its lines about a seductive land with a delicious air that finds its way into your heart.

The pain in his head came and vanished like a hard rap on the door of his conceit. Kyle tried not to think or feel. He fought his way ahead, referring at intervals to his cell phone to keep track of time. It didn't occur to him to use one of the newfangled apps to pull up a map. Not even the most advanced ones would be of help out here. He dared to hope that he had no bleeding on the brain, no other grave but deceptively quiet injury. The pain in his head made him feel like that Vonnegut character, what was his name, Harrison Bergeron, the guy in a future world who can't pursue a thought for more than a few seconds at a time. A lot of people are that way in quite normal circumstances, Kyle thought.

In the spaces overhead the texture of the light was changing. Time was moving on into the late afternoon, yet there was no sign he was getting anywhere. The pain in his head did not get worse but nor did it fade. Kyle began to toy with the idea of calling the emergency operator. But then he'd be turning over his life, his fate, to strangers. The locals would notify his family and his employer and they might detain him. He fought his way forward. The crackling of the twigs seemed to voice the annoyance of the natural order. He began to hope that he would find, if not a stream, then at least a pond with water fresh enough to drink. The dryness of his throat had grown noticeable over the pain in his head. Maybe that meant the pain was finally fading. Or maybe not. Perhaps his only chance to save his life was to call someone now. His fingers tightened around the cell phone in his pocket.

The waning light above had that leisurely quality that sometimes reminded him of how blissfully the world would carry on after his death. Of course, he assumed that he was alive now. His grip on the phone was firm. Then it was out of his pocket and his fingers moved gracelessly over the keys.

Now he made out a clearing about forty feet ahead. Moving further, he saw a wide rectangle fashioned of logs with a black shingle roof. He put his phone away. From his position in the trees, he could not make out the rear half of the place. But he saw lights in the windows and he heard the mellow appeal of jazz trombones and the low but animated voices of people having a good time. He paused, overcome with the strangeness of the moment. Was he alive? Seconds ago he'd felt a growing terror, and now he longed for a mirror to check his hair. After smoothing out his clothes a bit, Kyle walked into the clearing and advanced to the front door of the long structure. He opened the door and entered.

Here was a dance hall, sixty feet long and forty feet wide. It had elegant wood panels and ornate chandeliers hanging from points on a spotless ceiling. The chandeliers cast light on young guests standing in clusters of four or five, mostly in the rear half of the space. At first glance, Kyle thought that well over half the guests were young men. Then he thought the real figure was more like seventy percent. For the most part, they were fit handsome men in their twenties, clad in dress shirts and trousers. Here and there a light vest or a brightly colored tie scored the monotony of their dress. Kyle's impression was that here were guys from the area who felt acutely aware of their standing in the community, their status as young men with no permanent attachment as of yet. They had reached a critical moment where they must either make a commitment or race ahead into a reality they and their families dared not imagine. Looking at them, he knew that not just any woman would do.

When Kyle succeeded in forgetting about the crash and the pain in his head, which was now a fraction of what it had been, he could not fail to notice a lithe form moving among the young men. Here was one of a handful of women in the place. She moved gracefully and confidently among the good people of the community. She had short hair the color of acorns and pale skin. But her eyes compelled Kyle's attention more than anything. He felt like a child who has grown up in a troll's prison and at last gets out and sees clear, striking blue. Kyle had to force himself not to run up and grab her and stare. There was something merciless about her beauty.

She continued to move lithely among the guests, pausing at intervals before one of the young men. Kyle couldn't hear her voice but he thought she was making an offer and a request. Would the young man like to dance? So far not one of them agreed. Gazing from his position at the front of the hall, Kyle tried to understand why. None of the other women were ugly, but none were as beautiful either. Kyle couldn't guess what held the young men back. There must be something in their concern for their standing in the community, or in their self-schemata, that her charm could not overcome. Then again maybe it was pure fright at the idea of going out on the floor in front of everyone.

Kyle set off across the hall with his eyes on a point on the far side where people were serving themselves punch from big bowls on a long table. He thought that at any moment someone must grab him and demand to know what right he had to show his face here, where nobody knew or had any reason to trust him. Manners and morals were the foundation of communities like this one. He planted his feet before the table, reached for a plastic cup, and poured some punch. Then he turned, cup in hand, toward the floor, where the whirls and embraces of a brave few had begun to capture people's attention. He looked around for the woman with the striking blue eyes. He spotted a pair of comely blondes with slight builds, but they both quickly found a partner.

The punch was smooth and sweet. He gazed out at the whirling bodies and drank. Soon more people were dancing. He thought, *Am I alive?* Whatever the answer to that question, he heard quite clearly when a stranger to his right addressed him.

"Do you see anyone you'd like to marry?"

The voice belonged to a guy, about twenty-three, with brown hair and a faintly nasal voice.

"I'm still taking in all the scenery," Tanner said.

"Well, there's a lot to take in, I'll grant. I don't think I've seen you in here before."

"I'm passing through."

"Are you friends with someone?"

"No. But I'm sure I'd get on just fine with almost everyone here."

The young guy grinned.

"Well, now. You might want to be a little careful here. I'm Dan, by the way."

"Dan. I'm Kyle."

"Welcome, stranger. Enjoy that punch. It goes down real smooth."

"What did you mean when you told me to be careful?"

Now there came another voice, from Kyle's left.

"He means that not everyone here is an obscure person growing up in a flyover state."

Kyle turned with annoyance to the other stranger. Here was a Native American, probably a Lakota Sioux, with straight hair parted down the middle, in jeans and a flannel shirt that didn't quite restrain his gut.

"I do find cryptic statements irritating. Your answer doesn't expand on what Dan just said."

"You sound well educated. Where are you from?"

"Minneapolis."

"What are you doing here?"

"Drinking punch."

The Sioux laughed.

"I'm Mike."

They shook hands.

"Dan. Mike. Why do I feel like you both need to warn me about something?"

"We're just watching out for you, Kyle. We wouldn't want you to get drunk on that punch and go try to fly a plane or something."

Dan and Mike both laughed.

Kyle put down his empty cup and moved out onto the floor. All around him the young people moved gracefully, their bodies swayed with a kind of casual discipline. He gazed around the hall, trying to spot the blondes who had caught his attention earlier but had denied him a proper appraisal of their looks. They eluded him. He kept looking around until he felt people might find it unseemly. Maybe it was time to resume drinking until the punch blurred the outlines of all recent experience.

The luminous blue eyes appeared before him.

"Do you want to dance?"

He was a total stranger and these were her first words to him. He could not fail to note the fragrance of her hair, like the aroma of a bakery where they are grinding nuts, and the contrast her rich red lips made with her skin. She was here, before him, and was his to dance with if he desired.

Kyle was about to reply when he felt a hand close around his elbow. Someone pulled him back and to the left, leaving the woman standing there bewildered, her lips an image of thwarted expectation. Kyle turned in anger. Before he could make sense of things, Mike was pulling him through the whirling bodies toward the wall. Mike's manner suggested he had something he really, really needed to share with the visitor. Kyle reluctantly went along until they both stood at the wall, where Kyle felt a rush of the loneliness and frustration that had troubled him for much of his life. He thought that Mike's timing could not have been more disastrous had Mike set out to play a cruel prank, and maybe he had.

"You don't even want to talk to her, man," Mike said.

"*Why not?*"

"Are you telling me you don't know who that woman is?"

"Of course I don't."

"A man like you deserves a nice woman to go through the years with. She's not a nice woman, Kyle. She's a low-class girl from Seattle. A criminal. She's got relatives around here."

"If she's a criminal, then tell me what's she doing walking around free."

"Legal and factual innocence aren't remotely the same."

Kyle sneered.

"Thank you, Judge Judy! Why don't you let me decide whether she's all right to associate with?"

"I look at you and I see an as yet uncorrupted spirit."

"*What?*"

"Your mind is corrupt but your spirit is not. Not yet. When I tell you to avoid that woman, I'm acting in your best interest, Kyle. Please believe me."

Kyle laughed.

"Why do you laugh at me?"

"Look, Mike, I know you don't know how I ended up here. Let's just say I really don't have a great deal to lose here tonight."

"Kyle—"

"I'm not asking you, I'm warning you to leave me alone."

Before he could observe Mike's reaction to these words, he turned and made his way back to the long table with the punch bowl and cups. He looked around but didn't see Dan. Well, it was better if no one saw him drink the way he needed to now, with total abandon, with no concern for the image he might present to the folk around him or the locals who had to do something about the wrecked plane and help him get to Seattle. At this point he didn't care. He drank resolutely, trying to affect a blasé attitude about the whirling bodies, the palpable joy. He thought about Seattle. He tried to recall how long it was now since his feet had tapped on the dank pavement of Pioneer Square on a cold night. He would get there. Yes, he would reclaim all the dark spaces absent of life in the hours after the young people retreated to the wine bars and the comedy clubs and the flats where they could pursue all their vices in private. He recalled the smell of the frigid rain, so persistent and so indifferent to everything it hit, the images of bundled forms moving on the slick pavement in search of an alley offering a bit of shelter. Perhaps in one of the alleys there was the possibility of an edgy experience, an encounter with a girl who'd run away from her hidebound family across the water in West Seattle, or a mid-level dealer who needed to liquidate his assets at no matter what price, or a bearded and tattooed freak with a cardboard box growing damp and moldy and appealing to people to peel away the flaps and to see what lay inside, to discover a pale face looking up at the sky.

Kyle felt now that it was a mistake to grow so self-absorbed in the midst of all this revelry. He had walked in here and had been touchy toward people who could justifiably have tossed him out. But they had let him wander, let him do as he pleased. He could show his appreciation by joining the fun. He drained his cup again, set it down, and moved back onto the floor. As he darted and weaved, there came to his ears a tune that did not receive wide airplay today but would never seem the least bit dated. It was an old Carole King song. "*It doesn't matter whether skies are gray or blue. / It's raining in my heart because I can't be with you.*"

Enjoying the retro feel of this event, Kyle moved toward the center of the floor, dancing more and more aggressively, not caring if others mocked him for dancing alone. Soon he recognized one of the pair of blondes he'd admired from afar a bit earlier this evening. She turned away from a young man with a gaunt figure and stubbly black hair, presumably after having declined an offer. Viewing her now, in a moment of clarity afforded by a parting of bodies, he saw that her hair had more of a platinum hue than he'd realized from his remote vantage point. Kyle walked up to her and dared to place his hand on her shoulder. The blonde smiled, but then quickly moved off to a remote point in the room. He covered his face with his hands, feeling hot and anxious. Maybe it was time to retreat. Though his thoughts about this evening were a blur, he knew that some rogue, some bastard had denied and might still deny him company tonight. Maybe it was time to retreat to the ruins of his little plane, to a space that was, even now, his to manage as he saw fit.

Kyle felt a hand on his shoulder. It was so light that he had to be in a hypersensitive state to notice it. He turned, and there before him once again were those blue eyes. They probed and searched without a hint of self-consciousness. The woman was curious about him, and there was a playful quality to her curiosity. At this moment he desired nothing more than to satisfy her curiosity, and his own. He leaned his face forward, within a few inches of hers, and began to ask her where she'd been for most of the night.

Now he felt the twitching grasp of a lunatic's hand. It fell on his left shoulder and pushed him forcefully away from the woman. Having accomplished this task, Mike toppled forward and deposited the contents of his plastic cup on the woman's dress. He laughed hard right up until the moment of this disaster. Though his actions were clearly deliberate, he appeared to want to convey the impression that he had been in a hurry to get across the floor, and had tried to push Kyle gently aside but had applied too much force. Then the appearance of the woman in his path had so jolted him that he'd spilled his drink. For all Mike's apologies to the woman, Kyle didn't believe it. He thought the woman was going to slap Mike, who richly deserved it, but she mumbled a few words he barely caught, and then set out toward some point in the building where she could clean her dress. The left Kyle to face Mike, the destroyer of a sublime moment. He looked at Mike with fury, on the edge of violence.

"Kyle. Hey, man. Sorry about that."

"*Sorry about that?* You fucking idiot. I was on the verge of something really rare for me. What did you do that for?"

"Kyle. Come with me."

"What?"

"Come outside. I want to show you something."

"I'll break your face."

"Kyle. Please come with me. I'll explain myself."

Mike began half guiding, half pushing Kyle toward the back exit. Kyle didn't know whether he should go along or act on his threat, but for now the rush of events was too fast and fierce for him to try to assert control over it. They passed across the floor and through the back door. Kyle found himself outside on a little porch with narrow slats. Then Mike ushered him down a flight of steps and onto dirt and grass. Mike's strong arms guided him away from the building, and off to a region of muddy turf that rose and fell without rhyme or reason and trees with thick branches. Kyle gave up trying to keep track of the path Mike was cleaving over the mounds and pits. His muscles felt limp, his tongue lay flat in his mouth until Mike deposited him on a swell in the mud and grass not ten feet from where Dan sat. Dan raised a bottle in a mock toast. Then he reached into one of a few six-packs at his feet, pulled out a bottle, opened it, and handed it to the visitor.

Kyle felt resigned to letting them explain themselves to him. The plane was down, he was stuck here, but even now he had in his mind a notion of progress, of a lonely man making his way over barren pavement in a city synonymous with rain, moving toward a remote bookstore that remained open later than other businesses on Pioneer Square, a store with multi-hued lights flashing in its windows and casting a glow over bodies in motion. For all the frustration of this evening, he could not help feeling that his experiences with strangers here at this point in a rural state might help put his vision of a night in Seattle into context.

Mike grabbed a beer and began to drink. Kyle still felt an urge to hit the Sioux man who stood before him, leering, grinning, daring Kyle on some level.

"Why did you interrupt us when I was just starting to get close to that woman?"

"I beg your pardon."

"Don't avoid the question, Mike. You saw us there. I was right about to dance with her."

"Do you know who she is?"

"Some local gal."

"No, Kyle. You're drunk and you're forgetting things. She's got family here but she's from Seattle."

"Exactly where I was going."

"What?"

"I'm really fucking sick of this. No, I don't know who she is. Tell me."

Mike fixed the stranger with a fierce yet somewhat condescending look.

"You *have* heard about the case, Kyle. It may have melted back into the flow of tabloid drama but don't tell me you've never heard of it. This woman's a phenomenon. They convicted her, twice, of the murder of her housemate in a university town over on the other side of the pond. You don't recognize her?"

Kyle thought hard, thought of those lucid blue eyes, but he did not make any associations. These were not the conditions for any kind of mental effort. Maybe he'd seen black and white photos that didn't do justice to her unforgettable eyes. Mike continued.

"They put her in jail, but her family mortgaged two houses and kept hiring independent experts to question one or another piece of the prosecution's case. If you do that for long enough, you can foster a feeling that reasonable doubt exists, even where it really doesn't."

"So you don't doubt the evidence, Mike?"

"Oh, no. It's pretty overwhelming. You should read the trial transcripts and the judges' opinions, not just the accounts of people her family hired."

"So none of the experts' testimony was valid and she still got off. You must have a pretty dim view of the justice system over there."

"On the contrary, Kyle. It's this woman's supporters who refuse to believe that the courts over there could have convicted her fairly. There's a ton of evidence against her but they slander the authorities over there. Contamination. Coerced statements. Incompetent or rogue cops and judges. All that nonsense."

At this point, Kyle was barely listening. He brooded about the woman over there in the elongated wood structure from which merry noises rose into the night. He thought about the open trusting spirit that drove her not once but

twice to approach a stranger, to flatter him with her attentions. Maybe these guys had come up with ploys to keep her
available for some other man, or for themselves. He turned
toward the dance hall. Then one of the guys put another beer
in his hand.

"Hang out some more, Kyle," said Dan.

Kyle thought that either these guys were liars or they were
fools who refused to believe what experts who'd spent decades
analyzing forensic evidence had to say about the young woman's case. Drinking his beer reluctantly, he considered ways to
remove himself from this situation. Maybe he was too polite.
Maybe he should walk up the slope and enter the hall again.
He set his beer on a rock.

"Hey, Kyle."

It was Mike. Kyle decided to ignore him. He started up
the slope.

"Kyle! Please wait!"

He heard lumbering steps behind him, and then Mike's
hand was once again on his shoulder.

"Just listen to me for a minute, white man."

Kyle looked at Mike with loathing.

"Kyle. I know you find her beautiful. We all do."

"So what's your stunningly original point about beauty,
Mike?"

"You want to know what's deep, Kyle? It's my commitment
to certain kinds of experience available to us in this world."

Kyle laughed really hard.

"Oh, this is too much. The wise Native American urges
the callow white man not to act on his shallow vain impulses.
To get in touch with what is deep and meaningful. Tell me
something I haven't heard in a thousand bad movies."

Mike grimaced as if recognizing something unconscio-
nable, a racial insult, in Kyle's words. At the same time there

was a hint of resignation in Mike's manner, as if he really expected no better from Kyle.

"I'm not talking to you as a white man with white values. Oh no, Kyle. I'm speaking with your best interest in mind. Listen to me. You don't know a *thing* about that woman."

Now Mike had gone still further in his efforts to belittle Kyle and to insult his judgment.

Kyle swung so hard he felt a bright burst of pain at the impact of his fist with Mike's face. Mike's head jerked back and he fell to his knees. His position was ideal for a good hard kick. Mike groaned as his wind left him and he tottered backward, unable to steady himself on the mud and grass, until a second kick settled the issue and he flopped on his back, spitting blood.

"Kyle! Are you fucking crazy?"

Kyle looked up and saw Dan, whom he'd forgotten, coming toward him. Dan didn't look as upset as his words suggested. Dan was drunk. He held out a beer toward Kyle.

"I'm sorry. I really didn't like the way he spoke to me," Kyle said.

"It's okay."

Kyle took a look at the barely conscious Sioux man lying on the ground before him.

"I know, Kyle. He's a little supercilious. Come on, don't walk away from us now. Please come and have a drink with me."

Dan must be so drunk you could impale someone in front of him and not upset him. Kyle felt that if he could get a buzz going, he'd be ready to walk into that hall and approach the woman without a bit of self-consciousness.

"Oh, all right."

He followed Dan to a point about a hundred yards from the rear of the hall. Dan reiterated what he'd said about Mike's tendency to talk down to people and the need not to let it rankle. Kyle sat on a mound, leaned back against the trunk of a big tree, drank his beer, and enjoyed the feel of the crisp cool air. He decided he kind of liked Dan, who so far had acted kindly toward a stranger who had walked into the hall with no invitation, no pretext beyond his own needs and impulses. Maybe when Mike came around, it would be appropriate for Kyle to apologize. For now, Mike lay inert. Perhaps Kyle had done more damage than he'd realized, and Mike would never get up.

"I think maybe our Sioux friend is choking on his blood," Kyle said.

"No, he's fine."

Kyle wondered how Dan could know that. He breathed deeply of the cool air. Once again, he wondered: *Am I alive?*

"So tell me, Dan. Are you being kind to me because you like me? Or maybe it's because you've got some idea that I'm a man from the city, and I know a lot of lawyers and politicians, and there's some kind of imperative for you to make an impression."

"Oh, no, Kyle. Mike and I both like you a lot."

The talk turned to really banal matters, work and money. Soon he thought of asking Dan for yet another drink, but Dan lay slumped against a trunk, looking at the stars.

He remembered the plane, out there in that field. They were going to discover it sooner or later, if they hadn't already. He could have used the past hour to talk with his lawyer and come up with a plan. Right now, he needed another drink. Wiping leaves and dirt from his pants, he advanced toward the beer. Then he thought of that woman, over there in the hall, he recalled the almost unbearable beauty of her eyes, and he thought perhaps she clung to a fading image of him as she moved about the floor amid all the handsome young men.

He set off toward the hall. Now the force that gripped him from behind was even stronger than in the harrowing incident when he'd been about to dance. Mike had him by both elbows, and Mike knew how drunk he was. Mike pulled him roughly in a strange direction. Kyle alternately walked backward and let his feet dangle as Mike moved him toward a point behind the hall and about fifty yards south of where he'd hung out with Dan. Having glimpsed this area earlier, Kyle could not fathom why Mike would bring him here. He murmured words of protest but Mike ignored him, the way you ignore any drunk idiot.

"Hey, Mike, tell me what the fuck you're doing."

"Shut up, Kyle."

"The wise Native American tells the bigmouthed white idiot to shut up."

As Mike continued to pull Kyle over the grass, Kyle glanced back at Dan, picking himself up, cleaning leaves off his clothes. Then he looked up. For all their number, the stars looked proud and secure in their own private spaces in the vast dark. Finally Mike let go, and Kyle collapsed. He looked up again and discerned the outlines of Mike's features in the light from a rear window of the remote dance hall. Kyle picked himself up and addressed Mike with a sneer.

"Where have you brought me to, Mike? I suppose this is an Indian burial ground."

"It is."

"What?"

Mike fixed Kyle with a severe look.

"Bigmouthed white idiot. Shut up."

Then Mike was gone. Kyle straightened his posture and rubbed his eyes. The hall was so far off, he wasn't sure he was actually seeing the lights in the rear windows, or mentally reconstructing them. He tried to shut them out, thinking he must let this place he stood in be what it wanted to be.

And so it became. The hall, the trees, the two men with whom he'd talked and argued fell away. He looked up and his mind sped across the continent, over the plains and fields and forests, the cities where men in dress shirts and ties plotted revenge on their past, the beaches where women challenged a puritanical order but could not quite bring themselves to flout it, to run after prurient ten-year-old boys with the edges of their vulvae dangling in the sun. But he had barely exhausted the distances, the spaces extending beneath the ferocious sun and the lucid moon. Kyle saw further, and further still. He made out the point on the far horizon where the cobalt sky met the aquamarine waves, and he was hurtling across the ocean, and then finally, at last, reaching a coast, a shore where rocks freckled the clay a few yards up the beach, a shore that became an unattainable ideal for thousands of dark-skinned migrants from the continent below, but Kyle had at last attained it. He had at last crossed the border of the country containing the town that had risen to global fame following the actions, admittedly the disputed actions, of a certain American guest.

At last the town appeared before him. His eyes roamed over the rooftops of the medieval buildings, the stone streets and plazas, and then the fringes of the town, the areas where they told you not to go alone at night. The cottage he found here wasn't ugly, it would do for a quartet of girls of varying backgrounds who could spent about three hundred Euros per month, but the cottage was on the edge of a car park where drug deals went down. Kyle's mind moved inside the cottage.

But Kyle was not in that town or that country. He stood on a tract of earth in Montana, imagining the setting of a murder that had fixated the world. His mind had the agility to summon images of such distant places, but it did not feel more nimble or unfettered than it had before. Now he vaguely recalled seeing pictures of the crime scene in some tabloid. Yes, he had glimpsed them and then had completely forgotten about them and about the case, and they acted now as an unbidden aid to reflection. But he could not help thinking that something had happened to his consciousness purely as a result of standing here, on what he'd jokingly called a sacred spot, a place with profound resonance for certain of the Sioux.

He really was unsure where he was. His balance was off. Once again he wondered whether he was alive. The vividness of the experience was no answer. Where was he? Now a being rose in front of him. An agglomeration of mist. But the mist moved in rhythms and it assumed a precise form before his eyes. He was looking at the victim. She had lain on the floor of her room in the cottage with her throat cut, and she was before him now and was not in the same position but her body had the same quality of limp helplessness, of violated purity, as in the images in the tabloids. This young woman, this mist-figure, could not communicate with him in words, but through a mere effort of will she could present all kinds of other images to his eyes. He saw what the tabloids had hinted at or, against the advice of their lawyers, had clearly stated. There came to him a knowledge of the case so intimate that if he had these secrets in some concrete form he could sell them for millions. He watched now as the woman sat in her little room in the cottage, and the other woman, the one with the striking blue eyes, came in with two men and began fighting the victim. The victim screamed as her head slammed into a wall behind the bed and the fingers of the blue-eyed aggressor dug into her throat. Then the knives came out. Blood gushed in four directions, people began slipping in it and falling and trying desperately to erase their tracks and prints. The victim cried out deafeningly as one of the young men plunged a knife into her neck from the left, and then the woman with the blue eyes averted a second scream with a strike, from the right, with a bigger knife. Now the blood was gushing far more liberally, filling the room.

Kyle's mind could not stay in the room. It focused on the blue-eyed woman and followed her, move by move, from the town in Italy to points all over Europe and North America, including points in the Pacific Northwest. He saw her in contexts that most people who followed the case never imagined. Here is the woman on the lonely frigid streets of Pioneer Square, but the streets are not quite as empty as she might wish. One of the bundled forms up the street turns, sees her, and advances toward the seemingly vulnerable young woman. When the menacing figure draws near, his furious eyes leave no doubt how far the drugs have advanced throughout his system. His hairy hands extend toward her, ready to rend her pale flesh, but she does not retreat. The woman breathes an air which passes quickly into the man's lungs and makes them swell. Soon his lungs explode and the deadly air makes his entire body swell grotesquely until his eyes burst from his face and he screams and falls dead to the wet pavement.

The most widely jeered aspect of the case was the suggestion that the blue-eyed woman had committed the murder as part of a ritual, in order to persuade the ruler of hell to confer certain powers on her. Kyle saw now that this was no lie. Yet she clearly retained human traits. Her sight and hearing were like the next person's. She could feel rejection as acutely as anyone.

He saw the woman walking through deserts, in fields, on prairies with giant white peaks in view. Then she was in a room where men regarded her with rising alarm, cried out, and tried to flee. They felt the murderous wind enter their lungs and knew a few seconds of terror before their bodies erupted and the floor vanished beneath a stream of blood with limbs coursing fast on the surface. Kyle wondered what he could possibly be seeing. He thought the woman had only recently won her appeal and come back from the jail in a foreign land to her home. He could not guess what opportunity for carnage might have presented itself. Then, with Mike's bitter and condescending words in his ears, he realized that he was a fool for thinking so literally, that time did not conform to any linear model when you stood on this burial ground.

Kyle pulled his hair and slapped himself as hard as he could. He looked desperately around.

"We have to get up there now," he said with a gesture at the hall.

Dan gaped at him in bewilderment and alarm. Mike didn't appear to have heard.

"The men in there must have all rejected her by now. We have to warn them!"

Dan didn't set his beer down. From the hall arose the noises of some kind of commotion.

"Come on, Dan! Come with me now!"

Reluctantly, Dan picked himself up.

"Run around the front and be ready to turn the lights off," Kyle told him.

Just then there came cries from the hall, as if a fight had broken out on the dance floor. Then more cries, rising in pitch.

"Come on. Right now."

They began to move in the direction of the hall. Kyle felt Mike's strong grip once again, on his left elbow.

"Mike. Let go."

"Are you sure you want to go up there? You're awfully drunk."

"*Please, Mike.*"

The cries from the hall grew still louder, and the wail of sirens came from some point off in the night.

"Tell me why you'd heed the words of a walking cliché, a Native American with a wiser and more spiritual cast of mind."

"You've made your point."

The sirens grew louder, then stopped.

"Tell me why you care about any of those strangers up there," Mike said.

"Please let go of me!"

"No."

They heard a loud blast amid the screams. Noting Mike's distraction, Kyle swung his right arm as hard as he could. He caught Mike in the jaw, and Mike fell.

Kyle ran to the back of the hall, Dan ran to the front. They went inside. In Kyle's mind, the experience formed an analogue to his dream of making it to that bookstore on Pioneer Square on a wet frigid night, going inside, and engaging at last with the controversial woman. But as soon as he was in the hall, he feared he would vomit. All around the floor lay the bodies of the young men he'd found so handsome, with flaps of skin dangling around holes where the pressure had grown so fierce that their organs and muscles and blood could not stay put. Blood was on the walls, the chandeliers. It diluted the punch in the bowl on the table. A heart lay by itself in a puddle on the floor, busily beating away. Half a dozen men, drenched in blood, still stood at points around the room. Over by the building's southern edge, the wall on your right when you entered from the front, lay the bodies of a sheriff and his deputy. The deputy still clutched a shotgun.

As her gaze alighted on Kyle, the woman's smile grew still warmer, still more effulgent. The smile conveyed her utter delight that at last Kyle had overcome all reservations about coming to her. He set off toward the fallen deputy. A young man lying on the floor, with bloody holes where his eyes had been, grabbed Kyle's left ankle and spat up about a pint of blood. Kyle kicked the man in the head with his right foot and continued across the floor.

The woman had seen him. He sensed her will, her malevolence, drifting across the room in a weightless ethereal form. At a signal from Kyle, Dan turned off all the lights. Kyle felt relatively safe. As soon as he moved again, he tripped over a mutilated body and fell onto yet another corpse, his hands landing in a puddle of blood. He got up and moved tentatively forward. But there was no way he could cross the hall in the dark. He called out to Dan. The lights came on. He leapt over two more corpses and took shelter behind one of the few standing people.

When he moved again, the woman fixed her gaze on him. Kyle felt the deadly air enter his body. Seeing Kyle choke, his veins bulge, Dan killed the lights again. This air lacked certain properties of air. It was akin to a laser that is either on or off. Now it was gone once more. Kyle exhaled in relief, but he feared he would never cross the room. He called out again and the lights came on. Now he moved in Olympic leaps and dashes over the remainder of the space. The air entered him again. He seized the shotgun and cocked it. All his blood was in revolt and he felt his limbs begin to swell grotesquely. His tissue and guts were moving toward points of exit. He groaned and staggered and fought to keep his balance on the bloody floor. He whirled toward the woman and raised the shotgun. The smile broadened even further beneath those gorgeous eyes. Kyle steadied the shotgun, taking careful aim at her head. He squeezed the trigger as the fatal air coursed through him and his eyes burst from his face.

About the Author

Michael Washburn is a Brooklyn-based writer and journalist. His short fiction has appeared recently in *Concho River Review, Green Hills Literary Lantern, Rosebud, Weirdbook, Serial, The Tishman Review, Meat for Tea: The Valley Review*, and other publications. Michael's story "Confessions of a Spook" won *Causeway Lit*'s 2018 fiction contest. Two other collections, *The Uprooted and Other Stories* (2018) and *When We're Grownups* (2019), are available from Adelaide Books.

www.ingramcontent.com/pod-product-compliance
Lightning Source LLC
Chambersburg PA
CBHW022246020726
47496CB00004B/1087